MW00390339

GOD'S
ANGRY
BABIES

To Atoya,
My hard working,
Jamaican student!
(Yeah, right! ☺)
Take care of you and
yours.

Ian   11/6/06

GOD'S
ANGRY
BABIES

by Ian G. Strachan

A THREE CONTINENTS BOOK
LYNNE RIENNER PUBLISHERS
BOULDER & LONDON

A Three Continents Book

Published in the United States of America in 1997 by
Lynne Rienner Publishers, Inc.
1800 30th Street, Boulder, Colorado 80301

and in the United Kingdom by
Lynne Rienner Publishers, Inc.
3 Henrietta Street, Covent Garden, London WC2E 8LU

© 1997 by Lynne Rienner Publishers, Inc. All rights reserved

Library of Congress Cataloging-in-Publication Data
Strachan, Ian G. (Ian Gregory), 1969–
   God's angry babies / I.G. Strachan. — 1st ed.
   ISBN 0-89410-828-X. — ISBN 0-89410-829-8 (pbk.)
   1. Mothers and sons—West Indies—Fiction. 2. Family—West
Indies—Fiction. I. Title.
PS3569.T67575G63   1996
813'.54—dc20

                                                96-7474
                                              CIP
                                              AC

British Cataloguing in Publication Data
A Cataloging in Publication record for this book
is available from the British Libraray.

This book was typeset by Letra Libre
1705 Fourteenth Street, Suite 391, Boulder, Colorado, 80302.

Printed and bound in the United States of America

∞ The paper used in this publication meets the requirements
of the American National Standard for Permanence of
Paper for Printed Library Materials Z39.48-1984.

5 4 3 2 1

For Senorita,
who took six with her and saved the books

Acknowledgments

There are a number of individuals without whom this novel would never have appeared in print. First, I must thank Phyllis Rackin for reading the manuscript and for doing everything in her power to see me through. The insight and difficult questions of Farah Griffin have made this a better work: Farah, you are a gift to the world. Rebecca Bushnell has never said no when I have come to her in need of help and advice, and she deserves a thousand thanks. Greg Cohn has given me many extremely useful suggestions, and for that I am truly grateful. I must thank Kristin Hunter Lattany, as well. She is a fine human being, with an honesty and an openness that are priceless. John Roberts, Romulus Linney, and Herman Beavers were also extremely helpful during this process and they have my undying gratitude. I thank my friends at Penn who have taken the scholarly journey with me: Ntshonda Tynes, Roseanne Adderley, Eugene McGarry, Rhonda Frederick, Robert Barrett, and Crystal Lucky. Krista Walkes lent her keen eye to the proofreading of the manuscript; I hope to return the favor! I thank Senorita Gloriana Moss, for her strength and bravery. Chanti Seymour has suffered through it all with me during the writing of this book. I can never repay her. And last, to Donald E. Herdeck, who never hesitated.

The persons, places, and events depicted in this novel are all products of the author's imagination. Any similarity between them and real persons living or departed is completely coincidental. But if da cap fit . . .

The First Part

◆

T E N

And the Lord spake unto Moses and Aaron in the land of Egypt, saying, This month *shall be* unto you the beginning of months: it *shall be* the first month of the year to you. Speak ye unto all the congregation of Israel, saying, In the tenth day of this month they shall take to them every lamb, according to the house of *their* fathers, a lamb for an house . . .

—*Exodus 12:1–3*

It is the curse of the masses always, now as then, that those who have shouted most always quail when the time for action arrives, or worse still find some good reason for collaborating with the enemy.

—C. L. R. James, *The Black Jacobins*

"Ten, ten, the Bible ten."

—A Bahamian Obeah Incantation
Used to Ward Off Evil

1

The streets of Pompey Village had no names and no one cared. But there were potholes. These were the sign posts. The directions. Big potholes and little ones waiting to become big ones. That's how it was all over the island, except along the strip of towering hotels that lined the western end of Waterfront Road. That part of Grand Santa Maria had to look good for the tourists. The roads that led to the hotels were all smooth and covered with fresh white lines. Everywhere else it was mostly potholes. And that's why the huge, rust-eaten honey truck with faulty brakes marked "Charlie's Pumping Co.—We Suck It Out Without a Shout" collided and totally wrecked Johnny "Yellow Man" Roberts' "Harder Than the Hardest" Route 13 Bus, late on a November afternoon, causing children who were shooting marbles and spiking tops in the twilight to scatter like dogs dodging stones, spraying glass over the street like diamonds, and leaving a brown, funky ooze flowing steadily into Crazy Mr. Burke's front yard.

Had there been no potholes in the street, had Yellow Man and the driver of Charlie's Pumping Co.'s brakeless and uninsured truck not been drinking while driving and making fifty miles per hour in a neighbourhood where the limit was actually fifteen, the accident might not have happened. The potholes, at least, could not have been prevented. The road men usually came by in the summer time, once every five years, to do repairs. On a day when the sun was hot and bright and no clouds threatened rain, they would show up bare-backed, with shovels, a steam roller, and a stinking tar truck. Around Election time they would fill the holes with dirt and spread tar over them, leaving dark spots in the road where the holes once were. And somehow the roads would stay smooth up until Election Day. The minute it rained after that point the potholes would return. But no one expected Elections to be called until the following summer, so no one cared about the state of the roads. They knew nothing would be done until it was closer to Election time, and accepted it.

Since blacks had been in charge in Santa Maria, everyone had grown to expect holes in the road four years and eleven months at a time, and they would not have felt at home otherwise. The older ones, the ones who could remember the Union Jack, Empire Day, and "Rule Britannia" and the many places they could not enter because they were not white, appreciated just having the roads in the first place. They were grateful to the Government because they could remember when there were no roads, only white limestone tracks that strained through the bushes where they made their homes. So everyone took the holes with more than a grain of salt. The holes were one of the things that identified the island as *their* island, made it distinguishable from the streets of Miami or any of the other major American cities that the people saw on their momentous excursions to the Mainland. The potholes were a strange source of identity, even a sick sort of pride. And the five-year cycle of repair was somewhat of a comfort to everyone. Even those who made a pretense of truly despising their elected leaders.

It was like the first warning of gale force winds that came over the country's only radio station, ushering in the hurricane season. Everyone knew to expect it. Counted on it. Secretly felt good, excited when it came. The fixing of the roads created that same atmosphere of anticipation that people sensed at hurricane time. That secret pleasure at the thought of something unpredictable coming your way. A spectacle. The only difference was that during a hurricane people seemed to come together; there was less bickering in communities, in households. At Election time it was every man, woman, and child for him or herself.

The fixing of the roads meant that the politicians from the two parties would be coming around again to count the heads of eligible voters in each household. It meant that there would be open season on bribes, and neighbours would jostle to see how much free beer and money or how many job offers and free T-shirts they could get for themselves and for their children by promising to vote for either of the two parties.

The bribery, the promises no one expected fulfilled, and then the rallies. These would commence in the middle of the night. Theatrical performances to rival the evangelical gymnastics of the best pulpits. Political talent shows, replete with profanity, soca music, dance, alcohol consumption, slogans, and slander.

It was an exciting sign, this fixing of the roads. And people believed that was how it was meant to be. So they would only smile when the potholes, as usual, returned after the first post-Election rain. Only smile at the predictability of the thing (and grit their teeth too) as their cars banged in and out of the many craters. The return of the holes meant the beginning of a new cycle. So no one complained too earnestly.

More people than would have confessed it to outsiders believed that the Prime Minister of the Santa Marias—whom many suspected to be an obeah* man because he always called for General Elections on a date that added up to the number ten—had made a deal with Lucifer, who, in accordance with the contract, had agreed to spare the roads until after Elections so that the Opposition could not make the condition of the streets or the administration of the Ministry of Works and Utilities a big case against the Government. (The agreement also meant certain people would encounter no bumps on the way to the polling stations.)

That was the way things went in the country. The Prime Minister, who had won the last five General Elections, could do virtually

---

* The glossary on page 281 provides definitions for many of the colloquial terms used in the book.

whatever he wished and the people would find something admirable in it. It was the privilege given a black Moses, given the man that had led them out of captivity and put the lash to the Conchy Joe's behind. Being Moses meant you could work for both God and the Devil at the same time.

So nobody cared that there were big potholes and little potholes waiting to become big ones. And nobody cared that the streets in Pompey Village had no names. Although, it did cause problems for the driver of the wrecker that was called to clean up the mess of the crash. He was forced to turn off the Southern Road—the busiest of the island's two main thoroughfares—and come looking for a particular spot in front of a particular house of a particular colour on a particular street in an area that everyone simply knew as "Pompey Village," an area mapped out according to mango trees, basketball rims made from milk crates nailed to lamp posts or coconut trees, and old, broken down, abandoned cars.

And it didn't help that the houses in Pompey Village were all the same colour—white with yellow trimmings—and were almost all the same size—two bedrooms and one bath—and were not numbered. Nobody in the Village cared about that either because they knew where everything was. It was the outsiders' problem. And if you pestered them long enough, the older folks would probably remind you that the ruling Progressive National Front—seeing as next year was an Election year—had now decided to number all the homes on the island. Not all the buildings. Just the homes. Not that anyone considered this a step forward. The people of Pompey Village didn't, anyway. Rather, it was seen as a new wrinkle in the five-year cycle of ritual displays of concern for the environment in which people lived. Most people thought they were funny, these Election gimmicks. They were quite the topic of conversation. Some people in Grand Santa Maria got used to the idea of calling off the number of their houses, although many in the newer housing districts still could not say which street they lived on because these had no names. Word was that the Ministry of Works and Utilities would be getting to them shortly, but that for now they were busy numbering in the wealthier neighbourhoods and those constituencies with M. P.s who had significant influence in the Government.

This offended no one because it was integrated into their totaliz-ing conception of the cycle. If there was anyone on whom to place "blame," those who liked to be contrary, and even those who sup-ported the PNF, would most likely have laid it on Thaddeus McKinney, the fifty-two-year-old Member of Parliament for Pompey Village and the surrounding Hawkins Town Constituency. Their line of argu-ment went as follows: had Thaddeus not converted to the Jehovah's Witnesses and refused to attend Parliament at least a fifth of the time like the rest of the Back Benchers, then he might have been able to lobby for the boys in the Ministry of Works trucks to come around sooner. As it stood, no one ever saw him. He had appeared at people's doorsteps as the new candidate a month before the last Election, escorted by the heavy brass of the PNF. He spoke at two rallies, won the seat easily—it is rumored that many people who were known to have been dead for over five years were registered and cast ballots in the election—and then disappeared. He didn't even open up a cam-paign headquarters in the constituency, but used the neighbouring headquarters for Columbus Town instead. Few were shocked by his behaviour. Everyone knew that the only reason he had gotten the seat in the first place was because the PM owed him one.

It could have been worse for Pompey Village. Although it was rumored that Thaddeus could barely read and could not stay out of The One For The Road Restaurant and Bar even on a Sunday, he was not sitting in Her Majesty's Prison, which had been the unfor-tunate fate of his predecessor, who, despite pleading insanity, could not escape being sent to jail for stealing $100,000 from his own law firm. So everyone on the whole was more comfortable with Thaddeus, a man who was never seen and was not the most astute of politicians but was at least smart enough not to get in over his head. And smart enough, one might add, to know when to lie and whom to lie for. He wasn't really so bad anyway: men and women alike would tell you that the only reason he had converted to the Jehovah's Watchamacallits was because his present woman—the mother of two of his three outside children—was herself a mission-ary of that religious group.

No, it was all the fault of the drivers, not of the potholes or of the Honourable Thaddeus McKinney, MP, that Yellow Man's

"Harder Than the Hardest" Route 13 Bus had collided with such impending nastiness into Charlie's Pumping Co.'s rust-eaten, brakeless, and uninsured honey truck, driven by Harry "Sleepy" Rolle, causing Crazy Mr. Burke to march outside, Bible in hand, and holler (ankle deep in ooze) about signs from God and the wages of sin. Both drivers, it was later discovered, were drunk. Sleepy, because that was his usual condition on a Friday afternoon after being paid and driving en route to Fredricka's Place to play pool with the boys. Yellow Man, because it was knockin' off time and he was celebrating with his lone passenger, Mark (the last son of the school teacher Maureen Bodie), who everybody in Pompey Village—for what reason few knew—just called "Tree."

It was all the fault of the drivers, neither of whom was looking at the road when they ought to have been, but both of whom, from opposite directions, turned the corner on which Crazy Mr. Burke's house stood too wide and, without slowing down or blowing their horns, rammed the living daylights out of each other. Yes, it was clearly and equally the fault of the drivers. Each man turned as wide as he did without slowing down because he had not been looking at the road, and when he had finally looked, saw, to his great consternation, a patient pothole, its cavernous mouth ajar, in the middle of the narrow street.

Hence, both drivers were forced to delay their festivities and spend their Friday night in the Emergency Room of Queen's Royal Hospital, waiting for Tree to receive medical attention. Both men gawked pathetically at Tree, who sat there for hours clutching an acceptance letter to University abroad in the clenched fist of his aching left arm. And both men were suppressing inebriated smiles, smiles that betrayed that sick satisfaction Santa Marian drivers have felt all too often: the steady thrill of knowing that, as always, the passenger had been the one to suffer while the drivers got away without a scratch.

•   •   •   •   •

Rastafarian Dives off Santa Maria Bridge

—M. E. Bodie, Daily Report Staff Writer

At 3 p.m. yesterday afternoon, August 17th, students of Grand Santa Maria Island were given a special treat on their way home from school. And they weren't the only ones either. Tourists, who usually buzz in and out of the stores that line the bay front shopping area of downtown Safe Haven, stood on both sides of the street in awe. Traffic moving in both directions along Waterfront Road, as well as on the bridge, was at a stand still. The shouts of approval from peanut boys and the honking of bus and car horns rose above the blaring megaphone-shouts of the police, who were unable to get to the root of the matter before the amazing feat was performed.

Just as the police got within yards of him, Russell Phipps, alias "Slinky," a well known Rastafarian, wearing variations of red, green, and gold clothing and a pair of Oakley shades, leaped from the highest point of the Santa Maria Bridge, arms spread wide like a seagull's, to the roar of the crowd, and landed head first into the shimmering waters of the harbour with hardly a splash.

Mr. Phipps, according to one onlooker who wishes to remain anonymous, was for many years a diver for conch and tourist coins in the harbour after dropping out of school, and is presently a seller of peanuts and Ital foods residing on Twiddle Corner in the Churchill District area of Grand Santa Maria. *The Daily Report* received an anonymous phone call at about 2:00 p.m. on the afternoon of the 17th, notifying us of a planned demonstration to commemorate the birthday of the founder of the Black Star Line, Marcus Garvey, who was born on that day in 1887.

The newspaper was not told what form the demonstration would take, and Mr. Phipps was unavailable to answer our questions in regard to his decision to dive from the 90 ft. arch of the bridge or about the accuracy of the onlooker's information. He is being held by officers of Her Majesty's Royal Santa Marian Police Force on charges of disturbing the peace and resisting arrest.

It took some time for the crowd to disperse on Waterfront Road due to the chase that ensued on foot between Phipps and the four policemen, who pursued him in and around the buses and stores before finally pinning him down beneath the giant Black Crab sculpture that stands at the roundabout at the foot of the bridge.

Regular flow of traffic did not resume until about 4:30 p.m.

2

"What I tell you 'bout riding around dis bloody islan' wit' dis donkey's behind?!"

Tree's mother was a tall woman with smooth, brown skin the colour of dried coconut. She wore no jewelry or makeup and had her hair tied in a short ponytail. Gray lines ran all through her hair. But except for that, her features were those of a woman twenty years younger than her three score and one. She commanded respect. Not because she was rich and influential, or the wife or sweetheart of someone rich and influential, but because she was strong and unselfish. Strong, unselfish, and never betrayed herself by wearing her suffering like a new dress. As a teacher, a woman of the church, a person both young and old came to for advice, and the rock of her extended family, she had served as a mother to many.

"Mamma, it ain't Yellow Man fault. Seerus. It ain't."

"Don' gimme dat horse fart! I know is his fault you in here. Dese boys from Pompey Village cyaa do nuttin but find trouble for people chirren. Don' know how dey parents raise dem but it sure ain' wit' sense! Every time I turn roun' one a my chirren in trouble. What God give me sons for but to test me? Give me strength, Lord."

She was not shouting. And her facial expression never changed. She was tired and annoyed. She looked weighed down just then, but the words were shot out of her. She had the eyes of someone grown impatient after years of toleration. Someone who had tolerated, and then one day, and forever, decided she would tolerate nothing more. Eyes that always scrutinized, that missed little, especially another person's true intent. But she was conscious of the public spectacle of pain that surrounded them in the Emergency Room, so she was careful to remain poised. She knew everyone's eyes were on her as she stood, with her beaten leather bag in hand, papers bulging out of its unsealed zipper, the sweat stains at the armpits of her blouse, the chalk on her fingers and in her hair. She was tired. The heat outside was almost unbearable and the smell of hospitals usually made her nauseous. But she had come here to get one of her sons. She was not unused to having to do that. She wore that quiet resolve on her face, that same expression she wore on the many occasions she had pulled herself out of bed in the middle of the night to get Firsborn out of jail; that expression she wore when she had come home before a summer downpour to find her oldest son ready to commit murder and was forced to wrestle him to the ground in the middle of the road and take him to Crazyhill. She took a deep, exhausted breath and frowned.

"Miss Bodie, it wuzzan my fault you know. Seerus. Is dis jackass, Sleepy. He stay gettin' in accident. Is da second time I crash wit' him. He gat bad luck. Every time I pass him on da road I is have ta cross my finga. Dis time I didn' see him comin' 'til was too late. He is drink."

"Yellow Man please hush ya mout', because you done do nuff damage. If my child was more hurt than he already is I would have to kill you dead."

This was the language of choice with her. Perhaps, if Yellow Man were not there, and the eyes of the other sufferers in the Emergency Room seeking diversion from their own sweat and open wounds had not been on them, she would not have used this language. It communicated her annoyance. It let everyone know that she was Tree's mother. That *he* was the one she had come all the way downtown to get. Not the other two, who, although she would do whatever she could for them, were not her flesh and blood but were, in this instance, so clearly at fault and deserving of disdain. If she and her son had been alone she would have spoken differently. Perhaps, she would have spoken in the language of her childhood teacher, Fanny Harrington. A language of classrooms and offices, lawyers and library books. A language which she understood to be a door to the outside world. She had taught herself to speak that language and to write it, and she had conveyed the same idea of its importance, its power, to her last son.

"Boy, what happen tuh ya arm? Answer me. Mark Etienne Bodie. What happen tuh ya arm?"

"I don' know, Mamma. It numb. I t'ink it break."

Another woman might have exclaimed and struck Yellow Man over the head several times with the handbag. But she would not reveal herself so easily. There were still the suffering eyes. Still the pride of her son to consider. She did not raise her voice.

"You *t'ink* it break?"

"Yes, ma'am."

Tree shifted in the chair. He thought about all the backsides that had sat in it before his. He thought about Elsa. He needed to call her. He hated hospitals. His arm hurt. He still clutched the letter.

She stared impatiently at Sleepy, who was sweating a thick shiny sweat and was reeking of spilt beer. At first she thought to question him but decided it would be a waste of effort. She did not know this young man and would have to deal with him later. She turned to Yellow Man, who immediately looked down at his Clarkes to avoid her annoyed, assessing gaze.

"And what happen to you?"

"I gat dis cut on my leg from da glass. But oder dan dat I fine."

"Yellow Man, where is your father? Does he know about this? Or did you expect him to read about it in *The Beacon?*" She was gaining more of a sense of what the moment required of her, and altered her tone. She felt as though she were about to discipline a third grade boy for lifting up a girl's skirt and had to be certain that the boy understood why correction was necessary before actually dealing out the punishment.

"He still drivin' da oder bus. He don' know 'bout da accident. I was gern tell him when I get home tonight."

"And have you two talked to the police?"

"Yes, ma'am."

"Mark Etienne. How long have you been here?"

"Two and a half hours, Mamma."

He was in pain. He was tired. But most of all he hated these scenes. He never looked up at her. Instead, he kept his head bent, his eyes on the dull tiles. This was his signal to her that he did not wish to speak, that he just wanted to get out of the Emergency Room, to go home. She knew this posture: it communicated his feelings perfectly, no further words were required between them. He would soon be twenty and still he was the moody boy she always knew. University would change him. The sooner he got out of Santa Maria and got on with his education the better off he would be. *University made all the difference in my life. If I had stayed under Mercer Stone I would have nothing today. My sons would have nothing. Leaving has made all the difference.* The sooner he got away from bad influences like Yellow Man and Small Pint, and the Rasta they called Jahown, young men to whom the future was closed off . . . she would feel better when he was in University and learning. Then he could make something of himself, and all the people who had misused her and written her and her children off, Mercer Stone's family, Mercer himself, would see what a wonderful thing God had done for her. What God had wrought in her life, without the help of those who thought she was dirt.

"Young man. What is your name?"

"Harry, ma'am. Harry Bowe. People is call me Sleepy. I work for Charlie's Pumpin'."

"I see."

That gaze and all it communicated made Sleepy uneasy, ashamed that he had made this woman come to the hospital to discover whether her child was dead or alive. He had never met her before, but he could tell she was a schoolteacher. And she reminded him a little of his own mother in the way she was looking at him. His mother was a maid at the Sheraton. They both had the same way, he thought. The same look of disappointment, outrage, and for-giveness all at once.

"Miss. I didn' mean to hurt ya son. Hones'. I ain' never been in no trouble like dis. An if dey take my license I gattie quit dis job. I just get dis job, Miss. It wuzzan my fault. I done tell the Constable how it happen. He turn da corner too wide ya see. An' das how we crash."

"Listen boy, don' talk no shit! Hear? You 'pose ta stop at da damn corner!" Yellow Man pointed a finger in his face. Neither man wanted to admit to guilt in front of her, and they both would have fought right there and then, in the Emergency Room, even though they were more than a little dizzy, to save face.

Still the suffering eyes. The heavy smell of disinfectant. So thick and heavy you carried it with you when you left and everyone said you smelt like hospital. Tree was still looking down at the tiles, thinking about the backsides, feeling a little dirty. He was wonder-ing if he would need shots. He hated shots. He was still clutching the letter.

Maureen Bodie's mind was made up.

"Watch your language, Bertram Roberts. At this stage it truly doesn't matter to me *who* is to blame. A magistrate can decide that." She paused and considered the three of them together, one last time. *My baby have to leave dis place 'fore he en' up like Firsborn: drag down in the dumps wit' no way out. He need his chance like I needed mine. He just dat kind dat need dey chance.*

"Mark, let's go. I'll take you to a private doctor. You could be sprawled out on the floor with your head split open and these people would not 'tend to you. Next time I see the Minister of Health on the road I will give him a piece of my mind about this hospital! When he sick, he is climb on a plane an' fly to Miami or New York. The res' a us 'pose to dead. Bertram Roberts, I suggest you call home and tell your sister where you are and what happened. I don't know how many times you must crash in your father's bus before you learn sense. If you aks me dere ain' one safe jitney driver in all a Safe Haven puttageda. As for you, Mr. Bowe, I don't know who your people are, but—"

"My ole man is Felix Bowe. He's a palice sergeant."

"Yes. Well, I'm sure you'll be needing to call him. Goodnight." She turned abruptly and never looked back. The eyes followed her until she disappeared and then returned to their own suffering. Tree got up, said "Check ya," and followed her out into the parking lot to her car, a white Toyota that needed a paint job. By the time they had pulled out of the parking lot and turned onto the hysteria of the Friday night streets, Tree noticed that Yellow Man and Sleepy had yet to come out of the big swinging doors marked "EMER-GENCY."

* * *

It was very late when Maureen Bodie and her son returned from the doctor's office. The x-rays had shown a slight fracture just beneath the left elbow. He came home with his arm in a sling and a package of pills, and had to explain everything all over again to Frankie and Firsborn, who were both sitting at home wondering when their mother would come home to cook them dinner. And as tired as she was, after working as Vice-Principal of the East Ridge High School, then teaching a literacy class for extra money and going to the hospital, she still went into the kitchen cluttered with dirty dishes and garbage that had not been thrown out to cook for her sons.

And it was only then, with the noise of fish frying and the dogs barking in the back yard and Frankie and Firsborn laughing at something on the television, that Tree showed her the letter from abroad and told her he was accepted to University, as she had been accepted in her day, as Firsborn had been accepted without ever finishing. She was proud of her last son, and told him that nothing which God had set aside for him could be taken away.

He said he would save all his money from *The Daily Report* and that he would try to go the next September, and that he couldn't help her with the bills as much as usual. And she said that that was alright, that she had appreciated his help and would continue to because, except for Kevin, her other sons had never given anything to her in return for their shelter. They were like their father in that way. And she said he must apply for scholarships, and go and get his transcript from the College, and ask for a letter of recommendation from his favourite teachers. Especially the Government Scholarship. Didn't he know she went to University and took the four of them with her on a Government Scholarship nearly twenty years ago? He would certainly get a Government Scholarship. His grades were good enough. But what about the demonstrations? Not to worry about that. That wouldn't change anything. She was a PNF woman and the Ministry people knew that. They would take care of her and her own. Hadn't she done her fair share of work for the Party? And what had she asked for in return? Couldn't they at least ensure that her last son had a chance at a future? But why was that even necessary? Why did a person have to be for this or that party to get a scholarship? Weren't his grades good enough? Couldn't he just deserve it? Couldn't he have just earned it? Why did it have to matter who he was or who his mother was? But don't be foolish. Of course it mattered. Did he think that if the Opposition FLP was in power they wouldn't watch out for FLP people and their children first and foremost? And besides, in this life everybody must know someone. Did he think it was different anywhere else in the world? Did he think the American politicians weren't corrupt, didn't take care of their friends and family? He'd learn. But he must go to the Ministry of Education and apply. And what's more, he must go see his M.P. What the hell for?! What the hell must he do that for?! He must watch his language, first of all. She expected that from her other sons, from Frankie and Kevin and Firsborn, but not from him. Thank God Kevin moved out because he and Firsborn fighting all the time was getting impossible. But Mark should know better. Wasn't he the one who said not long ago that he wanted to be a priest? Now all that has changed. But he must go, because Thaddeus McKinney is a good man. She met him when she taught in Crab Bay, St. Mark's Island. McKinney's people were from there and he would come down to visit the school every so often. She helped them organize a campaign for a PNF candidate way back when. Black people must stick together. Mark remembered Crab Bay didn't he? On St. Mark's Island? Well, he was just a little boy. But he must go speak to McKinney, a good man, a humble man from Crab Bay. And do what? Beg him for a scholarship? He didn't need to beg anyone. Don't be foolish.

She never begged for anything in her life so why should he? He should simply go and meet him, tell him what he wanted to do with his life. He wasn't sure. Well, go talk to him anyway and hear what he had to say. Tell him he was her son, Maureen Bodie's son. She helped organize for him last Election in Hawkins Town as well, and had never asked for or taken anything. Thaddeus is a good man. Go and see him. Tell him he worked for *The Report* and that he just got accepted to University abroad and that he hoped to go off next September. He would be making a mistake if he did not go. Just introduce himself. That's all he had to do. And then he could wait and see what happened. She just heard that evening on the news that Thaddeus was made the new Minister of Education. Wasn't that something! Thaddeus from Crab Bay, with hardly any formal education, who worked his way up from a bus driver. A man could be anything in Santa Maria. Mark must set his hopes high. Minister of Education. Wasn't that something!

* * *

Later that night, after everybody but Firsborn had gone to sleep—Firsborn never slept at night—Tree called Elsa up and told her about the accident, the hospital, the letter. It was after twelve, but she was up reading a book, waiting for his call. She was happy for him; upset too. She wondered if he would go in to work the next day. And after he promised he would be fine, they shared pleasantries: about her day at the firm, news and gossip they had both overheard. He could tell that she was worried about him, and he told her that he would borrow the car the next night and come over to visit. Neither of them mentioned leaving Santa Maria, but it was on both their minds. Tree tried to sound upbeat about it, to make it seem as if everything would be wonderful, even if they would not see each other for many months and would be separated by thousands of miles.

Elsa was planning on going away too, but she had not yet applied to a school abroad because the deadlines were still months away. She had been saving her money ever since graduating from Santa Maria College with an Associates Degree and starting work as a clerk for Forbes, Bassett and Hill, the American trust company that was promising to send her off to finish her schooling. Everything in their world seemed accelerated now, and Tree could tell that she was not as excited about the prospect of being away from home as he was. For him it was escape. For her it was what one had to do to get ahead. And it was that sharp difference in outlook which prompted him to exclude all mention of Thaddeus McKinney or the debate he had had with his mother.

He was very surprised at himself, disturbed by his own secrecy. Surprised at this new, unexplainable willingness to conceal things from her. He told himself that it was not the same as lying. He couldn't really lie to her anyway, she knew him too well. As well as his mother did, he thought. But if he could not lie outright he could conceal, he could simply neglect to say things. And that is what he fell back on, the ability to neglect to say things. Because he knew that at the mere mention of his mother's proposal Elsa would be angry. Angry and certain that, after everything they had been through at the College—the march and the demonstrations—he would refuse outright to see the new Minister. Elsa would have echoed the very same sentiments he had earlier expressed to his mother if she had been the one urged to go and see Thaddeus. But there was one other difference between Elsa and himself. She knew for sure she would get the money from the firm. All she needed was an acceptance letter. Tree, on the other hand, was beginning to feel a little desperate, less resolute in his willingness to starve himself for a cause he was no longer sure meant anything. For him, at that moment, the only real cause was getting out of Santa Maria. As far he could see, refusing to compromise one's ideals, speaking the truth, being a crusader, got you nowhere. And yet, it bothered him that he had let his mother convince him so easily. It bothered him that he could conceal things from Elsa, whom he loved, whom he had shared everything with since the first day they started going together.

When he hung up and went out through the front door he could hear Firsborn in his new room laughing and talking to himself, but it wasn't as bad as it used to be with him. He thought for a second about the fights Firsborn and Kevin used to have, and how Kevin had left home to move into his own apartment because of it. Kevin was married now, with a baby daughter. He worked for the Government-owned phone company. It seemed one or all of them was always leaving someplace to go somewhere else. Maybe even Frankie would get tired of sharing a room with him, would save some of the money he made as a croupier at the casino of the Diamond Beach Hotel, and get a place of his own.

He walked down the nameless street, chasing Sheba and Racer back into the yard with a stone. Under one of the lamp posts where bugs flew in a frenzy, he could see the shapes of Small Pint and Yellow Man. They were playing a game of Round the Clock on the basketball court they had all put up so many summers ago. When he got up to them and said hello he noticed that a light was on in Biggity Miss Francis' house. He thought of how angry she must be that they were bouncing that basketball in the middle of the night. Small Pint had just gotten off duty. He was wearing his blue Defense Force uniform. When Tree approached, his two friends did not acknowledge him right away.

Small Pint: Yellow. I tired tellin' you to learn how ta damn drive. I don' know when the police ga realize you buy your flippin' driver's license and t'row you in jail.

Yellow Man: I ain' da only one buy license in Safe Haven. Plenty people do da same ting. Why you have to bring dat up every damn time you see me?

Small Pint: Oh? I t'ought I is only bring it up when you buck-up in ya bus. But since you say is everytime I see you I guess is so. Dat mean you mussie does crash every damn day, hey?

Yellow Man: En I tell you it wuzzan my fault? Why you have ta keep carryin' on, dread? You like man, hey? Tell me now. You like man? Drop ya pants den!

Small Pint: Ma buhy, I ain' cause you mash up ya ole man bus, ya know. I just knock off. I only come check ya see if ya dead or alive. You cyaa take a joke? When I do foolishness yooz da firs' one open ya yella mout' to say sumtin. So deal wit' it. You mash up ya bus again. So what? All dat make you a man.

Yellow Man: I done tell you it wuzzan my fault. Is dat ass Sleepy. Aks Tree if it ain' true. Dey should take 'way *his* flippin' license.

Small Pint: He buy his for fifty dollars too?

Yellow Man: Man, fuck you!

Small Pint: No t'anks. I'll take ya sista dough. *(To Tree)* Hey, buhy! You still livin'? I hear dis ass almos' kill ya dead. O damn. Homey arm in sling! Yellow break it forya, hey?

Tree: I awright man. Just a fracture, das all. Crazy fella in a honey truck ram us right up in front a Burke yard.

Small Pint: Yeah. Das what I hear. Da way people describe it to me I t'ought da two a ya'll done get duppy. All I see is glass bottle in da road like sand. You awright?

Tree: Yeah man. I rightcha. Whayasay, Yellow?

Yellow Man: Yeah, buhy. My ole man likes to tear off my head, dread.

Small Pint: He need ta kick ya in ya teet'. Wit'ya license buyin'ass!

Yellow Man: Anybody talkin' ta you, panties?

Tree: What he say?

Yellow Man: Who?

Tree: Your ole man?

Small Pint: Say he mus' pay all ya medical bills. An' fix da honey truck out he own money too or else he gatta go fin' a real job.

Yellow Man: Why you don' stay outta man business, nigga?

Small Pint: Sorry, girl.

Tree: You ain' gat to go t'rough all that Yellow. Is only a fracture man. I ga be fine. Mamma say she ga claim insurance.

Yellow Man: Cool runnin's.

Tree: How about you? Why you don' jus' claim insurance for the bus too?

Yellow Man: No dread. You don' wan' see how much dey ga charge me for my payments after I claim for dat accident. They likes to kill you wit' da taxes boy!

Small Pint: Dat ain' why, hear! He cyaa claim cause his ole man tell him he mus' pay out he own damn pocket. *(To Yellow)* You should look where you goin' nex' time.

Yellow Man: Why you don' seckle, buhy? Tree, tell dis nogoodnigger Sleepy cause dat accident, hear!

Tree: Well, to be honest, neither a you was looking at the road. Is just one a those tings. You have to be careful. Is my fault. I was talkin' to you.

Small Pint: Don' try take blame forrim. Is his fault. He's da driver.

Yellow Man: *(To Small Pint)* You hear him! Nobody was lookin' an' he was aksin' me sumtin. T'ink you know damn everyting! *(Hitting himself in the head as if he forgot something crucial)* Oh shit, I almos' forget! Small Pint, guess what? Ya boy get accepted to University in the States.

Small Pint: Stop storyin'!

Yellow Man: Seerus.

Small Pint: Ya get in?

Tree: Yeah man. Take um long enough ta let me know.

Small Pint: Sheeeeet. I shoulda pay more attention ta dem GCE 'steada lif'in dem gal gown tail.

Yellow Man: You! You only take one GCE, an' ya fail dat!

Small Pint: I make the Force right? *(Yellow sucks his teeth)* Right?

Yellow Man: Yeah yeah, ya make it. But dat ain sayin' nuttin.

Small Pint: It sayin' plenty. At least I earn dat. I ain' buy it.

Yellow Man: Buhy, kiss my black ass!

Small Pint: Your ass ain' black. You forget, hey? Das why you name Yellow Man.

(Tree and Small Pint laugh hard and long. Small Pint has won the battle this time. Tree joins the game of Round the Clock)

Tree: So what about the police? You have to go to court? *(Small Pint and Yellow laugh. Tree looks at them confused.)* What happen?

Small Pint: Court? What you t'ink dis is, buhy?

(Tree still does not understand)

Yellow Man: *(Smiling as if he has just gotten off the plane after winning the Florida Lottery.)* You forget dat drunken fool say his pa is a palice hey?

Small Pint: I forget you did wan' be a priest. You still have too much good ways. You know dis crooked yellow boy don' like go ta court.

Yellow Man: Sleepy tell his daddy to go down to Road and Traffic and tear up the report. Dat acciden' ain' never happen!

They all laughed so hard Biggity Miss Francis came outside and cussed them stink. But they kept playing their game late into the night. So late in fact, that Jahown, who had been in his shack painting and working on his Junkanoo costume, came out to join them. And then Stooley passed in his policeman's uniform, just getting off work at the Dolphin Street Station. And they played several games of Twenty One, quite a few of which Small Pint won by cheating on his score. And even though Tree could only play with one hand, they all laughed, and joked, and teased one another about this or that. So much so, that it was almost like old times between the five of them.

3
Mamma

M' riddle m' riddle m' randio. M' fada had a ting.
M' riddle m' riddle m' randio.
M' riddle. M' riddle. M' riddle.
Back then. Back then, the games went late into the night. The
story telling and the singing. The girl Maureen and her six sisters,
her two brothers, on Runaway Island. She did not know exactly
where her people came from. No one told her, no one remembered.
It was enough to know the name and birthday of the English King.
Enough to have the *Royal Reader.* No shoes to wear in the schoolyard.
One skirt to wear in the schoolroom. One teacher at the All-Age
School. And all roads in the town led to the well. Tree's mother would
talk of the ways things used to be:

When lightnin' come it dance on the wall and scald everybody
back. Lightnin' come straight in the school and scald everybody
back. I ain' lie. Tings was tough. Good, but tough.

One day her father bought her a bicycle. Iron donkey speeding
on the dusty trail. Because she was the smartest. Never had to be

punished. One day her father bought her some shoes. Too small. But good shoes for church.

Not for the schoolyard. And the games went late into the night, as did the storytelling and the singing.

M' riddle m' riddle m' randio. M' fada had a ting.

She did not know from whence she came. The past began with her grandmother. A black woman. Some said she was taken off a slave ship. Some said she was a pureblood African, captured from a slave ship. Captured from a ship going to Cuba in 1860. Set free, but never to return home. Some said her grandmother was a pureblood African. But the girl could not know. The grandmother died before she was born. The grandfather she knew. The grandfather she could see, from a distance, aging. The grandfather was half-in-half. Himself half-a-black man, half-a-Scotsman. Light brown skin, blue eyes, and nappy blondish hair. Light brown skin, blue eyes, and nappy blondish hair. And the games went late into the night. As did the storytelling and the singing.

M' riddle m' riddle m' randio. M' fada had a ting.

Back then. Back then, her grandfather was a farmer and a fisherman. A fisherman and a man with land.

Land he get from he white pa. Land he get from he white pa. He white pa from Scotland.

Her grandfather was a man who knew how to use a gun. A man who never was afraid of anyone. He had a daughter named Jewel. Jewel, the girl Maureen's mother. Jewel was a brown-skinned girl with long black hair. A brown-skinned girl with long black hair. And her suitor, the girl Maureen's father, was a black, black man. A black, black man with no land and no money.

My Daddy, John Bodie, was a boy didn' have no schoolin'. He use to go roun' with a long-sleeve shirt on and no pants and no boxers. Back den tings was tough. Tings was good. Good, but tough.

Back then. Back then, John Bodie asked for Jewel's hand. But he had to ask from afar. Every time John set foot on the half-a-Scotsman's land, whose wife had died in childbirth, and who had one daughter named Jewel, the half-a-Scotsman would fire his gun. Fire that big gun. But John got himself his virgin bride. John got himself his sixteen-year-old bride.

♦ 26 ♦

Back den ya had ta be a virgin or dey would put you to shame. Dey use ta check da sheets. And dey'd put you to shame. Man wouldn' wantcha no more. Make ya sit inda back a da church.

The half-a-Scotsman never liked John Bodie and made him swear. Made him swear Jewel would never sweat. Made him swear she'd never work a day. The half-a-Scotsman never liked John Bodie because he was a black, black man. And the games went late into the night. As did the storytelling and the singing.

M' riddle m' riddle m' randio. M' riddle m' riddle m' riddle.

The boy John Bodie used to stand under the trees. Stand under the trees with his friends and preach. Stand in his long shirt and no pants and no boxers and preach. And when John Bodie became a man and took a wife he worked the land. He worked the land the half-a-Scotsman gave and was a deacon in the Baptist Church. And Jewel never worked a day. She bore him children, many children, some who died right away. And when the others were old enough they did the chores she used to do. And Maureen was the smartest and the hardest-working child among them. And never had to be punished.

From I know myself I use to iron, cook, and clean. Wash and fetch water from da well. My ma never had to raise a hand once she had me. And my sisters nor my bruddas needer. Back den tings was tough. Tings was good too. But tough. An' da games used to go late intada night. Anda storytellin anda singing.

Once upon a time it was a very old time. The monkey chew tobacco and he spit white lime.

And Maureen was the smartest. And the hardest-working child among them. And never had to be punished. But she was not a boy-child. And John Bodie, though proud of his daughter, would not send her to the Government New School. The Government New School they had set up for black children in the capital, Safe Haven. The new school they had built for the smartest of the black children of the colony there on Grand Santa Maria. That privilege was reserved for his two living sons. His two sons, who would always carry his name. And not a daughter. Not Maureen. Maureen didn't need high school. Maureen needed a husband.

Das jus' how Daddy was. I don' hold it agains' him. But I always think how everything might a been different if Daddy let me go to the New School in Safe Haven. Maybe was 'cause Grand Santa Maria was far away. And he didn't want trust me wit' nobody. Seem always sumtin stood in my way. Always. Even long before I was marryin' age I shoulda know. When Mae Gibbs strike me in my head wit' a sharp rock one day after school. I shoulda know. When I aks her why she fling rock at me, she say cause I get a perfect score on da test da teacher give, while she get duck egg. I shoulda know. You believe I end up teachin' Mae Gibbs chirren twenty years later? I tell you tings gat a funny way, a funny way . . . Yes. Tings was tough. Good. But tough.

Once upon a time it was a very ole time.

Maureen Bodie had a choice of two men and married the lesser of two evils at the age of eighteen. By then one brother had left the islands for the States and the other was already in Safe Haven studying at the Teacher's Institute. One of Maureen's sisters had gotten pregnant at the age of seventeen and John Bodie chased her away from the house. The sister's name was Annabelle, but they called her Bell. Bell married the boy but John Bodie didn't care. As long as he kept his wits he never spoke to either of the pair. But when John Bodie could no longer shave his own face or control his bowels, Bell took good care. Bell took very good care. And the games went late into the night. The games, the storytelling, and the singing.

Once upon a time was a wery ole time. Da monkey chew tabaka and he spit vite lime.

Maureen left the other sisters in Runaway. She left the week after her grandfather, the half-a-Scotsman, passed. He had spent his last days in a house on a hill overlooking the huge, rough sea. He died alone and spoke to no one. No one, save his daughter with the brown skin and the long black hair. The brown skin and the long black hair. The games, the storytelling, and the singing.

Come here, Mark Bodie. Lemme talk ole story witchoo. You ever hear me talk old story? I ga tell you dis storee my daddy tell me when it was t'underin' and lightnin' outside an' all a us was huddle in da house in Runaway. He use to talk dis jus' before we go sleep wit' da kerosene lamp down low.

One mornin' B' Bouki and B' Rabby gone on da bay an' pick up one keg a butter to carry home. An B' Rabby say, "Nah, B' Bouki, we mightaswell cut fiel' tageder." Say "You gee me a han' today an' tommorow I ga do da same." So dey gone start cuttin da fiel'. When ya look, B' Rabby holla out, "Say wha'?" Bouki spin roun' and ask him say, "'B' Rabby, who callin' you so?" B' Rabby suck he teet'. "Dem people over so mussie callin' me ta come name dey damn chirren. I don' know why dey cyaa name um dey se'f. I ain' gern nohow." B' Bouki say, "Man you better go 'head cause only you could name pickney roun' here." B' Rabby say, "O.K. I goin dis time; but if dey call me again I sorry but I ain' settin' foot." Dat time B' Rabby gone and start eatin' from out da keg a butter. Soon tereckly he come back and B' Bouki aks him say, "What da chil' name?" B' Rabby rub he belly an' say, "I name him 'Begin um.'" Next ting you look B' Rabby holler out again like somebody callin' him, "Wha' ya wan' now? I ain' gern nowhere nomore!" B' Bouki say, "Don' mind me, go head. En you know you is da only one could name dese chirren?" So he gone. An' when he come back B' Bouki aks him what he name da chile. B' Rabby say he name him "Quarter um." Nex' ting ya know B' Rabby call out again. "Huh?!" An' he gone and he come back. He tell B' Bouki he name um "Half um." Den he gone and he come back again. An' he tell B' Bouki he name da chile "En um." Nah, after work done finish, B' Bouki want some a dat butter bad bad. So he say, "B' Rabby, les go open dat keg a butter so we could have some fa dinner." So he open da keg. And when he push he hand up in it he come out wit' 'lone nanny in he hand. So B' Rabby try jump slick. He say, "You eat all da butter!" So B' Boukee get dead vex. He say, "Me? You lef' me right dere in da damn fiel' all day! Is you eat da flippin' butter." So B' Rabby say, "O.K. Le's lay out in da sun and which ever one da butter melt outta das da one who eat um." So B' Bouki lay down and fall sleep. An' B' Rabby spread butter all over him. And when B' Bouki wake up, B' Rabby say, "See! See! I know is you eat all da butter and try blame me!" An dey start ta fight and B' Bouki kick one kick so hard B' Rabby fly and buck up right inta me and knock me here to tell dis story.

The man Maureen married was himself a teacher. She told him that's what she too wanted to do and he didn't seem to mind. The two went off to live in Safe Haven, a growing town after the War. The two went off to live in Safe Haven and left John and Jewel Bodie and the daughters at home. But each daughter in her turn would marry and leave.

The man Maureen married was from a good black family. Not too too dark, and not that poor. He was not a Baptist. The man Maureen married came from a small family. He was Anglican but he went to the school for boys run by the Catholic Church in Safe Haven, and his daddy was one of the first black schoolmasters. Maureen's mother with the brown skin and the long black hair named Jewel warned her more than once. Warned more than once that the man her daughter wanted to marry had bad ways. But Jewel, in her time, never listened to the half-a-Scotsman, and Maureen wasn't going to listen now. The man Maureen married wasn't a black, black man, and he came from a family with a good name. Jewel would have kept her tongue because she liked that. But Jewel felt the family and their son had bad ways and thought Runaway people wuzzan wort' nuttin. The man Maureen married was the colour of dead leaves and tall. Broad shoulders, a moustache, the colour of dead leaves, and tall. He was called Mercer Stone.

And the games went late into the night . . .

● ● ● ● ●

Dr. Harcourt Fitzwilliam To Run in Bi-Election
—M. E. Bodie, Daily Report *Staff Writer*

Dr. Harcourt Ulysses Fitzwilliam, a former Professor of Political Science who has held posts at numerous prestigious American universities, and a well-known lecturer at Santa Maria College turned independent politician, has declared his candidacy for the upcoming December 1st Browne's Town Bi-Election. The Professor, who heads the People's Christian Socialist Party, has entered every bi-election on the island of Grand Santa Maria in the last twelve years and has tallied fifteen votes collectively in that time. Dr. Fitzwilliam says he is not discouraged by this lack of confidence on the part of the Santa Marian voters however, and has assured *The Daily Report* that his unique brand of "restoration politics" will eventually "open the eyes of the blind proletariat and bring about a revolution beneath the coconut trees that will usher in the long awaited downfall of the brain-dead black bourgeoisie and their white merchantocratic puppeteers."

The Browne's Town seat became vacant after former Minister of Education, the Right Honourable Sir Eugene A. Thompson, stepped down as Member of Parliament for the constituency and vacated his post in Cabinet in September. Sir Eugene resigned after accusations by the Leader of the Opposition led to an investigation revealing that more than one third of the $1 million donated by the Taiwanese Government for the building of a National School for the Deaf and Blind had been misappropriated under his administration. (Sir Eugene has since been appointed Santa Marian Ambassador and High Commissioner to Switzerland.)

Interviewed outside the Office of the Parliamentary Registrar, Dr. Fitzwilliam was evasive when asked to give an estimate of the amount of support his Christian Socialist Party has garnered in Browne's Town and in the country at large since the last bi-election almost a year and a half ago. He urged *The Daily Report* to tell the people of the nation, whom he described as "drowning in a funky sea of political spittle and sermonic semen," that his message of restoration could be heard every day except Sunday, from 8 a.m. to 2 p.m. at the intersection of Malibu and Russell Streets.

This reporter can attest to the truth of this statement as he has, on numerous occasions, witnessed Dr. Fitzwilliam at the aforementioned junction (except when the rain was coming down with special force), standing on a red milk crate, delivering his political message to drivers on the way to work — as well as any pedestrians who care to stop and listen. The lamp posts at that corner have been decorated with nailed strips of rotted plywood on which the letters PCSP have been painted in bright red colours. Similar wooden signs are to be seen along the more notoriously depressed streets of

Safe Haven. *The Daily Report* has tried to discover whether or not the good doctor has a permit allowing him to carry out his promotions in this fashion. However, a spokesman for the Ministry of Works and Utilities said they have no record of any such permit being granted but no effort had been made to make Dr. Fitzwilliam remove the signs from the public property on which they were so advantageously displayed.

4

When you grow up you mus' treat a woman wit' respec'. Ya hear? Don' be followin' ya pa example. When you grow up you better try ya hardes' to resis' dat side a you, boy. I see it in ya bruddas. Dem is Mercer Stone t'rough and t'rough. Dey hard head, dey cheap, and dey gat bad ways. Strugglin' to make ends meet, I ain' never had as much time to spend wit' dem as I have wit' you. So you better mind. I never listen ta my mudda, Jewel Macintosh Bodie, ya see. I never listen. But you best mind what I say. Ya gat ta fight dat side a you. The Stones is a set a people wit' bad damn ways. Mark me. I know you too young to remember, so I tellin' you.

I was raise ta treat a man wit' respec'. In John Bodie house he had da final say. An' he use ta beat, and beat hard too, when you cross da line. But I never in my life had no complaints, aldough he use ta curry favour for he sons. Dat was just Daddy way. John Bodie was a good man. You favour him plenty, have his same dark features. Even walk like him. He always provide for his children. Never one day we want for nuttin. You hear me? Never one day. An' my ma never had to raise a finger around dat house. Jus' as my daddy swear to the half-a-Scotsman, so he keep his word.

I spend my life slavin' and I know what is like to have a man keep you down, to have a man try to suffocate every ounce a dignity outta you. Take woman for a donkey he must ride 'til it dead. And for fifteen years I tolerate his shit! I was loyal ta him, cook his meals, iron his clothes, fetch him water, clean his shoes. Only ting I never do for dat no good man was wipe the shit from his ass! You hear? Fifteen years I lay on my back and let him have his way. And I get pregnant for him six times. Six times! And never once did I see Mercer Stone put his hand in his pocket to buy so much as a candy for one of his sons. Mercer Stone would go to Kentucky Fried Chicken to buy food, and sit right in the living room and eat every last piece. Suck the bone dry, while his sons watch him wit' dey mout' white. And never offer dem so much as french fry! Den he ga turn to me an' tell me, "Woman, you better cook cause ya children hungry." I tellin' you dese tings 'cause you too young to remember. I tellin' you dese tings so you'll learn the difference between real man and play-play man. You hear me? I tellin' you now, while you still a green plant dat could bend. You must learn ta do for yourself. Don' be ridin' no woman like she's a damn market donkey. Don' be tellin' her to fetch dis an' do dat. You hear me? A man and a woman is partners. Equals. Slave days over.

Been a cart horse all my live long life. You see, back when I was a girl in Runaway, my daddy had to leave and go to the States to work on da Contract. He been all roun' dere in the States: Florida, Georgia, North and South Carolina, Alabama and Tennessee, even as far north as Pennsylvania working on the farm. Say he even know a fella who get lynch while he was over there. Say the white folks accuse this fella, a Santa Marian fella, a rapin' this white girl. But it wuzzan so. Her bruddas catch her wit' him and kill him ta save face. I ain' storyin'. Boy name Wilbert Cash. His people was from Finnegan's Bluff too. Couldn' a been more dan twenty-three. White girl offer him little bit and he en' up dead. Shoulda know better, but John Bodie say he wouldn' listen ta sense. Say he gone all around da town paradin' wit' da gal. When they was finish they toss what was lef' a him on the side a da road.

Well, while John Bodie was away all dat time we had to fen' for wesef. Kill da hogs an' chickens, feed goat, work da farm, an' keep da house up. An' I learn from den to work hard and take care of my sisters and brothers, and my mudda Jewel too. She teach me how to cook, and once she teach me I use to do all the cookin', an' mind da chirren, an' iron all deir clothes. Was no 'lectricity. Use ta have ta put da iron on da fire. It was hard times wit' John Bodie gone so long, but we manage. I know he didn' want to go. He just gone right so, because money was scarce, and dey was gettin' paid good American dollars on dat Contract. John Bodie take care a us good. Was plenty chirren walkin' 'round in flour bag for clothes.

But Runaway life was still a good life. I use to go to the All Age School that was run by an English woman name Fanny Harrington. And I was in da Girl Guides and Red Cross, too. I was head of the Guides for a while. An' church time was a good time. We use to have singspiration, rushin', and jumpin' up session 'til mornin' come. I even remember t'ings what happen during da War. I was a little girl den. Use ta sit right dere on Pleasant Place yard—dat was da name a our yard; Daddy name it Pleasant Place because it was good land, plenty acres, and the house was up high wit' lots a trees— I sit right dere under a sapodilla tree on Pleasant Place, looking dere on da Ocean-side, an' see the warships pass 'cross da 'lantic Ocean. Runaway life was a sweet sweet life. An' when my daddy come back he had boxes a tings for everybody. We gone to the dock to meet him when he come on da mail boat. An' he pick me up and spin me roun' an' roun' four times in his arms, and he give Ma Jewel a long hug an' a kiss. We was oh-so glad to see him come home, 'cause was plenty a man who gone on the Contract what never come back, and plenty a woman who man gone on da Contract wuzzan fait'ful. But John Bodie come back. And Jewel Macintosh was fait'ful. So it was a fine fine day. I remember it like it jus' gone. It was day clean, and the gulls was singin' up above. And Daddy spin me roun' and roun' so much 'til I was dizzy. Those was da best days of my life.

Just t'inkin' 'bout dose days make me wan' cry. When I t'ink a how marryin' Mercer Stone nearly ruin my life, I wish I was still a little girl in Runaway in my fada house on Pleasant Place.

Whatever you do, no matter how bad you hurtin', Mark Bodie, don't let people see you cryin'. Is none a deir business. When my daddy die and I see them place his remains six feet under ain' no one know what pass between me and him. Only God know. Only God see the tears.

Same for Mercer Stone. As much as dat man try to break me, he never could one day say he had da best a me. God is my witness, I do right by dat man, but he never ever do right by me, nor a single solitary one a his children. But he ain' never see water fall off my cheek yet, save it was my sweat from all my hard labour. 'Cause I never let him see what I had inside. The day a man know what you have inside a you for him is the day he gat you. He gat you. Good as gold, he gat you.

Don't smile. Dis ain' no smilin' business. I tellin' you dese tings, because the sins of the fathers shall be visited upon the second and third generations. Take heed. Being a real man is a damn hard t'ing in Santa Maria. And I don't want you to grow up t'inkin' 'cause you have a cock between your leg you is man. Dat'll be your biggest mistake.

I see I need to let you know 'bout Mercer Stone. Let you know why when I divorce him I give him back his name and wouldn' let none a yall keep it. Let you know why it is when he come visitin' dis house what he ain' contribute five cents to buil', I is have ta leave and go in my room and lock my door behind me. You know why I leave and don't say a word to him?

Why I leave and let yinna entertain ya pa? Because if I open my mout' to speak I might have say some tings what God ain' ga be please wit'.

Hmph! I ain' shame to say I didn' know nuttin 'bout man when I was a young girl. Dat was how I was raise. I was a virgin who never see man penis to know to call it dat. I talkin' plain wit' you because ain' no one ever talk plain wit' me 'bout dese tings. When Ma Jewel was tellin' me Mercer Stone was a cheap-no-good-bastard I didn't pay her no mind. I was seventeen and all I could see was his nice clothes, his broad shoulders, and dat fake smile. He come to Runaway as a teacher fresh from Safe Haven Teacher's Institute. I was Fanny Harrington's teacher's aid, but I didn' have no high school diploma or GCE's because Daddy didn' let me go to the New School, even dough I pass da Common Entrance exam wit' flyin' colours.

he walk in dat school Mercer Stone was
t. He couldn' wait for school to out good
ie and talk sweet in my ears. But I was
know no better. Because I was so tall and
n Finnegan's Bluff never waste deir time
look my way was a ass name Ezekiel
he couldn' tell lef' from right. So, natu-
the attention this city man, who grow up
school, ain' know what is like to fetch
y or scale a fish or pluck a chicken, and
well, was payin' to me. If only I'da know
noes a year later!
in' signs. But when you want sumtin bad
enough you make yourself see what you want to see; make yourself
blind to what you wish to remain blind to. "To be forewarned is to
be forearmed," Fanny Harrington used to say. Yes, and I was forewarned plenty. Jewel Macintosh, nosey woman dat she still is, start
snoopin' around to see what dirt she could find 'bout dis tall brown
man who come to marry her hardes' workin' child. Sure enough,
she come to tell me one mornin' before I gone off to school dat
Josephine Symmonette swear to her dat "Mr. Stone pinch her on da
behind while dey was standin' on da line at the All Purpose Shop."
Say he whisper sumtin in her ear 'bout goin' in da bush on Sunday
after church. Now, a story like that is enough to give any woman
concern, and I was hurt to hear it at first. But because it was comin'
from Jospehine, who was a certified fool, and was worse off than
me when it come to man givin' her a second look, I was oblige to
dismiss it.

But when a hurricane hit Finnegan's Bluff dat October and
destroy ole Abel Hanna's house, Jewel was sure I was gone catch
sense. Even Daddy, who stayed out of my business most of the
time, had ta nod his head in agreement. Everybody was 'pose to
chip in to help wit' da supplies to rebuild Abel house. Problem
was, big and bold, when the collection plate was passin' in church,
(Mercer Stone wuzzan Baptist, but he use to sit wit' da men in ole
Mt. Sinai because he was tryin to impress my parents), when the
collection plate was passin' Mercer frown at the man carryin' the

money from aisle to aisle, whisper to da fella next him that "They mussie take him for a natural born ass to be givin' his hard earn money to some ole fool who was dumb enough to build his house too near the sea," proceeded to change a big bill in da plate for smaller ones, and never hand over a single penny!

Now I see you laughin' in disbelief. Is funny now, yes? But it wuzzan den. I marry him against my parents wishes. As much as he was from a good family, Ma Jewel never feel proper 'bout Mercer Stone, and what Jewel feel John Bodie use to feel almost without fail.

And I know now dat he never love me. I was just a wife to him. And a wife to Mercer Stone was a servant. A wife to Mercer Stone was supposed to do the chores his mother did for him his entire life. He never loved me. I was just a Backadabush Baptist. And das just where he wanted me to stay: in da back. And on my back. And if I was big black and barefoot nine months outta twelve all the better for him. Because that way he could have some fun and didn't have to worry about draggin' me behin' him to make him look bad wit' my "island ways."

You see that pot-bellied man that is come here visitin', sitting in my living room and smilin' at you like nuttin ever pass between me and him that justify my cuttin' his shrivelled ting off and t'rowin' it in the crab pen? That man try his damndest to kill my soul. If I was a woman wit' a bad head I woulda fix his ass long time and done wit' it. But I is go ta church, and I don' go see da obeah man right after.

Once we been livin' in Safe Haven long enough for me to get my "O" Levels and graduate from the Teacher's Institute, we gone to live on Ferdinand Island. And I don't want you t'ink he was encouragin' me eider, because aldough he say he didn't mind me studyin' before we was marri'd he change his mind fast once that ring was on my finger. Dis was still before you was born. He wanted me to stay home and mind his chirren. So when he get appointed headmaster of a school dere in Charles Town, me and Firsborn and Kevin gone wit' him. He see to it that I get posted to the same school. We live on Ferdinand Island eight years. I want you to understand dat. Eight years. And the Ministry of Education used to send all the teachers' cheques to the principal in order to be distributed. I want you to know that for eight years, eight years, Mercer Stone never give me my money. For eight years Mercer Stone take my cheques and I never see one red cent. If I ever had money in my hand, it was to go and buy food, and it was money he give me for that purpose. Eight years that man took what was rightfully mine. What I work for. What I earn. His excuse was he "takin' care of the family." He was the head a the house.

I could see you don' believe dere could be a man dat cold walkin' on dis here earth. But you wrong. You gat to realize what he see me for. You gat to realize what a woman count for in dis country. What a woman say don't mean shit in Santa Maria. What a man say is law. If a woman cheat on her man she is a whore and a slut. If a man sweetheart he is real man. Das reality.

Mercer Stone used to take all his money and go buy the fines' clothes for himself. I use to be up and down Charles Town in the cheapest rags. Had to make clothes for myself and my children outta any old cloth I could find. All the women used to look at me and say how sorry dey feel for me. But I ain' say nuttin', see. I know my day was comin'. I trust in God. He ain' never fail me yet.

Don' t'ink I exaggeratin' when I say that Mercer didn' care 'bout anybody but himself. When we leave Charles Town, Ferdinand Island, we come right back to Safe Haven to live in the house on Daley Street that his pa give him. And after keepin' my salary all those years he still couldn' spend any money on his children. Only reason I make a little money after we come back to Grand Santa Maria is because I gone to work in a different school from him. And when you and Frankie was born? Shoot. He act like he ain' never see ya'll in his life. When I tell him I ga leave him if he don' change, he use ta laugh in my face. But that was fine. 'Cause it didn't take me long to see dat I had to take care a things on my lonesome. I was done plannin' my way to freedom.

I remember the day Frankie get knock down. A truck come speedin' through Daley Street and Frankie was bouncin' a basketall in front of the house. Sure 'nough, he lose the ball and it roll 'cross the street. When he gone 'cross the road for it the truck was passin'. Knock him seven feet in the air. I watch it all happen, 'cause I was sittin' on the porch shellin' peas. I t'ought my child was dead 'cause I done tell him don' be bouncin' dat ball in the road, but I was too tired to beat his behind. I run in the road to look after him screamin' like I see ghos'. Everybody on Daley Street was out dere. Well, Mercer Stone was inside the house gettin' ready for a banquet. Mind you, he ain' never aks his wife if she want to go out wit' him. And he ain' had no time to go outside and see if his third child was dead or alive. He ga get dress and jump in his car to head on down the road to his banquet. And I know he hear me run out into the street screamin' for my chile. When he pass me in the road with my child in my arms he gone poke his head out da windah and aks if Frankie alright. I aks if he look alright. He suck his teet' and tell me to call a ambulance 'cause he cyaa afford to be late. Jus' pull off and gone 'bout his business. The man who knock Frankie down had to carry him to the hospital for me.

Never see such a full-a-shit man as your pa in my whole life. And dat sister he have dere name Ann Marie ain' no better. When Kevin was in trouble wit' his schoolwork I say to Mercer Stone, let me send him to St. Luke's. Now, I tell you before, das where Mercer hese'f been to school. Is a private school and it cos' money. That ole fool gone complainin' to his family 'bout how I want to send my chirren to expensive school. Ann Marie come to my house to aks me if I t'ink her brother rich. I say, why you say dat? She say, 'cause I want to send Kevin to St. Lukes. She say, "If you did wan' educate your children you shouldn' a have so damn many!" You ever see? I tell her I never aks Mercer Stone to pay for Kevin to go to St. Lukes. I was gone pay for it myse'f. You ever see anyting like dat. If I did wan' educate my chirren I shouldn' a have so damn many. So I commitin' a sin by wantin' my son to get over his learnin' problems. Dis from Ann Marie! A dunce if I ever see one! And where her daughter is now? Sellin' earrings on Waterfront Road in the Conchy Joe man jewellry store. My son Kevin done graduate Santa Maria College and makin' good money at the telelephone company. Dey might even send him off for more trainin' one day. Small-minded people. All dem Stones.

Fifteen years I put up with that shit. But I catch sense. Never had no ambitions for his own children. Didn' want his wife to have *a better education dan him. Didn't want his wife to show him up. Das why he never want me to study. But I use to wait 'til he go sleep and read my books by candlelight in the kitchen. I study when he wuzzan lookin'. When I take my "A" Levels in English and History I was nine months pregnant wit' you. Two days later, when my water break, my neighbour, Ms. Delancey, had to take me to hospital 'cause Mercer Stone was in da bar watchin' football. An' Mercer Stone ain' know how I pass exam while I was pregnant yet. I pass wit' Distinction too. And when I was accepted to University abroad he was mad. He wan' know what I need BA for. He try raise plenty hell when I tell him I plan to go away to University. Plenty hell. But he know better dan to lay his hand on me. Ain' no man ever lay a hand on me in my life, not even my pa. I woulda kill Mercer Stone dead and gone to jail if he hit me once, I tell you dat much. I wuzzan checkin' for him. I tell him I was going no matter what. I tell him if he was a real man he would come and try and further himself too. But he didn' want dat. He tell me I get too big for my own shoes. Tell me I want wear da pants.*

I even een mind him. I pack everyt'ing up and send you all to stay with ya Aunt Bell 'til I was ready to fly to University. He was such a no good father dat he didn' even realize his children wuzzan in the house for two whole days. And their clothes and belongings was out the house two weeks before that and he never notice. Mercer Stone use to go from bedroom to bathroom to livingroom and das it.

When I leave him to go on that plane I tell him dat if he still consider himself my husband he could come to University and be with his wife and family. I done clean up after him, and cook his meals all dat time. And I never once complain. But he couldn' find it in his heart to support me when I want to educate myself and do better for our children. And to top it off he never give two hoots about how yall was livin'. So I leave him.

And when I gone I see just what kind a man he was. I was all the way in school for three years and I didn' have time to look at a man, I was so busy studyin' and workin'. But soon as I call the house on Daley Street, not more than two weeks since I leave Safe Haven for University Campus, a strange woman was answerin' my phone as if she live dere all her life. Right dere an' den I know I reach the end a da road between me and Mercer Stone. I don't know how long he was seein' her, but people tell me she was a woman who teach to the same school as him and they was chummie for quite a time before I leave Santa Maria self.

I tell him straight and plain, I ain' do nuttin to deserve bein' treat like trash. In all da time I been marri'd to him he ain' do nuttin 'cep' treat me like a no good nigger. I tell him I was goin' to divorce him and that I never want to see his face again. And I won' tell you all the hell dis country is give woman who try divorce her husband!

Some man cyaa tolerate a woman unless he between her leg. Mercer is one a dem.

But I learn, baby. I learn da hard way. I took the four a yall to University wit' me, and build a house for you, and will put the four a you through school, God willing, out of my own pocket. And watch. Dat same man who ain' had nuttin to do wit' raisin' you ga be the firs' one to stand up and claim responsibility if any a yall make sumtin a yaselves. Don't look for him oderwise, because he ain' ga be nowhere to be found if you end up in trouble. But that's just fine. Perfectly fine. Because God still sit on da T'rone.

Bullfrog eat plenty fly today and feel good. Tomorrow snake gone take his time.

5

The Honourable Thaddeus McKinney might seem to have made the transition from bus driver to Minister of Education with the confidence and ease of a man rescued from the bulrushes, but he was no Moses.

Before becoming Tree's representative in the House of Assembly, a position as Vice-President of the Taxi and Tour Bus Drivers Union had been his only claim to fame for nearly ten years. The unions had become power blocs when the pressure for black enfranchisement and universal suffrage got into full swing in the 50s. Back then, Thaddeus was just a follower. The kind of hard-nosed, self-sacrificing follower it takes to get the dirty work of any grassroots movement done. And he still was a follower at the core. It was his specialty.

The Vice-Presidency had not fallen to him until the late 60s, and by that time the political battle had been won. The white minority National Democratic Party—or "The Egyptians" as the people called them—were overthrown by the black ballot, and no blood had been shed. Once the PNF took power, these slaveowners' grandsons and immigrant businessmen disintegrated and reappeared later in the FLP, the Free Liberal Party. This party was funded by the whites and many of them remained candidates, but most of its members were the blacks who had become disenchanted with the machinations of the nation's new leader.

Independence followed shortly after Majority Rule. Britain did not have much to lose in granting it. The real battle on Santa Marian soil had been between the rich white merchant and the poor black. With the white government enjoying something close to self-rule, Britain had been little more than a biased referee for over a hundred years. So just like that, the chain of islands named Las Santa Marias by that misinformed Genoese sailor, Columbus, became a united, independent state, and a member of England's Commonwealth of Nations. And Thaddeus, a man in his early forties by then, with a wife, three children by her, his sweetheart, and an outside child there also, was rewarded with the Vice-Presidency in return for what had by then amounted to almost twenty years as a staunch union organizer.

He was well liked. He was one of the fellas. He drank, he slammed dominoes, he cussed stink words late into the night. He played the numbers, and he had his little flings like the other man. He was reliable. Not smart, not ambitious, but reliable. And he was totally loyal to the PNF, especially the Prime Minister.

Then, after ten years in a position that meant little, the opportunity to gain even greater favour with the man at the very top came during the Commission of Inquiry. Both the Prime Minister's poor judgment and Thaddeus's own previously inconsequential role in the country's affairs worked to his advantage, providing him with an opportunity to join the ranks of the king's men. The Commission of Inquiry to Investigate Government Corruption taught the Prime Minister an invaluable lesson. It made him painfully aware of who his true friends were in his own party and in the country he had ruled for over fifteen years. To be considered one of the loyal made all the difference in one's political future. Thaddeus was one of the loyal.

The Prime Minister had established the Commission to clear his name and to convince his voters that he was not involved in drug trafficking. And that only became necessary after several major American newspapers and a national news show featured exposés that accused the Santa Marian Government and the Royal Santa Marian Police Force, top to bottom, of being corrupt middlemen in the trafficking of illegal drugs into the United States. But the Commission turned out to be a bit of obeah that backfired in the face of the ones who worked it. Instead of preserving reputations, the Commission implicated everyone. The PM did not foresee that such a Commission, which had been instrumental in removing the whites two decades earlier, (it was called to investigate mafia bribery of white government officials for the privilege of owning and running casinos in Santa Maria), would have the same negative effect on his own administration. From the confines of the palatial Whitehall Mansion—which he had privately built in his own honour and would later try to sell to the Government at a profit—the PM seemed to have remained unaware of the extent to which his own Cabinet, and men and women throughout the islands, were benefiting from drug money. There were resignations. A threat to his leadership emerged from within the Party. Even the second in command of the PNF (a man who had fought at the Prime Minister's side for countless years) stepped down, and then called on his leader to also resign before it was too late.

Although the Commission failed to directly connect the PM to any of the large cast of international outlaws that were discovered to have dealings with Santa Marian lawyers, elected officials, policemen, and private citizens great and small, it did point out that he had somehow amassed tremendous financial resources and built himself a mansion, which was impossible on his known sources of income.

Later, many of the less informed speculated that the Prime Minister had only been able to win over the people's support by agreeing to an internationally televised interview with some of his accusers on the American morning news show that showcased the scandal. This faulty reasoning posited that the sight of their leader, their Moses, confronting and talking hard to his white detractors for all the world to see, had won the sympathy of the many who still saw him as the champion of the man from Backadabush.

Nothing could have been further from the truth. The Commission and the PM's angry unravelling on American television were both uncalled for. In fact, they were the first tangible signs of his falling out of touch with his people in the fifteen years since he had led them out of Egyptian bondage. Of course, no one close enough to him had the courage to tell him that, or to tell him the truth about his most trusted men, if indeed he needed to be told.

The American newspaper stories had caused no serious damage that one impassioned speech delivered at Safe Haven National Park, (a huge, brightly lit clearing in the heart of a ghetto of clapboard houses), one speech about imperialist CIA lies and white minority racist plots, could not have trampled forever. Instead, the Prime Minister had overreacted and exposed himself to the greatest threat to his political power that he had ever experienced. The word among the women of the Straw Market, among the bus and taxi drivers, and among the fishermen on the docks, was that during the Election campaign which followed the Commission, the PM worked his obeah harder than he ever did before. They said he had brought in a special *hougnan* to add greater potency to his supernatural operations. Some swore they had friends working in Whitehall Mansion that saw him with "his Haitian" handling a boa-constrictor and chanting a mixture of *vodun* and obeah spells. (The snake wore a red bow tie, just like the ones the PM was fond of wearing at least once a week). And his technique of keeping the nation guessing at what combination of the number ten the date of the Election would fall on left the Opposition frustrated and petulant—winning him further admiration from the poor black people of Backadabush, who (like small town folk everywhere) admired anyone who could keep his mouth shut about something for any length of time.

The Commission and the interview had been unnecessary self-flagellations because, to Santa Marians, their Prime Minister's corruption and that of his leading men were non-issues. That following year's General Election victory by the PNF taught the Opposition as much. They tried to use the Commission's Report as a tool to discredit the Government, and their attempts failed miserably. People didn't care about corruption. Many might have confessed that the PM and his Ministers were doing nothing that any Santa Marian would not have done if given half a chance at a piece of the long-withheld pie.

In the years preceding and shortly following the Commission, things were good for everybody. Drug money had given the society an economic boost that rivaled days of piracy past. And as long as the wealth was being shared—which it was—it didn't matter to people that record numbers of men and women were becoming strung out on drugs, so long as their brothers, sons, cousins, were getting rich and spreading the wealth around. Every plane that flew over the islands in the hours before the dawn was a gift from God. And no one wanted to mess with such blessings.

So for many years, thanks to this influx of American dollars from marijuana and cocaine transshipment, and the small population of the country, it was not uncommon for the son of one family to be trafficking in the very drugs that wound up perpetuating his first cousin's addiction, much less that of some anonymous basehead in New York City. For a few years, the numbers of addicts per capita was among the highest in the world. Young men went to Florida academies to learn how to pilot single-engine planes. People started driving the most expensive cars money could buy and parked them outside their clapboard houses beneath the satellite dishes that dwarfed their homes. Branches of banks opened on the remoter islands of the archipelago with little infrastructure and reported remarkable amounts of deposits in American fifty and hundred dollar bills. And once in a while, a woman's son might disappear in the night to show up in a car trunk burnt almost beyond recognition, or tied to a tree with a bullet hole between the eyes, or washed up on the shore. A number of young men crashed in planes trying to land on airstrips under cover of darkness, or ditched them trying to escape the U.S. Coast Guard. More than a few fathers, sons, and brothers populated Floridian jail cells. Colombians disappeared from Her Majesty's Prison without a trace, days after being captured, charged, and convicted. But no one talked. The drug dealers were glamourous and exciting. The money was good, real good. And the Police and Defence Forces, disappointed that they were no longer the country's premiere rude boys, sold what they confiscated whenever they could. In short, Santa Marians lived the high life.

It was during this state of affairs that Thaddeus, the humble man who had come to Safe Haven as a picky-head boy from Crab Bay, the bus driver turned union man, the reliable fella, the man like other men, stepped onto the witness stand of the Commission of Inquiry, looked around the room at lawyers, reverends, and other self-declared leaders of men, and lied with a straight face, thereby placing himself on the road to wealth, status, and admiration.

During the Commission, the President of the Union was more interested in saving his own behind than protecting the reputations of Government Ministers. He had amassed a small fortune by pocketing Union funds for twenty-five years, so when he testified he was prepared to implicate stray dogs if it meant he was not going to jail. Thaddeus, on the other hand, had never been greedy. Besides, he lacked the know-how and access, even as Vice-President, to embezzle. He had nothing to lose by testifying. Broke and having a hard time supporting his two families, both Thaddeus's wife and his sweetheart encouraged him to commit the noble deed, hoping it would win him favour with the Prime Minister and the top brass.

So when the time came he said what he was told to say and the DEA, on pressure from U.S. top brass, (who feared that wholesale extradictions might jeopardise a treaty to sustain their naval base on Short Cay), had to let the Minister alone. Good fortune followed. The Presidency of the Union. And eventually, the easy seat in Hawkins Town. A dream come true for the boy from Backadabush. With nothing more than Grade 4 at an All Age School to his credit, he was now rubbing shoulders with lawyers and doctors, rich businessmen, and knights, betwixt the old pink walls of the House of Assembly in Victoria Square. He was now a man of the world. He was the Honourable Thaddeus Rudolph McKinney, Member of Parliament for the Hawkins Town Constituency and President of the Bahamas Taxi and Tour Bus Drivers Union. Titles galore. He was now a muck-a-muck of the highest order.

And with his new-found status came a flash of understanding, an epiphany that had eluded him all the while he had been Vice-President of the Union. It dawned on Thaddeus that this was the road the black man in Santa Maria had to take. To get anywhere in a place where whites may have lost the power of office but maintained a centuries-old economic stranglehold on the country, a man of his background, a man without benefit of years of University education which could enable him to be an accountant, a lawyer, a doctor, or an engineer, was faced with one of two options: to be a preacher or a politician. These were the only two jobs that held sway. These were the only two jobs that brought a man like him wealth, status, honour, women. And Thaddeus knew already that he lacked the shamelessness to preach. His eyes, thanks to his Prime Minister, had been opened.

But what Tree might not have known on the morning of his visit to Thaddeus's office in the old Great House that had been turned into the Ministry of Education—had Santa Maria not been a place where no one could keep a secret—was that, mixed with his obvious good fortune, the Minister had met with more than a modicum of bad luck.

It was common knowledge that Thaddeus's troubles began as soon as his first step up the political ladder was taken. (To whom much is given, of him much shall be required!) His overnight leapfrog into parliamentary eminence precipitated a variety of transformations in the man. Prompted simultaneously by his wife and his sweetheart, Thaddeus had now to project to the general public an image of great affluence and sophistication that heretofore had not been expected of him. The first sign of this impending metamorphosis was the receipt of his new, blue license plates with black lettering that read "MP 22." It was an awe-inspiring moment for him, and he knew, with a tinge of foreboding, that he was headed across strange frontiers. Up to that point in his life the only vehicle Thaddeus had owned was his old white Nissan twenty-five seater. But he couldn't very well put the new license plates on that, or pull up at the House of Assembly in it. (He might be poor but he was not a poppy show!) He took out an interest free loan—thanks to his new status and salary, such wonders were possible now—and bought himself a BMW. Navy blue, the colour of choice with PNF big shots. (A blue beamer communicated power, authority, calm under fire, refinement and sophistication, steadfastness and reliability, German engineering, etc.) Then, of course, he had to dress properly, as befitting a member of the nation's legislature. Each being unaware of the other's advice, his wife and sweetheart carefully observed other MPs and decided that the bush jacket and matching trousers, not the coat and tie, were fitting for him. Brown, navy blue, white, gray: he wore them every day. Then (of course) he had to move out of his old cramped neighbourhood into a district with fewer black people, and houses that had more yard space. "Space for a lawn, not mango tree and plantain sucker," his wife had said. Before he knew it, Thaddeus was a new man.

And perhaps that would have been enough for him: the blue license plates that said "MP 22" in black letters, the new car, the new clothes, the new home, the nice lawn instead of mango tree and plantain sucker, the special treatment he got from the police, the people at Santa Maria Air who always stopped everything to deal with him and put him in first class no matter what his ticket said, the sundry women that came out of the woodwork and from whom he was able to extract sexual favours in return for a job here or a promotion there, the customs officers who let his buxom sweetheart bring all her expensive New York shopping through the airport without inspection or charge (his wife was never afforded such extravagances as shopping trips), the sound of his name on Radio One, his picture in *The Beacon* and *The Safe Haven Times,* the genuflecting protocol officers and Channel One cameramen who followed him everywhere when he was in the company of the PM at some ribbon cutting or other, the never waiting on lines anywhere for anything, the look of envy and admiration on the faces of the people on street corners as he whizzed by in the blue BMW that communicated power, refinement, calm under fire, etcetera, etcetera, the unceasing attention of all his flattering, supplicant Hawkins Town constituents. Perhaps all that would have been enough. It was certainly more than he had ever hoped for. He was a follower after all. He was not greedy after all. He was not smart after all. And more than anything, he was already eternally grateful to the Prime Minister for choosing him, for elevating him, for picking him up from the dirt, dusting him off, putting a shirt on his back, and making him a man. Eternally grateful, eternally loyal.

But such devotion made him unfit to remain just as he was: safe and satisfied in the work-free, not-too-bright stardom of the typical PNF Back Bencher. The Prime Minister liked him. And that was trouble. It was always trouble when the Bigger Boss liked somebody. That he "liked" you usually meant that he saw you as a threat to his power, a rising star that promised to draw attention away from his own bright sun. And in that case he would either have to "deal with you"—meaning he would intimidate you or victimize you, thereby silencing your big fat mouth—or he would "take you under his wing"—which meant that he would give you a cushy position that demanded obedience, thereby sapping your strength and very life-blood as would a vampire. Santa Marians weren't joking when they said that in the PNF there was only room for one man with balls and that man was the PM.

Fortunately, the Prime Minister's affection for Thaddeus did not stem from any fear of him, any notion of his dangerous potentiality, a potentiality that needed to be contained, channeled, and slowly, gradually, destroyed by accumulated privilege, ever worsening complicity, and steadily increased body fat. Thaddeus was no threat at all. The PM's affection for him was born of the best intentions. He *admired* Thaddeus.

Now how could a man of the PM's education and training, a man who had risen to such awesome stature in Santa Maria, and, indeed, in all the Caribbean and the Commonwealth of Nations, admire a barely literate tour bus driver? You really didn't have to look any further than Thaddeus's humble beginnings to find the answer. Anyone could see that this is what endeared him to the PM. In the Prime Minister's eyes, Thaddeus was a man after his own heart; a man who, like him, had known poverty and deprivation, but who, unlike the PM himself and his party protégés, had not been slavishly driven to acquire countless academic qualifications in order to feel like the white man's equal. And should Thaddeus have been faulted for that? Should he have been considered unfit to lead, unfit to become a man with power and responsibility, simply because he was not a "trained professional" of some sort? So Thaddeus had not won a scholarship to the Government New School, the PM must have said to himself. So he didn't spend countless years of his life at Cambridge reading law or at Harvard's medical school. Big damn deal! He was a man. A black man. A black man with acute sensibilities. It was just like these niggers to think that they had to follow behind backra like monkeys, do everything he did, mimic his every word and mannerism, in order to be considered human, to be considered men! Rubbish! This same Thaddeus, this same simple, broad-nosed, picky-head man had been loyal to him when others, men with the best educations scholarships could buy, men with wives of the lightest hue and longest hair status could attract, his very own right-hand man, had sought to rip out his throat and carry away his privates in a jar. This man, Thaddeus, deserved anything that could be given to him. So convinced of all this was the Prime Minister that he proceeded to shower unprecedented blessings on McKinney. Blessings that left other PNF men—who had spent years prostrate and thought their time had come—baffled, envious, pouting.

But there was one tiny problem. It was not that the PM's thinking had been wrong about what was required in a leader—certainly, anyone with half a good brain could see that you didn't have to be a lawyer to know what was good for the country and what wasn't. The PM had simply misjudged Thaddeus's capabilities. Perhaps the crisis Moses had just been through with the Commission had affected his judgment, made him more sentimental than usual, no one knows. Certainly, Thaddeus appeared to fit the description of the "common man," of that typical Backadabusher whom the PM could elevate (in his graciousness) and make one of his most cherished and loyal disciples. As the old folks say, "Jus' cause ya have book learnin' don't mean ya have sense." But Thaddeus, sadly, was doubly denied: he was both uneducated *and* lacking in common sense. So for every seedling the Prime Minister planted in the soil of his fortune, Thaddeus found a way to let the caterpillars and the goats eat it just when it sprouted green and promising.

The biggest gift the Prime Minister dropped in Thaddeus's lap, on top of making him chairman or consultant on two or three boards that gave him extra income, was a once in a lifetime chance to run a Japanese car dealership. This turned out to be an absolute disaster. Thaddeus had no business head.

Every Tom Dick and Harry flammed him. And when he wasn't being flammed he was squandering his money left right and centre. So much so that within three years of opening the dealership the Japanese withdrew their support, refusing to do business with anyone from Santa Maria ever again.

In that brief time Thaddeus built a new home overlooking the sea that cost half a million dollars, bought a brand new top-of-the-line Mercedes Benz (blue), lent every boyhood friend he had oodles of money and permitted them to drive off with cars without meeting payments, sent his wife's children to boarding school in England, bought his sweetheart a brand new Jaguar (red convertible), sent *her* child to boarding school in Massachusetts, and invested bales of money in a handful of business ventures that all failed miserably, flushing his freshly acquired financial solvency down the proverbial toilet.

Then, as if bankruptcy was not embarrassing enough, was not sufficient to give him peptic ulcers and high blood pressure, Thaddeus started having personal problems. Woman problems. And, to make it even worse, these problems were played out on the public stage.

It happened just after the Japanese had told him, in syllables he could not understand, to piss off. He was sent no new cars, and his only income was coming from repairing old ones. But even this was getting harder because they stopped supplying him with spare parts. At this point Thaddeus wanted nothing more than to lay low for a few months and recover. In fact, he decided to go to New York for a week. He told his wife it was on business.

His wife, Marjorie, had gone to the bank to make a withdrawal. "She was lookin' wery ole and hang down," the tellers and other customers would later recall when they told all their friends about the incident. "Mussie 'cause her man wuz cheatin' on her from God make Adam." And by some terrible trick of that same God, Thaddeus's sweetheart, Anavee Rolle, a flamboyant woman twenty years Marjorie's junior, who loved to talk about "huh man and what he buy huh," also happened to be making an unscheduled visit to withdraw cash from the savings account Thaddeus had opened for her. "She say her and her man was goin' on a trip to New York," the tellers and customers would later recall. Unfortunately for Thaddeus, Marjorie had been having a particularly bad day, and she knew damn well who Anavee Rolle was. Everyone who cared about her welfare had told her the truth about her husband years ago, but she had pretended not to see until that day. "An' nex' ting ya know all hell bruck loose."

* * *

Old Ezra Darling, the stuttering bank security guard who tried to part the women without success, began to describe the scuffle in the following manner to the young constable who eventually took both ladies (handcuffed and still spitting at each other) in the back of his blue Grand Fury while the siren beckoned stray dogs to howl in reply all along the ride to Central Station:

"I is a prayin' man o-officer. I jus' wan' you know dat. I is a Christian. I don' believe in why-whylence."

An onlooker, fed up already: "Stop talkin' foolishness and tell da man what happen. Everybody know you does drink!"

"You-you see officer? You see what I does-does have to deal wit' in dis bank. Temptation. Da fiery darts a Satan flyin' at me every, every day I work on dis job. I don' know what ga happen nex'. Las' week two mens dem come in the bank wit' cutlass de-demandin' money. W-what I 'pose ta do? I-I don' have no gun."

The constable, sweating and getting impatient, is already nervous about having to write up a report, so he don' need no more wexation. "Jus' tell me what happen, boss. Hurry up!"

"I-I ain' da offenda ya know officer. I-I was jus'-jus' d-dooo-in' my job. Dese people here accu-accu-accusin' me of drinkin' and I ne'er touch a drink, drink in my life."

"I believe you. Nah go head and tell me what happen!"

"Well-well, dis l-lady here, da one in the h-h-h-high, high heel shoes and da t-tight skirt. She come in da bank t-talkin' loud for errybody ta hear. T-talkin' 'bout how she gat ta hu-hurry up pull some money out her account. S-say she goin' to Ne-New York wit' her man. Say heeza, heeza, heeza MP."

Anavee, seeing her chance: "Das right. THADDEUS McKIN-NEY! Ya hear me say it? He is my-damn-man! An' when he catch wind a how yall treat me ALL A YINNA LOSIN' YALL JOB!"

"You see you have any God damn man, ya dirty bitch?!," Marjorie responded. "You ain' nuttin but a t'ree cent whore! If you have man let me see ya marriage certificate! Yinna Santa Marian woman always tryin' to tear people household apart! Let dis palice take dese handcuff off my han' an' ahll rip your lyin' tongue right out ya smelly mout'!'"

"Don' start wit' me, bitch! Is 'cause you all dry up now he come to look for a REAL woman!"

The bystanders, enjoying themselves: "AAAAAWWWWW!"

The constable, really losing his cool: "Now listen, be quiet before I start makin' up charges ta add ta dis report! Go on nigger!"

"Well-well dis lady here, in the brown dress, was mindin' her own, own, own business officer. Wuzzan disturbin' nobody. Nex' ting ya look, dis woman, woman here in da r-red catch eye a her, an', an', she, she mussie figa she ga make poppy show outta her. So, so she walk off da l-line and pat her on her back an' aks her if sh-she know who her husband goin' New-New-New York wit' tommora. So da woman answer, answer, answer, say, she don' know, but whoever she is, sh-she is a no good slut. And das when everyt'ing gone stock crazy in da place."

From that point, Ezra proceeded to tell the officer that it was Anavee who threw the initial blow, which came in the shape of her red, cosmetic-laden handbag. It was this unorthodox gauntlet, delivered briskly to the cheek, which prompted the duel and caused Marjorie McKinney, "hang down" as she was, to spring to life. She did so by delivering a flurry of blows in that furious, uncharted fashion of women, all of which landed with incredible violence on the jaw bone and eye sockets of her attacker. The crowded bank was flung into hysteria as some people ran for cover and others ran to form a ring around the sparring pair. Stunned and insulted, Anavee countered with additional blows to the head, chest, and back of the MP's wife, again with her battle-tested handbag. She struck so many times and so hard that first the strap popped, and then the handbag burst, freeing all her beauty aids onto the polished tiles of the bank. Before the stuttering security guard could leap from his seat, each woman was cussing and spitting at the other remorselessly.

It was at this moment, people would later recall, that Mrs. McKinney resolved not to let herself be dishonoured by her husband's mistress. ("They was gern talk 'bout her anyway, so they might as well have sumtin' good to say," the tellers and customers figured.) So from that point on until they were parted—this took some time, not because Ezra could not separate them as he told the police, but because he and the men who eventually helped him were enjoying the view—Mrs. McKinney beat Anavee soundly. This was primarily achieved by pulling the weave out of her hair, punching her wildly in the face, ripping her blouse and bra off, (to the delight of the men in the now packed bank), and digging her teeth and fingernails into the flesh of her back and face.

Ezra concluded his story by showing the constable his later-famous scratch marks, but the entire event did not come to an end until Thaddeus dragged himself to Central Station and tried to decide which of his two women to bail out of jail. As unimaginable as Santa Marians later found it, the beleaguered MP bailed out the wrong woman, his sweetheart, and left his wife behind bars. And as if that were not sufficient proof of his temporary insanity, he still went on his trip to New York.

Thaddeus mussie figure if he hattie dead he mightaswell have he fun firs'. To no one's surprise, the trip to New York was a terrible mistake. Anavee insisted that he get a divorce (the temerity) and Thaddeus was obliged to refuse. On returning to his beach house he discovered that all his clothes had been stuffed into three garbage bags and tossed on the lawn, the keys for his Mercedes were mysteriously missing from their hiding place in the utility room, new locks were on all the doors, and his telephone number had been changed.

When it was all over Marjorie had divorced him and taken the house and the car—a precedent in Santa Maria divorce cases. Anavee left him for a young police sergeant. The business was shut down and the property repossessed by the bank. Thaddeus, broke, beaten, and hungry, disappeared from the face of the earth. He stopped going to the One For the Road. He stopped playing the numbers. He never went to Parliament sessions. He resigned as President of the Taxi and Tour Bus Drivers Union. He didn't even show up to PNF General Meetings. It seemed as if his career was over. The last anyone had heard from him, he was shacking up with a Jehovah's Witnesses woman who had just had twins for him. He became such a recluse that he even sent this woman to the bank each month to withdraw what was left of his MP's pay check after the law suits and other bills were paid off.

Certainly, no one expected Thaddeus to run for the Hawkins Town Constituency seat in the next election. They were all certain that the PM had realized his mistake by now and would unceremoniously drop Thaddeus from his ticket, as he was prone to do. But such second-guessers had never properly understood the Prime Minister's esteem for this man, who, despite some bad luck, was unquestionably and forever his loyal follower.

Thaddeus deserves a second chance, the PM must have thought to himself. *It's like these niggers to pull a man down, to laugh and celebrate when he fall on he face instead of trying to help him up. That's the problem with black people. They too like damn tear down!*

Out of the blue, Thaddeus's phone rang. It was the PM himself on the line. Thaddeus was overwhelmed. (That he should stoop to speak to him in person, after all he done do wrong!) And for the second time, the PM was there for him. Ready and willing to pick him up from out of the dirt where the hard cruel world had dashed him, to dust him off, etcetera, etcetera.

The Prime Minister never mentioned the incident in the bank, his resignation from the Union, or his absence from Parliament. (The PM never went to Parliament meetings either—he had no time for small time showboating.) Instead he told Thaddeus that he had just the job for him, that he had been waiting for just the right moment to give him this opportunity, and that he hoped Thaddeus had no intention of withdrawing as the incumbent candidate for Hawkins Town in next year's Election. Thaddeus was dumbfounded. The Prime Minister was offering him a place in the Cabinet. Cabinet! The position of Minister of Education had been left vacant since Sir Eugene A. Thompson had skipped town for Switzerland. As usual, the PM had been taking his own sweet time in naming a new Minister.

And now here he was, offering it to him. "God is good," thought Thaddeus, "God truly good." Minister of Education. Wuzzan dat sumtin.

* * *

"What happen to your arm?"

"It's just a fracture. A little accident."

"Hmmm. So who is your people again?"

"The Bodies. Maureen Bodie is my mother."

"Yes, yes, das right. I shoulda recognize you long time. You favour her. How ya mammy doin' ?"

"Fine, sir."

"Good. Good. Me and her go way back. Way back."

"Mmm."

"Yeah, man. She ain' tell you?"

"I think she started to, but . . ."

"Yeah, man. Me and Maureen Bodie meet down in Crab Bay. Das where my people from, ya see. I born on St. Mark's Island. And ya mammy was a schoolteacher, I think, a senior mistress down there or something. When da PNF use to come dat way she use to help cook food an' campaign an' ting. A good woman. Raise the four a yall on her own, hey?"

"Yes, sir."

"Yes, yes, a strong Santa Marian woman is a precious ting. I had a mind put a ring on her finga once. She tell you dat?"

Getting uncomfortable: "No, sir. She never mentioned it."

"No matter. I fancy your mammy wuzzan interested in me in dat way. Besides, I was done marri'd!" He laughs almost hysterically. Tree forces a smile without teeth. Thaddeus catches himself.

"So. What can I do for you today, young man?"

"My mother suggested that I come see you . . . To introduce myself . . . Seeing as we live in Pompey Village, which is a part of your constituency, she thought that I . . . I . . . ah . . ."

"Oh. You the one working for the newspaper. Yes. Everybody said that rascal Curry find hessef a good young writer. Is you. Yes, yes. It figures. Your mother is a smart woman, so it don't surprise me."

"I finished the New Government School three years ago. I did a two-year Associates Degree in English at Santa Maria College. Been working for *The Daily Report* for a year. I'm quitting at the end of next August, though. I've been accepted to University abroad."

"I don' blame you. Dat paper is publish too much damn gossip anyhow! Curry, the Editor, is a FLP stooge if you aks me. Never ever gat anyting good to say 'bout da Government . . . University you say. To study what?"

"Well . . . I'm not really sure. I think I may finish in English, or do History, or Political Science. Something like that. I haven't really . . ."

"A fella like you should be a lawyer. Law is the thing man. All these fellas in politics is lawyers. Excep' me. I mean you gat other fellas, like doctors and businessmen and so on, too. But if I could I would do law. So I could know da ins an' outs. And how to get tings don' wit'out a hassle. Can't no one take advantage of ya or pull da wool over ya eyes if you know da law. Das what all my children gern study, I guarantee you dat."

"My mother always said there are so many lawyers in Santa Maria we don't need criminals." Tree is smiling broadly.

Thaddeus does not laugh. He looks at the young man with suspicion.

"You was at the College, right?"

"Yes, sir."

"You wuzzan involve in dat ruckus a year or so back, hey? Wit' those students marchin' an' so on. Young people these days don't seem to appreciate what dis Government done do for them. If it wuzzan' for the Prime Minister there wouldn' *be* no College."

Tree senses that he had better be careful. "I agree, sir. The Government has done a great deal."

"Yes. A *great* deal."

Still scrutinizing the young man. Only the air conditioner makes a sound.

"Actually, sir, my mother suggested that I come to see you because I have just applied for a scholarship to help with my educational expenses. And she thought that if I spoke to you, you would do what you could to help, seeing as I am a student living in your constituency."

"I see." The Minister understands now. He smiles. Triumphant. "How are your grades?"

"I graduated with a 2.9 average. It could have been better but I was a little too involved in extra-curricular activities . . . like the College paper and so on."

"I see. I see. Well. You realize dat da recommendations of the Scholarship Committee are not final. Dey are merely recommendations. The final say res' with the Minister, who happens to be me. If I feel dat a candidate is not needy I have the right and da power to strike deir name from da list."

Silence. Tree avoids eye contact with the gray-haired man behind the desk. Thaddeus almost snickers.

"In life you scratch your friend's back and he scratches yours. You agree?"

Tree's heart is pounding. He is growing angry. "Yes, Sir."

"Very good. I'm glad you agree. People have to remember that when they want sumtin done for dem they don't expect to be told no. So when it comes to us in the Government needing sumtin' we won't accept no for an answer either."

What do you want from me you no good sonofabitch. Spell it out! "Your mother is a smart woman, a hard worker, and a good PNFer. But don't believe that what has been given cyaa be taken away."

Shit. Why I come here today anyway? I tell her. I tell her. What the hell you ever give Mamma!? Hey, bastard?! She work like a damn dog for everything she have! People have to t'ank you, worship you for the clothes on dey back, for the shoes on dey feet? Yall mussie gods, hey? Why people must bow down and give burnt offerings to you?! Just because yall bloated sucknecks was at the wrong place at the right time yinna expect us . . .

"I think you could help me wit' sumtin, young Mr. Bodie. Matter a fack, I almos' certain you could help me. I have a slight problem dat a man of your skills could solve very easy. Very easy. You scratch my back, I scratch yours. Right?"

Sonabitch politicians.

"Right?"

"Yes, sir."

6

Firsborn

"No. No. Uh uhn. Um hum. Yeah. Yeah. Uh uhn. No. No. Uh
uhn. Um hum. Yeah. Yeah. Uh uhn. No. No. Uh uhn. Um hum.
Yeah. Yeah. Uh uhn. No. No. Uh uhn. Um hum. Yeah. Yeah. Uh
uhn. No. No. Uh uhn. Um hum. Yeah. Yeah. Uh uhn. No. No. Uh
uhn. Um hum. Yeah. Yeah. Uh uhn. No. No. Uh uhn. Um hum.
Yeah. Yeah. Uh uhn. No. No. Uh uhn. Um hum. Yeah. Yeah. Uh
uhn. No. No. Uh uhn. Um hum. Yeah. Yeah. Uh uhn. No. No. Uh
uhn. Um hum. Yeah. Yeah. Uh uhn."

Shaking his head. Shaking his head. Nodding his head. Nodding his head. Nodding again. Shaking his head in exasperation.
Holding his index finger to the bulging vein beneath his left
temple. Looking up to the ceiling. The smell of his own semen.
The smell of grimy, unwashed clothing. The smell of a hundred
cigarette butts tossed beneath his window sill. The ceaseless,
meaningless blare of the transitor radio locked forever on a Cu-
ban radio station. Spanish he cannot understand, the world he
cannot grasp.

Spanish he cannot understand, the world he cannot grasp. Span-ish-he-can-not-un-der-stand-the-world-he-can-not-grasp . . .

And living for the rock. Hooked on the rock. Everything is the rock, the rock, the rock.

"No. No. Um hum. Yeah. Yeah. Uhn uhn. No. No. Um hum. Yeah. Yeah. Uhn uhn. No. No. Um hum. Yeah. Yeah. Uhn uhn. No. No. Um hum. Yeah. Yeah. Uhn uhn. No. No. Um hum. Yeah. Yeah. Uhn uhn. No. No. Um hum. Yeah. Yeah. Uhn uhn. No. No. Um hum. Yeah. Yeah. Uhn uhn. No. No. Um hum. Yeah. Yeah. Uhn uhn. No. No. Um hum. Yeah. Yeah. Uhn uhn. NO! NO! UM HUM! YEAH! YEAH! UHN UHN!"

"Firsborn! Firsborn!"

Knocking on the door. Pounding on the door. Knocking on the rock. Pounding on the rock. Everything is the rock, the rock, the . . .

"Firsborn! Firsborn! Who you talkin' to in there?"

Spanish he cannot understand, the world he cannot grasp.

"Mercer, Jr.! Answer me boy!"

"Yes, ma'am?"

"Who you talkin' to in there, son?"

"No. No. Um Hum. Yeah. Yeah. Uhn uhn."

"You cyaa see he gone crazy? Dat shit mess up his brain, Mamma. I tell you dat. I see him walkin' 'roun' wit' dat pipe dey is use. Stupid ass 'round here talkin' to himself. Lookin' like he in outerspace, man. Make me sick! I jus' feel like shootin' him ev'ry time I see 'im!"

"SHUT UP! Shut up Kevin. If you can't have anything good to say about your brother then just SHUT UP!"

Banging on the door. The door . . . the rock . . . the door . . .

"Mercer! Mercer Bodie! Open this door!"

Open this door. Open this door. Open this rock. The rock, the rock, everything is the rock . . .

"Please baby, open the door for Mamma. Turn the radio down and open the door!"

"What the hell he listenin' to in dere any damn way! Some Spanish station, man! He crazy, man! He flippin crazy! I tell you kick his ass out long time!"

"SHUT UP! When you have a child you could kick him out your house if you want. But dis my house and he is my child, so stay outta it! Now go! Go on back in the living room or go outside or sumtin'! Jus' moo from this door! I tellin' you for the last time!"

Eyes closed now, gently tapping on the door, her heart painin' her. Frankie and Mark sitting in the living room pretending to be listening to the t.v. Kevin storms out of the house.

"Firsborn. Open the door, baby!"

But he is fighting those voices in his head. Answering those voices in his head. Fighting, answering. Voices telling him to do things, bad things, or not to do them. Telling him to seek the rock, or to fight the rock. Seek, fight, seek, fight. Fight Firsborn, fight buhy! Fight Firsborn, fight for your life!

And from behind his door, he hears her voice. His mother's voice. Mamma voice, callin' to him. Her hand caressing the door painfully, lovingly. Salt water, no one sees, sliding down her cheek for her son. Her forehead resting on the door. Wishing she could force it open. Her soft voice seeping through to him. Seeping through to her child. And he cuts the radio off. And he rocks back and forth in the bed, crying silently. Afraid. So afraid, confused, and desolate.

And she speaks to him, soft, as if whispering a secret through the door.

"Listen baby, sit right there. Don' mind Kevin. He don' know no better. He never suffer, you see. He never suffer like you or me, so he don' know no better. Lemme tell you da story 'bout how B' Rabby make B' Bouki he cart horse . . ."

The Second Part

◆

VOICES

Be not afeared, the isle is full of noises,
sounds and sweet airs that give delight and hurt not.
Sometimes a thousand twangling instruments
Will hum about mine ears; and sometimes voices
That, if I then waked after long sleep,
Will make me sleep again; and then, in dreaming
The clouds methought would open and show riches
Ready to drop on me, that, when I waked,
I cried to dream again.

—William Shakespeare, *The Tempest* II, ii, 140-148

He listened with great attention, and received with pleasure the notion of Jesus Christ being sent to redeem us, and of the manner of making
our prayers to God, and His being able to hear us, even into Heaven; he
told me one day that if our God could hear us up beyond the sun, He must
needs be a greater God than their Benamuckee, who lived but a little way
off, and yet could not hear till they went up to the great mountains where
he dwelt, to speak to him . . .

—Daniel Defoe, *Robinson Crusoe*

I knew them all,
the "swell-foot," the epileptic "*mal-cadi*,"
cured by stinking compounds,
tisane, bush-bath, the exhausting emetic,
and when these failed, the incurably sored and sick
brought in a litter to the obeah-man.
One step beyond the city was the bush.
One step behind the church stood the devil.

—Derek Walcott, "The Divided Child"

7

The smell of paint always reminded him of Christmas . . .

Everyone cleaned and painted at Christmas time. He didn't know why. But he knew that when December came it was time to scrub, dust, push, pull, rearrange, and paint.

And later, when he and his family were settled in the new house in Pompey Village, with the journey to the Other Country and the years they had spent in Crab Bay behind them, it was painting at Christmas time that inspired him to think of the house in which they lived—the house with no number on a street with no name in a neighbourhood of houses all of the same colour—as the Yellow and White House, as opposed to a white house with yellow trimmings. And once that occured to him, it never looked like the others again.

> *Ma Ma bake dat Johnny Cake*
> *Christmas comin'*
> *Christmas comin'*
> *Christ-mas-com-in'!*

For him, no Christmas was an exciting Christmas until they moved into the Yellow and White House.

Turpentine and paint on hands rubbed underneath the water tap, the paint falling off in flakes. A holiday favourite on Radio One: Stevie Wonder singing "One Little Christmas Tree." Old newspapers spread all along the tiles. His mother with big jars of raisins and nuts soaked in rum turned upside down for fruit cake, singing something happy and solemn all at once as she worked with her back to everyone in the kitchen. And in the Sinking Church they would sing "O come, O come Emmanuel": his favourite, for its beauty, and its sense of anticipation.

Before that, he remembered small gifts given to him by a mother with little money. Gifts given away from the smells and the sounds of Santa Maria at Christmas time. Gifts given in transit.

A yellow Tonka truck. The indestructible toy.

That money had been hard to come by, but her baby could not go through Christmas without a gift.

"But who buy you a gif' Mamma?"

"Mamma alright child. I don' need no present. I have all a you."

And once, a set of toy guns. He remembered playing with them and destroying them promptly, as boy children always do. *Pull em out fas'. Bang! Pow! Spin em on ya finger and pop em back inside. Slam!* That fascination with the hero and his pistols continued long after the toys were tossed away, broken. There would be many trips with Small Pint to Saturday matinee reruns at the Bridge Street Theatre: *Trinity, High Plains Drifter, The Outlaw Josey Wales, Rooster Cockburn,* and *My Name is Nobody.*

Firsborn standing on the roof of the Yellow and White House trying to fix the antenna so they could watch the Saturday Night Movie on WNIN Channel Nine in Miami. *Tonight, Clint Eastwood, Lee Van Cleef and Eli Wallach star in Sergio Leone's* The Good, The Bad and The Ugly. *Blondie, know what you are? Just a son of a . . .*

But playing with the truck on the livingroom floor was the oldest memory of the past his mind offered him. The gift of the yellow truck with big black wheels from his mother, the student with four children living in the Other Country at Christmas time. That was his first memory.

He never remembered seeing the man his mother said was his father until he was nine and they had moved into the Yellow and White House. And by then Mercer Stone was nothing more than an intruder.

"Who dat is parkin' in our yard, Mamma?"

"Das ya pa."

"He comin' inside?"

"Hush. Talk ta him when he come. Kevin, tell him I sleepin'. Firsborn, watch your mout' boy. Go say hello to ya pa. I in bed if he aks. Tell him I sleepin'."

Christmas time away from Santa Maria: the memory was a little painful, and he would guess it was so for his three brothers also. The problem was that they were all children away from the country of their birth for the first time in their lives. And at the busiest, most exciting time to be there, and in its capital, because Christmas meant Junkanoo Festival. Although they made friends while their mother studied in the Other Country, Christmas could not have been the same outside of that place where everything meant so much more. They were slightly out of rhythm.

Even back in his own country, in Crab Bay, the holiday was not as sweet as it should have been. When he was a boy playing cops and robbers in the grass with Will Richards, the American couple's son, he wondered why white people put popcorn on their Christmas trees, and told Will he didn't care how many G. I. Joe dolls and electric race car sets his mother gave him. It was not as it should have been because Christmas, in the days before the Yellow and White House, was always celebrated in a place that was not truly theirs. The yard was not theirs. And the house was not theirs. For, in the Other Country, the house was rented. And in Crab Bay, on St. Mark's Island, where his mother was appointed as a Senior Mistress after returning from University, the house really belonged to the Ministry of Education, and they were merely its temporary occupants.

"Why don't you have more toys?"

"Don't aks me no stupid questions like dat."

"That's not a stupid question. My Mommy and Daddy buy me lots of toys at Christmas time. I'm going to get a brand new B.B.

Gun. You know how I know? I saw it. They hid it in the closet underneath a blanket."

"Man. I ain' checkin' for what you get. Le's go for sea grape if you goin'."

"My Mommy says you don't have a daddy. She says your Mommy teaches at the new high school in Salt Creek. Says you have no daddy. Is that true? My daddy is an engineer. He works for your Government. Is it true you don't have a daddy?"

"You gern down the beach for sea grape or not?"

"Not until you tell me."

"We ain' gat no daddy."

"That's stupid. Everybody has a daddy. If you don't tell me the truth I'll box you!"

"Try it!"

"Owww! You punched me in the eye!"

"Das good. I hope it swell. Go home an' tell ya Yankee daddy I buss ya in ya eye!"

But when they moved into the Yellow and White House in Pompey Village, the land and the house were theirs and that meant something to all of them. Especially to his mother.

It was her house. Not John Bodie's, not Mercer Stone's, and not the Government's. Hers. It signified the end of her dependence on others. It signified the end of the days when men could hold her back. It was God's way of telling her that the pain and the shame of her difference, and the loneliness she had suffered for her soul's sake and for her children, had not been in vain.

He remembered sitting at the dining-room table of the Ministry's house on top of the hill in Crab Bay, with Maureen his mother and his three brothers, looking at the architect's plan of the house. And she asks them, *Do you want a blue bathroom or a yellow bathroom? Blue. Blue. Blue. Yeah, blue.*

And so it was that on returning to Safe Haven he, and perhaps all his brothers, associated Christmas with the smell of paint. For when they finally moved into the new house in September, after all the delays, they did not like the paint on the walls. It was fading already. So Christmas came and they did it all over.

"Slaves had free time at Christmas," his mother said. "Das why we still clean up roun' den."

The smell of paint, and of freshly cut pine . . .

He loved that. Going to cut the pine tree at Christmas time. It was always an adventure. They would set out like men going off to war. And their mother would stand in the door of the Yellow and White House waving to them and shouting something as though she would not see them again for a very long time, for they were off to do some great deed, to battle in some crucial war that required men of their caliber. Yes, men of their caliber and singularity. They were her men. The only men she needed after she left Mercer Stone, for she never remarried. *Look at my fine fine men of whom I am oh so extremely proud and in whom I am utterly delighted.* She would talk that way, so properly, and they would laugh and then she would say jokingly, *Da next man I marry ga have to be rich. And he ga fetch my breakfast and dinner and do all the work. Otherwise he better keep outta my face. 'Cause I cyaa break my back for no man no more. Dem days over. I'll talk to ya. But when I ready for you to move on ya bes' move on.* But they were her men. And they were good little men, all four. She needed no others. She would speak to others. Be with others. But ever so discreetly. For no man came to her house to boss over it or lay in her bed next to her. Tree never knew such a thing was possible. Would have hated the man who tried to boss her, rule her house, lay in her bed. And she in turn was funny when it came to her sons. Protective of her boy-children to a fault. Worried that the girls they saw would eventually take them away from her forever and she would be left all alone. She lived for her sons.

On the first day of Christmas
My true love sent to me
A partridge in a pear tree

"Whuzza patridge Mamma?"

"Iza bird, dummy."

"I ain' aks you nuttin Frankie. Whuzza partridge Mamma?

"What's a partridge? It's a bird, Mark Etienne Bodie."

He liked how she pronounced his name.

"Come, look with me in the dictionary. That's how you learn words you don't know the meanings of. Webster's. Partridge. Do you know how it's spelt? P-a-r-t-r-i-d-g-e. From the Greek word 'perdix.' Medium-sized game bird of diverse plumage."

"Whuzza 'game bird'."

"A bird men hunt for sport."

"Whuzz 'plumage'."

"Those are feathers."

"Aw, fedduz."

"Feathers."

"Feathers."

The smell of paint. And of freshly cut pine.

Me and Firsborn and Kevin and Frankie. The four a us used to go in the Pine Forest in the mornin'. Maybe ten or so days before Christmas come, and go lookin' for a tree. We use to have a worl' a fun. We use to eat some slam bam, or corn flakes and roll out. Mamma use to say, "Let Firsborn or Kevin hol' da cutlass." Not me or Frankie 'cause we was too small. Man dat was a sweet time. Everybody use to bundle up in all kind a clothes. From head to foot. 'Cause you know, is be kinda chilly in the mornin around Christmas time. I like it when it cold roun' Christmas time. It don't feel like Christmas if it ain' cold. But we use to wear all dem clothes too so we don't get stick wit' prickle or catch no poison ivy. Firsborn use to wear his old jeans jacket. That was nice. Everybody wish dat was deirs. He buy dat while he was in University in the States. It look real decent. Da res' a us use to make sure and wear long sleeve pants and shirt so we don' catch no itch. We use to look like we was goin' crabbin' instead a goin to cut one tree. When we was living in St. Mark's Island, in Crab Bay, we use to go catchin' land crab when it rain heavy in da summer time. Dat was fun! We use to dress jus' like dat. But den it was 'cause mosquito is bite hard on da Out Islands. White crab is da big set. It have a big claw and when you catch dem and put dem in da pen dey is never want touch each other. Black crab is the small set. And they always sparrin' and walkin' on each other and jam up inda pen. Dey's pile on each udda an' none cyaa reach da top a da pen 'cause da res' 'll pull um down.

Sometimes it would be hours before they selected the tree that was just right. It had to be so tall and so wide, with leaves and branches that went just so. Otherwise they'd move on, walking through the paths in the Pine Forest that a tractor had made long before, sometimes abandoning the trails altogether to forage in the prickly undergrowth, walking in and out of pockets of soil that gathered in the holes formed in the eroded limestone, chopping away at vines and thatch trees in search of the Christmas tree that was just right, the one that they always thought they saw for sure just a little ways further. And then Firsborn and Kevin would take turns chopping. Hard, vicious strokes. Each uttering an expletive as he spanked the spine of the rock-hard tree. And when they were halfway they'd let him get a chop or two, so he could learn how to swing a cutlass. *But be careful, is sharp.* And Frankie would swing too. Already Frankie could swing hard. Frankie was stronger 'cause he was six years older. And when the final blows were delivered that would break the tree's back, they would look to see which way it would fall and they would be concerned for each other. And they enjoyed those last blows and would accentuate them with cries of *Beas', Beas', Bitch, Bitch,* and *Suckatakedat.* And it would fall and he would cry *TIMBER!* like he'd seen the lumberjack on Sesame Street do time and time again. And they'd take the pine tree, the soldier they had slain in battle, back to their waiting mother, their queen. Back to the castle. And the four of them would hold a part of the pine, as though it were the four limbs of a man they had killed. They would walk as though in procession. And their walking was awkward because the pine needles stuck through their clothes. And they would take the captive home and she would say, *well done boys, well done.*

Christmas was the smell of paint and freshly cut pine. The soothing sound of carols being sung in the Sinking Church that were wafted gently by the night breeze and carried into the Yellow and White House. They lived just around the corner from the Sinking Church.

Christmas was decorating the pine tree they had slain. Spraying fake snow on the leaves. Gently laying little shiny pieces of plastic that glittered silver all along the branches. The package the strips of shiny plastic came in said they were "Icicles."

Christmas was ham and turkey and fruit cake. Christmas was the Michaelmas service at the Sinking Church. The service began very late and Tree would be eager to go home right afterward and open his presents. He had the most presents because he was the youngest. He would look at the clock until 12:00 struck. Then he would know it was Christmas at last. They sang "Joy to the World" and "Beautiful Star of Bethlehem."

Christmas was the manger built by the men of the parish and placed with devotion at the back of Sinking Church. The manger with the Baby Jesus and the Virgin Mary holding him in her arms, with Joseph looking benevolently over them, and the animals all looking on as the blonde Angels sing hosanna.

Christmas was his mother smiling at him as she sat on the settee in the living room of the Yellow and White House. She would watch him unwrap his presents by the light of the tree with the fake snow and fake icicles. And through every front-room window of every house in Pompey Village, the green and red lights of a Christmas tree, however modest, could be seen blinking in the crisp night.

Christmas was Tree and his brothers laughing at the cheap gifts each of them received from their father, Mercer Stone. Christmas was Maureen Bodie's mixed expression of amusement and annoyance at the sight of the gifts their father had sent to his sons. Gifts given too late, that were too meagre to matter much. Neither love nor forgiveness nor reconciliation would ever be possible between Mercer Stone and the family he seemed never to have wanted.

And Christmas meant cow bells, whistles, bicycle horns blown from jubilant lips, goatskin drums invoked with fire, crowds of black faces, bending knees, behinds shaking, costumes bouncing, a crescendo of masks. Christmas was Junkanoo Festival.

And Junkanoo was where his brothers would take him to sit on a wall on a side street to watch the parade go by. Not Waterfront Road, they couldn't take him with them to Waterfront Road, 'cause Maureen Bodie say people dere is carry on too crazy.

Junkanoo was roasted peanuts sold by the RastaFari, mashed corns, chains ripped from necks, women's behinds being pinched, and bottles being broken across hard heads in the hustle and vengeance of the crowd. Even on the side street he saw all this, safe and perched on a wall, sitting with his brothers until the coming of the sun announced the end of the masquerade.

Junkanoo was the boys from Pompey Village who all had that special wall to sit on that no one else messed with. And Tree would sit there protected by his brothers, until he was big enough to find his way there on his own, and watch the big groups rumble and the scrap groups scuttle, like big and little crabs in a procession.

Sitting there on that wall with the sea of spectators moving just below his feet, he felt suspended in air. The shock of drums and the stun of whistles dissolved that border between dream and the real in the dew of a fading night. And in the midst of the music and the masquerade, in the heart of the drum shouts and horn riddles, the world became a place—even after Kevin told him that Santa Claus was killed in a plane crash—where strange magic could be worked, where ordinary people on the most unlikely occasions could be crowned with power and robed in magnificence.

8

Eenie, meenie, mynie, moe
Catch a nigger by his toe
If he holler let him go
Eenie meenie mynie moe
I-say-so

He likes school. School is a good place. Because the children are almost his age. Not like his brothers; they are much older than he is and don't like to play. Except Frankie, sometimes. He and Frankie fight too much. Frankie picks on him. Kevin and Firsborn too, sometimes. Still, he likes his brothers. And he likes school. Grade 6. They just moved into the Yellow and White House. All the boys play pawkin' in the schoolyard before school and at lunch time. They never played pawkin' much in Crab Bay. But they played rounders. He likes playing pawkin'. Getting hit in the head is shamin' but hitting someone in the head is good. He likes to clown around. The boys all call him Joker. That's because he watched the Joker on *Batman* on t.v. and he could imitate the way he talked. He could do the Penguin really good too. *Waaaak waaak waaaaak waaaaak.*

Chitty Chitty Bang Bang sittin' on a wall, try'n'a make a dollar outta fifty cents. He miss! He miss! He miss like dis!

Grade 6. And the girls are all bigger than the boys. Dagineau is a boy in his set. Set 1. *All the girls like Dagineau because he have light skin.* All the girls like Dagineau. And Patrick is funny. Patrick eats his lunch standing up and has bow legs. Charles Farmer brings his lunch from home. A bowl, a small jar with milk, and a tiny box of Frosted Flakes. *But I like barbeque cornchips and slush from the slush stand.* Slush is all red and gets on your shirt and Mamma will be mad. *Have the Orange Drink instead Mark Etienne, because you make a mess of your shirt. I ga make you clean it yase'f nex' time.* Dagineau and Patrick are the best at pawkin'. Dagineau hits really hard and Patrick can stand right in front of you when you have the ball and you'll never hit him. How does he do that?

Boom. Pine. Apple. Win'. Say boom pineapple win' dollar fifty all the time. Say boom!

Dagineau has a girlfriend. Her name is Sheila. Sheila is bigger than all the boys. Charles says the teacher caught Dagineau with Sheila hiding in the cupboard. The girls are all bigger than the boys. That girl Sheila is a bully. She hit him right in the back so hard he wanted to cry. He hates girls. When his mother left him in the schoolyard of this new school after they moved into the Yellow and White House, he cried. And the teacher, who knew his mother from the Teacher's Institute, put him on her lap and dried his eyes.

"Big boys don't cry. Don't you see everyone looking at you?"

"I don' care. I could cry. I ain' as ole as dem."

"I know. You're a year younger than they are. But that's fine."

"I don' like dis school."

"But why not? This school is nice. Where did you go before?"

"Wilberforce Primary in Sunrise Settlement. It was right on da beach and was plenty sea grape outside our class."

"Well, I can see why you'd miss a school on the beach. But you're living in Safe Haven now. Come on, you're a bright little boy. You'll fit right in at Ponce de Leon. Come with me and I'll take you to your new class."

Now he likes this school. But he is a year too young to be in Grade 6. He is eight going on nine. Some of the children tease him because he is short. He wants to join the softball team.

Dis a way a bellabee, bell, bell, a bellabee. Disaway a bellabee all night long. So step back sassy, sa-sa-salassy, step back sassy all night long. So walkin t'rough di alley, al-ley, al-ley, walkin t'rough di alley all night long.

He is in the school play. The play is the story of B' Nansi and B' Snake and B' Rabbit and B' Donkey and B' Frog. *Mark, you'll be B' Frog. Yes, Miss Russell.* B' Frog wears green tights and a mask with goggle eyes. The boys tease him about the green tights. But everyone is in the play. It's fun. The teachers have made sound effects and everything. The noise of crickets and birds in the night and thunder and stuff like that. They were rehearsing and this girl named Kate said she wanted to use the bathroom. She said she'd run off while the teacher wasn't looking. Tree told her she musn't go until they were finished or else he'll tell Miss Russell and she'll be beaten. But the teacher wasn't paying attention anyway. She didn't go but wet herself up on stage instead. He felt bad for telling her she would get in trouble if she went to the bathroom. It was bad for that girl. She was playing B' Donkey and everybody always talked about her bad. Said she was real poor and smelt funny, and that she had a picky head. Tree felt sorry for stopping her from going to the bathroom. Never saw her again after Grade 6. But the play was good and Mamma came to see him in it. And Frankie and Kevin too. But not Firsborn. Firsborn was away in University in the States.

Sauchiss in dere! Loaf a bread right here. Take ya penny sauchiss an' stick it right in here. You ain' know where? Right in here. Devil roun' da corner say stick it right in here!

He likes school. School is a good place. He learns all sorts of things about his country at school.

"Look on the cover of your exercise books children. Who do you see?"

"The first black Governor General."

"Look on the dollar bill, who do you see?"

"Her Majesty the Queen of England."

"And who is in this picture on the wall, class?"

"The Rt. Honourable Prime Minister of the Commonwealth of the Santa Maria Islands."

"Very good. And who is this picture of?"

"The Honourable Deputy Prime Minister."

How many islands are in the Santa Marian chain? And what is the capital of our country? Of St. Mark's Island? Of La Ventana Island? Of Runaway Island? Of Ferdinand Island? And when did Christopher Columbus discover the New World? And what is the national flower? And the national bird? Very good. No. Yes. Very good. And what is our country's motto? Dagineau, be quiet. Patrick, give Charles back his pencil. Sharlene, sit down. Patrice, it's not break time yet. Mark, don't sit in the chair on only two legs. Next week is the school spelling bee.

One time he pee himself up. It was because he made the same thing happen to Kate, the girl with the picky head who everybody said smelt funny. At least that's what he told himself, that it was because of what he did to her.

Red rover red rover let Marko come over!

It was three o' clock and he was waiting for the bell to ring because he wanted to pee. Brrrrrrrrrrrrrrrrrrrrrrrring. But they can't leave. The teacher is mad because Set 1 was rude today. They talked too much. So they must stand behind their chairs. They pick the chairs up and turn them upside down and rest them on the desks so the janitress can mop. They close their eyes and put their hands together to say the Our Father. But he is moving his legs back and forth and almost bending over because he wants to pee. The teacher is mad and everybody keeps talking. *Sssshhhh. I want go to da bat'room man. Stop talkin'. Ssssshhhhh. Maaaaaaaan. Teacher mad.* Why don't they shut up so he can go pee. But the teacher is mad. They keep whispering and opening their eyes. He feels like his doggie will burst. They pray now. *Our Father, who art in Heaven, hal-low-ed-be-thy-neem.* She is still keeping them after that. Punishment. Is because he do dat to dat girl. Is too late. Too late. Is hot. All wet now. He shame.

Ma chirren, ma chirren?

Yes ma'am?
You hear me callin' you?
Yes ma'am.
Well why you don' come?
I don' feel like comin'.
I ga set ma dog on ya.
I don' care.
I ga set ma cat on ya.
I don' care.

He is a year too young because he missed grade four when they were in Crab Bay. It wuzzan his fault. The teacher couldn't spell. It wuzzan his fault. His mother came home from work and found him sitting on the steps of the house on the hill. He'd been there since one o'clock. Pulled up in the car and found him picking leaves from the stem of the croton tree. Said he came home at lunchtime and caught a ride with Mr. Bradley, the carpenter. He was passing by in his truck. She wanted to know why he had walked out of Crab Bay Primary. He looked down at his shoes and frowned. Said he left because the teacher couldn't spell.

"Young man, what do you mean the teacher could not spell. Talk fas'."

"I don' wan' go back to dat school. I wan' go back where we come from. Why we always movin' all over the place, Mamma? Da teacher tell da class spell 'plane.' 'Plane' what does fly in the sky. Ain' nobody spell it right, and 'cause I don' know nobody dere I didn't say nuttin. Den she write 'P-L-A-I-N' on da board. An' I tell her say dat ain' how you spell 'plane' what does fly in the sky. Das 'plain' when you mean land. And I tell her it spell 'P-L-A-N-E.' And she tell me hush my mout' an' go outside. So I gone outside and I ain' gone back."

He is too young because he missed grade four while they were in Crab Bay. It wuzzan his fault. Maureen Bodie went to the school to talk to the headmaster and the teacher. The teacher was mad. She wouldn't take him back. He did not want to go back. *My son is not rude or unruly. He's having difficulty adjusting. He has lived in Safe Haven and with me in University abroad and now Crab Bay, all in his short lifetime. He becomes impatient and frustrated when things are out of order.*

Maureen Bodie sat in on the teacher's class for half an hour and agreed with her son that she could not spell. So he went to another school. A school built on the beach with sea grape trees standing outside his classroom. He liked that school. It was his third primary school since he left Safe Haven at three years old. He skipped grade four and went to grade five. He had a hard time. The teachers at the school on the beach said it was all the moving up and down. But he was very smart.

One of his problems was that he had "developed a slight complex about how words ought to be spelt." That's what his report card said.

There's a brown girl in the ring, tra-la-la-la-la. There's a brown girl in the ring, tra-la-la-la-la-la. Brown girl in the ring, tra-la-la-la-la. An' she look like a sugar in a plum plum plum.

Now Dagineau and Patrick and Charles Farmer are leaving the new school he came to after his family moved to Pompey Village. This is his fourth primary school. He cannot graduate with them. The teachers say he is too young for Junior school and needs to repeat. He does not like how that sounds. But he likes this school. They will let him join the softball team. He likes softball. He plays third base.

The next year the boys still play pawkin' before school starts and at lunchtime. The girls are still bigger than the boys. There is no school play the next year, but the children have ring play in the yard as always. He likes to watch the ring play, and to listen to the songs. Sometimes he even joins in. But only if other boys do.

The next year the school introduces a new rule. Everybody must freeze when the bell rings. Everybody must stand perfectly still when the bell rings at the end of lunch and break time or they will be beaten. No matter where you are. He and his new friends like this new rule. They like to watch the first and second graders make up awkward positions to freeze in at the ringing of the bell.

The next year he finishes first in his class. Nobody teases him about his age and how short he is now. And he has grown a little. He is the prefect in Set 1. But he never volunteers for spelling bees.

Good mornin' Mr. Fisher
Good mornin' Fada Brown
Have you any sea-crab
To sell me one or two?
Bonefish bitin',
No bait to catch dem,
Every marri'd man
Gat he own bonefish.

• • • • •

Woman Hit by Truck

—*M. E. Bodie,* **Daily Report** *Staff Writer*

The streets of Santa Maria almost claimed the life of their fifteenth victim yesterday, as Sue Mortimer, originally of Duncombe's Town, Ferdinand Island, was struck when she walked in front of a speeding truck at about 9:30 a.m. Miss Mortimer, known to everyone in the Churchill District of Grand Santa Maria as "Crazy Sue," is reportedly forty-eight years of age. Mortimer is an unmarried, homeless woman who lives in a cardboard box across the street from The One for the Road Restaurant and Bar on Infantry Street, where the accident took place. Childless and abandoned by her family because she was "her head bad," said one elderly woman who wished to remain anonymous, Mortimer took lodging on the side of the street and was living off the kindness of others. "Usually she just eat out the garbage like potcake," said Rico Tynes, a thirteen year old who says he walked past Crazy Sue everyday on his way to school. "Every morning she used to come out her box and stand up in the road with one blanket wrap round her," young Tynes added. "And if she see one man pass in a car, she use to drop the blanket. She use to be naked underneath there."

Several other residents of Infantry Street and the surrounding area confirmed Tynes's claims. One bystander, Rev. Jacob Turner of Golgotha Baptist Church, expressed the opinion that there were far too many liquor stores in Safe Haven, outside of which "drunkards and bums who should be receiving spiritual guidance become trapped like flies in a spider's web of sin." He said that Sue Mortimer was one such "unfortunate fly."

Harry Bethel, another eyewitness to the accident, stated that he was just on his way into The One For the Road to order breakfast when he saw Mortimer standing in the middle of the road, "arms spread out," and her blanket down around her ankles. According to Bethel, she did not seem interested in getting out of the way of traffic nor in crossing the street. "She just stand in the middle of the road in her birthday suit with her hand stretch out and the driver of the truck ain't try to stop. Maybe he figure she was gone jump out the way."

Police have Mr. Curling Frasier of Daton Alley in their custody for further questioning. Frasier's lawyer, L. C. Jackson, Esq., told *The Daily Report* today that his client did not have time to brake, and feared that any attempt to swerve out of the way would have endangered more lives because the street was cluttered with pedestrians, among them women and children.

This reporter spoke yesterday evening via telephone with the owner of The One For the Road Restaurant and Bar, Mr. Pat "Lone Ranger" Darling, to get his interpretation of the events and his response to the accusations lodged against his establishment by Rev. Turner. Mr. Darling objected emphatically to having anything to do with the condition of Ms. Mortimer. If "people want to know why that woman attemp' suicide," he asserted, "they must ask themself why Crazy Sue was crazy in the first place and livin' in the bush." He said it was not his liquor that was responsible. "Ask the fella who leave her standing at the aisle on her wedding day 'cause he gone run off with other woman. Ask him how come she been walkin' round about the place buck naked and countin' lam' pole all these years." Darling would not identify the man of whom he spoke but said he was a prominent politician whose favourite number was ten.

Ms. Mortimer is in stable condition at Queen's Royal Hospital.

9

Small Pint was the boy living across the street whose grandmother always chased him with a broom screaming, "I ga beat ya damn backside." His real name was Paul. At least, that's what the grandmother with the broom called him. He used to ride up and down the street with no name on a red bicycle with his face screw pretending he was a bad dread on a loud motorcycle. To create that effect he stuck a soda can in between the bicycle frame and the rubber tire so that it made a wailing sound every time he peddled. Mark got his nickname from Small Pint the summer before he entered the seventh grade. He got the name because he lost a bet.

It rained all the time during the summer, the wet season in the Santa Maria Islands. The heat would beat down on you like the bottle in a hand beating conch, and the sun would make the asphalt soft at the same time that it made the loose dirt on the side of the road almost as hard as stone. People would say to each other on such days, "Dis a good day to go to da beach." Then, in the afternoon, grey clouds would gather, blacken, swell, and then burst. But always, just before it fell, the air would be full of that smell, that creation-smell of the rain's arrival. And the first drops would fall heavily, singly, as if God were releasing the rain from heaven drop by drop. And it continued like that for some time, drop by drop, until, almost imperceptibly, the single plunks of rain would accelerate in their frequency; quickening until it became impossible to distinguish one from the other with the human ear. This progressed until it all came down hard, showing no mercy. Surely, somewhere someone had been unlucky, had misread the signs the clouds made, had waited too long to take shelter and was now getting completely drenched while white Papa God laughed up above, his great grey beard shaking as he watched the person scurrying for cover. The shower would fall in such steady, determined sheets that, if you sat on a porch and looked at it coming down, you might think it possible to run into the streets and wrap yourself up in those folds of rain, as you would a bed cover.

Then the downpour would end, abruptly, and everything would be dripping water. A dripping that seemed to have a life of its own, that had a healing sound to it. And if you lived in a generally quiet neighbourhood like Pompey Village, you might spend long moments just listening to that dripping, that sweet sound of the sky's water falling off and into man-made things. The entire earth seemed to have been cooled, cleansed.

It was on such a day that Mark got tired of sitting on the porch of the Yellow and White House and looking over at the boy who was always chased by his grandmother with a broom screaming "I ga beat ya damn backside." He had finished his chores—which were few because he was spoiled—and was nibbling on a cup of frozen red Kool-Aid he'd bought from "Mr. Tingum Shop" for fifteen cents. Small Pint was doing something while bent over a small mango tree in his front yard. All the homes on the street with no name were without walls or fences, so everything going on in people's yards could be easily seen.

Casually, Mark walked to the edge of his front yard and sat on a rock, letting his bare feet touch the brownish dirt at the edge of the road. It was dark and moist because of the rain. He looked over at Small Pint, who was bent intensely over the little mango tree with something in his hands.

"Hey."

"Hey."

"Hey. What you doin'?"

"Shush!"

"Hey."

"Hey."

"Hey, buhy. Whachooname?"

"Shush . . . Small Pint."

"Small Pint?"

"Yeah. Shush!"

"Whachoodoin?"

"I tryin' ta hang dis damn lizard. But if you don' hush your mout' you ga make me scared him off. So shut up."

"Shutcyaagoup"

"See. You make a little noose wit' a piece a leaf spine, an' you edge up on 'em real real slow. An' ya HOOK UM! HA HA! BEAS'! GETCHA!"

He caught the lizard and dangled it for Mark to see. It was a bright, almost fluorescent green. It wiggled frantically, and that made Small Pint smile with pride.

"I t'ought your name was Paul."

"Yeah. But ain' nobody is call me dat."

"How come?"

"Ain' nobody does get call by they family name in Pompey Village. Das too dead."

"I have a nickname in school. They is call me Joker."

"School don' count. They is only be tryin' to play wit' ya head in school. Is what ya friends home is call you what count."

"I neem Mark."

"Mark! Das as bad as Paul. You see me look like any Paul? I is Small Pint."

Mark liked this boy already. He seemed extremely confident in himself. And he was very stringy, with long limbs and funny bow legs that reminded him a little of Kermit the Frog. He seemed to Mark to be that special kind of boy that was good at everything. And even if he wasn't, he was at least good at making it sound as if he was.

"Who give you dat name?"

"Some fellas in da bar dere on da Southern Road. Teddy's Bar."

"Why they call you dat?"

"Because Yellow Man dare me to go inside an' buy a drink. So I gone and aks for a pint a Bacardi."

"Dey give it to you? En das agains' the law?"

Small Pint smiled, toying like a kitten with his dying lizard, pleased that he was impressing his partner in crime to be.

"So? Teddy don' care. He give it to me anyhow. All he want is the money."

"Muddow."

"An' from den everybody is call me Small Pint."

"'Cept dat woman you live wit'. She is your grammy hey?"

"Yeah. I livin' wit' her 'cause my daddy say he cyaa raise me. Say I is too much trouble." This impressed Mark to no end. He tried to imagine what it would be like to be sent to live with his grandmother because he was "too much trouble." Jewel Macintosh Bodie would spoil him stink—if it were possible to spoil him stinker or pamper him any more than Maureen already did.

"She is beat you?" Mark knew the answer but asked anyway.

"Yeah. Sometimes. When she catch me."

Mark had never been beaten in his life. And he found the scenes between Small Pint and his grandmother funny. He never took them seriously, nor was he ever afraid that the old woman would pound the boy to death with her broom, primarily because Small Pint always seemed to be laughing at her when she chased him; laughing mockingly even on the few occasions when Mark had seen her succeed in capturing his new friend. "She mussie cyaa beat hard," he thought.

Small Pint was getting bored with the lizard. He dropped it in the tall grass as if he hadn't spent all morning trying to catch one. He stood hands akimbo and surveyed the street with no name.

"I goin' go sail boat," he announced.

"Boat what on the sea?"

Small Pint laughed. Mark didn't mind.

"No dummy. Toy boat."

"Where?"

"Don' worry."

Small Pint walked off in the direction of his backyard. Mark had not moved from the rock at the edge of his mother's property. The sun was beginning to peep through the remaining grey clouds and streams of rain water were flowing down the street with no name. He did not know where the water was going. He felt awkward. He wanted to follow Small Pint but did not want to seem like a pest or a sissy. Without turning back, Small Pint hollered, "You comin' or what?"

For the rest of that day, and for the entire summer, Mark and Small Pint were inseparable.

Mark followed the skinny boy into his backyard and watched him as he cut a makeshift boat out of a piece of two-by-four and adorned it with a paper sail and a nail for a rudder. He simply marvelled at his friend's ingenuity. Together they ran through the puddles of water and made a swift cut into the bushes at the end of the street with no name. There Mark realized that a track road wound its way through the bushes, a fact he had not been aware of in the year and a half he had lived in the Village. The tiny path led to the small pond that stood directly beside the Anglican church on another street with no name. Tree had never realized that it was possible to get to the church by such a route and he would later use the track road whenever he went to church service, even at night.

It was in this pond that Small Pint placed the boat and then jumped in himself so as to steer it properly. He pretended to be Christopher Columbus sailing from Spain. Speaking like a Shakespearean actor, he talked of adventure and gold and spices as he helped move the wooden boat along the water with his hand. Providing his own theme music with his mouth, he decided to carry the boat to the other side of the pond so that he could discover Guanahani to the sound of trumpets and drums. Mark, who had seen a picture in one of the books that adorned his mother's big bookshelf, thought that Small Pint, standing waist deep in the muddy water of the pond and pulling the boat behind him, looked more like Gulliver than Christopher Columbus, but he kept the opinion to himself.

Nevertheless, it didn't take Mark very long to lose his inhibitions and jump feet first into the pond. It was his idea that they fight a battle at sea. Small Pint would steer the warship with a stick down the length of the pond, while he would attempt to bomb it by tossing small stones in its vicinity. Each simulated the noise of the ship's engine and the explosion of the bombs as the stones fell into the water with little plops. It was like being in a movie.

This went on until they were both soaking wet and laughing so hard their stomachs ached. Then Small Pint remembered that although he had escaped his chores by sneaking out when his grandmother fell asleep, he hadn't had anything to eat. Nurse Culmer's guinep tree was full and ready to be pillaged.

"You hungry?"

Mark had not thought about eating since gorging on the cup, but now that Small Pint mentioned it . . .

"Yeah, buhy. I dead hungry."

"You want some guinep? I know where one tree is what so full a ripe guinep ya belly'll buss from eatin' um."

"Where it is so?"

"Mrs. Culmer yard."

"Which one dat is?"

"Das da white and yellow house round da corner."

"Don' be stupid buhy, dey all white and yellow."

"Da one wit' da monkey tamarind tree in front and da broke down Volkswagen on the front lawn."

"Aww. One guinep tree in backadere, hey?"

"Yes, man! Full-full. You ain' never been walkin' round here to see what in dis neighbourhood, hey?"

"Uh uhn. Not too much. Mamma is don' want me wandering round by myself too much."

"Sheeeeeet. Les go man. Lemme show you what you been missin'."

They began running back toward the track road, their tennis shoes squishing water with each footfall. They hadn't taken them off before jumping in the pond for fear of stepping on something sharp at the bottom. Their minds already on the fruits they were going to enjoy, they neglected to take the boat out of the water.

They left it there in the pond for other children to claim, floating somewhere between history and make-believe.

"I bet you so backward you cyaa even climb a tree!"

Mark hated bets and dares. He usually lost them to his brothers, but he was feeling courageous.

"Oh yeah? Ain' no tree in the Santa Maria Islands I cyaa climb, buhy!"

"O.K. O.K. I wan' see you climb dis guinep tree in Nurse Culmer yard. You don' know when it rain the trees does be slippery, hey? Ya's have to be careful."

"Don' worry 'bout me!" Mark felt good sayin' that. "Just tell me one ting dough."

Small Pint stopped jogging and looked at him. He was an inch or two taller than Mark. "Wha' happen?"

Mark was panting now. They were now at the end of the track road. He stopped running and bent over with his hands on his knees in an attempt to rest. "Dis woman . . . Nurse Culmer or whatever her name is . . . she home right now?"

Small Pint sucked his teeth. "No man. She does work in the hospital all day. And all her chirren so old they don' even live home no more. Les' go. Ev'ryting cool dread. Trus' me."

Even though Small Pint had insisted that no one would be at home, they snuck round the back as if they were avoiding detection. There was no sign of anyone but they crept round the back like prowlers just the same. It perpetuated the in-a-movie feeling.

Mark, eager to prove himself, was the first one up the huge, slippery guinep tree. Small Pint did not begrudge him. He watched him appreciatively, but half hoped he would slip and lose the bet. As Mark danced up the branches of the huge fruit-laden tree, drops of water fell off the leaves and onto his head, and on Small Pint, who was standing at its base with his hand on his chin like a judge at a gymnastics competition. Then Mark began dropping guineps in bunches, which Small Pint adroitly caught and, after breaking off the leaves, placed in a plastic grocery bag he picked up in the yard.

"Yeah ma buhy, you could climb for true."

"I tell you dat, buhy. I use to live in Crab Bay. We use to climb mango and almond tree all the time. I won' talk 'bout dilly." Mark was feeling oats he hadn't known he had. "Dis one bet you was bound ta lose, dreadie."

But Small Pint hated losing. He figured he'd make it a little more difficult for his friend. "See dat branch right dere what stickin' out? Plenty ripe set on dat one. If you could grab dem you is da bes' tree climber I ever see!" He talked like B' Rabby trying to trick B' Bouki once more for old time's sake.

"What?! You fool hey? You mussie want me fall and bus' my behind!"

"Youzz da one say ain' no tree in the Santa Maria Islands you cyaa climb. Climb out to dat branch an' grab dat big bunch a guinep and you win da bet!"

"And what I gettin' if I win?"

"All the guinep in the bag is yours if you do it!"

Mark had already proven that he was not afraid of heights. He had climbed to the very top of the guinep tree and could see every house on his street. He could even see the Anglican church in the distance. But to get the guineps Small Pint spoke of, Mark had to climb down to about ten feet and walk along a long thin branch that he was not totally certain could hold his weight. And what was worse, there were few branches that he could hold onto on his way toward the ripe fruits. Small Pint had picked carefully and Mark began to hate himself for taking up the challenge. He tried his luck anyway.

Halfway along the branch he started to feel as if he was going to succeed. It was sustaining his weight and he was able to steady himself by stretching out and holding onto a branch higher up that was just barely within reach. But to grab the bunch of guineps, he would need to release his safety branch. Small Pint watched the sweat gather on his buddy's face and he smiled with the glee of a devil.

"Gone buhy! Grab da ting an' you win!"

"O.K. O.K. Don' rush me!"

Mark's palms were moist and his throat was getting dry. He released the safety branch and stood there like a man in a high-wire act. He took hold of the bunch of fruit and wrenched it loose. But just then, from the corner of his eye, he noticed Small Pint spin round as if startled by something. And as a drop of sweat slid from Mark's forehead and trickled into his mouth through his slightly parted lips, he heard Small Pint holler "OH SHIT, SHE COMIN'!" and saw him take to his heels as if a Doberman were after him. Distracted, Mark lost his footing on the wet branch and fell straight into the mud, guineps in hand. His reflexes were quick enough for him to use his free hand to break the fall but he could not protect himself from a face full of muck and a burning ache in his backside.

The pain in his backside was nothing compared to his embarrassment. No one was coming. It was all a prank. Small Pint stood over him laughing hysterically, a guinep seed rolling around on his tongue and tears of delight forming in his eyes.

From that day forward Small Pint called him "Tree," and the name stuck. Soon everyone in Pompey Village knew him by that name, and only his family called him by the name his mother had given him at his christening.

The event never caused ill feelings between the two boys. Tree was not seriously hurt and he suffered no cuts or ugly bruises that he would not normally have incurred during his usual antics in his own backyard. So the charade on Nurse Culmer's property was forgotten promptly, as boys are prone to forget what they do to each other in jest—however dangerous and irresponsible—and the two went back to Small Pint's house that very same day to eat the guineps.

To ease the pain Small Pint let Tree have most of the plump green fruits. And they had a real raucous time of it until Small Pint's grandmother came outside calling the name of the Lord vigorously and brandishing her broom. Tree ran home with what was left of the booty, figuring his mother would soon be back from summer school anyway, and left Small Pint to fend for himself. From what he could tell from across the street the old lady must have felt renewed after her nap because Small Pint wasn't laughing as heartily as usual.

* * *

During the remainder of that memorable summer, Small Pint taught Tree some of the invaluable lessons of Pompey Village boyhood. He learnt how to catch poggy fish in the pond by the Angli-can church. He learned how to make slingshots from rubber tubes and clothes hangers, and how to knock a chimmey from the branch of an almond tree from twenty feet away, skin it, and then cook it. He learned how to build two-wheel scooters using old two-by-fours and the wheels of food-store shopping carts or roller skates. He learned how to make and race go-carts, and he was taught not only how to spike tops in the middle of the road but how to make them out of fresh wood.

Small Pint showed him how to ride a bicycle with no hands, how to patch a flat tire, and how to wheely the distance between one lamp pole and the next. He taught him how to shoot marbles and win at games like Knock Tar Take and Puttin' in Jail. He taught him how to build wooden shacks underneath the shade of tama-rind and gum trees and how to dive and touch the bottom of the Government-built canals that began where the Pine Forest ended. He introduced him officially to all the boys, girls, and young men of Pompey Village with the simple declaration, "He name Tree."

Small Pint even proved to be an authority on the history of Pompey Village. In fact, he expressed amazement at how little Tree knew about his own neighbourhood. He passed on the history of Pompey Village as if he were the only soul who knew it, and not as if his grandmother and others had been the ones to tell it to him a few years before.

According to Small Pint, Pompey Village had not been Pompey Village for very long at all. The entire area had been a part of the huge expanse of fertile land that stretched from the Southern Road to the edge of the Pine Forest, all of which belonged to old Mr. Stirrup, a half-a-Conchy Joe who had inherited it many many years ago because he was the bastard son of a white bootlegger. He had swindled the inheritance away from the bootlegger's legitimate son, who had been thrown in jail for killing a man. But whether his claim to it had been legitimate or not, the land that people now called Pompey Village was once all Stirrup's land. And because it was once all Stirrup's, his four overgrown sons terrorized the young people of the Village whenever the inclination hit them, and acted as if the Village was all still theirs to handle as they saw fit.

Many considered the land on which Pompey Village stood to be blessed with the finest soil in the south-central district of the island. Despite his having sold most of the land, Stirrup's house was on a sprawling estate full of mango, dilly, and grapefruit trees into which only the brave of the Village tried to sneak at twilight in order to help themselves. It was fenced around with barbed wire and protected by pit bulls and Stirrup's four boys, all of whom knew how to handle a shotgun.

On those occasions when he ventured out alone Tree had walked past the large white house which stood aside the Southern Road. He often stood at a section of barbed wire fence and looked into the shady grove of trees that began where the white house ended, stretching into the very heart of the Village. He would gawk at the huge ripe mangolas that were too many for the lone Haitian worker to gather. He often saw them fall to the ground where they would rot and be eaten by bugs. But he had never gotten up the nerve to sneak over or under that fence.

In his first year in the Village he saw Stirrup's eldest son, the one that everybody called Raccoon, catch a boy who had decided that letting the mangolas rot was an insult to God that should not be tolerated. Raccoon held him in the middle of the street police-fashion, forcing the captive up on his toes by grabbing him at the back of the trousers, twisting them around in his hand, and pulling upwards. The child, who was about Tree's age, was still in his school uniform and started to cry the moment Raccoon got hold of him. The bully made him put the barrel of his sawed-off shotgun between his teeth. Only after the boy had wet himself in front of an audience of children and cussing adults did Raccoon let him go. Nothing was done to Raccoon and the grumbling passed.

According to Small Pint, ten or eleven years before Tree's family moved into Pompey Village, Stirrup's bootlegged inheritance began to dry up. While on his death bed, he had wanted to make some big money fast so that his sons could open up a new business. He decided to break his property up into small lots and sell them to the public. He made a deal with a local contractor and they decided to build a neighbourhood of identical houses on the land and call it a "suburb of the future." A place where blacks who had come into a little money since Independence, blacks who wanted to escape the poor conditions of the Safe Haven clapboard districts, could get a new, lower middle class lease on life.

The old man made a killing. People were allowed to buy the lots on the condition that only Stirrup's contractor build the houses. And the houses were not pre-fabricated like the new ones the Government was building. Compared to the people of Pompey Village, low-cost home buyers had a little less to spend. Their Government-subsidized houses were built on swamp land, so every time it rained the neighbourhoods got flooded. Water came up through their toilets or rose from the street into their living rooms and people couldn't pull their cars out of the yard for fear that they would stall. Pompey Village was built on a slight elevation, so the rain never damaged people's property. It drained off and settled on lower ground.

It was all called "Pompey Village" because Stirrup had liked the story of the ruined city as a child, and he thought it added a certain style to his manufactured neighbourhood. People didn't complain. They were just happy to have new homes. And the soil was so fertile that they didn't mind Pa Stirrup's insistence that all the houses be painted the same colour. They didn't mind the nameless streets either. Small Pint said that people who came from the older parts of Safe Haven were used to street names that meant something, that had a history, like Congregation Street, where the slaves used to meet under the silk cotton tree to talk and carry on their business without interference from backra, or Davis Car Lane, which was named after a man who lived there who had happened to be the first black man to own a car on the island. Small Pint figured that to have given the Village streets names out of the blue, which is what they were doing in the Government projects, (officials used names like "Hibiscus Boulevard" and "Lignum Vitae Avenue" just because they felt like it and where there were no hibiscus or lignum vitae trees), would not make much sense. So people were contented, planted fruit trees in their yards, and, after a few years, began extending their houses: a carport or utility room here, an extra bedroom there.

Small Pint knew the story of how the Anglican church was built as well. A Rastafarian named Jahown had explained to Small Pint that the church was actually sinking. Pressed to give a little land to the church before crossing River Jordan, and having been an Anglican all his life, Pa Stirrup spared a plot of land from being sold and donated it to the Diocese. Problem was, it was the worst strip of land old Stirrup owned. The land he donated had been impossible to sell because it was adjacent to the pond and was virtually all swamp. It was land that stood at the bottom of Pompey Village and had no protection against flooding. Before the church was built all that could be seen in that area were tall reeds and dragonflies, and the only thing that could be heard was the plop of fish and the deep-throated grunt of bullfrogs. So when they built the church they attempted to fill in some of the swampy ground. But every time it rained the pond rose, the land flooded, and the water climbed up to the church door. Cars were regularly stuck in the mud and one or two even slid into the pond. The muck from people's shoes covered the red church carpet every time there was even a slight shower. One woman slipped and broke her hip, and after that people started staying at home on Sunday if rain clouds threatened. Tree had heard his mother complain more than once about the mud, but he never knew the actual reason for the church's poor location.

Tree's world expanded after he built up the courage to approach Small Pint. From that summer right up to the day that he entered the twelfth grade of high school, no one was closer to Tree than his neighbour. He was a teacher and a friend to Tree; a protector too. Even Maureen was prepared to tolerate his association with her son, within certain limits. It was Small Pint who introduced Tree to Jahown, to Yellow Man. And it was Small Pint who taught him the ways of the street and the bush, made him think of St. Paul's Anglican Church as the "Sinking Church." But though he saw Small Pint do it a hundred times after that day, Tree never mastered the art of catching lizards by the neck with the stems of leaves.

10

Before Firsborn tried to jook Raccoon with a pitchfork in the middle of a street with no name, there were only three mad people in Pompey Village. Mudda Mae, the obeah woman, Crazy Mr. Burke, the Walker, and Tree's good friend Jahown, the Rasta.

Strange legends surrounded these three Villagers. They were talked about, avoided, stared at with a mixture of amusement and fear, evoked by parents as threats to disobedient children, and occasionally taunted by the bolder boys of the neighbourhood. They were Tree's first taste of the unconventional. He would remember them when he began working at *The Daily Report* and writing about the bizarre and embarrassing, remember them when he began writing stories about things Santa Maria people hesitated to mention in public because they did not wish to be considered troublemakers.

Mudda Mae

Mudda Mae was the most feared of Pompey Village's so-called lunatics, but strangers who passed her on the street wouldn't think she was crazy at all. Even the children at the school where she worked had nothing substantial on which to base their suspicions—except, perhaps, that the other janitresses at Prince George Primary kept a healthy distance and lowered their voices around her. Without any proof of her malevolence, these children ran when they saw her coming, and each would threaten to make Mudda Mae fix the other.

There could be no proof because Mudda Mae's madness did not manifest itself in highly noticeable ways outside the confines of Pompey Village. The old lady was sane enough to hold down a regular job, and that was saying something. The modest clothes she wore to work (as opposed to those who often cleaned toilets and mopped floors in fine dresses and gold bangles) certainly marked her as conservative, but not crazy. She had no crooked walking stick with idolatrous runes etched all along it, no shark bones hanging around her neck. She had no wicked toothless grin or deranged witch's cackle. She never gave anyone the evil eye or carried animal limbs in her purse—or if she did, no one had seen them.

Obviously, she would not have been able to keep her job had she suffered from fits of hysteria or shouting matches with invisible adversaries from the netherworld. Now, you might have found it peculiar that a janitress would travel on the jitney and walk in the street, to and from work, with the tools of her trade (the first potential sign), but unless you saw her toting her bucket, broom, and mop every single day, you might just as easily dismiss such behaviour as some eccentric display of zeal. Either that or you'd figure she was *t'iefin da people dem supplies* and think nothing more of it.

If anything qualified this silent recluse—forever without visitors, never going anywhere but to work but always receiving boxes from the Out Islands—to be an obeah woman it was that yard of hers.

Firs' a all, Mudda Mae is keep chickens. Plenty-plenty chickens.

She was the only person in Pompey Village to do so. They cockadoodledooed every damn day and woke people up an hour before sunrise. They roamed all over people's grass and ate the seeds of green corn they planted in their backyards. They chased each other up and down the street and raised a ruckus in the bushes. And no one would complain too loudly or touch one feather of their loud, greedy little heads.

Other than the sprawling Stirrup Estate, hers was the only structure in Pompey Village that was fenced in. Barbed wire fence at that. In fact, on three sides of her yard she had become dissatisfied with the effectiveness of this criminal deterrent and had added sheets of corrugated iron to her fortifications.

Da gumpshun to t'ink dat somebody wan' t'ief from her. Crazy damn woman! Who she t'ink she is? You see anybody else have fence? She mussie forget she black like da res' a we!

Mae left one end of the yard unboxed with this imposing material so that her fiendish fowls could wiggle beneath the fence and forage for food. Thanks to this architectural peculiarity it was impossible to see anything other than the roof of her house unless you stood in the bush on the one uncorrugated side of her yard. Few had the guts to look into the yard through the space between the corrugated iron that was made to accommodate the tiny front gate that swung outward into the street.

Stand in da road and look straight t'rough da woman gate for her to put mout' on you? You mussie crazy.

People said it was just as well because of what that yard had to offer. Not one blade of grass would grow in Mudda Mae's yard. It was scandalous.

The ground surrounding the house was just one smooth expanse of brown dirt. The boys in nearby houses, who stood on their roofs and looked over, insisted that she made cryptic designs in the dirt with her rake. "Nuttin could grow in dat groun' no how, not 'less she want it to," Small Pint had remarked. "Is dat obeah she does be workin'. She done frig up the soil an' all."

The only thing Mudda Mae wanted to grow in that yard of hers was a huge sapodilla tree which bore more fruit with each new season. It shone with green leaves and juicy brown fruit every summer and could be seen from quite a distance. No one touched it, ever. Mudda Mae herself never went up in it nor sent nimble boys to pick some for her like other women of the Village did with the trees in their yards. She just let the dillies drop to the ground. Darrell, a plump boy who went to Junior School with Tree, claimed Mudda Mae picked the fallen dillies up off the ground each night. Said he would see them from the side-bush one day and they would disappear the next.

A huge branch of the sapodilla tree rose over the barbed wire and corrugated iron to cast a shadow in Mrs. Deleveaux's yard. But as notorious as Mrs. Deleveaux's boys were for t'iefin people dem fruit off dey tree 'fore it even have time to ripe se'f, every single dilly that fell onto the Deleveaux's property rotted where it fell. No one ate them, touched them, raked them up.

People in Santa Maria always said that if you put something out there for everybody to see you had better share it because black people would take some anyway. It was a common practice in the summer months for young men in Safe Haven city to take guineps from people's trees, place them in small plastic bags or a crocus sack, and sell them in the street. One time the police tried to crack down on the practice, claiming that the fellas ought to have licenses to sell the guineps. The public disapproved so strongly of this pointless display of zeal (and of being denied guineps) that the crackdown was quickly brought to an end.

So in Pompey Village, as in the country at large, the rule was that you were asked the first time around. If you said no, people decided that you were gravalicious, and they had a right to get some of what grew in your yard by any means necessary. Usually, the children were the catalysts of this peculiar form of wealth distribution, and only Mr. Stirrup and Mudda Mae were exempt. Stirrup was immune because he didn't give a damn if he was ostracized by the community and because he would shoot you dead if you trespassed on his land. Mudda Mae was left untested because everybody was convinced she was an obeah woman. She stood apart from ordinary people because she had the power to fix.

Everyone said Mudda Mae had banged nails into the dilly tree and placed bottles, cans, strings, and ribbons of different colours all over it. That was a sure sign there was mojo on the tree. People young and old even swore that they'd seen the tree move from one side of the yard to the other and back again, in broad daylight.

Stories of this nature were rampant and new ones were added to the repertory every year.

Children were so terrified of her yard that tennis balls accidently knocked into Mudda Mae's yard during rounders or tossed over the fence during a game of pawkin' were considered irretrievable. No one ever called over to have them returned or requested permission to shake a branch of the tree so that they could fall to the ground. No one ever leapt over the front gate to grab a ball and hurry back into the street. Boys never walked by the house on her side of the road either. And no one ever stole anything from the house. The very dust of the place was enough to kill you dead.

Now, there developed between Tree, Small Pint, and the other boys their age a precocious rivalry when it came to performing acts of daring. This business of being reckless was just the sort of thing boys in the neighbourhood did to prove they was man, to add their names to the annals of the Village, be numbered among the legends of the place. Legends like Tyree, who had been bitten by a tiger-shark, lost his arm, and made it on the front page of *The Beacon,* or Scalawag, who was arrested and sent to jail when, to win a bet on Discovery Day, he sprayed "TEEF" in red paint on the statue of Columbus that stood outside the Governor General's Mansion.

Like the deeds of these young dreads, any voluntary contact with Mudda Mae or her haunted house was considered the height of bravery. So naturally Small Pint and Tree endeavoured to challenge the old obeah woman every chance they could get. They took to throwing stones at the dillies and chasing her chickens. They would ride by the house on their bikes and holler out her name as they flew past. They would wait in the bush and watch her walk home from the bus stop and make bird noises. At the pinnacle of their amazing valour they even threw rocks at Scabies, the cat. (This feline, people said, was really Mudda Mae's missing husband, whom she transformed because he had cheated on her.) They never tossed these rocks accurately; but the act itself was the stuff of legend among the younger children.

Tree and Small Pint tried everything short of going up to the front gate, opening it, and knocking on the front door, or actually eating the dillies they knocked down from the tree. They picked one up with a glove after Tree had sprinkled it with holy water from the entrance of the Sinking Church. They set it on fire just to see what would happen. Nothing. It didn't burn very well.

Their interest in Mudda Mae would wane and then be rekindled after a month or two, but they could never bring themselves to face her on the road, call out to her or go by the house at night. It would be many years later, when Tree had given up pranks altogether and was Head Boy at the Government New School, that he would have his first and only face to face encounter with Mudda Mae.

All those years she maintained her ritual of carrying mop and bucket to and from school. One day Tree missed Yellow Man's bus and had to take a jitney called "Sunshine Chariot" home from school. Small Pint, who was also attending the New School, was staying behind for basketball practice. Tree sat by the door of the bus the whole time and never looked at the other passengers. He simply tapped his feet and nodded his head to the reggae that was coming from the bus's huge sound system and watched the world speed past through the window. When the bus finally skidded to a halt at the Southern Road entrance to the Village, two or three people got up behind him. Tree didn't pay them any mind. He was busy searching his pocket for fifty cents to pay the driver, who held out his hand impatiently and frowned. One of the passengers who got up was Mudda Mae.

As soon as Tree jumped out of the bus and onto the dusty sidewalk, a black purse fell down at his feet. He picked it up and turned to hand it to the woman behind him, who must have dropped it while trying to step out. Mudda Mae reached out with her free hand and took the purse while balancing the bucket, broom, and mop in the other.

"T'ank you chile. God bless ya, hear?," she said, with an affectionate smile, and walked down the street without missing a beat.

Numb, Tree couldn't walk down the road behind her. He took a long, slow trip in the opposite direction and sat on the shore of Rocky Beach until twilight. Then he made his way home, thinking of an excuse he could give his mother as the stray dogs barked and the street lights ushered in the night.

Crazy Mister Burke

Where Mudda Mae inspired fear and trembling, Constantine Aurelius Burke, because of the peculiar nature of his affliction, provided amusement for almost everyone in Pompey Village and beyond. He was known far and wide as the Walker, and with just cause, for that's what he did. He walked. The same distance, to the same place, by the same route, at the same time, every day except Sunday the whole year round. People could tell time by him.

Word was, Crazy Mr. Burke had once been a teacher and preacher of great repute. While still in his mid-twenties he was made Assistant Pastor of the Canaan Baptist Tabernacle on Duncombe Street. Whenever he was scheduled to preach, the congregation sat up straight in their pews. Arthritic women jumped up at the sound of his voice and shouted "Halleluyah!" right on cue. The most rheumatic old man, hat in hand, would charge into the centre aisle and dance to the glory of God as Young Burke gesticulated with the fury of a composer. People said that when he preached he would rock like a mad man and groan as though tormented in deep sleep by a nightmare. The Holy Ghost moved when he was preaching as at no other time. His scorching tongue spared no one. His exegetical brilliance enlightened the most clouded minds. In short, Reverend Constantine Aurelius Burke was the youthful sensation of Duncombe Street and the miracle of Canaan Baptist.

Everything he touched blossomed. When he took over the Youth Ministry the number of young people in the Church tripled in the space of one year. Even his job as a teacher at St. John's Baptist High was marked by success after success. His students always won the top prizes on Speech Day and achieved the best O' Level results at the end of the year. So his ascension to the full pastorship of Canaan Baptist Tabernacle at the sacred age of thirty-three was seen as an act of Providence, not coincidence. He was beloved, admired, and feared. But best of all, he was unmarried.

The women of the Church flocked to him. The young girls of the Youth Choir seemed ecstatic when their names were pronounced on his firm, thick lips. The solemn women of the Prayer Band giggled like school children when he approached. Love letters of every kind, addressed to him, circulated each Sunday from pew to pew. Many of these would appear mysteriously in his Bible and hymnbook, or in the pockets of his coat as it hung on the rack in the tiny Pastor's Office. But Constantine would have none of it. He was God's firebrand. His lips had been cleansed by burning coals, his feet dipped in a pool stirred by an angel of the Lord. He had no need for desires of the flesh.

Within two years of taking over as Pastor, Burke oversaw the expansion of the Church and the building of the New Canaan Baptist Tabernacle. It was four times as large as the first, with cushioned seats and central air. It was, as he put it, "A mountain of faith in the middle of a ghetto of despair." Its imposing structure was a testament to the power of a people forced to live amidst dirt, dilapidated clapboards, and rusty old rum shops. It was no wonder then that many of the young women who sprang from those same cushioned pews, who fell into his arms possessed by the Holy Ghost and speaking in tongues, showed little concern if their blouses became unbuttoned or their skirts rose too high in all the ruckus. They openly delighted in his touch, revelled in the promise of those dark, righteous arms. But never mind. Reverend Burke's eyes were open but they could see naught but the glory of God. His arms held gyrating damsels eager to please, but he felt only the warm glow that came from the Throne of the Almighty . . .

That is, until Brenda Gray. Until "that woman," bedecked in gold and black, walked down the centre aisle of the Tabernacle, dragging sin and tribulation behind her.

The minute she set foot in da place the woman dem face was screw.

That woman was a case and a half. And stuck up? Never said a word to anyone but her Rev. Burke. A peacock among hens, that's what she was. A woman who made "Sunday best" a euphemism. And the way she swung her behind about in those tight clothes! Which man with any blood left circulating between his legs could help but notice? The very essence of splendour promising excess.

Brenda Gray had a voice as sweet as night jasmine, but simply refused to join any of the choirs. She sang in Church for Burke and for Burke alone. She never opened her Bible or her hymnal unless he was slated to preach. No one knew what to do with her. Her reason for setting foot in that holy place was clear and she didn't give a damn what anyone thought. She had come to see this majestic man that people were talking about. This man who preached as though a fever was frying his brain, whose face prophesied Judgement Day, and by whose will a towering Tabernacle of concrete and steel had replaced four walls of rotted wood. She had come to see this man, and to win him.

With envy and despair the women saw their great leader, their holy raging saint, their sacred shepherd, fall prey to a pompous she-wolf, and they could do nothing about it. The men, captivated by her elegance, her outrageous beauty, never once tried their hand. It was as if they conceded defeat from the very first, as if they knew in an instant that fate had delivered her to be Pastor Burke's helpmate. They resolved to drink to his good fortune and health when the wedding bells rang and left it at that.

But the women of the Church would not trust her. How could they? Brenda shunned them all. Frowned on their Prayer Band, mocked their choirs with her voice, even looked on cynically when someone was filled with the Holy Ghost! They would speak to the Reverend in private, one by one if they had to. They would ask if it was not unwise for him, being already forty-five and turning gray, to marry a girl of eighteen. He dismissed their warnings. "Brenda is a gift from God," he would say sternly. "Do not suggest that I would become unequally yoked by taking her hand in marriage. The Lord said be fruitful and multiply." And that ended it. It also ended the days of the Reverend Burke they had come to know and adore.

Not long after dat tings change. Tings gone wrong. Dead wrong. Is dat woman cause it. Is like the fire gone outarim.

As the story went, Constantine returned from his honeymoon a radically altered man. He had lost the holy rage. When he stepped into the pulpit and preached, he no longer roared like a lion or snorted Judgment Fire from his nostrils. The man who could call down the Holy Ghost on their heads had vanished. The man who pranced and pounced like a maniac, who dealt mortal blows to the Devil in bloody combat, was now dead and gone. Only the creepy skeleton remained. "Marr'ed life," they said. "Dat woman suckin' he lifeblood."

Canaan Baptist tried to go on, of course. They still clapped their hands, stomped their feet, sang until it seemed their lungs could sustain them no longer, and prayed like the Lord had ascended to Heaven just yesterday. But Burke was now aloof, absorbed in far-off thoughts. He seemed exhausted and gloomy. He handed the preaching chores over to his subordinate ministers more and more. He stopped attending prayer meetings. And then, the bombshell. He announced that he was leaving the new house on Duncombe Street the Church had furnished for him and was moving to a place called Pompey Village. He said the family needed more space now that his wife had borne him a child. *Pastor Burke leave Duncombe Street? Move from 'mongst the people?* Rumours started spreading. Not a few women started saying Burke had been fixed by that woman. Not a few came to Church late at night and opened the Pastor's office to look for signs of fyak. Sister Talbot, the rock of the Prayer Band, said strange prayers over Pastor Burke's cloak while making the sign of the cross. She read special verses from his Bible while holding a candle, and even placed certain leaves in his Sunday morning tea, but to no avail.

Some of the men tried to be fair to Brenda Gray. They tried to see her side. The fact of it was that Brenda was young. She was having a hard time living by Burke's strict rules. People remembered that she worked for the Post Office before getting married but Burke had insisted on her quitting the day after the wedding. And Brenda was not allowed to go anywhere except to New Canaan or to visit her people in Collins Harbour, Ventana Island. She was stifled. And probably, they permitted themselves to say, she was not being satisfied by the old man. Being cooped up in the house all the time—a twenty-seven-year-old married to a man over fifty—with nothing to do but tend to their little girl, Charity, would drive anyone cuckoo. Some even mentioned the stories coming from Pompey Village folk. They claimed that at least twice, in the middle of the night, they'd seen Brenda run screaming into the street buck naked, and seen Reverend Burke standing there in the doorway of the house holding a leather belt and a Bible in his hands, wearing his preaching robes, calling her "bitch" and "whore" and telling her to bring her "black ass inside for he get vex," saying he "gat to beat the wickedness outta her flesh 'cause was woman bring sin in da world."

Strange tings was happenin' and not errybody in Pompey Village was convince is Brenda cause it all. People start to wonder if Burke head wuzzan bad from day one.

And then, another bizarre occurrence. Brenda began participating in everything. Prayer Band, Choir, Sunday School, counselling, the works. She seemed consumed. Sister Talbot was not fooled. Yes, Brenda had become more active, but she had also begun laughing with the young men of the Church and openly receiving their hugs as a form of greeting. Especially a big healthy boy named Calvin, who worked for John Capron, the contractor. Calvin was a wonderful baritone and when he sang his big hard chest forced its way up against his too-tight shirt. He was the most desirable young man in New Canaan. So when he and Brenda took to singing duets, rumours started flying again. Reverend Burke acted as if he saw nothing. He remained aloof, gloomy, lost in thought.

It was not long afterward that "Crazy Mr. Burke" became a legend in Pompey Village and all Santa Maria. Shortly after those duets Burke retired from St. John's Baptist High and resigned as Pastor of New Canaan Baptist due to "illness." That woman drove him mad.

This is how it was supposed to have happened; how it was that Crazy Mr. Burke lived in his house in Pompey Village with only his daughter Charity to comfort and run errands for him, how he ended up rising six mornings a week at six thirty, putting on his fine gray suit, taking his umbrella and hat, and walking from his house all the way to Safe Haven so he could watch the mailboats leave for the Out Islands, only to turn around and walk home again by precisely the same route. This is why Crazy Mr. Burke never went anywhere but downtown to Prince Edward Harbour. Why he would remain at home on Sundays and preach with rage to a congregation of one, his young daughter Charity. Why he would hurl verses from the Book of Job at the children who came into his yard to get water from his tap after a game of hopscotch or pawkin'. Why he was known far and wide as "the man in the gray suit who does walk up and down," as "Crazy Mr. Burke, the Walker." Sister Talbot knew the details:

Was all cuzz Brenda gone run off wit' Calvin Green an' leave him. She walk right down da centre aisle one Sunday when he was preachin', briss and bold. Preachin' hard and strong like he ain' never preach in years. And she stand in front da pulpit while he preachin' and holler at him. Make him forget what he was sayin'. Say "I sorry Constantine but I leavin' you. I leavin' you tomorrow. I goin' to my people tomorrow. I sailin' on the Flora Mae. Calvin goin' wit me. You keep Charity. She your chile. I ga send for her when I ready." And cold just like dat she walk out da Tabernacle. The Lord is my witness, Constantine Burke stand like Lot wife in the pulpit and ain' speak a word. Ten minutes gone by and he ain' move a inch. No one in the Church say nuttin'. Den he sit down and Rev. Williams take over the service. Church end early but Rev. Burke ain' even wait for it to over se'f. He gone out the door. Next day bright and early he was standin' in he gray t'ree piece suit, umbrella and hat in he hand, to watch Brenda leave on the Flora Mae. Half the Church was there too. People ain' gat no shame. Burke ain' never say a word. Just watch the boat leave Prince Edward Harbour. Watch all the boat dem leave. Den he turn round and walk Pompey Village. Never say a word to nobody. Just walk down the road same way he come.

Jahown

His name was not Jahown, though that's what Pompey people called him. He was christened in the Church of the Holy Virgin Mary as Michael Tyrone Cunningham, Jr. His father had been a music teacher and his mother a secretary for one of the white law firms downtown. They were both rather old, Mr. and Mrs. Cunningham. When Tree first saw them they were in their sixties and already retired. By the time Tree was about nine, Jahown was twenty-five and had been home three years. His real name was not Jahown, nor Tyrone Michael Cunningham, Jr. for that matter. His name, he would readily tell you, was Brother Nehemiah. But no one called him that. No one except the other Rastas who came to visit him at the shack he built in his parents' backyard.

They would come and he would greet them as Rastas greet each other, in that special language of their faith. They would sit together in the shack and smoke herb. They would sing hymns sometimes and read the Old Testament. Often they just talked. About the faith. About events and places in Africa. About politics and the police. And he would show them his artwork and ask them what they thought of it. Sometimes he would tell them what he believed his paintings meant, what he had tried to achieve by this or that line, shade, colour. They respected his opinions, these Rastas who came to visit. They listened to his advice about almost everything that affected their lives. Some were younger than he, others much older, but they came and listened. He was considered one of the wisest Rastafari in Santa Maria but he was not a priest or a leader. He was simply a man to be trusted. There was a peace and a simplicity about him that made you feel easy in his presence. A sadness to the truths he spoke that beckoned contemplation, quietude.

Tree would visit the shack just to talk. Sometimes he would sit by the door after school and watch Jahown paint or carve. He would sneak over and listen to the Rastas sing and pray and warn them when the Babylon was passin' by in they squad car. Everybody loved Jahown. He was the rock of the Village. He watched out for the small children. He kept his eyes open and checked on people's homes when they went away. He was a grown man but he would play with the boys when it suited him. He especially liked Small Pint, Yellow, Tree, and Stooley. They spent lots of time together while Tree was in Junior School. He would call them his pupils. They formed a small band, a gang, but he would never use the term "gang" to describe what they were. Everybody loved Jahown.

He was six foot four and his locks, on the few occasions he revealed them, seemed to reach below his waist. His beard was thick and curly. His eyes were a moist, dark, brown. He took his time in speaking, and each word was the sound of a pebble falling in deep water. He was a strong man but he never got in fights. He never drank rum, he never ate meat, he never spoke a profane word. He took care of his parents in their old age and kept to himself. Every morning he would take his paintings and carvings down to the harbour to sell at the Straw Market. He was clean and orderly in all he did. It was rumoured he had a woman but he never brought her to his parents' house.

They called him Jahown because he would always say "I and I is Jah child." They called him Jahown because to him, everything was Jah own: the fruits of the trees, the clothes on one's back, everything. He would say to Tree, "Bring I Jah chisel," or "I and I thirsty for a drink a Jah water."

Everybody loved Jahown. And that is why they felt it was such a pity what had happened to him. That's why they felt such sympathy for old Mr. and Mrs. Cunningham. Why they regretted that such a smart young man, a young, handsome, strong man with so much of a future, had come to what he had come to. A waste.

"Goin' away een for errybody," they would say. "Too much book learnin' ain' good fa da head," they would say. "Cunningham only chile gone off to foreign land and let them people set him crazy."

That's how they explained the striking transformation that took place in the Cunninghams' son. That was the only thing they could think of to explain what had happened to this brilliant young man. The books, the studying, had set him crazy.

When Tyrone was still in high school he was considered the finest student St. Luke's had ever produced. He was Head Boy, delivered a speech at graduation, and finished with twelve GCE O' Levels. All As. He sat the SATs and got one of the three highest scores ever recorded by a Santa Marian. Universities throughout the United States were inviting him to come to study, scholarships and all. He was guaranteed aid to study in England. The British High Commissioner himself had written a letter to his Principal saying he should apply for a scholarship. That, in itself, was unheard of.

The Cunninghams were the proudest parents in the country. Their boy was a prodigy. Mr. Cunningham, a man from the old school and himself a composer who had been one of the first to get a degree in music from an English University, had reared a highly intuitive and remarkably disciplined boy. Mrs. Cunningham's steady diet of fish, milk, and cod liver oil had nourished what was clearly the mind of a young genius. All Backadabush—the name given to the places where black people lived—celebrated in his stardom. Michael would have to be a doctor or a lawyer, nothing else would do. If he chose to read law, it was off to England. If he chose medicine, he would go Stateside. Those were Tyrone's choices.

When he told everybody at the dinner held in his honour that he wanted to study art he made his mother cry and his father choke on his food.

The sixteen-year-old was sent to University in the States where he got a degree, a year early, in Chemistry and Biology. He finished summa cum laude. At age nineteen he entered medical school with the intention of becoming a specialist in cardiovascular surgery. At age twenty-two he had only one year remaining to complete the medical degree, after which he would begin his Residency. In the seven years he was away from home the Cunninghams had moved to Pompey Village and retired. Tyrone had been home only twice in that time. He wrote letters constantly however. The Cunninghams had been to see him only once, on the occasion of his Baccalaureate.

During the summer before his fourth and final year of medical school, Tyrone returned to Santa Maria. Only, he was no longer Tyrone. He was Brother Nehemiah. He was a Rasta who had "turned his back on Babylon and the vain pursuit of the white man's knowledge." The Cunninghams tried everything to persuade him to go back and to cut his hair. His old teachers came to visit him. The priest who christened him came over to pray for him. He would not be moved. Mrs. Cunningham cried for three days. Mr. Cunningham didn't sleep for five. While his relatives wept over him, Jahown made trips to the Pine Forest. With the help of some of the boys from the Village he brought back pine wood to his parents' yard with which he built a shack where he could work. When it was finished he began to paint and carve.

They begged him to shave his head, at least, to get a job, and to use his degree. He said he got the degree for them and they could do with it what they wanted. He was no longer going to serve Babylon.

People expected that either one or both of the senior Cunninghams would shortly die of ulcers or a stroke. But Jahown's parents recovered by and by, much to the disappointment of those whose boredom made other people's suffering legitimate entertainment. Mr. and Mrs. Cunningham became resigned at last. They had missed their boy anyway. If he had not become a doctor or a lawyer, at least he was alive.

But people still talked. Some blamed them for pushing him too much. Most just said book-learning had set him crazy. The older ones cursed Rastafarianism as the scourge that was ruining the next generation. Jahown seemed oblivious to all the talk and looks of disappointment. He worked in his shack and enjoyed life. He seemed to never have been more fulfilled in all his days.

Let me show you dis vibe, seen. In life, man must follow his soul-riddim. Das what matter most. Life is movement. Soul is riddim. Black people get t'ief from Africa and stranded here in a strange land, but they have to keep movin'. I and I move back and forth between Ethiopia and here all the time in my dreams, in my visions, in my art, seen? I and I is two tings at once. What the backra do to de-I and what I and I bring from Africa, both tings is what make up I Ras Nehemiah. Santa Marian people is new creation on Jah eart', overstan'? When de-I dead, I and I soul goin' back to Zion, to Ethiopia, land of the Conquerin' Lion, seen?

You, Tree Bodie. I see you is a smart chile of Jah. You hear what dey say 'bout de-I? Dey say "Jahown crazy." De-I don' mind dem. They confuse by Babylon. You remind de-I of I-self way back. I and I had a t'irs' for knowledge. But now de-I t'irs' for knowledge not to advance in the things of this world, but to teach the Children of Israel the way to true overstandin'. Why must a man get a education? To make money? To become rich? To say heeza muck-a-muck? Big and bad like backra? Smart as the Conchy Joe? Smarter than the Englishman? The honkie? Let I tell you sumtin, Tree. And de-I tell you dis because de-I see in you the t'irs' for knowledge and wisdom that bringeth overstandin'. Where dis same Santa Maria gone wrong is the people want what they see backra dem have. They followin' too much in he footsteps, seen? The worst ting you could do is want to REPLACE your master. What sense that make? To replace your master? To what end, dreadie? To become master yourself? To become the nex' downpressor?

I and I eyes open Stateside, seen? De-I read the things dey don't let you read in these schools today because dey want to keep the children blind. Santa Maria own black leaders want to keep the people stupid and grateful, seen? I read Frederick Douglass, Booker T. Washington, Ida B. Wells, W. E. B. DuBois, the one Marcus Garvey, Martin Luther King, Malcom X, Angela Davis, C. L. R. James, Fanon, Césaire, Cabral, seen? I and I eyes was open. All that dese University and College teachin' people is vanity. It teachin' people to t'ief and to kill. To go along wit' the System, overstan'? It don't teach you how to live in the world like a man or a woman. It just teach you how to be a suckneck. How to suck the blood a da people. Neckbiters wit' degrees.

When de-I was Stateside I meet Fari in New York. They show me the Way the Trut' and the Light. I gone to Jamaica you see, the land a Paul Bogle and the mighty Maroons. I learn what Rasta is. I learn who Haile Selassie I, the Rightful Ruler is. I and I see the Blue Mountains and Cockpit Country. And de-I come to know Jah, seen?

Your mudda, Ms. Bodie, she's a good woman, Tree. She want the best for you. De-I people was like dat too. But you must follow your heart first, Tree. Don't be like me and live for other people. Don't be like I and I was and try to live out your parents dream instead a your own.

I and I see what happen to your brother. He was a great ball player. I see how the University shake him loose when tings get rough. Mercer, Jr. sufferin' now. I see it in he face. So you must be careful. Don' let the world blind you. Don' let Babylon blind you. Remember, life is movement. Soul is riddim. Remember who you is and what make you. You owe the place what make you. You owe the people who send you fort'. But you must decide how you gern pay back what you owe, seen?

De-I is face Babylon all the time, every day in the Straw Market. I ga tell you the trut'. I and I is don' want sell my paintin's to dem white tourist, you know? But I and I need to survive. I and I own Santa Marian people wouldn't never buy my paintin's 'cause it show dem dey true-true face. Truin, all dey believe a paintin' should be is sunset and flamingo. They don' believe they own black face, they own wide nostrils, belong on canvas and could get call Art. Is colonialism that mess wit' dey head so bad they even forget Africa, will cuss you if you call them African. Look how they walk pass the Ministry of Education and done forget it was a plantation Great House? They will cuss you if you say to them they great grand daddy was a slave! They forget what happen just thirty years ago but they know all 'bout Cromwell and King Charles. They shame a they own tings but love Miami, New York, and London. I and I people! Look how dey treat da Haitian 'cross the water. First people bring liberty to Africans. Is what make dem believe dey don' gat nuttin in common wit' oder black people?

I show you a vibe. De-I know why the tourist dem is buy dese paintin's and carvin's, you know? Is 'cause they think they "exotic." I show you dat, das how they t'inkin'. Is hurt me to have to sell my tings to dem, but my people don't believe they have artist who could say sumtin to dem wort' listenin' to. They rather listen to dese play-play politician talk foolishness all the live-long day than support the young people who tryin' to say what time it is fa true. Tell you da trut', de-I is feel like a whore sellin' dis work to dem touris' man, seerus. But de-I gattie eat. De-I parents pension ain' enough to keep tings goin'. De-I cyaa live off dem like a suckneck, seen? I and I have to contribute. But sumtin been formin' in de-I head. You see, is the touris' hesef who first say the sunset beautiful, so we t'ink ONLY the sunset beautiful, and we wesef ain't beautiful too. But I gat a way to show I and I people dat they is beautiful.

One a dese days Tree Bodie, mark Br' 'Miah words, one a dese days I and I gern rush in Junkanoo. I been dreamin' a dream 'bout dis costume I goin' to make. It gern look rumpin' when it finish, dreadie! De-I ga buss on Waterfront briss and bold and show da world what time it is, seen. Briss and bol', and show the whole wide worl' what we is and where we come from! Movement and riddim buhy, das da secret. Dey give da black man trial and tribulation but we keep on movin'!

11

Hers had been a long and bitter seasoning. And things didn't get better when Tree was born. Mercer Stone stormed into the Maternity Ward soaking wet, a scowl on his face, and nothing in his hands but a *Miami Herald* balled up like a policeman's billy. And with that tone of disgust and exasperation he used whenever he didn't get what he wanted, said, "Damn woman! You couldn't do better dan dat?"

To this she gave no reply. Mabel Jones, the woman in the bed opposite hers, just shook her head and clucked, feeling ashamed for Maureen Bodie that she should have to put up with such a fool-fool man. But Maureen held the child to her chest like a bag of rubies, and never answered. That was what she always did. Never answered. Just stared at him and let him make a fool of himself. It drove him mad.

On the day Mark Etienne was born it rained for hours on end. His father was furious. And maybe a little drunk. He walked from the parking lot in the afternoon downpour after having made a frustrating trip to the Sapodilla Lounge to watch the Dolphins game with the fellas. They lost. So he was hoping to be pleasantly surprised when he entered Queen's Royal Hospital with its foul odour of disinfectant, and made no effort to hide his disappointment when his wife gave him the news. Bloated and sweating in the humidity, Maureen put her lips to her child's forehead and announced, quietly, that it was another boy.

Mercer Stone figured three sons were enough and he wanted a daughter badly. But Maureen Bodie had lost the only two baby girls she had ever given birth to, and she believed that it was not by accident. It was the will of God that she should not have daughters. The girls, Barbara and Elizabeth, were born still. Two girl children asleep in the ground, never having screamed, never having uttered the cries which signal life's arrival. In that way she was very much like her mother before her, knowing what it meant to bring life and death into the world from the one womb. Three of Jewel's children had died at birth and were buried beneath a silk cotton tree at Pleasant Place.

A long and bitter seasoning. Mark and his brothers, Mercer Jr., Kevin, and Franklin, lived with both their parents for three years after he was born. After that Mercer Stone and Maureen Bodie separated. Maureen went to University in the Other Country and took her four sons with her, leaving no trace that she had ever lived in the blue clapboard that stood on concrete blocks, and creating a sensation among the gossips of Daley Street, not to mention the circle of Mercer's family and friends.

Scholarships were being offered every year as part of the Government's effort to provide University education to a generation of black folk that had been denied the opportunity by the white minority. No one seemed to notice that the whites weren't racing to schools abroad because they owned all the big businesses and could simply hand them down to their children from generation to generation. Black people were too embroiled in the process of becoming qualified to remember that they were broke, and that the majority of them might remain that way for years to come, despite an education. As far as Maureen was concerned, going abroad was more than scratching that old itch to prove she was as smart or smarter than any man, white or black; it was an opportunity for a new and better life. Many people said she was crazy to carry her four boys behind her to a foreign country, especially if she would be spending all her time in school. Who would raise them while she was in classes? And where would she find the money to feed them without a job?

"She mussie don' trust none a her own family dem to raise her chirren," Brisimae Williams snorted, a mother of seven by five different men. "Well chile if it was me, I was droppin' dese suckers off to dey Granma and I was gern partyin' soon as dat plane touch groun'."

Mercer's two sisters were the most cruel in their comments. After all, who did Maureen think she was to leave a good, respected man like Mercer Stone to go off on some crazy University course? The gall. What made her think that she should go off to University before Mercer had the chance to himself! No kind of respect for her husband. And why didn't she leave the boys if she insisted on going in the first place? What did she expect to happen to them but that they would come back Rasta chirren or something crazy like that? Mercer never should have stooped to marry a gal from Backabush like her anyway!

"Serve him right," declared Ann Marie. "Here he is, big time schoolmaster, and he have that cheezie woman and her four picky head sons behind him all the time. And livin' on dat street of all places. Wit' dose break down shacks all around. You t'ink he couldn' find a decenter place to live?"

"Serve him right. Too damn cheap!," Ruth barked, as if she was voicing a gripe she had held close to her chest for far too long. "Pa Simon raise him better dan dat. Dat woman een gat no broughtupcy at all! And gat Mercer going right behind her wit' dem niggerish ways!"

But Simon Stone cut to the chase. He told his only son, "Boy, you must learn to put your fist up side ya woman head. Then she won't talk fool." And as far as he was concerned the matter ought to have been closed. No woman of his was going anywhere unless he said so. The woman who tried would feel his foot coming squarely up against her backside. That said, the retired schoolmaster expected his son, his only son, who had followed obediently in his footsteps, to do da right damn ting.

But Mercer never dared tell his father everything about his wife of fifteen years. In all those years he never raised a hand to her or shouted an order. He had not even threatened her once. First of all, he had not done so because she never disobeyed him. Second, he was afraid of what she would do to him if he tried. There was a spooky seriousness about her. No doubt she was obedient. But there was something Out Island and rough, something Baptist and old, something unnervingly grave about her that said she was not to be tested. She was the kind of woman, he thought to himself, that would take your shit all morning and poison you that night. That was the reason he smelled every meal before he ate it, had her taste it first before he gulped it down. It pained Mercer to confess that as much as he had his way with his wife and was free to sleep around with women and girls as he saw fit, he still did not have control of this backwater gal.

What no one seemed capable of understanding, least of all Mercer Stone, was that Maureen's decision to pack her bags, load up her sons, vacate the clapboard house on Daley Street, leave her husband for good, and flee the country altogether, was not the spur-of-the-moment act of unmitigated brashness and crazy female emotion that everyone seemed to think it was. Maureen's exodus, though terribly hard to effect, had been rehearsed for over thirty years. Showing the resolve to leave her man, take her children, and depart from her own peculiar Egypt in search of greater opportunities for herself and for her sons was a great casting off, a breaking of time-honoured yokes. Along with studying for the "O" and "A" Levels by candlelight in the kitchen, leaving Santa Maria and going off to University was the first thing she had done in her entire life that was just for her. It was the first thing she had ever done that was not intended to fulfill her duty to her parents or to please her husband, win his approval, and obey his unquestioned authority.

The shaping of that determined, powerful, disturbing smile without parted lips, that assessing gaze that never betrayed the secret of a strength that came from on high, had both come to her through forge-fires that were set years before that courageous day when, the sun glaring white and angry, she had stepped onto the Air Santa Maria Jet and, never looking back, kissed her home goodbye for three years without once returning for so much as a Christmas vacation. The preparation for that act of leaving began when she was just a little girl at the All Age School, with the stone that was tossed vindictively by the obtuse hand of Mae Gibbs. The stone that struck her in the head and fell, blood-stained and ominous, onto the limestone trace. It was because she had gotten a perfect score and Mae Gibbs had gotten a duck egg. The stone was insurance. While insurance against the mischance that she might one day think she was sumtin and forget that all she was, all she would ever be, was a stringy, black Out Island nigger gal, a workhorse and a man's mattress one day, if she was lucky.

The seasoning got worse while she played the role of cart horse for her family, her mother, her siblings. It was intensified by John Bodie's outright refusal to give her the chance to see, unfettered, the world beyond Runaway when she passed the Common Entrance Exam for the Government New School. Because she was not a manchild. Because what she needed was a husband, not books. Because a woman didn't need to find work, there was enough of that to do in a man's house and in his yard.

Long and bitter. For fifteen years she was one of those women that worked in a rhythm. She gave birth in the wet season and got pregnant in the dry. And as if the indignity of perpetual pregnancy for a man who neglected his family and sweethearted was not enough, she had to reckon, twice in six childbirths, with the agony of two girl children born dead. What more obvious sign could she have been given of her own wretchedness?

So for fifteen years she did what a Santa Marian woman was born and raised to do for her man. She made his every meal, fetched and washed and ironed for him. She watched him take her money every month for eight years on Ferdinand Island. Watched him ignore her and neglect his children, his own flesh and blood. Said nothing when he walked out of the door and lied about where he was going. And her selfless giving had been her expression of love. Her dedication to the status of cart horse, the status of the daughter never punished, of the daughter who was smart but not a manchild, of the bearer of children, of the backward, poorly dressed Out Island wife of the snazzy teacher man from the city, all this had been her expression of a faith that life would get better, that prayers might be answered, that love might be returned, that the Lord would make a way somehow.

And yet, this leaving, this breaking loose had not been her first. The first had been leaving the security and love of Pleasant Place. At that time, the fear and the evil omens that surrounded her betrothal were hard to shake free from. The part of the truth that Maureen had told no one was that leaving Runaway and her father's house at Pleasant Place had been a last resort. She was going nowhere quickly being a teacher's aid at the All Age School. And being eighteen and unmarried at that time was peculiar. She was afraid she might never leave her father's house. So she suppressed her doubts and left her home, despite her mother's grumblings. Even when it rained cats and dogs on her wedding day, she forced herself to see it as a blessing and not as a sign of worse things to come.

Safe Haven had been a totally different and imposing world for her. Electric lights, radios, and telephones were becoming the order of the day in many Safe Haven homes. And the people were not as open and relaxed as on Runaway. The folks who lived next door to you were not necessarily neighbours. The hostility she encountered from Mercer's sisters and parents didn't help. They looked on her with contempt and condescension because she was from an island far south in the archipelago, an Out Island, and she was a "Catchin' The Sperrit Baptist." But she had endured all this and adapted, just as she adapted to sleeping in bed with a grown man every night. This was especially frightening for her, having never looked at a man in her life. As a child she had grown up sleeping on a grass bed with her sisters and brothers, but nothing prepared her for the demands a man made when the lights went out.

Compared to that first departure, leaving Santa Maria almost seemed easy to her. She was ready when the time came. She had suffered beyond tolerance and would not be held back any longer. Yet, there were times in Barbados, sitting in the living room of the apartment she rented with the scholarship money, when she would come close to despairing. She would strain to hold back tears and drift into a song she might have sung long ago at Mt. Sinai. She would shut her eyes in exhaustion and needful prayer. Then everything would be fine with her. God would provide. She need only believe. She need only put her trust in him. Look at the lilies of the field, she would say to herself. They neither sow nor reap.

Then, one day, she came very close to having absolutely nothing with which to feed her children. She contemplated skipping classes to go and work extra hours somewhere; even considered packing up and taking a semester off so that she could make some money. But she knew that if she returned to Santa Maria without her degree, there was no guarantee she was ever coming back. She also knew that there was no way she could pass her courses if she missed any more classes. So she went to class despondent and late.

That day the Prime Minister of Santa Maria was paying a visit to Barbados and had taken the opportunity to address the Santa Marian students that were enrolled at the University. Maureen missed the speech but was walking by the cafeteria where the Prime Minister and his wife were guests at a reception organized by the Santa Marian Students Association. As she walked past, distracted and anxious, the wife of the Prime Minister came running outside to greet her. She had never met The First Lady before, nor did she have any reason to believe that Lady would know her from Eve. The Prime Minister's wife came over to her and said she had never met her before, but that the other students couldn't stop talking about "the woman with four children" who was also studying at the University.

"I just came to tell you to keep it up and that I proud to see you striving for better." The Lady gave her one hundred American dollars, hugged her warmly, and kissed her on the cheek before returning to the cafeteria.

Maureen Bodie would later tell this story over and over again to Tree and his brothers when discussing her reasons for supporting the PNF. "She didn' know me and her heart gone out to me. The PNF is the only party that give a damn about black people!"

More than an explanation for her political leanings, to Maureen this act of kindness from a stranger, and a stranger of such great importance and stature, was nothing short of a sign from a listening and sympathetic God. A sign that miracles were real things in the lives of those who would only believe. A sign that her having suffered injustice after indignity had only been a testing, a preparation for a greater work, a process that would ensure that when the Bridegroom came, she would not be caught without oil in her lamp and be denied entry into the Banquet Feast.

● ● ● ● ●

Fourth Low Price Food Store Gutted in 3 Years

—by M. E. Bodie, Daily Report *Staff Writer*

The intersection of Brandy and Wilberforce Streets was the scene of large-scale hysteria yesterday as the fourth Low Price Supermarket in three years went up in flames. According to Lucilda Hill, the building became a wall of spewing flames and smothering black smoke at about 6:30 Monday morning. Mrs. Hill, a fifty-two-year-old straw vendor, believes she heard an explosion while she sat reading her Bible in the front room of her Brandy Street home. "I couldn't see no flames or nothing at first," said Mrs. Hill, whose house is located directly opposite the food store. "Then, about twenty minutes later, all I see was smoke smoke smoke. So I run call the fire engine."

The blaze, which lasted about two hours, was somehow contained to the Low Price and did not spread along either street, both of which are lined with clapboard houses. Mrs. Hill explained that about an hour after she saw the clouds of smoke and called 919, a fire truck arrived on the scene and began fighting the flames.

"I ain't never see nothin' like this in my born days," declared Brian Farmer, ten-year-old student of Cambridge Primary. "I run out the house fast-fast and come see. Cars was back up mussie for a mile in every direction. And one woman in curlers was screamin', say her chile gone too close to the fire to check tings out, and now she can't find him." (The aforementioned child was Tamiko King, a nine year old, who suffered minor injuries but was retrieved safely).

The fire was finally subdued at about 8:45 a.m., by which time two additional fire trucks had arrived at the scene. Miraculously, the four walls and roof of the the building remained intact and seemed to suffer only superficial damage.

Firemen were momentarily hindered in their efforts to quell the flames when a tall, bearded man dressed in rags, whom everyone called "Ezekiel Dry Bones," attempted to unscrew one of the fire hoses. Failing this, he leaped onto a parked car, pulled out a Bible, and began preaching to anyone who would listen, announcing the Second Coming of the Lord, calling all sinners to repentance, and inviting the bystanders to be baptised in the "cleansing flames." He was arrested promptly and taken to the Central Police Station.

When asked about reports of an explosion, Sgt. Carlton Rahming of the Police Fire Department said that there was no evidence of an explosion of any type, and that the short-circuiting of electrical wires probably caused the blaze. Low Price Supermarket officials have made no statement up to press time today, and they have been unavailable for comment.

Amazingly, of the four food stores that have caught fire, none suffered major damage to the brick structure of the buildings nor the roofs. And none of the supermarket fires spread to adjacent buildings. The first Low Price to be gutted by flames has since been rebuilt, furnished with more up-to-date equipment, and laid out in a more customer-friendly interior design. The other two LP's are being renovated and redesigned in an identical manner as the first. Citizens have complained for years about cramped conditions and pests at the Brandy Street LP.

The Daily Report was informed by an official of the Fire Department who wishes to remain anonymous that there is no one on staff trained to investigate possible cases of arson.

12
Las' Chile

The five a us start hangin' out little while after me and Small
Pint start talkin'. After dat we was always tageda. At least 'til I
start at the Government New School. Now I don' have much time
for playin' 'round in the road no more. I use to just talk to them on
the basketball court and visit Jahown or Small Pint now an' den. I
always ride in Yellow bus too, 'cause he is to let me on for free. But
them t'ree years I was in Junior School was when we had our own
li'l gang. We call ourself "the Rovers." We never use to do anyting
bad like these new gangs in Safe Haven—'cept t'ief fruits erry now
and den, break some windows playin' pawkin', or buss a dog wit'
rock jus' ta hear him squeal. But udder dan dat we never cause no
trouble.

Jahown was da leader 'cause he was da oldes', da bigges', and
da smartes'. He was the one give us the name "Rovers." The res' a
us use to bring up da rear. It was Jahown, me, Small Pint, Yellow,
and Stooley. Errybody had dey role. Jahown used to make da big
decisions and settle arguments. He never use ta curry favour, aldough

Small Pint always say he like me da most. But das only 'cause Jahown smart from studyin' how to be a doctor an' stuff. He just like to talk to me plenty cause I use to keep up wit' my studies. Jahown always tellin' me to read dis and dat, but Small Pint never check for no book learnin'. He use to go to school for errytning but class.

Den you had Yellow. He always had money and good tings in his house to eat and drink, and we could go to his place to watch bush karate. "Enter the Dragon," "Snake and the Monkey's Shadow" and "Drunken Master" was da best a all time. Yellow had plenty dirty books under his bed what me and Small Pint use to sneak peek at too. We never tell Jahown 'bout the books 'cause he is Rasta, and he have funny ways when it come to tings like dat. He don't even t'ink say girls should wear pants. Say dey followin' Babylon.

Yellow was the secon' in command. When Jahown was busy paintin' in he shack or doin' his devotions, Yellow run tings. Yellow real name was Bertram. He was Mr. Roberts' son. Mr. Roberts use to drive a Route 13 bus and had two taxi plate he used to lend out to people so dey could make money for 'im. Yellow dem always had car and bus park outside dey house. The first time I meet Yellow he was cleanin' one a da bus. Was one Satdie mornin', an' Mamma send me to Mr. Tingum Shop on Kevin bike. Errybody use to call him Yellow Man, like the reggae singer, 'cause he was light skin. Light like a ripe, hairy mangra. All his people was light too. They all come from Preacher's Point, Ferdinand Island, and they say errybody from Preacher's Point have mangra skin. But dey ain' really Conchy Joe. Dey jus' have light skin. Mamma say dey was white once but dey have some black in dem and you could tell if you look at dey hair. Yellow was finish wit' Grade 12 by the time me and Small Pint hit Grade 8. Me and Small Pint didn' go to the same Junior School but the two a us inda the Government New School.

Me and Small Pint use to do most a the sneakin' and t'iefin'. And Stooley was so small and sickly he was just the look-out. Everybody use to pick on Stooley back den. But now he ain' nuttin like how he was den. Now he tall like Jahown, and he say he wan' be palice.

Stooley dem live in the only house in Pompey Village what ain' white and yellow. Das 'cause it was dere 'fore Pompey Village get make in the first place. Stooley don' have no brothers or sisters. Is jus' him and his ole man, Mr. Lightbourne. Mr Lightbourne was from Flamingo Bay, Little Santa Maria. He come to Pompey Village from dere long-long time ago and buy piece a land from the half-a-Conchy Joe, Pa Stirrup. When the contractor dem come to build Pompey Village, Lightbourne say he wuzzan movin' and he wuzzan changin' his house to look like da res'. So das why dey house different and standin' by itself on a dead end. People say ole Lightbourne gran' daddy was a real African from Africa. I aks Jahown if das true and he say yeah. Say slavery abolish in Santa Maria first Monday in August 1834, but some places like Cuba and Brazil had slavery long after dat. Say the British use to catch the slave boat goin' to Cuba an' set the Africans free in Santa Maria, where wuzzan no slavery. Jahown say wuzzan tens a t'ousands a dem what dey bring, but was enuf dat a good few gat a connection ta Mudda Africa—das what he call it—what pretty recent. Mamma say my great gran' mudda, Rachel Macintosh, was a real African. But Mamma say she ain' never had chance to talk to her 'bout Africa and tings like dat 'cause she dead when Ma Jewel was born.

Stooley dem is the only people in Pompey Village with a real well like you see on the Out Islands. Even though they have plumbin' like everybody else, they used to draw water wit' bucket. The well have frog and ting livin' in it an' it dead deep. Whenever public water stop runnin', Mamma is sen' me and Frankie to fetch water from Mr. Lightbourne well. Das how me and Stooley get to be fr'en's. We start talkin' while me and Frankie draw the water. Is me give him his nickname, just like Small Pint give me mines.

You see, Ole Lightbourne had a big hairy mangra tree, and me and Frankie use to come down tada house when school out to t'ief lil bit. Stooley those house was right on a dead end at da edge a da Big Bushes, where da trail start what lead tada Pine Forest, da canals, and Rocky Beach. It was easy to sneak 'round back wit'out anybody noticin' 'cause dey ain' never had no fence. Ole Lightbourne was hard a hearin' anyhow, and he couldn' see too good neider. Wuzzan no trouble gettin' up dat tree and down again *wit' a bag-full. No trouble atall. Stooley always use to take long to get home from school for some reason or oder, so we never use to get catch.*

But dis Friday we was up in da tree an' out da blue, me and Frankie hear somebody screamin' loud-loud from inside the house. So we start wonderin' what was goin' on. Nex' ting I know, we see Stooley come runnin' out the back door intada yard, shoutin' and cryin' like dog was bitin' him. An he een even had on no pants or drawers or nuttin! And when we look close was a real live worm dangling out his boongie. Man, dat was the funniest ting I ever see! Nex' ting you know, Mr. Lightbourne come rushin' outside and holdin' ma lilly buhy down and pullin' the worm out wit' he bare hands. Dread, dat ting was long and reddish—make me want to jump out my skin. We had ta fight hard not ta buss out laughin' 'cause we woulda get ketch! And from den on I call him Stooley, 'cause he had worms when he was stoolin' and run outside screamin' wit' all he boongie an' ting showin'.

Stooley mussie was sick all da nex' day 'cause Small Pint say he ain' gone to school. Only me an' Frankie know 'bout dat day. I never tell nobody else why I call him dat, 'cause I didn' want shame him. It wouldn'a really be fair to go spreadin' it roun', since errybody is get worms. M'se'f included. When I had um I t'row mines up on the rug. Mamma give me medicine to get ridarum when I was small. When I was 'bout five or six I use to eat dirt after it rain and das why I get worms.

Anyway, I guess he figure out I was up in his tree t'iefin' when he hear me call him "Stooley" after dat. But he ain' never aks me 'bout it or get vex or nuttin'. Now he so use to people callin' him Stooley he is don' answer to Rufus Lightbourne no more.

Back den, in da summer time, we use to go errywhere. The canals, Rocky Beach, the ponds, mangrove, Pine Forest, and the Big Bushes after da houses too. We use ta change our headquarters erry couple weeks. Firs' it was the Big Gum Tree with the roots that come out da branches and down to the ground. Then it might be by a lignum vitae tree in da bushes down from Yellow dem house. Once we even build a shack outta pine wood and had some old car seat for chair. Dat was da life. We use to talk all kind a foolishness 'bout sports and what we want to be and tings like dat. An' Jahown always had sumtin interestin' to say. I know people mussie use to wonder why a grown man like him, wit' all dem brains, turn Rasta and use to hang roun' all day wit' a bunch a little snotty nose boys like us. But he jus' cool to dat, das all.

We use to play pawkin', karate, and rounders. Even hide-and-seek. We use to spike top and build scooter and go-cart. Erryting. We use to go bikin' too. Jahown is da best when it come tadat. He could pop longer dan anybody I ever see. He had a iron donkey once and Small Pint bet him he couldn' go the len't' a our street on one wheel. Dread, Jahown pop so long he even turn the corner and gone on a nex' street. He tell us he pop a whole t'irty-five lamp poles. Small Pint was good at poppin' too. He use to try pop and stan' on the bike the same time, like dem dreads who is ride the motorcycle is be doing. Jahown always say dat people like dem motorbike riders ain' have no "inner strengt'." Dey jus' do dem tings so people will believe dey hard.

"You sow da wind, you reap da whirlwind." Jahown is talk like dat all da time. And he make Small Pint stop poppin' like dat. But far as I concern, if Small Pint fall on his ass jus' once he woulda catch plenty sense anyhow.

Mos' a all we use to go walkin' through Pompey Village when people wuzzan home and t'ief mangra and plum, sour sop, dilly, sugar apple, banana, juju, coconut, guinep, sugarcane, coco plum and guava. And we use to pester Crazy Mr. Burke for cherry from he cherry tree, and tease people potcake and chap dem wit' rock, shoot chimmey out da trees wit' slingshot, and go 'round by Mudda Mae to see if we could catch her workin' obeah or vexate he cat. Jahown never use to like us to bodder Crazy Mister Burke or Mudda Mae dough, 'cause he know say errybody use to t'ink him and dem was bad in da head. He use to feel fa dem. Mosadatime it was just me and Small Pint. Yellow never boder wit' dem neider and Stooley was too scared.

One time Jahown gone in Biggity Miss Francis yard to t'ief hog plum and she come outside cussin' lone stink words. Biggity Miss Francis was a woman wit' t'ree chirren an' wuzzan never marr'ed. Da house she was livin' in was her sweetheart own. Her las' two chirren was for him. She was hard mout' and use to fight wit' her man once erry couple a months in broad daylight fa errybody ta see wha's what. One time she even t'row knife at her sweetheart and it ketch him right in he back. He fall in da grass cussin' and crawl ta he car and drive off.

So dis time nah, all a us sittin' in da road laughin' boy, 'cause we didn' expec' her to be home. But her oldes' son gone out in da car and she was inside waitin' fa her man to make he daily visit. Well, when she start her whoopin' we ain' run, 'cause we figure we was goin' watch see how Jahown handle hese'f. He always gat sumtin smart ta say to boof people, so we just sit back an' relax like we own da road.

Nex' ting you know, Jahown jump out da tree wit' a bag full a plum and say, "Daughtrine, rail not against the Children of Israel! Don't you know de Eart' is Jah's and the fruit dere of? So cease an' seckle! Dis JAH tree!"

Man, we buss out laughin' and start rollin' in the street. She get so screw, her eye gone blood red. Look like she was ready ta yuck up her gown tail an' go ta war. She say she was gern call da police on us. Say, her man leave his gun underneat' her bed and she have a mind go fetch it. So we break off runnin'! Nuttin' make us feel better dan makin' Biggity Miss Francis mad, das fa sure!

Man I tell you, da foolishness we use to do! And never really t'ink 'bout it, ya know? Just do it right so 'cause we get da inclination. We use to go down to Rocky Beach and walk over to the canals what the Government build there not long ago. Use to swim almost every other day in the summertime. Divin' off the highest rocks, try'n'a touch the bottom. Small Pint and Yellow was the best. Dem two could dive straight off the rocks and go down to the bottom, straight down. When they come back up they use to hol' up mud and seaweed in they hand to prove they touch the floor. Me and Stooley never could make it. We'd reach half way and stop. Stooley use to stop 'cause he was 'fraid a barracuda. But me, I use to stop 'cause my ears use to start hurting me dead bad and I use to look 'round and 'round in the water and be scared I'll never reach the top again if I go any further.

Whenever we gone to the canals we use to tease Jahown 'cause he never come in the water wit' us. He couldn' swim. His parents keep him coop up studyin' book so much he never learn. So when we use ta be foolin' around, divin' and doin' cannonball and flips an' ting, Jahown just sit little ways from the edge, on a rock, and smoke a spliff or just stare at the sky, the birds, or the Pine Forest in the far off distance. I use to feel sorry for Jahown then. 'Cause I know in his heart he want to swim too, but he was too ole to try learn. We use to splash water on him but we never even pretend to t'row him in or nuttin'. 'Sides, he was so big he coulda toss all a us in, him one.

Small Pint and Yellow t'ink they is man. I remember dere was dis one canal Small Pint and Yellow did like da most 'cause it had a refrigerator at the bottom. Dem two fools use to dive in the canal and climb in the fridge and close the door! First Small Pint would do it, den Yellow. Jahown use to be dead mad at them, boy, but they didn' care. Me and Stooley just look at them from the top and laugh. Damn, we was one big set a fools!

And don't let it be Halloween time! Man, we use to carry on so bad! Firecracker and rotten egg left right and centre. If ya get ketch outside after sunset Halloween night in Pompey Village you better be prepared for battle. Me and Small Pint use to save money all September for Halloween. Use to stock up on sky rockets and Air Bombs. We use to place da Air Bomb in the yard, knock on people door while somebody else lightin' it, den run like hell. KABLOW!

'Round six o'clock, when the buses making they last lap past Pompey Village, me, Small Pint, and Stooley use to hide in the bush side the Southern Road and toss rotten egg at the buses. And after the bus dem stop runnin' we use ta attack the cars! Jahown never condone dat kinda ting, but it was fun. 'Course, we never do nuttin to Mr. Roberts bus 'cause dat was Yellow Man daddy. Police chase us once or twice too, but dey wuzzan ready. They don't know Pompey Village like us, so we always get away.

Mind you, I wuzzan always so mischievous on Halloween, you know. I remember the first time I try do sumtin for Halloween. Was before me and Small Pint make frenz. I see the white children on t.v. trick or treatin', so I decide I was gone do it too. I was mussie nine den. Fool me, I gone over to Miss Johnson house, right nex' door. But ting was, I ain't had no money for no costume. I put a paper bag on for mask and punch two hole in it. I knock on the door and say "Trick or treat, money or eat." Miss Johnson come to the door and aks who it is. I say, "Is Cookie Monster." She look at me and just smile. Say she sorry but she ain' have nuttin, so I must go on home for I get in trouble. Boy dat make me shame! I cry underneat' dat paper bag. Das the first and last time I trick or treat. After dat I just trick!

And I'll never forget how that plane crash in Pompey Village. Seerus as a heart attack. Drug plane fall right out the sky and land on dese people dem place. Right around the corner from the Yellow and White House. It sound like I storyin', but is da trut'. Single engine plane, in the middle a the night, had to make emergency landing and was trying to do it on the Southern Road. Sucker land smack dab on top the people dem house! Wake the whole a Pompey Village up. Plenty people get rich that night. The plane was full a dope and was at least two briefcase in dere full a money from what I hear. First a all, everybody in the plane was dead but nobody in the house get hurt 'cause the plane jus' hit the ground and end up in they living room, and it ain' never blow up. When them people house insurance kick in they was able to build a two storey mansion in Pompey Village and start a construction company ontopadat! And everybody who gone outside there that night and reach before the police, come away wit' big bills. If you don' believe me you could pass by the house today. The plane still there. They use bulldozer and push it on the side a the street and lef' it right dere like it was a break down car.

On that same plane, me and the Rovers watch the PNF rally last Election Time. The house was 'cross the street from some bush what belong to the Stirrups, and he sell the property to the Government so they could build a basketball park. Well, they ain' never build the park, but they clear down the bush so they could have a rally dere and attract everybody from the Southern District to come and hear what they had to say. Ting is, they leave the plane right dere. So the night a the rally all us sit right dere on the wing what wuzzan mash up and listen to the soca music and all the politicians. Small Pint and Stooley even gone and get free t-shirt and food. All a our parents was in the crowd cheerin'.

Dat night the Prime Minister introduce the new candidate, name Thaddeus McKinney, to the people. Say he was their man, and he was going to keep the ship sailing in the right direction. Everybody was all into what the PM was saying. But it was like it didn' really matter what he say, they was gone cheer anyhow. Then McKinney had he turn to speak. Yellow say he was bound to win, 'cause Pompey Village people always vote PNF, no matter what, even if the Devil was the one the PM put up to run for Parliament. Then Jahown just laugh and shake his head like is the sad trut'. He say he don' know why he is bother listen to dem politicians. They all just suckin' the people dem spirit. He say backra come and see the islands and decide he want dem, so he enslave and kill the Lucayans. Den he decide he cyaa use he own people to work the fields 'cause they cost too much. So they bring us from Africa. Then, when they see they wuzzan makin' no more profit off bein' here they get tired a enslavin' the Africans and finally they just leave. But when they leave they put couple black politicians in charge; a set a lawyers who they train like monkeys in the circus. And dese same monkeys is who run the country for the white men abroad and keepin' us poor. Cyaa t'ink for they se'f. Cyaa do nuttin' differen' from how they see backra do it. And all the monkey dem is be in suits and drivin' fancy car. And when FLP and PNF start fightin' come Election Time is just monkeys fightin' over what the trainers leave behind.

I miss dem days, seerus ting. Now I is hardly see the fellas when I home. High School is so much pressure, so much work. I spend most a my time studying for dese GCEs. I don' want let Mamma down. I gat to do well if I ever gone get the chance to go to University abroad. Frankie and Kevin been to Santa Maria College, but ain' none a her children get a B.A. like her. Firsborn is the only one who wanted to go away, and he get kick out and had to come back home. I know Mamma feelin' now like ain't nuttin' get better since her days a strugglin'. I gat to make it. I gat to have my chance. I cyaa be stuck here livin' in her house and not doin' nuttin wit' my life.

I is still hang wit' Small Pint, but he gat his own frenz in school and I gat mine. I guess I hang out wit' the nerds. He is hang wit' the boys from his stream. They all act tough, ya know? His frenz is call the students in the top streams "the Soft Boys." And now, dis Head Boy business just make tings worse. Is like Small Pint don't want nobody know me and him is frenz. We'll talk as soon as we walk out the school gate, but while we in there he wit' his crew and I doin' my duties. But I know Small Pint. He is act hard but he ain' really the same as those boys who is get in fights all the time and get expel from school. He just act that way 'cause it cool and the girls like it. A dude like me, I cyaa never be one a the cool crew because the teachers pick me to be Head Boy. I is the enemy in school. I have to report all the students who come late, who don't wear the uniform, who fight, who wear makeup, who chew gum in class. Das all I do all day, report, report, report. It ain't fair. It don't make no sense. They shouldn't have students doin' the teacher job. How we 'pose to do all this plus study for GCEs?

One time I catch Small Pint standin' in the hall when he shoulda been at mornin' assembly. They make the prefects patrol the school durin' assembly time, das how come I see him. He was writin' sumtin on the wall. It say, "NO LAW." Everybody who t'ink dey hard is write "No Law" on the walls or shout it out in the headmaster face. Small Pint see me comin' and he just finish writin' what he was writin' like it was no big deal. Write it wit' a red marker, at dat. Then he put the marker away and just smile at me and walk off. I couldn' report him. Small Pint is my good-good fren. We just changin', me and him. Is like we goin' two diff'ren' ways. But I cyaa never forget where me and him come from. The two a we is Rovers.

13

Scratching Thaddeus' back proved even more unpleasant than Tree had initially imagined. He'd hoped his role in the political war would be carried out in secret. He figured he'd be forced to write a few campaign speeches and that would be it. No one would see him. No one would know his name. And no one would say that the snotty nose boy who raise all that hell with the rest of them at the College, 'bout "da Gobmen' dis" and "da Gobmen' dat," was changin' his tune come Election time. But with each passing week Thaddeus brought him closer and closer to the frontline.

"Jus' tell me what the hell it is you tryin' to prove wit' dese articles I see you gat dere in *The Daily Report* ?"

"I don't understand."

"You don' understan'? You damn right! Listen' bulla, I try'n'a win a Election here in the next eight-nine months. I don' need you over yonder writin' foolishness for Curry 'bout crazy women who use to go out wit' da PM or people settin' fire ta dey own businesses!"

"Shouldn't the PNF be glad to see somebody exposing some of the practices of the Egyptians? I mean, that's what we're fighting against right?" This was as close as he ever got to being rude.

"Son. Listen. Tings ain' dat simple no more. Certain people in our party have shares in Low Price. It still majority white-owned, but. . . . Anyway, just be careful what you write in that paper."

"I'll try."

"Do better than that. Stop your foolishness. And I need you to come meet the folks down at the Headquarters."

As with everything between them after that first meeting, Thaddeus was not asking Tree if he would like to come to the PNF Headquarters in Hawkins Town, he was telling him.

"But . . . I . . . I didn't know I would have to be involved. I mean, sir, I thought these speeches and such, like the one for the opening of the new library, would be enough."

"Bodie, you already involve."

Bodie, you already involve. He didn't want to hear that, but when he walked into the Headquarters and was greeted by all the party workers (mostly women) he knew it to be true. They all knew who he was. Maureen Bodie son. They shook his hand and embraced him as if they were proud to see another generation of Bodies dedicated to the struggle. As if it reaffirmed their belief in the rightness of their mission that at least one young person had not been lost by the wayside, (elders always, without fail, described his generation as "lost").

Sitting there listening to strategy, to plans for ordering t-shirts, posters, flyers, beer for an upcoming rally, hearing an estimation of the number of PNF versus FLP households in Hawkins Town, an estimation of the cost of radio and newspaper ads, speculations about the probable changes in constituency boundaries, etcetera, etcetera, Tree felt faintly sick. Sick and strangely special. It was like being allowed into a room that had been declared off limits for years and years. His mother had always been an active party member, but the nitty gritty of Santa Maria politics remained outside his experience. This was his own doing. Once he graduated high school she was always inviting him to join the youth wing of the party, but, caught up in the moment of Runne's Poli

Sci class, and later, the demonstrations, he always refused. Now, with his mother too tired to scrap for the PNF in the trenches, he had come into the fold. The old women occasionally smiling in his direction and the old men slapping him on the back made him feel like a long-awaited secret weapon, the smart young brain that would guide Thaddeus to victory. Thaddeus had virtually introduced him as such. Before all those witnesses Tree was tempted to say, "No I'm not! Go to hell! You people are insane! Leave me the hell alone! Win your own damn Election!" But he never did.

Before he knew it he was spending part of almost every evening helping to put up the huge posters of Thaddeus and the PM that the PNF had gotten made in Miami. He was sticking smaller posters to lampposts. He was knocking on people's doors and handing them flyers about Thaddeus's great rise from nonentity. He was giving out free t-shirts and bumper stickers. He was even writing articles for the PNF's organ, *The Clarion,* about the tremendous crowds that were showing up at rallies all over the country. (The numbers were always greatly exaggerated.)

Maureen: "I hear Thaddeus and the folks at the Headquarters like you alot. Say you doin' a good job. Das good, chile. It ga pay off. Fella wit' your brains? When you come back from University you might could enter politics yourse'f. The PM need young fellas like you by he side. Anyting is possible, Tree. Look at what Thaddeus do. Minister of Education. Dat could be you."

Dat could be you, boy. Dat could be you.

Thaddeus: "The PM say I must aks you for a idea for a ad to put in da papers. A full page ting. Sumtin what could remind people a how far we bring dem. A what at stake if dey vote FLP. Sumtin what could teach dese Backadabush niggers to be t'ankful for da PM and the party. You gat any ideas?"

The ad appeared in all the dailies and the weeklies too. At the top was the photograph of an old man with dark skin. A broad, noble nose. Proud, thick lips. His hair and eyebrows were white with wisdom. His eyes, slightly cataractous, looked confidently out to the reader. The trace of a smile was hinted by white teeth that offered themselves from behind the slightly parted lips. He wore a tie and coat: bust of a grandfather in Sunday best. Beneath the photo were the following words.

• • • • •

We Stood Together Yesterday.
We Stand Together Today.
We'll Stand Together Tomorrow.

My name is Zedekiah Rolle. I am a Santa Marian and a PNF. A Santa Marian who remembers the days when we could not get work in the banks and certain branches of the Civil Service, when we could not go into certain movie houses and restaurants. I survived those days. PNF history is filled with struggle, struggle on behalf of Backadabush. Our future, thanks to the PNF, is filled with hope, hope for our children and our children's children. The PNF is the party of hope, the party of action. In Santa Maria, because of the PNF's policies, Backadabushers have risen to the top of every profession in a short twenty-five years! In fact, today one of my sons is the Manager of a bank where formerly blacks could not hold jobs, and my granddaughter is employed in another bank as well. The PNF has done this! But what will you do? More than ever, it is vital for us to realize that there are still people in this society who want to turn back the hand of time. We must stand together. We might not be able to change history, but we can make certain that no one plays games with our future in this country!

• • • • •

The workers at the Headquarters loved it. The PM sent word down the line that young Bodie was a "damn genius." But Thaddeus was not happy. There were frightening signs of discontent in the constituency. The lamppost posters were being torn down. The big posters along the roads were being defaced and crude phrases were being written on them. These things had never happened before. More and more people were wearing FLP t-shirts and putting FLP stickers on their cars. The crowds at the FLP rallies were getting bigger and bigger. Election was coming and the streets had not been tarred. The Public Treasury was low on funds and the five-year tradition would not be upheld in any of the constituencies in the country. Thaddeus was in trouble.

"Gaddam Maxwell Brown!"

The gaddam Maxwell Brown to whom Thaddeus referred time and again before Election Day was his rival in the Hawkins Town race. He was not like other politicians in Santa Maria. He talked about things they never talked about. For a long time he had been a member of no political party. He was an advocate of things and for people that other lawyers and politicians never wasted their time on. He complained incessantly about the prisons. He talked all the time about "Human Rights." He raised hell because no one in Santa Maria seemed to remember that August Monday holiday was really Emancipation Day. He organized events to truly com-memorate the occasion, events that did not involve rum and beach picnics. He was the only politician who tried to be objective about the Haitian situation in Santa Maria and who talked about refu-gees instead of illegal immigrants. He was the only politician who criticised the government's control of Radio One, who called for them to permit independently owned stations on the air waves. He criticised the nature of business in the House of Assembly. Once he dressed up in golfing attire and practiced his stroke on the House of Assembly's lawn: he told the press that the people's money would be better spent if MPs did this at the House rather than pretend to be handling the affairs of the nation. He was a clever lawyer. Young people listened to him. They identified strongly with him and what he had to say about the youth's "growing sense of frustration" at graduating high school without skills and without opportunities for employment. He never failed to accept invitations to speak at community events. He represented poor people in labour disputes. But Maxwell Brown, supposedly, could never get elected in Santa Maria. Everyone should have known that.

Was because "he like man."

Once Maxwell Brown had been a rising star in the PNF heav-ens. A man the PM had handpicked to take his place one day as leader of the party. His first bright moment occured while he was still at St. Mary's Catholic High School. In the twelfth grade he almost brought about his principal's resignation by protesting the excessive school fees, fees that, years after Majority Rule, kept St. Francis three-quarters white. Then, on his first summer break from law school, he organized a protest march against the Queen's Visit. Her arrival had precipitated a "city-wide" cleanup and the repaving of downtown streets. Young Brown and his companions complained that the PNF government would never have made such a costly effort had Royalty not been coming to town, that this worship of the Queen was a sign that they as a people were still "colonized," and that the dirtiest and most ramshackled corners of Backadabush were as always being ignored and would certainly not be part of Her Majesty's tour of Safe Haven. That was enough. When Maxwell Brown finished law school the Prime Minister took him under his wing and promised him the world.

But Maxwell Brown spoil everyone plans because he like man.

People said that one day during his lunch break Maxwell Brown—he was party Vice-Chairman at the time but had not yet run for public office—approached an eighteen-year-old in the men's room of the downtown Public Library. No one knows what the two discussed but a good many have speculated. The young man, who worked in Bullard's Hardware, struck Maxwell Brown in the head with the dustbin and charged out of the restroom. Marching angrily downtown he ran into his brother, the policeman. This chap was busy directing traffic on Waterfront Road and taking pictures with smiling white female tourists in straw hats who thought he looked good in his starched old-fashioned uniform. But when his younger brother told him what had happened he left his duties and proceeded to further avenge his sibling's honour, this time on the steps of the Public Library where Maxwell Brown stood reeling from the blow to his head.

The news spread: "Maxwell Brown like man."

It was a popular saying in Santa Maria, to "like man." If one boy wanted to shame another during an argument that others were witnessing, he would ask him loudly if he "like man." If two boys went to the Bridge Street Theatre to watch a movie and they sat next to each other instead of with a seat in between them as they should have, somebody in the crowded hall would ask if one or both of them "like man." The two would move apart as derisive laughter echoed all around them. Girls in Santa Maria could hold hands, could sleep in a small bed together, could bathe together, could even kiss. But a boy who was so inclined was a "boongie bandit," he like man.

The results of the men's-room episode were swift and cruel. Everyone heard about it. Maxwell Brown became known as "Badboy Brown." The Oppostion FLP had a field day at their political rallies. Maxwell resigned the office of Vice-Chairman, quit the law firm where he would have quickly made partner, and left the country for almost twelve years. And for a time, he fell from the people's memory.

What had actually "ruined" Maxwell Brown's career was not that "he like man" but that he had not kept that inclination out of public view. Yes, people might whisper it. But if he had been willing to do what many other so-called boongie bandits had done, those who were highly successful and powerful but had done what they felt they had to do in order to win tolerance if not acceptance, in order to keep the whispers from becoming shouts, Maxwell Brown might have been a Cabinet Minister by the time Tree Bodie graduated the Government New School. People could point out these men. They could say to you, "So and so is a big time sissy." But the men in question were safe, if not from rumour, from open ridicule and violence. Most were safe because they chose to enter marriages of convenience. They made their offering to a society that was willing to let things slide provided you kept it out of sight. If you called yourself a public figure but you were open with it, if you refused to marry or at least be seen with a woman regularly, if you flaunted and advertised your preference for men, then the facade was shattered, the game was called, and people began to cringe and recite Bible verses to ward off the demons.

Maxwell Brown would not obey the rules that permitted man who like man to rise to prominence and power in Santa Maria. In fact, he had behaved like someone terribly ignorant of the rules on that midday when he approached a handsome fella in the men's room of the Public Library and asked him if he would like to have lunch with him. Either he was ignorant of the rules of the game or he was ignoring the game altogether. In any event, it cost him his career. Or rather, it changed it forever.

The birth of Badboy Brown that bright day was actually a blessing for Maxwell Brown and for the country at large. What it gave him was his freedom. Freedom from the pattern of outrage and silence that all young firebrands got caught in who became the adopted sons of the Prime Minister. Freedom to speak his mind about any and everything without fear of being repressed by the party machine. Freedom to live his life in a manner that he could stomach. Freedom not to pretend.

When he reappeared in Santa Maria and opened his own law office in downtown Safe Haven he returned a man without a future, a threat to no one. He was, after all, a man who had been named, and his name was a constant reminder of his shame. No one had to worry about him. There was no chance of his rising in politics. He was a misfit. An outcast who had gone away to lick his wounds and had returned at long last. This meant that Maxwell Brown could say or do anything without having to worry about losing public support or alienating his voters or upsetting party heads. As a man who like man, as someone who had been run out of town, as Badboy Brown, he had no supporters, no voters, no party. He could call for people to rise up, set fire to the hotels, bulldoze all the banks, and sink the statue of Victoria that stood in Victoria Square into the sea. No one would care. Supposedly. Being Badboy Brown and having the guts to come back to the scene of the crime meant that he was granted his own frequency, but a frequency that no one would ever tune into. He became another sideshow, like Dr. Harcourt Fitzwilliam.

But people *did* listen to what he said. People *did* care. He had been gone so long that an entire generation was learning his name, his original name, for the first time. They did not know of the transgression years before and if they were told about it they might not have believed it. To them he was special, an engaging voice. Even for those who claimed they remembered, the story had grown cloudy, had ceased being fact and had become rumour. Those among the older generation who were helped by Maxwell Brown, those elders who actually believed in Maxwell Brown, began to reshape him in their minds, they began to doubt or simply deny what twelve years ago everyone knew for certain to be true. Only the vindictive swore they knew the details and embellished in the retelling. Most of the elders, out of sheer surprise that the man had had the courage to return and start his life again as though the whole affair had never happened, refused to bring it up in public. They felt as if they themselves would be losing face if they tried to "t'row lowness" and call him by the name he had been given. It was as if he was daring them to say he should shut up, move to the side, sit down.

So this new Maxwell Brown emerged in Santa Maria. A new Maxwell Brown who inspired silence on all sides among the elders but was fast becoming the champion of the young, the poor, the prisoners, the refugees, the so-called misfits like himself. (He represented some of the wealthy as well, or he would never have gotten food to eat.) It was a silence that said, "But doesn't he know that at any minute we can call him by that name we have given him? We can bring it all up again? We can say it out loud? We can say that he like man?" But no one ever did. And as a result, Maxwell Brown became the most promising politician in the country, but one no one ever expected to see him sitting in the House of Assembly.

Of course, he tried. He would run as an independent in the bi-elections. He even ran in the last General Election. But always he finished third. He and the FLP candidate would split the votes of the discontented between them, and the PNF man would win again and again. His friends said he needed to play the game, and this time he agreed. But he didn't mean what they meant by playing the game. Everyone knew that there was not a single Member of Parliament that was not married or seen in public with a woman regularly. And everyone also knew that some of them like man. But they were playing the game to keep people quiet. Maxwell Brown refused to take a wife. He refused to bring a woman along with him to keep the whispers from becoming shouts. But he understood that though you could not disregard the game, you could play it without obeying all the rules. You could cheat. And cheating without being caught was the mark of a smart player in most sports. He would not marry or hire a chaperon, but he would make sure that his preference remained a private matter. He would be asexual in the eyes of the people. He would appear to have no one, to "like" no one. What people couldn't see they couldn't throw stones at. This was not complete victory, but it was not defeat either.

He also had to come to grips with what it took to win votes in Santa Maria. His activism had won him the support of the young, and they would be of voting age in the next General Election. But he knew that he could not win a three-way race. He would have to join the FLP or get an agreement from them that they would not offer a candidate, and with the growing mood of discontent in the country, there was no way the Opposition would not run a candidate.

Because he spent every extra cent he had in Hawkins Town for the five years following the last General Election, the people had come to know a Maxwell Brown who was not only vocal, but who backed up his expressed concern with his own, hard-earned money. People in Santa Maria would listen to you all day and night, but Elections were about putting bread on the table, not about ideals. It was a dirty business, but he was prepared to suffer the means to achieve the end: the House of Assembly. Once there, the people would see that he was not an inexhaustible well that they could run to for water whenever the sun got hot. Cyaa put da cart 'fore da horse.

The FLP, after long debates in Council, took him into the party. Maxwell Brown was a man who could not be ignored. They would take a risk on him, provided he kept his speeches in check. They made him their Shadow Minister of Education and the candidate for Hawkins Town.

Thaddeus called Tree into his office.

"Dis gaddam Maxwell Brown. He gat ta go."

"What do you mean, sir?"

"I mean he gat ta go, Bodie. He gat to go."

"You mean you need to figure out a way to beat him nex' year in the Election?"

"I mean, we gat ta do sumtin ta make *sure* we beat him in the nex' Election."

"Maxwell Brown is a serious opponent. I mean, he's very popular, sir. People my age especially . . ."

Even more irritated. "You aware a who dis man is? A what it will mean if he get elected?"

"What it will mean?"

"Heeza damn sissy! He like man. Heeza a boongy bandit. A abomination. Possess by the Devil. Consume by a evil spirit. You ain' never hear a Sodom and Gomorrah boy?"

Tree did not like where this was going at all. He had never seen the Minister so out of control.

"Well, what you have to say?"

He blurted it out: "I don't think . . . I mean, if I were a voter . . . I mean, as a voter it doesn't matter to me what a politician's sexual preference is. It's not my business. I mean, you don't hear people accusing the Deputy Prime Minister of being unfit to lead because he has illegitimate children all over the place. I really don't think the people will care one way or the other when Elections come around this time. Sir."

Thaddeus considers him.

"You sayin' to me that you refuse to write a article for me reminding the Santa Marian people of what a moral disgrace this man is? You sayin' you refuse to remind these forgetful fools what Badboy Brown IS? You too young to know, hey?"

"I was simply saying that I think he should be criticised for what he has had to say about the way the country should be run, not about his sexual orientation. As long as he ain' do nuttin criminal . . ."

"He damn well IS a criminal! Buggery is a sexual offense in dis country!"

Tree looks down at his shoes.

"Listen Bodie. I need to remind you dat to get a U. S. Student Visa to go to school you need a Police Record clearance form? A little white piece of paper with a red stamp on it. See one before? I need to tell you dat it only take a call from me to make sure you never get one a dose white piece a paper? I need to remind you dat your brother work to the *Government* owned phone company and I could have him sent home TODAY? I need to remind you dat as

Minister a Education, I could make it so your mammy have to teach at da rickettiest damn school in La Ventana Island 'til retirement? Hmm?"

Tree is looking at his shoes.

"Good. Get crackin'. Gaddam Maxwell Brown."

* * *

Later that evening Tree got a visit from Jahown. It was brief. He stood in the doorway with one of the flyers that Tree had been handing out. Every household in Pompey Village had gotten one. And when people were not home, Tree left one on the doorstep. Seeing Jahown standing there in the doorway, looming tall in its frame and with darkness settling, Tree almost thought he was being visited by a strange spirit. The Rasta did not say hello.

"Is *you* put dis in de-I mudda hand, Tree Bodie?"

The voice like great waters moving.

"Is you put dis in I and I mudda hand? *You* working for da politraitor now, young Bodie? You ain' never learn nuttin what de-I try teach you?"

"I . . ."

"Listen."

Jahown handed him the flyer. Thaddeus's grinning face on the flyer stood out in the pale fluorescence of the lamppost on the street with no name. Thaddeus grinning like an old decrepit imp in his left hand.

"The Prophet say, 'Never let a politician grant you a favour. He will always want to control you forever.' Yout' Tree, ya never hear dat song before, hey?"

The look of disappointment was cutting Tree up inside. He could not speak, he could not explain.

"Don' bring dis 'round I and I house no more when de-I away seen? Mark de-I words, Tree, and strive for overstandin'. Leave off Thaddeus McKinney. He will kill ya spirit, seen? He will kill you dead."

The moist eyes looked forebodingly into Tree's and then disengaged. "One love, dreadie." And he was gone.

The Third Part

♦

C L A S H

Now the people gather on the beach
And the leader try to make a speech
But Dread again tell them that it's too late
Fire is burnin'
Man pull your own weight
Fire is burnin'
Man pull your own weight

—Bob Marley, "Ride Nattie Ride"

14

He first became acquainted with Death and Hell at the age of seven. At that time they were still on St. Mark's Island. His mother was the Head of the English Department at a new high school the Government had built in Dove Creek. She would drop him off at the second primary school he attended on the island, the one in Sunrise Settlement that was built right on the beach. His three brothers went with his mother to her high school, which went from grade 7 to 12. In Crab Bay, Maureen's sons could do just about whatever they wanted. They went all over the settlement after school and on the weekends. Firsborn and Kevin made lots of friends, but none that Tree would remember very well when he grew up. The brothers went to the beach, went crabbing, and rode their bikes up and down. They also spent less time in church than Maureen might have liked because the nearest Anglican church on the island was many, many miles from Crab Bay. This not going to church was a pattern the boys had gotten used to in the Other Country, where they didn't go at all because Maureen worked or slept whenever she was not in class. None of that would change until they moved to Pompey Village. Then they were expected to go to church every Sunday.

One night during a storm, Tree and his brothers sat at the table for a game of dominoes. They played by candlelight because the power had gone out. Kevin started teasing Tree about the Chickcharnee, while the lightning and the thunder went wild and the waves crashed against the rocks where the hill on which they lived became a cliff that dropped violently into the huge, rough sea. But Tree was feeling animated and a little brave that night, and with Firsborn and Frankie's support, he had dismissed the idea of an owl with a man's head as ridiculous—this from a boy who was still terrified of the Abominable Snowman he had seen on WNIN.

Frustrated and disappointed that he had not provoked the usual tears from his little brother on mentioning bogeymen and the like, Kevin resorted to religion. He informed Tree that seven was the age at which people became responsible for their sins. Kevin told Tree that he was a certified sinner, because he had done many bad things since his seventh birthday, and for that he would die and go to hell, burn in hell fire, and be tortured and eaten by Lucifer himself and by "Bellzabub and Mefastofaleez" and all the other beasts of the Inferno. Then, to Firsborn and Frankie's amusement, Kevin went into the other room where his mother lay sleeping and brought back her huge Bible with Concordance and began reading from the dreaded *Book of Revelation*. He quoted extensively from passages about the Fall of Babylon, about the Horsemen of the Apocalypse, the last days of war and natural disaster, and about the Throne of God, which was surrounded by a sea of glass like unto crystal, and out of which came the seven spirits of God and lightning and thunder and infinite voices, and around which stood beasts with eyes all over that saw the sins of men. And Tree would be called to Judgement and he would be found guilty and all his secret little sins of "t'iefin' an' lyin' an' tings of dat sort" would be punished. And the whole entire Universe would see "erry stinkin' ting he ever do in his whole entire disgustin' life." And he would die an everlasting death of damnation, shame, and torment.

This had been sufficient to evoke tears and screaming from Tree, who, although he did not understand "sin," "death," and "revelation," understood monsters, fire, being eaten, having one's misdeeds exposed for public consumption, and so on. And this encouraged Kevin to continue his taunting until such a commotion was created that Maureen Bodie got out of bed and almost cussed them all and told them to leave her last child alone. And told Tree that he could come to her room if he wanted to. Which he liked. Because then he was safe. And her bed was warm. And she always had a little snack for him that she kept in her purse or under her pillow. And she would lay him down and give him a sheet to sleep under. And she would clear the bed of books and clothes, then tell him to go to sleep. And everything would be fine.

Tree was able to wrestle with his occasional bouts of fear for four years after that stormy night on which he was introduced to the peculiar terrors of John's *Revelation*. He was never completely comfortable lying awake in the dark but he had compensated for the evil faces people's clothing made in the night time by covering his head with his pillow. This served the double purpose of blotting out all vision and of stifling his hearing as well. In the dark, this second feature was important because his imagination got the better of him and he would often think that the Yellow and White House was full of sinister voices beckoning him to leave a limb hanging out of the bed so that a monster could drag him off into the bushes and devour him. He would even have sworn that, on more than one occasion, as he felt himself gasping for air in the throes of a dream-sleep, the Old Hag had come for him and was trying to take his breath away. So he slept with his pillow over his head, and he slept with the sheet covering every inch of his body to fend off mosquitoes and to trick monsters into believing he wasn't there. He would enter the world of the unconscious in this fashion every night, even after he grew to adulthood.

In his eleventh year, both his grandfathers died and were buried within three weeks of each other. Their deaths made Kevin's words more concrete. They forced him to think for the first time about the fate of his soul; made him reckon with a rule of the world that as a child he had found inconceivable: that he should come to an end.

It was not surprising that he should have such a self-centred reaction to the funerals he attended, that he should be so detached in the midst of the wailing and gnashing of teeth. He had not become unfeeling and callous at age eleven. He was simply incapable of feeling loss for these men. He had not known them. He could not love or miss that which he had not known existed.

Simon Stone, his father's father, had died first and was buried in an old graveyard near Prince Edward Harbour. The service was a sedate one. There were a few moans of despair, but when the coffin was lowered into the ground no one attempted to leap in after it to show their conviction. He and his mother sat in the church like spectators at a play. His other brothers were given the choice of coming or staying at home and had all elected to stay at home. But Maureen had made up her mind that Tree should be the one to know, to take account, remember.

Tree watched his mother closely during the service. Her face remained blank. Most of the people in St. Joseph's Anglican Church didn't seem extremely shocked or heartbroken at the man's passing. The wife of the deceased was the principal person doing the crying and hers was a polite whimpering from beneath her veil, punctuated by muffled groans of pain as the service progressed. Mercer Stone and his two sisters sat beside their mother obediently and they all looked solemn and distressed, but none of them was in tears.

As Simon Stone's body lay in the coffin, Tree realized that he had only seen his grandfather alive once. That was a year ago, and even then Mercer Stone's father was already an octogenarian and an invalid. On that occasion his father had come and taken him to see his grandparents on the Stone side so he could "know who he family is." Frankie was also forced to go and took his slow time getting dressed in protest. The entire visit proved to be an uncomfortable experience for both of them. Everyone his father introduced to them as an uncle, aunt, or a cousin was a total stranger, and he found himself faking smiles in an effort to return what he sensed was the false warmth they offered to him. He felt absolutely no connection between himself and these people and couldn't wait for the visit to end.

At the funeral Tree marvelled that so many people he'd never seen before in his life could be related to him. He read through the funeral programme restlessly, following each activity on the agenda with the impatience of a person with better things to do. He concluded during the funeral that his only family was his mother's family, and that all others were strangers to whom he owed no allegiance. Getting to know the Stones and make friends with them seemed permanently out of the question. Even if he had wished it, to have done so would be to betray his mother and he could never do that.

When they left the grave site Tree asked his mother about Simon Stone. Maureen seemed pleased that her son had asked the question. Perhaps she wanted to be the first person to tell him the truth about his grandfather. Tree later believed that his mother had taken him to the funeral just so she could tell him who his father's father *really* was. She said that he was eighty-seven years old and had been sick a very very long time. She said that all the wonderful things they said in the eulogy were only one side of Simon Stone. "He was a pompous, evil-tempered man," she said matter-of-factly. "Is no wonder he raise his son to mistreat woman."

His mother seemed as relieved as he was to leave the scene. But when she spoke he heard more in her tone than the bitter disappointment he was accustomed to when she referred to his father and his family. There was a trace of regret that confused him. When they returned to the Yellow and White House she turned to him, exhausted and a little sad.

"Well, Mark Etienne, your grandfather has passed away." She turned and looked through the living-room window, which was just a white glare because of the sun, and seemed to be thinking of a long ago past. "And you never knew him from a man on the street. It wuzzan me who make it so."

They were silent for some time after that and she didn't speak again until Frankie came in and asked her about the funeral. She didn't answer his question directly. "Dorothy Stone gat some nerve to cry dem crocodile tears in dat church," she said as she took off her shoes and massaged her aching feet. "Dey use ta have ta pull dat man off her when he start lickin' her up side her head. And she sit dere in that Church and cry for him. Hmph." Again, she was silent for a moment.

"Anyway, I gone to show my face because I was marr'ed to their son. Is common courtesy. It was the decent thing to do. And I know is more than he'll do for me if any a mine pass."

Three weeks later John Bodie died of heart failure. He had been living in Bell's house in Poinciana Park for four years. When he and his wife became too old to take care of themselves, Maureen and the rest of the family brought them to Safe Haven from Pleasant Place. They could get better medical care in the capital. They were both too sick to walk, and it was clear to everyone that John Bodie did not have very long left to live. He no longer spoke intelligibly and he had lost all control of his bodily functions. It was in this condition that Tree had first seen his grandfather at the age of nine. It was also at nine that he saw his father for what seemed like the first time, because the last time he sat in his presence he was only three and he had no memory of it.

Though his mother's parents were also strangers to him, he became somewhat accustomed to them because Maureen insisted on him visiting regularly. At first Tree had difficulty overcoming his child's fear of the old and of sickness. He cringed involuntarily when he was made to hug and kiss his grandmother and he received her gifts with hesitation. It would take years before he finally got used to her and was the one to initiate contact.

When Maureen Bodie announced that her father had been sent to the hospital and was on death's door it meant more to him than the news of Simon Stone's demise had. He had seen this man alive on more than one occasion, even if only barely alive. And more than that, John Bodie had been a romantic figure in his past, a presence in his mother's stories of growing up, a man to be respected. Someone he might regret never having known fully. And yet, he had *not* known him. There could be no terrible sense of grief.

John Bodie's funeral was remarkably different from Simon Stone's. First, there was a wake at Bell's house. More food was cooked than Tree had ever seen in his entire life. People he had never seen before streamed into the tiny house and when the house was full, sat on the grass in the chairs Maureen had brought from her school. They ate chicken and pig-feet souse all night and they sang songs until the early morning hours.

Tree fell asleep on his aunt's sofa and woke up when his mother nudged him so that he could help her clean. As he picked up the plastic bowls and cups that were scattered everywhere, the image of dark faces contorted in song and the sound of feet stomping to the rhythm of a rake-and-scrape band remained with him. It struck him that people seemed as happy as they were sad at the wake. Old men with canes got up to tell stories of their days with John Bodie on the Contract in the States or in Runaway. People embraced and laughed, and even Ma Jewel seemed determined to wear a smile despite her loss. The songs made him want to dance and to cry at the same time, and he couldn't remember how many bowls of chicken souse and slices of Johnny Cake he had devoured.

The funeral for John Bodie was held at the grand old Gethsemane Baptist Church, off West Road. Vibrant, mournful hymns were sung, many long unseen people from Runaway came, and John Bodie was given the respect and ritual of a deacon of the church. There was much more action than at Simon Stone's funeral in St. Joseph's. And even though his death had not been a surprise because of his long illness, the congregation marked his passing with wailing. All of Tree's brothers attended the funeral and each of John Bodie's children placed a rose on the coffin as it was lowered into the ground to a steady chorus of moans. But Maureen's face never betrayed emotion, nor her eyes tears. And through it all, Tree, though seduced by the wailing, was unable to cry for his grandfather who had left the world of the living.

This composure and detachment lasted until he tried to fall asleep in the Yellow and White House. When he closed his eyes beneath his pillow, with his sheet wrapped about him tightly and none of his limbs sticking out of the bed, he was harassed by visions of the dead. Both his grandfathers, their heads shrunken and their skulls gleaming through the loose skin, confronted him. Out of the crack made by the unclosed door of the closet he saw the grinning white fangs of a horned, snake-eyed Satan. Burrowing his head into the pillow he simulated the suffocation one might feel if caught alive in a coffin. All life proceeded as usual above him, but as he lay in his hot, airless box, the worms seeped through its cracks and began chewing on his flesh. They dug their way into his stomach and down his throat, they nibbled through the sockets of his eyes and mined his brain. He let out a muffled scream into the pillow and fell out of the top bunk onto the waiting tiles.

Feeling nothing, he leapt up, sheet still wrapped about him, the pillow in his hand, and slapped on the light switch. A mosquito cried around his earlobe as Kevin mumbled profanities. He cut the light off, made his way into the living room, and turned the television on. He would not think of death. He would not think of dying and worms and coffins.

It was not as late as he thought because Channel One was still broadcasting. Church was the only thing on. An American evangelist was preaching to a huge congregation as a number to call if you wished to make donations flashed across the screen. Rattled, Tree sat down to listen, hoping it would calm him down. The man's sermon was remarkably akin to Kevin's tirade on the night of the storm. The evangelist, crisp in his shiny suit and brandishing the Word of God like a sword, insisted that the wages of sin was death, that Satan was the ruler of the world and that Christians should be in the world but not of it. He spoke of Armageddon with relish and prophesied that the Second Coming was just a few years away. He spoke of the day the dead would rise again and be called to account at the Throne of Judgement. He said that only those who accepted Christ as their personal Saviour and begged for the forgiveness of their sins could enter the Kingdom of Heaven, where they would be spared the hell fire and eternal torture that will be meted out to all sinners. You must be saved and put on the whole armour of God. "Death has no victory over Christ," he said, banging on the pulpit with sanctified urgency. Death has no victory over Christ. "Through Christ comes the forgiveness of sins and everlasting life." Everlasting life.

Tree cut the television off and sat straight up in the settee. Death is not the end, he thought. There is heaven. If I ask for forgiveness of my sins I can go to Heaven and I won't be eaten by Bellzabub or burn in hell fire. My body will turn to dust but I can live again. But to get to Heaven I have to die first. Maybe not. Maybe Christ will come before then. The preacher said He'll come in a few years. I wonder if my grandfathers will go to Heaven or to Hell. What if my mother went to Heaven and I went to Hell? What if my mother went to Hell? Dat wouldn' be fair. No way. She don' deserve to go to hell. No way.

He jumped up from the settee, sheet and pillow dragging behind, and opened the door to his mother's bedroom. She was quietly sleeping.

Her breathing was soft and steady. He watched to see if her chest was going up and then down. Good, he thought. She's still alive. But suppose she dead tonight? What he ga do den. Oh God! What if she dead!? What I ga do if Mamma dead?! She still breathing though. Still breathing. Still . . .

* * *

At six the next morning Maureen Bodie got up to pray and cook Sunday dinner. She found her son asleep on the floor beside her bed. She carried him back to his room in her arms and went about her morning chores. Tree woke up not knowing how he managed to get back into his bed but relieved to see the sun.

That morning he was full of questions but he couldn't bring himself to ask his mother. He simply hovered around the kitchen as she stood at the stove with her back to him. Finally he said, "Mamma, I don' want to die."

She stopped what she was doing, turned, and smiled at him. "Everybody have to die, baby. All things living must die. You can't fight it. It have to happen. And it will happen, someday. But don't be afraid. What you must do now is live, darlin' heart. Just live."

She turned from him and went back to cooking, but she was quite aware that he was still standing there.

"Mamma . . . you miss Granddaddy?"

"'Course I miss him. He was a good man. A good man to all of us. But the Lord say let the dead bury the dead."

"How you mean?"

She started cutting carrots for coleslaw. Still her back was turned to him. "Get me the cabbage from the fridge." He obeyed.

"Was a time nobody on Runaway even know what fridge look like." She said this as if it were to herself that she was talking. He handed her the cabbage and she looked him up and down, thinking

♦ 159 ♦

of where she had found him the night before and wondering if he was old enough to understand such things as the power of the dead.

"You was dreamin' las' night?"

"Yes ma'am."

"Hmm."

She considered him. He looked down at his bare feet to avoid her gaze.

"Try don't t'ink 'bout it no more, you hear? Mindin' the dead is a seerus business. When I was a little girl I use to have plenty dreams. See all sorts a things in my sleep. Sometimes I still do. But is not sumtin to play wit'."

"I dream I see John Bodie las' night."

The look of concern on her face intensified.

"You musn' dream dat no more . . . And if you do . . . Just don't dream dat dream no more. Dead people don't have no business dealin' with the livin' unless is time you go to join them. When I was a little girl a ole-ole woman name Naomi Cumberbatch pass away. She use to live down below Pleasant Place in a little shack. People say she was a hundred-and-ten years old. Say she was friends with my grandmother, Rachel Macintosh the pure-blood African. When she pass they lay Naomi out in the church durin' the night. Daddy send me and my sister Pauline to the well and we pass that same church. The door was lef' open and the casket was sittin' there in front of the altar, big and bold. I never been so scared.

"When I sleep dat night I dream I see my grandmother, the Half-a-Scotsman wife. But Rachel ain' her real name what she born wit' when she come from 'cross the Ocean. Don't nobody know her true name. Is lost forever cause only the Half-a Scotsman who see her when she come off the ship know her true name; and he keep it to himself up there in that house where he wouldn' speak to nobody 'cep' Ma Jewel. Wouldn' even tell his daughter his wife true name. Hol' it from her, 'cause Africa was sinful to him. Rachel Macintosh come here when she was just six years old. The government set her to live and work for a white minister in Safe Haven. Half-a-Scotsman come and t'ief her when she was fifteen. T'ief her and carry her wit' him to Runaway. Never had no chirren 'til she was thirty-eight. Stillbirths only. Dead when she was thirty-eight

♦ 160 ♦

years old. And Ma Jewel had me when she was done thirty-eight too. Had t'ree before me and four more after.

"My grandmother *talk* to me dat night. She talk to me just like I talkin' to you right here now. But I tell you I ain' never even see dat woman amongst the livin' in my born days. She dead when Ma Jewel was born. And only ting I ever see a her is dat ole picture the Half-a-Scotsman had a her in the house on the hill where he never come off till he pass away. An' I ain' see that picture since. But she talk to me dat night, and she reach out her hand to me and I reach out and hol' hers."

"And what happen?"

"When I wake up next day I tell Ma Jewel. She mos' had a fit. She tell me you don' never take the hand a no dead person in ya sleep 'cause dat mean is your time to dead too. She gone out the house direckly I say dat to her. Gone straight to the graveyard, draggin' me behin' her. She stand by the gate a the graveyard and she hold my hand tight and she raise her next fist like she was rowing. She holler out, "You listen here Rachel Macintosh. Dis my favourite chile! The one I could count on! She just start her life and she ain' goin' no where! So you just sit still where you is an' don't be troublin' her. Is me take you out dis worl' when I come in it, so if is anybody you come to take 'way it bes' be me too! You hear?! YOU HEAR?! You done t'ief two a my chirren! Leave my daughter alone!" And she turn 'round and walk off wit' me behind her. Halfway home she take off her shoes and shake off the graveyard dust off um and I ain' never dream dat dream no more."

"Rachel Macintosh comin' to get you?"

"No baby. When is your time is your time and not a minute before. You just gat to know how to *deal* wit' the dead, das all. Now go outside . . . and don' be dreamin' no more foolishness. Le' Mammy finish cookin' in peace."

Still amazed by his mother's story Tree went outside to find Small Pint. It wasn't long before they were rolling old chrome bicycle rims down the street with clothes hangers. The warmth of the morning sun began to wipe all the fear away.

"Small Pint, you scared a dyin'?"

"Me? Scared? No dread. En errybody hattie dead? What I must be scared for? When I t'row crop I want dem bury me on my belly wit' my boongie pointin' to da sky."

"Why?"

"So da whole world could kiss my black ass!"

They both laughed hysterically. Small Pint had heard someone say this before and was waiting for a chance to use it himself. Tree appreciated it to no end. It made him forget about his behaviour the night before.

But that night, when everyone was asleep, Tree found his way to the living room once again. He knelt in a corner of the room and tried to pray. He prayed often in school and in the Sinking Church, but this was different. No one was watching him here. Only God, he thought. God and the Devil. He tried to close his eyes and forget about everything. He would pray and ask for forgiveness for the bad things he had done. He promised to be good. He asked God to bless his mother and his brothers and to bless Small Pint too. And then he thought of Nurse Culmer's guinep tree and the prayer was ruined. He started all over again.

15
Las' Chile

August 25

First day of classes at Santa Maria College and I met a special girl. She was leaning against a bookshelf in the library. Beautiful. But I didn't think that right away. She doesn't seem like the girls everybody usually likes. She doesn't have that mango skin that everybody is so in love with. And her eyes are a dark brown, like coffee. They aren't light, like everyone flips over. If your eyes ain't hazel or something like that, you just ain't happening. That's why I say she was not beautiful to me, at first. Not magazine or beauty pageant beautiful. Not one for the Miss Santa Maria contest. Her features are too black for them. At first she was just nice. Her smile. And her eyes. I liked her eyes. They made me feel good. Don't ask me why they did. I feel kinda corny writing it down, but I guess they had something in them that I could almost feel. Like she knew me from some place before. Yeah, where you hear that before, right? But I serious. It was like I wouldn't have to be anybody I wasn't to impress her. Like she liked what she saw. And when I got closer to her, and looked at her for the first time, you know, like you look at a girl, I saw that she was beautiful.

There was something fine about her. I don't mean that she was cute or womanish or acted so delicate. Girls like that piss me off. She was, I don't know. Quietly fine. Soft and sweet to look at. Those eyes. They glittered, man. And she seem so self-assured. Not hyper at all. A real woman. Full of what makes life sweet. And she had a certain elegance. But not in a false way. I know girls who paint everything, pack on makeup and eye liner and eyeshadow. And they even wear fake nails. She didn't have any of those things. She was just herself. Plain. But bright. A natural kind of beauty that needed nothing to accentuate it. I can't even remember if she had on earrings.

I could see she was in the world like the rest of us. Only, she ain't never let the world beat her down to where she ain't had no hope for the future. I can't believe I didn't even notice if she had on earrings! Too busy looking into those eyes that was making four with mine. Deep eyes. Made me feel right at home. No slyness in them. Just the truth. I just meet that girl and I believe in her already. I know I come across something truthful when I meet her today. But I ain't had the guts to ask her name. Next time.

September 2

I remember the first time I started liking girls. Because for a long time I didn't like them at all. I hated them with a passion. They use to piss me off. But even so I was curious. I remember one time in Crab Bay, me and Cheryl Ramsey went in the bushes to the edge of the pond with the gaulins always around and played a game. "I'll show you if you show me." But that doesn't really count, because I didn't know what I was doing anyhow. Didn't even know what a hard-on was or where I was going to put it if I did. The first time I stopped playing around and seriously had a crush on a girl was Junior School. Sherine Knowles. Boy, I had a serious crush on that girl. But she treated me rough.

September 8

I found out her name today. Elsa. Her full name is Elsa Lynette Farrington. I like the way she talks. It's not in that foolish way girls talk when they think they look good and playing cute. Her voice is almost hoarse. It isn't squeaky. It isn't high. It's alto. It's smooth. Like her motion. Like the motion of her hands when she talks. Like her smile. Soft like talking into a pillow. It's ancient and beautiful, like her eyes. She was talking to her friends from high school when I saw her by the cafeteria. Not many of my classmates from the New School are here at Santa Maria College. No dinero. But a lot of hers got in. She from a private school. St. Luke's. It's a Methodist School and use to be all white before Majority Rule. It has a pool and everything. I been there a couple times to play against their soccer team. Seems to me the students at that school are stuck up and don't like Backadabush folk, but maybe I ain't being fair. After all Elsa is from Backadabush like me. Her father and mother spent a lot of money to give her the chance to get ahead. I don't think I ever would have met any St. Luke's or St. Peter people if I didn't come to the College.

I don't think they are better than me. But I think things are tougher in a government school. There's more fighting and the school is run down. The bathrooms don't work and you don't have good desks to write on. My desk in Home Room was always rickety and too low for my knees to get under without the rust staining my pants. Most of these rich private-school children spoilt and think we beneath them because we don't live by the beach and the hotels or in Sherwood Estates. But she from Backadabush too, and she have her head screw on right, like they say.

I liked the Government New School. That's the school my mother couldn't go to because she was a girl and my grandfather had funny ways. All our leaders went to the New School. It was a bigger deal back then, when The Egyptians had power, than it is now. It was like a private school almost. A place to send the brightest niggers. Not anymore. It's just like the other government schools now. But I still liked it. I could have gone to St. Matthew's on a scholarship because I did good on the qualifying exam in Junior

School, but I didn't want to. St. Matthew's is full of white children, most of them American and English or Conchy Joe. And all my friends was going to the New School anyhow. I'm not sorry I went there. Funny that they call it the New School. It's pretty old and broken down now.

September 15

Elsa live in Oakdale. That's Backadabush but ain't many people live all the way out there. It's mostly just farms what people start on land they get from the Government. But Pompey Village is a good neighbourhood too. And it clean, except for a broken down car or two, and the houses are made of brick. It's better than the house Mamma say we used to live in on Daley Road. A clapboard on bricks. But that wooden house still standing, so it must be good for something to survive hurricane every year.

I wonder if Elsa even know how to find Pompey Village? I bet she never catch a Route 13 Bus in her life. She probably just take the Route 18 all the way out to Oakdale and call it a day. This island small but people live so separate. So many places I never even see in Grand Santa Maria! Like where the whites live. I know they live good. On the beach and everything. In Grand Santa Maria they own everything. But in the other islands black people own land, good land. Like on Runaway. My grandfather owned acres of land that passed on to his children. Mamma say it overlooking the sea too. I need to go to Runaway some day and see that land that we get after slavery, see Pleasant Place.

September 26

Just come off the phone with Elsa. Her voice sounds nice on the phone. We talked a whole lot a stupidness. I know exactly where her house is now and how to get there from the bus stop. I ain't never been all the way out Oakdale in my life.

October 25

This fella, Bain, in my Poli Sci class. He really serious. Stuff he talks about I never even think about. Him and Dr. Runne get along real good. They talk politics while the rest of us listen. Seem every class is just a conversation between Runne and Bain. The rest of us just eavesdropping. And everything they say is against the Government. Hell, before I come to this place I never even think about who was corrupt and who wasn't. Never even matter to me. Mamma is a PNF and that's that. I just take her word for it. All a Firsborn those vote the way she tell them. I can't vote yet so it don't really matter to me yet. Now, when I do vote I ain't so sure I could vote PNF after the way these two fellas is be talking in my class. The big thing with them is how the Commission of Inquiry prove the Prime Minister and everybody was crooked. Today Bain ask me who I for, PNF or FLP. I say I don't know. He look at me as if I was simple. Tell me I have to know who I for. Say I have to side with somebody. And if I side with the PNF I on the side a corruption. You see some shit? He running next semester for President of the Student Government. Want me be Secretary on his ticket. Next thing he'll have us marchin' in the street like them chirren from North West High. Protestin' poor conditions in the schools.

February 9

I know I ain't write in a long time. My English lecturer, Miss Williams, recommend we keep a journal for our first year, but she didn't say it was going be this hard. I just write to say that me and Elsa going steady now. She tell me she love me first, so I wasn't in danger of making a fool of myself. It feels good, man. It feels good. We can do anything together. Just talk fool all night, it don't matter. But she don't take no shit either, if you know what I mean. Thing is, I don't know if I'm as wonderful as she seems to think I am. This might be the thing I been waiting on since I start to take my life serious. I know I sound stupid, but is true. I could marry her. She good for me, man.

March 12

Well, like a ass, I do it. I let Bain talk me into running for Secretary and his whole slate win! And I'm not even sure I like him. But with things heating up the way they are and all these students demonstrating in the high schools against the Government, I wouldn't want his job. I don't know what I really think about these politicians and Education and stuff like that. I still figurin' it out. Elsa more on top of this shit than me and she ain't even interested in Student Government or politics. Far as she concerned the politicians only out for themselves and ain't nothing they say is worth believing.

Anyway, Bain seem to have all the answers so we'll have to see what he does. The trainers and the monkeys.

July 15

Going to the beach with Elsa and her baby sister, Tamika. Elsa in a swim suit! Yeah, I know, I'm thinking with my you know what. Anyway, I tried this journal thing for a year. And maybe it helped in the long run to put these thoughts on paper. Maybe it will make me a journalist some day. The SGA newspaper I started for Bain is working out O.K. and that's a start. But looking over these pages in this journal I don't see too many grammatical sentences! "Is one language to write in and one to talk in." That's what Mamma say. Or one to be proper in and one to be yourself in, I guess. But if I ever try writing like this in a exam I'll fail for sure.

October 26

Don't know why I see fit to write in this fool notebook again anyhow, but here it goes. Guess there's nowhere else to turn. Can't talk to Mamma because she won't understand. She's just like most of these old folks. Don't understand when we complain about the Government. Don't understand when we say that the PNF ain't interested in educating the people. They want to keep the young people stifled so they can preserve their power. Can't talk to her. First time in my life I can't trust my own mother! I know she love me, but she just don't see the situation like I see it. I don't even know what'll happen now. The piss miss the bowl, big time. Stupid Minister of Immigration, Employment, and National Security ordered twenty foreign lecturers to leave the country in 48hrs! Say the College must hire Santa Marians before foreigners. Why the hell they didn't think of that when they decided to pay these lecturers so little money? No Santa Marian with qualifications will teach at the College when they can make twice as much elsewhere, and don't have to be hassled with the Minister of Education breathing down their necks, telling them what they can and cannot do, threatening to retire them "in the interest of the public" if they criticise the Government.

They talk about nationalizing the workforce with one breath and hire foreigners left right and centre in the next. Look how many foreigners, how many white foreigners are working in these Ministries. The so-called "experts." Everytime they want something done they go hire some white man and pay him more than that selfsame foreigner could ever make in his lifetime in his own country. Why not train your own people? But they always complaining about foreigners. They complain about the Egyptians having all the money and businesses but they don't do anything to give Backadabush people a chance to start nothing. They talk about foreigners but consult them on everything. The truth is they don't believe in their own people. And to tell the lecturers to leave in the middle of the God damn semester! What the hell is the point of that? And some of these lecturers have been here for twenty-five years or more. Longer than I been alive!

Bain call a meeting with the Student Government Executive Board. Dr. Runne, our Faculty Advisor, was there too. We plan to march on Waterfront Road and block traffic in front of the House of Assembly until something is done. Everyone is saying the Minister has to go. I just hope I don't nanny in my pants when the Riot Squad grab hold of me.

16

He found it hard to be as good in the light as he was in the dark. It was one thing to promise to be faithful while visions of Hell tormented you, but it was another thing to be good in broad daylight. Tree knelt in the corner of the living room almost every night and tried to concentrate on God and stave off the advances of the Evil One.

But as the months passed it grew harder and harder. Finally, he realized what the trouble was. He was not saved. It was just as the white American preacher on television had said. It was fine to beg God's forgiveness each night, but to be able to defeat Satan you had to be saved, dressed in the "whole armour of God."

Actually, it was the first time he'd heard the term, "saved." Fr. Dandridge, the priest in the Sinking Church, who went to seminary in England and spoke with an English accent, certainly never used it. And no one in the Church's congregation, not even his mother, ever mentioned it either. The closest thing to it in their vocabulary was "Salvation." And that had a completed quality to it. "Two thousand years ago, Christ died for our salvation. But to get *saved* seemed to be a thing that had to be in the present. An event that each individual could experience at any given moment.

By his twelfth birthday Tree was still not saved. He felt incapable of becoming so. He was not only uncertain as to how one went about it, but something strange was happening to him. He was changing. No longer was he the child of those primary school days. In the many months that had passed since the dream of his two grandfathers, Tree had entered an entirely different world. The teacher of his Health Science class at Junior School called it "Puberty." His voice was breaking, he was growing hair all over his body, and he was noticing girls in a different way. He was having dreams too. Dreams he never had before. Disturbed by it all, he wondered if he was possessed by an evil spirit. That's how a girl in his class, who went to a Baptist church, described people who kept on committing a particular sin.

One day Tree and Small Pint stole some books with naked white women in it from under Yellow Man's bed and they sat in the Big Bushes looking at the pictures and laughing. Seeing the women naked did something to him. He laughed a lot but his heart was beating fast. He went to bed that night and didn't think about Death or God or the Devil. He didn't think of praying in the corner of the living room or sleeping with the light on. He crawled under his sheet, closed his eyes, and thought about the white women in the book.

Noticing girls more, sneaking peeks at dirty books, asking God's forgiveness in the corner of the living room whenever the fear hit him, running around with Small Pint and the other boys of the Village, sinning all over again: these fluctuations persisted for almost two years. And always, guilt plagued him to the point of distraction. He felt trapped. He could never reach a state of perfection, which is what being a "Christian" meant to him. He watched the people in Junior School who said they were Christians. They brought their Bibles to school, they quoted scripture as if it were ordinary speech, they sat quietly, they dressed modestly, and they read from the Good Book during every recess. They never cursed or told dirty jokes. They were the most boring people to be around, for sure, but there was a certain holiness about them that impressed him. As much as he liked to talk and joke in school? He could never be that way, act that holy. Look that solemn and serene. And to top it off, he would only have been made to feel stupid by the boys at school if he started carrying around a Bible and going to Student Christian Movement meetings at lunch time.

He tried reconciling himself to being dirty minded and evil. His only moment of purity came at the very instant he successfully completed a prayer. Every second that proceeded his "Ah-men" was tainted by his flesh, his sin, his evil imagination. The moment he ended his prayers and put his head on the pillow, he fell into a pit out of which there could be no escape. He couldn't help himself. He couldn't control his impulses, as much as he tried.

Just before his fourteenth birthday, a young woman named Louise Gibbs came to Pompey Village. She came to visit her cousin and her grandaunt: Small Pint and his grandmother of the brandishing broom. She came from Little Santa Maria to Grand Santa Maria for two weeks, bringing with her boxes of fruit and vegetables from her people at home and a body the likes of which Tree had never seen before, not even in Yellow's dirty books.

Louise became Tree's principal obsession. She was never really a person with a story he wished to hear. He had absolutely no wish to know what she was about or what she may have wanted to do with her life. It never occured to him to find out, for instance, what her favourite things were. He had dabbled in sweet talk with the girls from school but this was more serious, more urgent a matter. He wanted to have sex. She was a thing to be possessed by him, felt by him, entered somehow, someway. He communicated this with every look, every pathetic greeting. His very posture betrayed him. "I just want piece," he told Small Pint. "Just wan' get some. Once!" He heard the boys in school talk in this fashion, had heard Frankie and Kevin and Small Pint talk that way. Now it was his turn. He was man.

For those two weeks Louise became so many outrageously tempting body parts, so many points on a map that he had to cover, had to reach, to know as thoroughly as time and energy would allow. His greatest hope became that this obviously knowledgeable young woman would release him from the embarrassment of his virginity, free him from the pressure of knowing nothing at all, enable him to have something truthful to say under the juju tree at school when the boys talked about "juicin'," "feelin' up gals," and "grindin'."

Louise was the topic of conversation among Village males from ages twelve to forty-five. She walked like a woman who could tell just what men had on their minds. She was not a person to them but a cause. First prize in a contest. Small Pint introduced Tree to her on the fourth day of her stay and winked at him. And later, Small Pint added meat to the bait by telling Tree that his cousin was hot for him, that she was seventeen, knew a lot about sex, and wanted to be alone with him so they could talk.

"An' what you say 'bout me? Hey man?"

"I tell her you's a damn ass and you don't know your doggy from your right hand, you spend so much time pullin' on it."

"Don't talk fool, man! Dis seerus business. What you tell da gal?"

"Don' worry man, I swell her head up dead good. Don't worry, I tell ya. Louise fresh-fresh. She like man since she was twelve. I use to play dollhouse wit' her mase'f. You know what dey say, cousin make dozen." He winks again.

"Stop talkin' fool, man. She like me or what?"

"She like you, man. Relax. You ga hit it, take it from me. We jus' hafta wait fa da right time."

Whenever Tree saw Louise after that, washing clothes in the tin tub at the back of the yard with her poom-poom shorts on, or walking to Mr. Tingum Shop for ice cream in a loose-fitting blouse and no bra underneath, Tree started trembling and felt himself getting erect. On such occasions she just smiled knowingly at him, amused and charmed perhaps. Flirting, plotting, he told himself.

Whenever he lost control of his organ in public he half expected God to strike him down with lightning, rip all his clothes off with a gust of wind, and reveal his sin to the world. He feared he would be exposed and laughed at like Julian Thompson had been at school. Julian was called to the front of Math class to work a problem on the board. But, like most of the boys in class, he had been looking at young Miss Hanna's backside and not at his *New General Math-*

ematics. So when he was called to the front the entire class erupted at the sight of the bulge in his gray trousers. But nothing of this sort happened to Tree. He was permitted to keep his guilt concealed beneath his t-shirt and he took that as a good omen.

All in all, Tree and Louise barely exchanged more than two words on any given day. But Tree's gawking sent the message. He could only hope that Small Pint would come through as he had promised. And he did, on the night before Louise was to take the mail boat back to her people in St. Mark's.

It was a Sunday night and Small Pint and his grandmother were set to make their second trip to the Big Jumper Church for the day. Tree's mother was about to perform the same twice-a-day ritual, only she was going to evensong at the Sinking Church. Unlike Small Pint, Tree was not required to attend night service if he had been good and gotten to mass on time at 9 a.m. Frankie was on the phone, Firsborn was locked up in his room as usual, and Kevin, because Mamma went in the car to church rather than walking, was stuck watching Channel One. Louise was supposed to go to the Big Jumper Church as well, but she had come down with a mysterious bellyache that forced her to bed early. So that she would not travel the next day without God's blessing, Small Pint's grandmother assured Louise that she would pray for her. The coast was clear. Small Pint called Tree to let him know the big event was finally going to happen and that Louise would blink the living room light when she was ready. The in-a-movie feeling.

But the whole thing happened very quickly, and before he knew it, Tree was back on his top bunk in the Yellow and White House, trying to remember what their naked bodies had looked like on Small Pint's twin bed with the loud springs. As the antique radio in the living room broadcasted a service from the Holy Saviour Baptist Church, Louise had sex with him twice and then rushed him home so they would not get caught. It was not at all the way Tree'd planned it.

After all the sweaty anticipation, wishing for so long to have her, to feel her body beneath his fingers, to find himself between her smooth thighs, he was surprised at his tentativeness, embarrassed by his own ignorance. He had not known what to do. As a lover he was totally lost. She directed him to her breasts, to her lips, and between her legs as she would have guided a child who was trying to tie his own shoelaces for the first time.

The sight of her naked body had made him excited, but he could not possess her as he thought a man ought to have done. Tree's idea of sex—acquired by talking to other boys—was that the man *does* the woman. He performs and the woman moans and cries in a mixture of physical pleasure and disbelief at his prowess. He should have hit "it," manipulated, done things to "it," provoked this or that reaction by touching and caressing "it," but none of that had been possible. Afterwards, he felt like he didn't know women at all. Her body had overwhelmed and, finally, intimidated him. He was adrift, ineffectual. The whole time, rendered stupid by the newness of the whole thing, he felt alienated from himself, somehow outside of his own body and what was being done to it. Exposed and naked for the first time before someone who was not a member of his immediate family, he felt cold and conspicuous. The smell, the very logistics of the sex act were unsettling to him. He found it impossible to close his eyes.

Once it was finished, the fact that "love" had not been a part of his first time angered him. Strange that he should think of love at this point when before he could have cared less, but for some reason he began contrasting his first experience with the romantic ideal he sometimes entertained. His intentions were from the start bankrupt of any pretension to romance, but now he was angry that such had been the case. Not only was he not in love with her, in the idealized way he conceived of it, but he was sure that she felt nothing for him either. Hoping to have plundered, he now felt exploited and lied to. Tricked. Balled up in the bunk with the act of sin only moments behind him, he decided to hate her. He cursed her under his breath. He was glad that she would be gone early in the morning so he wouldn't have to face her again. He told himself that she was a slut, a whore. He tried to thrust out of himself that dirtiness he had been harbouring since the day he first saw her. Tried to blame Louise for what he knew deep down had nothing at all to do with her but with him, with his own filth, his own sin. He was in that pit again. No escaping.

Lying there on the twin bed with the loud springs, she had been the one cradling him while looking up at the ceiling and not the other way around. It all went wrong, he told himself. It was all a mistake. It was not the way he had planned it.

Then, before he had even recovered from the shock, she decided it was getting late and sent him home. She kissed his lips vaguely as she covered herself with the blue bathrobe and held the door. He stepped out of the house no more a man than when he had entered it, thief-like, two hours before.

"They soon come," she said, smiling in a way that gave away nothing. "I ga see you. Take care." Then she closed the door and he heard the lock being turned. He stood there in front of the door for at least five minutes after she cut off the porch light and went back to bed.

• • • • •

Senator Adams FL(i)P's to the PNF

—by M. E. Bodie, Daily Report *Staff Writer*

Senator Kevin J. Adams, President of the Electrical, Sanitary, and Water and Sewerage Workers Union, defected from the Opposition Free Liberal Party and joined the governing Progressive National Front. At a press conference yesterday, Senator Adams announced that he was leaving the ranks of the Opposition because he no longer felt they were "committed to the cause of the workers." Adams is one of the two Party members who hold office in the Senate and are leaders of a union at the same time. The other is the Honourable Mrs. Juanita Charles, President of the Straw Weavers Union and a representative of the PNF in the Senate.

In response to the defection of Senator Adams, the Honourable Leader of the Opposition informed *The Daily Report* that as an FLP appointee, Adams is holding a seat intended for the Opposition and he cannot leave the Party to join the PNF and still remain in office. The Leader of the Opposition said that his party is "as committed to the neglected workers of Santa Maria as ever." Senator Adams, the Hon. Opposition Leader remarked, "has left the

FLP for no other reason than this one: He will not be on next year's Election slate. And because we are not putting him up as a candidate in any of the constituencies, he has decided to go over to the other side. Good riddance. We won't miss him!"

The Rt. Hon. Prime Minister of the Santa Marias also issued a response on receiving word of Senator Adams's conversion. According to the Prime Minister, the PNF is delighted to welcome him into the ranks of the only party which is truly concerned about the people. "Senator Adams," the statement continues, "has always been a champion of the workers and there is nothing in the law which states that he must relinquish his Senate seat." The Prime Minister stated further that, "The disaffection and disillusionment Senator Adams has experienced is not surprising and should be a sign of warning to all those who mistakenly consider the FLP a viable solution to our present economic woes. You better come back before is too late!"

Ten years ago Senator Adams originally withdrew his support from the PNF to join the ranks of the Opposition. His words at that time bear a striking resemblance to the ones he spoke only yesterday. On the steps of the Union Headquarters, Adams declared that the PNF had "betrayed its mandate from the people"; that the party which achieved Majority Rule on the backs of the unions was "no longer committed to the cause of the workers," and that he would rather "live like a dog" than work with the Prime Minister any longer.

When asked at the press conference if he was not returning, like the dog, to its own vomit, Senator Adams grew somewhat indignant. "Return to my vomit? Damn right! That suppose to be a shot at me? Look here, I not only ga return to it, I ga swim in it!"

Senator Adams is expected to speak tonight at a PNF rally in Pineville; his theme is "Regurgitation."

17

November 5

I ain't never see nothing to beat what take place today in Victoria Square. Students been boycotting classes for three days now. The College virtually shut down and the administration seem to have left it up to us students to fight this battle against the Minister. Their hands tied. If they open their mouth they lose their jobs, "retired" like the last leader of the Teacher's Union.

All the students congregated in the auditorium this morning at about half past nine. The Student Government and the administration and a few faculty (the ones that wasn't afraid of losing their jobs) stood up front. There were at least three hundred students. Someone, I think it was a student, said a prayer. Then the Principal spoke. He was solemn. He explained the situation, but he didn't say anything we hadn't already heard by word of mouth or on t.v. and radio. Then he said that if we the students wanted to continue the boycott or march to Victoria Square there was nothing he could do to stop us. "The law prohibits me from encouraging students to protest, so I won't. But I won't discourage you either. I simply ask you all to remain peaceful and remember that your behaviour is a reflection on the College."

We all felt sorry for him. It make us forget that we were the ones whose future was in real jeopardy. Bain notified the police of our intention to march but they didn't grant us clearance to make a procession. And I ain't tell Mamma what was going to happen to-day neither. If I was arrested I was going to be in serious trouble. Everybody know Mamma is a big PNF. What it look like, her son marching in the street against the Government? It might cost her her job. It might cost me a chance at a Government Scholarship. Bain instruct each Executive Board member to write a speech. I write one. But right there in the auditorium I chicken out. I decide to be one of the crowd. I didn't want to stand out. I wasn't Presi-dent or Vice-President, so why should I put my head on the chop-ping block? I give my speech to the Treasurer, Sharon, to read. She was glad to do it cause she ain't write none herself. I pretend like I gone looking for something. I leave the auditorium soon as the SGA speeches start. When I return I don't go back to the front. Bain was walking toward the podium. I find Elsa and her friends and stay with them instead.

Bain was the last to speak. He didn't seem nervous at all. In fact, he seem to be enjoying himself. He was smiling the whole time. It was as if he was cherishing the whole thing. Like he was just waiting for something like this to happen, and now that it hap-pen he was going to live it to the full. He said we shouldn't be afraid. He said the police would be in the streets waiting for us but we needn't worry, Central Station didn't have enough space for four hundred people. Everyone laugh. He was oh-so calm the whole time. Not even a bead of sweat was on that forehead while he stand there in that hot auditorium, with them dark shades on, and a coat and tie too. He remind me of pictures I see of the PM in his early days.

He say we was going to march on Waterfront Road and de-mand justice. Say we was going on Waterfront Road and demand that this victimization end. "A nation that seeks to cripple its youth cripples itself." He say it so good make me want to forget was Dr. Runne who say the same words over and over again in Poli Sci.

"We will not be stunted by this oppressive and backward gang of brainwashing, corrupt politraitors!" Man, he was good. People start shouting left and right. Next thing you know he take up a placard and with the Executive Board walking behind him, lead everybody out the auditorium and along the route we decide on last week. I didn't make no effort to join them at the front. The truth is I's a coward. All I could think about was myself and my future. I just melt in the crowd, shouting and singing. I hold Elsa's hand and she smile at me like she think it was a joke I was playing, not going up front with the rest.

So we walk out briss and bold, and I there thinking, "I wonder whether or not any of these students scared like me or they ain't checking." Cause they was all laughing and excited. Like it was just a game we was playing. I wonder while I walking in the street if they was really behind Bain for true and was prepared to go to jail or whether this was just a excuse to make a poppy show and get on t.v.

Meantime the police ain't even stand in our way. They just act like escort. That give us confidence, so we march faster and make more noise. When we reach Waterfront Road we meet traffic already block off, like they was expecting us, like the whole a downtown get tipped off to what we was gone do. The tourists stand outside the souvenir shops smiling and taking pictures. It was like a party instead of a demonstration. We just sit in the road and start up different chants, calling for so and so to resign, saying this and that about the education of the youth. I still ain't sure what we was expecting to happen next. We really ain't had no plan as such, least not what I know of. We just sit there in Victoria Square singing. Bain and them take up position in front of Queen Victoria statue, outside the House of Assembly, and start talking through one megaphone. Dr. Runne was standing beside Bain looking well pleased. Channel One News show up. They interview Bain and Timmy Marshall, the V. P. Even Dr. Runne say his piece for the camera.

Then the bigger boss come to show what time it is. I don't think nobody really expected it. The Prime Minister himself come down from the Raleigh Building into the crowd. I sure he could hear all the shouting and fuss from his office, cause it right there on the other end of the Square. I was wondering when I first see him there in the road if we remind him of himself when he lead all them demonstrations on Waterfront Road twenty something years ago.

When everybody see it was the Prime Minister they cheer like crazy. It was as if they just hear the news that everything was going back to normal. But they ain't hear no such thing, not yet. It was just that him coming down into the street make them celebrate. They surround him and shake his hand and grin from ear to ear. They even start to chant his name. He smile back at everyone. It was like the greeting a person is get when they return home after being away a long long time. Bain and the Executive Board stand their ground by Victoria statue. Bain was holding the megaphone but he ain't say nothing. They just watch the PM approach. They were the new kids on the block, he was the old master. Was like we all, without knowing it, wanted the PM to come down and talk with us. And now that he come we felt rescued, relieved that everything was gone be alright and nobody was gone get in any trouble.

When he reach the statue he say something to Bain, Dr. Runne, and the Executive Board. They all laugh—all except Dr. Runne. He shake all their hand and then Bain give him the megaphone. Everybody in the crowd was smiling, thinking we straight. He hold the megaphone to his lips and started to speak. His voice have a real deep, resounding quality. He seem so poise today, with all that crowd and the tourists and the police and the sun beating down. Like he had a speech all memorize for just such a occasion. As if the whole thing wasn't no surprise to him. Like he was on our side the whole time anyhow and the fools who cause his children to be inconvenience was gone be dealt with. He talk to us like he was proud of us for marching, proud of us for coming to him and asking for his help. He assure us that everything was under control, that there had been a mistake, a "misinterpretation by the Minister of the Government's policy on nationalizing the work force," but that the whole business was gone be cleared up immediately. The lecturers would be allowed to stay. The Government understood that the youth was the future. Nothing would jeopardize that. The Government build the College, "why would it destroy what it had taken such pains, in the very first days of Independence, to build?" Everything was gone be fine.

Then he invite Bain and the Executive Board up to his office in the Raleigh Building. He say he wanted to hear what they had to say and he would carry out whatever needed to be done. He tell us we came and made our statement and he was proud of us. We should disperse now and go home. The lecturers would return. He would speak to the student leaders.

Cheers ring out all over the Square. The PM shake Bain hand enthusiastically. He lead the SGA leaders out the Square and into the Raleigh Building. For a second Bain and Dr. Runne exchange some words. Runne look dead mad but Bain ain't seem to study him. He turn away while Runne was still talking and follow the PM. Runne didn't go with them. He stand by Victoria statue shaking his head. The crowd dispersed. Me and Elsa take the bus to her house.

January 25th

Is all over now. The teachers back. Bain get invited to speak at the annual National Convention of the PNF. He speak live on radio and television from the Neptune Ballroom of the Hotel Impérial. He attack corrupt politicians and governmental neglect. He make the front page. But everybody saying he will probably end up a politician himself, maybe a PNF man. The PM like him. At the end of the semester two of the original lecturers was told to leave the country again. This time there wasn't no uproar. No one make a fuss because they didn't stand to be set back in their classes. Maybe if the Minister waited until the semester end in the first place there never would be no boycott, no marches. People only holler when is their own corn what mash. Other than that, too damn bad. The explanation for the Government not renewing their work permits was that they was "threats to national security." Last November the SGA raise hell about the sudden threats of deportation but they never say nothing about the policy of annual work permits that allow the Minister to terrorise foreign lecturers in the first place. Nothing about this Government's hypocritical nationalizing policy. Anyway, I don't care. Nothing really change. The public schools still run down. The College still understaffed and lacking resources. What we was trying to accomplish anyway?

Dr. Runne leaving Santa Maria College after this semester. I gone to see him day before yesterday. He was sitting there in his little office looking distant. He say he had enough of this country and its pettiness. Say there ain't no "intellectual climate" in Santa Maria. Say the politics of the country is gutter politics. "Santa Maria is a vulgar society," he say. And he ain't want no part of it. He going off to the States to teach. Say he won't come back unless things change in Santa Maria, until people get the courage to really change things. Say he feel stifled, like he ain't accomplishing nothing.

April 1

I going to be glad to finish with Santa Maria College. This place make me miserable. I feel like the only thing what make this worthwhile is Elsa. Other than her I don't believe in nothing or nobody no more. All our talk ain't accomplishing diddly. And Bain simply gone through all that to be the next in line for the House of Assembly. What about the people?

Shit. Who I kidding? Ain't no people. Is everybody for himself. No one care about nothing but themselves. And I ain't no better. I had a chance to stand up, to say my piece, and I couldn't do it. I ain't no damn better than all the rest.

18
Elsa

Gat dem t'ree grown man up dere in dat house like they still chirren. Kinda sad if you aks me. T'ree grown man walkin' roun' in dat house talkin' 'bout "Mamma dis" and "Mamma dat." An' don' look like any a dem ever plan to get up an' do a bit a work around dere neider. Gat her runnin' aroun' cleanin' up after dem like they still toddlers. Hmph. I'll be damn if I care for any Santa Maria man hand and foot. See my ma doin' the same foolishness. These some ole fashion woman. Slave to man wheder dey is husband or son. No joke. My daddy refuse to dish up his own food or wash a cup! But I wan' see Tree Bodie try dat foolishness wit' me. He'll wait 'til the sun fall out da sky.

Nah, as spoil as my daddy been all his life, he at least is a fait'ful husband and he know his responsibilities to his children. Mummy don' even need to aks for nuttin twice, and she don' never need to wonder where he is or what he doin'. So I feel for Maureen Bodie. She had a hard road to travel. To be hones', I don' know how she manage it all dese years, raisin' four sons her one, and takin' all a dem to University wit' her too. Lord!

But she gat to stop doin' ev'ry little thing for dem sons a hers. Dey ain' ga never be men if she fight all dey battles forrum. Every time dey get in a little jam she come runnin' to save 'em. Sometimes you gat to let them sink or swim on dey own. My parents gat to learn to stop studyin' my brudda Julian too. He t'ink his head bad. When he get a feelin' for da rock he start shoutin' an' cussin' at my daddy. An' 'cause my daddy gatta mind his heart he is let Julian talk to him any kind a way. Mummy a little bit better. She'll slap him in his mout' if he cuss her to her face, but she still let him ack like a fool 'round da house. Me, Stephan, and Tamika always tellin' her to t'row him out but she say she cyaa do dat. Don' mind we gat to hide everyt'ing from him and lock up all our possessions for fear he ga t'eif and sell it. Humph! And always bailin' his little narrow behind outta jail! I tell her she should leave him in jail just once. I hope nex' time she listen, 'cause he ain' ga never change so long as he know dey ga come runnin' ta da rescue.

As much foolishness as people is have to go t'rough for dey kids, I don' know what get in me to still want a baby. But I want me a baby girl one a dese days. I cyaa deal wit' no sons. No boy chirren for me. Is like dey come in da worl' angry, or mix up, or sumpm. And I definitely don' want no chirren 'fore I get married. I done tell Tree dat if I get pregnant 'fore I have a ring on my finga I gettin' a abortion. And I ain' even aksin' him no questions. I'll jus' hand him the bill after is said and done. Dese man like to talk you outta stuff, but dey ain' da ones carryin' da chile aroun' for nine mont's. O don' get me wrong, I believe is murder. But I ga have ta do it anyway. Ain' nuttin standin' between me and what I have to achieve. And ain' no way I havin' no shotgun weddin' or bringin' no baby in dis worl' outta wedlock. I'll jus' have to live with the guilt.

Yeah, I want me a little girl. But I ain' so sure I want her to have these mood swings I see Tree Bodie havin'. Happy an' jivin' one minute and solemn and morbid da nex'. Peasy hair and black skin don' trouble me. But dat boy gat some scary moods. Sometimes is like he don' care what he doin'. Like life don' mean nuttin to him. Like he could jus' convince himself outta the clear blue sky dat life ain' gat no meanin', dere ain' no God, an' derefore he could do whatever the hell he feel inspired to do. And when he don' get his way? Shoot.

You should see Maureen Bodie, girl. Is like Tree cyaa do no wrong! Ev'ry time he buil' up his face she up and down try'na please him. A mamma's boy, any which way you look at it. Spoilt stink. I swear, dat woman is indulge him WAY too much. Couldn' believe it when she tell me she let Tree use a milk bottle 'til he was five. Five! Say he use to clean da damn t'ing hese'f. Jesus Christ! (Forgive me, Lord). But five? Dat ain' nat'ral, any which way you look at it.

I een try'na be disgustin'. I jus' try'na figure dis stuff out. I try'na understand dis woman. I know she strong. Strong like iron. I know she been t'rough some mighty painful t'ings. But dat ain' give her no right to look at me like she is look at me. I is notice her watchin' me. Sizin' me up. Lookin' at me like I come to her house to t'ief her prize possession. Lookin' at me and all she gat in her eyes is disapproval and suspicion. Da other day I gone Pompey Village in my new miniskirt and you should see her look me up and down. Like I was sumtin da cat drag in. I ain' no tramp. I wear what I please. Was hot as hell outside! And I was comf'table in it. Shoot, I LIKE what I had on! Why should I dress like dese Jumper Church girls in dese ankle-long frock. Dey force dem to dress stiff an' proper, clean and holy, while da men in the church out jumpin' in ev'ry bed what vacant. 'Cause I wear a miniskirt mean I slack? I should tell her the name a the one man a sleep wit' in my life. I truly wonder if he get me pregnant if she'll claim it wuzzan him who do it. And what if I WAS slack. All dat mean is I do what men do. Shoot.

It don' matter no how 'cause I know what the deal is. She want to see what her son gettin' into. I cyaa blame her. Ev'ry mudda mussie the same way sometimes. Is jus' I t'ink she is carry it too far. Dem eyes a hers. Try look right into you. Right t'rough you. But I know I is bug her, 'cause as hard as she look she cyaa see da real me.

An' da t'ings she is say sometimes! Me and Tree havin' a argument da oder day in da car. We gone to pick Maureen up from work. Now, usually, when da t'ree a us inda car I is keep quiet-quiet, 'cause she like to pull you into trouble wit' her funny questions. But dis time Tree was runnin' me hot. All dis time I t'ought me and him see eye to eye when it come to dis PNF government: dey gat to go. But dis day he change his tune. Talkin' some foolishness 'bout how the PM ain' so bad and is da men unda him what is the crooked set. And before you know it, Maureen jump in wit' her two cents. So I had to set dem straight. I had to let dem know jus' how much people the Prime Minister RUIN on dis small island. Had to let dem know how jus' because my Uncle who is teach Phys. Ed. was RUMOUR to be a FLP, jus' 'cause someone spread lies 'bout him promoting the FLP on da job, (my Uncle Carlton who nobody know which side he vote for from one Election to the nex' 'cause he so close-mout'), 'cause a dat, dey transfer him to the worst school in Grand Santa Maria and refuse to give him his increment for mussie six-seven years! And what about Sir John Forbes, who ain' never get his pension YET 'cause he cross the PM ten-fifteen years ago. Sir John Forbes who was deep in the struggle before the PM even come out law school! Maureen Bodie might could tell her good stories 'bout how wonderful the PM been to her and her family but it ain' so for ev'rybody, chile, I show you dat.

But you know what dat woman tell her son? The nex' day she ga tell Tree he need to find a woman what ga agree wit' him, what ga obey him. I couldn' believe it when Tree tell me. A woman what ga OBEY him! You could see some tings? Now you know mankind do a job on women when MAUREEN BODIE gone tell her son, he need a woman what ga agree wit' him in every conversation! Maureen Bodie who had to fight toot' and nail wit' dat jackass she had for a husband. Maureen Bodie who never get to go to high school 'cause she didn' have a dick between her legs. Who in Santa Maria don' know Teacher Bodie who struggle and pull herself out a ditch and buil' a house for her chirren on her own? Teacher Bodie, who ain' never had ta whore herse'f or be nobody sweetheart? SHE tell her son he need a woman who ga obey him. Ev'ry so of'en da runaway slave is wake up feelin' for his chains.

She need to ease up wit' dat foolishness, man. And furdermore, I don' like da fack dat she t'ink I ain' good enough for her son—if *da's what she t'inkin'. I love Tree Bodie. I know he special. But hell, I special too. I gat sumtin to offer dis country a ours as well. He ain' doin' me no FAVOUR by goin' out wit' me. I gat as much brains an' ambition as him. And more discipline. I mean, look at me. Wha's wrong wit' me dat she gat to find fault wit' ev'ryting I do?*

Tree tell me she don' like how I come to her house an' refuse to eat her food. He say when you come to people house, you insult dem if you don' take what they offer. Well I sorry, but I jus' don' eat any and errybody food. I ain' try'na say is beneat' me or da woman try'na poison me or nuttin, but da's jus' how I is. I notice Tree. Whenever he in people house an' dey offer him sumtin he say "Yes, t'ankyouverymuch." Claim he bein' polite. An' no matter how foul it look or taste he grinnin' and eatin' it. Now, sayin' "No t'ankyou," why da's bein' rude? If I een hungry I een hungry; I don' mean no offense.

Tree tell me sumtin a while back I beginnin' ta t'ink is true. He tell me she want him to go out wit' one a dem girls what is go to dey church. Say das what she want for him. Someone she could keep a eye on. Someone she know like da back a her hand. Someone she could say dis and dat to and dey ga say, "Yes Ms. Bodie," "Das true Ms. Bodie, you een lie." She wan' pick one a dem obeyin' wives for her son. And I don' jus' mean obeyin' Tree, I mean obeyin' her as well. Nex' ting you look she tellin' you how to raise ya children, not to mention how to please your man an' wash his draws jus' right. Girl, I ain' mean to sound bitter but I jus' don' know what to do. All the boyfriends I had I ain' never once been made to feel dis way by any a their parents. And Tree come to my house and fit right in like he is mummy and daddy son. It ain' fair.

Maureen Bodie is a good woman. But is possible to love a chile too much. And sometimes when you do that they reach the point where they cyaa stand to be around you. The burden get to be too much: livin' for you and not for themselves. He say she gat a command over him he cyaa explain. Hmph. A tie like dat ain' all good. Is a kinda love and obligation where you could tell he cyaa never make a move in his life wit'out t'inkin' if his ma will approve or disapprove. I only repeatin' what he say, but I believe I see it wit' all a dem in dat house. She gat to cut dat birt' string. Tree is a funny creature. Never know what he gone do sometimes. Gat some strange things in his head. Gat a troubled spirit. Da one you spoil the most might spoil ya plans.

He don' know it but I find out where he is be goin' at night when he don' come to see me. He t'ink I don' know but I find out he is be workin' for Thaddeus McKinney. And I didn' go spyin' on him to find out eider. People come to ME wit' da news. Das how Santa Maria people go, always spreadin' sip-sip. One of my cousins tell me dey see him at the rally last Tuesday in Churchill. And my aunty what work to the Ministry of Education, she tell me he is be up dere in the Minister office two-t'ree times a week writin' speeches forrim. Santa Maria small. Cyaa hide nuttin here. No such ting as a secret.

An' now dis. Dat fool man Mr. Braynen at the firm is a big PNP. He come in the office wit' a copy a da Clarion. And he readin' dis article in it out loud what slandering Maxwell Brown, the candidate who runnin' 'gainst McKinney in Hawkins Town. No by-line, but I know the style. Is Tree write it, I know. I know his style anywhere. And Mark Etienne know why he never mention none a dis to me. 'Cause I'd a let him know from da get go ain' nuttin' good ga come from it.

I mean, what if Maxwell Brown gay? So damn what? Dese Santa Maria people need ta check dey se'f. Dese politicians makin' illegitimate chirren lef' right and centre, an' nobody never say one word 'bout dem not bein' fit for office. Dese man sexually harassin' woman inda work place ev'ry hour on da hour, an' you cyaa say nuttin' ta dem. An' wors' a all, you gat dese t'irty-year-ole man gettin' dese t'irteen-year-ole girls pregnant and ain' nuttin bein' done about it. Is wrong ta be a boongie bandit but you could be a poompoom bandit all ya want in dis country. Tree know better dan ta encourage dat. He know dat ain' right, but two-to-one, 'cause he scared to say sumpm to upset dat ole fart, he goin' along wit' his mudslingin' foolishness. But ain' nuttin to be scared of in dis life but God. Thaddeuses come and go. Da people put him dere and dey ga move him too when they ready. All we gat in dis life is our integrity, an' if you gat ta sell dat ta get ahead you ain' gettin' ahead at all.

I understand sometimes you gat ta do tings you radder not do. But you gat ta draw da line. You gat to listen ta what ya insides tellin' you. Sure, I workin' for Forbes, Bassett and Hill. But I know what side I on. You think I plan ta work for this Conchy Joe firm when I get back from school? Girl, I know what they doin'. Gat us here doin' the small-fry work while they make the big money an' makin' all da decisions. I just waitin' to get my degree. Den I goin' inta business myself. Sumtin a our own. A Backadabush project. Sumtin in da community. I might even teach a little Maths on the side.

Dese politicians talk an' talk but dey ain' down at da people level where da real fight is. Tree talk and talk but he ain' gat no plan. He figure he could hang wit' dem and learn da rules a da game, but da game dey playin' ain' helpin' nobody. I workin' it out. I gone start me my own business. A Backadabush project. Our own ting. University is jus' da means to a en'. I'll be damned if I sell my soul to Forbes, Bassett and Hill an' spend da res' a my life countin' da money a some rich American swindler who want ta avoid payin' da IRS. Dere gat to be more ta life.

19

He sat at the water's edge, took off his shoes, and let his feet touch the water. He listened to the sleepy lapping of the waves that broke against the man-made shore. No one was swimming anywhere along the canal. Although this pleased him, it also made him afraid that something might go wrong. He looked about nervously, surveying the harsh white rubble and sparse, green-brown foliage. He took deep, slow breaths. Suddenly, he had the feeling that somewhere—perhaps somewhere behind him—someone was watching. Behind the trunk of a cedar tree. Or maybe crouched and grinning like a devil beneath one of the burnt pines that ended abruptly in a line where the rocky earth on which he sat began.

Sitting there at the edge of the water and thinking of the thing that had driven him out alone to the canals, he felt a little foolish. Anything could happen to him out here. A group of boys could come and beat him up. He might jump into the water, catch a cramp, and drown. No one would ever know where he was or what had happened to him. But no matter how foolish he thought he was behaving, he was resolved. Pretending to be a crusader in that manner that he had perfected while walking home alone from the Junior School to the Yellow and White House, he was now outside of himself and witnessing his actions as through a camera lens. He convinced himself that he could hear absolutely nothing. Even the undulating water that beckoned just beneath his toes offered up silence. It just rolled, green and blue, shimmering in the light of the sun. He was almost blinded by the reflection. Shards of light that promised redemption, that beckoned him, almost casually, to enter and risk his life.

He thought he should at least have heard a dove, a seagull, a black crow, something. Nothing. It confirmed his nagging suspicion that he was not alone.

But wasn't that the point? That he was not alone? That God was there with him? That He was watching the entire affair? That when Tree emerged from beneath the tree where he had spent most of the afternoon meditating, God saw that very movement, understood why he had found the solitude necessary, why he had found what he was about to do necessary?

Ever since he became afraid of dying, Tree had convinced himself that his heartbeat was irregular. It beat even more irregularly now.

He had to do it soon or he would have to try again another day. It was getting late and before long the sun would be setting. Maureen Bodie would want to know where he was and what he was doing out so long.

Jump! Jump! Do it now! Now man! Go on! Say the prayer and jump!

The ridiculousness of the thing hit him again. For a second the camera turned inward. Perhaps it was really unneccesary to jump into the water, unnecessary to give himself again to the Lord. Hadn't he done that already? Anglicans did things differently, that's all. Differently. *The Baptists do things their way, we do it ours. You're baptised as a child, then confirmed. And you live your entire life in communion with the Lord. But does baptism when you're a baby count? Suppose, after years of believing I was saved, I died and went to Hell just because I wasn't baptised when I was grown? I can't afford to take chances with my soul! So does that mean God will condemn all Anglicans and Catholics because they baptised when they still babies?*

An' if you have to be born again to go to Heaven, when the baby is be born again? At Christenin'? But how a baby could confess he sins and accep' Christ, when he cyaa even t'ink for hesef?

Like Friday reckoning with the nuances and contradictions of Crusoe's religion, he didn't know the answers to those questions. And he wasn't bold enough to confront other people about what he was thinking, least of all his mother. For if he raised questions, he might single himself out as an unbeliever. And he did believe. He simply knew, deep down in his heart, that he was not saved. That if the world ended right there and then, if Christ came again with Fire and Judgement, he would be cast down into the fiery pit of Hell, just like the white evangelist on television had said, just like Pastor Ferguson had said that Sunday in the Big Jumper Church, two weeks before his Confirmation. Sneaking to the Jumper Church with Small Pint had affected him drastically. It exposed him to a whole new way of worship. Not out of books, with recorded prayers marked by the calendar and scripted "Amens." But a Church of spontaneous fire, cleansing emotion. And that is what he needed, cleansing. He had to wash himself clean. He had to rid himself of all the filth. If he could wrench it from his guts he would have. If he could just rip the sin out of his eyes, find the strength to sever his unclean hands from the rest of his body, he would have willingly bled to death there at the water's edge. But sin, as insidious as cancer, had infiltrated his entire frame and contaminated him to the core. If only there was a way he could undo the horrible thing he had done on the Lord's Day, there on the twin bed with the loud springs.

Dear Lord forgive me for i have sinned against Your Holy Name in thought word and deed and in what i have left undone. Forgive me, O God! i accept You as my Lord and Saviour. i do. i swear i do. i confess my sins. InthenameoftheFathertheSonandtheHolySpirit-AH-MEN!

Da water ice cold.

* * *

Jesus Lord, You know i try to serve You, Lord Jesus. You know i try to serve You Lord.

but is hard Lord.
all this temptation and sin, Lord Jesus.
Lord, You know i thought i was call to be your servant, Lord.
You know i wanted to serve You.
You know i wanted to be Your priest, Lord Jesus,
ever since i gone to the Jumper Church
and answer the altar call.
you speak to me dat day, Lord Jesus.
and i feel your spirit for the first time, Dear Lord.
feel it move in my soul, O Lord.
and people speak in tongues
and catch the Sperrit, Lord.
and das why i gone to get baptise again, Lord.
so i could serve you.
and you know i sit in the sinking church
and i listen to Father Dandridge preachin'
and i see how content he was and i say i wan'
be just like him Lord, want be Your messenger Lord,
to speak to the people, to minister to the people,
to save souls los' like i was los' Dear Lord.
but O Jesus, sumtin terrible happen today, Lord.
sumtin, i don' even want believe is true.
so much sin and temptation. so much.
i don't t'ink i could be the kinda priest you need, Lord.
i don' t'ink i could live that straight a life, Lord.
i weak Fada, i still ain' gat the faith i need, my Saviour.
Lord, i know you see what happen in Church today, Lord.
was a big disgrace, Dear Jesus.
and i see it clear as day
cause i was serving up high in the Altar.
das why i say i havin' a change a heart Lord.
change a heart.
Lord, is sacrilege, Fada.
i is think bad things in Church too, Lord,
but dis diff'ren'.
dis wuzzan no t'inkin', Lord,
dis was doin' right dere in Your House so.

i come early to Church Lord,
so i could carry the Crucifix.
i come to polish it for the Seven o'Clock Mass.
wuzzan nobody 'pose to be dere in the Church, Lord.
only Fada Dandridge shoulda be in the back makin' ready.
low and behol', Dear Saviour,
what i see when i gone behind the Altar
to the changing room, Fada God.
i 'xpect to see Fada Dandridge going over the lesson
an' ting for the Service Lord, but dat ain' what i find.
O Christ Jesus!
Lord, the man there, wit' Mrs. Josey, from the choir.
gat her t'row over the counter Lord.
same counter where dey is count Your Offerin's, Lord.
he gat her bend over on the counter and her gown tail
toss up over her head, and he standin' dere behind her
wit' he pants an' ting down roun' he ankles!
Sweet Jesus, ah almos' dead!
most dead dere and den Lord God!
You know how i respec' Fada Dandridge, Lord.
You know how i wan' be a messenger like him, Lord Jesus.
but it wuzzan right, Lord.
wuzzan no messenger of the Lord
'pose to do dem sorta tings.
an' in Your House, Fada.
wit' a marri'd woman, an' him marri'd hissef.
i run outda Church, Lord.
they so caught up dey don' even see me yet.
i ain' cut out fa dis, Fada God.
please forgive me.
i jus' ain' cut out for dis.
when You look, i get catch sinnin' behin' Your Altar?
is a Sign, Lord. i know is a Sign.
i don' have what it take to be your messenger.
if Fada Dandridge could do dem tings, imagine me.
i gatta find a nex' way to serve You.

20

Dear Doc,

How you? I know I promise to write you sooner but things been hectic here in Santa Maria since you leave. I think about you up there in that University and I say, "Dr. Runne probably had the right idea." At least you don't have to deal with this stress. I hope you staying clear of all that racism, though. I hear they is be shooting black folks in the road for no reason. It don't seem they like people our colour up where you is. But even so us Caribbean folks keep coming for more.

Anyway, I hope to be in the States in late August, if I survive this Election. I'd like to see snow and Autumn leaves.

But that's not what I wanted to tell you. I get myself in a big mess. All that ruckus I help make in College kind of backfiring on me now, because I end up working on the wrong side. For a PNF politician. I know what you must be saying. I can't believe it either. I guess I kind of walked into a trap. And I don't seem to have the willpower to get out of it. It's almost as if I <u>wanted</u> to get trapped. I mean, I was kind of curious. I wanted to see how they operate.

How these politicians think. To be completely honest, a part of me finds it appealing. The life they lead. Not so much the wealth and privilege as the spotlight. It must be good having all those people hanging on your every word. If I was totally honest I would have to say that I was even a little jealous of Bain back at the College. I guess I got hooked when I was Head Boy at the Government New School, standing in front of a school of two thousand students reading announcements and giving speeches. Seem this country starts training its politicians early.

So as I say, I been working for Thaddeus McKinney, the new Minister of Education. The man don't know the first thing about educating nobody, but that never stop our great Prime Minister from appointing whoever he feel like appointing. I write boring speeches mostly. Stuff he says at dull ceremonies or at rallies. Even had me handing out flyers for him. Background stuff. Grunt work. It didn't even seem like nothing where no one would have to know my name, and I liked that. But all the Hawkins Town Headquarters people treat me like I was their long lost sheep. And then I get catch once by a close friend of mine giving out some of those retarded flyers.

And I wasn't finish making a fool of myself either. Thaddeus tell me write this "article" in *The Clarion* about Maxwell Brown. Smearing him, you know. I should have drawn the line right there and then. I mean, Maxwell Brown is someone all the young people could respect! It was really a bad business and I shouldn't have done it. But I keep giving in to his pressure. He keep threatening to get my mother in trouble or to keep me from going off to school. I ought to stand up to him but I don't. I feel like I sinking. Like I turning into what I hate.

I telling you Dr. Runne, Thaddeus scaring me. It's like he gone crazy.

This Election is like a obsession with him. He scared he going to lose. Scared bad. I mean, Maxwell Brown popular in Hawkins Town. He been working that place for five years. All the fellas on the blocks could rap with him. And when they get lock up they want him for they lawyer. He ain't like these PNF politicians who show up every five years. And Thaddeus believe we all should be

GRATEFUL he is our MP. He can't understand why he getting the cold shoulder, why they doing all the PNF candidates this way. He expect to get in and he ain't doing nothing for nobody. He expect to get in on the name PNF alone. And every time someone mention Maxwell Brown he run hot and he say "Don' worry, I ga deal wit' him soon directly."

Then he receive word that he going to be on the Queen's New Year's List. So Thaddeus will soon be "Sir" Thaddeus. And he pull me waist-deep into all this nanny, as if knee-deep wasn't already deep enough. Say he want me to introduce him at a rally in Pompey Village. ME! Say it will mean something for a young person to endorse him. And especially how I been to Santa Maria College and going off and all. Say the young folks will listen to me if I endorse him. Ain't nobody tell him wasn't no young people going to be at no PNF rally in the first damn place!

So now I sure you could imagine the irony of it all. Here, after I run scared at the protest march, was my chance to speak. My chance to blast the powers that be. To shock the hell out of Thaddeus, the Party members, and all those old faithfuls, including my mother, that was standing there praising God for the PNF. I flirt with it. I truly did. I show Thaddeus one speech and I write a totally different one for this special occasion. One calling Thaddeus a no good victimiser, a fraud, a disgrace, a weight about the neck of the people, a cancer that had to be removed, a foul orifice on the body politic that had to be washed clean. I think up some metaphors that would make you proud. I even took both speeches up to the podium with me to add to the personal suspense. The PM was there. Thaddeus was there. My mother was among the hundred or so faithful who come to hear the message from on high. And I couldn't do it. I got caught up in the cheers. I was in the limelight. I had them in the palm of my hand. I gave Thaddeus a introduction like none he ever had in his whole entire political life. The PM was smiling at me with approval and nodding to Thaddeus as if to say, "Boy, you snag a good one. We can't let him slip away."

And then it happen. Out of the shadows come that friend of mine I mention earlier. His name is Jahown. Baptise Tyrone Cunningham. Re-baptise Ras Nehemiah. And in his hand was a bunch a ripe banana he cut from his backyard. He rush up to the stage while I was in mid sentence. He toss the bananas on the stage and he holler out, "HERE MONKEY, EAT! EAT!" He had seerus fire in his eyes, Doc. Rage and disappointment, you hear? Before the police know what was happening he disappear into the night and through the bush like he come. I couldn't speak. I couldn't say a word. The crowd try clap. Weak at first, because they was trying to recover. Then when the PM stand up and clap for me they get stronger. Then Thaddeus come and give me a hug and take the podium. You believe that? The bastard hug me!

I think Jahown lose all respect for me, Doc.

Yours,

Tree

21

Mercer Jr. failed. Failed himself, failed his mother, failed his country. And the pain of that failure, the anguish of that falling short, fueled his rage, led him to freebase cocaine.

Firsborn had been famous. A talent. A very good basketball player in high school. One of the best the country had ever produced. A white American scout came to the island championship to see Firsborn play. Firsborn was given a scholarship to go to a University in the States, a school up North where it snowed. Maureen was proud.

Firsborn was tall, strong, and gifted with his hands. He could make things, anything it seemed, if you gave him the raw material. He could carve, paint, draw, repair cars, fix any appliance, even play the congas. Maureen told him to go to school and learn to do something with those hands, to come back, to make something with those hands that people could look at and say, "See, dere is sumtin Firsborn do."

Firsborn was a gift from God. Maureen use to tell everybody about her son who was playing basketball in University up North where it snowed, who was tall, strong, and gifted with his hands, and who had made her proud.

Mercer Stone, too, had been proud. He came to Firsborn's high school graduation and sat up front, his head held high. He posed for pictures with Maureen and Firsborn. For an instant—that moment it took for the camera to flash—the three of them made one neat little happy family. But only the daddy in the picture was smiling.

The day before Firsborn's flight, Mercer Stone gave him fifty dollars to take with him to University up North and tried to say "Goodbye" in that mechanical, stiff-assed way he always said things to his children. But before he could turn to leave, Firsborn tossed the money back in his face and hollered, "Stuff dis up your ass, man! What in the hell you t'ink *fifty dollars* could do?!" Mercer Stone thought seriously about slamming him across the mouth like he used to when Firsborn was a little boy. But he thought better of it. Firsborn was a man now. He picked up the money and left without saying a word.

Maureen Bodie didn't witness this exchange because she was in her bedroom with the door locked and gospel music playing loud on the boom box she'd bought on her last trip to Miami.

Firsborn was the only black player on the team. One of the few blacks at the University, period. He was the focus of attention. He quickly got himself a girlfriend. A white girlfriend. He sent a picture back to Maureen Bodie. She didn't show anyone this picture. Tree saw it many years later in a drawer full of old discarded letters and cards. The white girlfriend in the picture had her hands around Firsborn's waist and she was kissing him on the cheek ever so tenderly.

Firsborn was the star of the white basketball team at the University in the North where it snowed. He sent a picture of himself in a big coat and boots, standing in the snow. Maureen showed this one to everybody. He wrote letters. She read these to everybody, skipping out the uncomfortable parts.

Firsborn was tall, strong, and gifted with his hands. He scored lots of points for the white basketball team and made the papers. He sent clippings to Maureen which she showed to everybody. The newscasters at Radio One interviewed Firsborn by telephone a couple of times each year and broadcast the conversations during the evening news. The Safe Haven newspapers would run articles about his performance in big games as well. Firsborn was famous, tall, strong, and gifted. A talent. A gift of God. He made his mother proud. Mercer Stone, too, held his head high: "Tha's my oldest boy."

But in his junior year everything went sour. He stopped paying attention to his work. The University in the North gave him tutors. But Firsborn wasn't taking classes that would teach him to do something with his hands like his mother told him. He was doing Accounting. He said he wanted to be a CPA. His mother asked him, "Why you wan' do dat and you know you cyaa do Maths and you don't have no head for business?" Firsborn said he wanted to do Accounting. He said he wanted be a CPA. All his friends were doing Accounting.

But Firsborn "got in with the wrong people" and partied too much. He missed too many classes and tutoring sessions. By this time he was smoking herb almost every day and drinking heavily. He broke team curfew. He missed some practices. He was suspended from the team. He flunked Accounting I and Calculus, then Macroeconomics and Statistics. He went on academic probation. He played in a pick-up game against the coach's orders and tore up his knee.

Then Firsborn got into a brawl with members of a white fraternity on campus. Two of them called him a "porch monkey" as he walked toward the cafeteria with his white girlfriend. He broke one guy's nose and kicked the other in the stomach. Then some of their friends came along. Firsborn was expelled. The white fraternity members were reprimanded. (They were not allowed to wear their paraphernalia on campus for the remainder of the semester.) Firsborn's white girlfriend left him.

Maureen Bodie made the long journey by plane to get her son at the University in the North where it snowed. They said nothing to each other the whole trip back home.

Firsborn came back to Santa Maria beaten and disgraced. He couldn't look anyone in the eye. He hardly spoke a word for two months. The papers covered the story of his being dropped from the team and his being expelled for "disciplinary reasons." Everyone whispered when they saw him; whispered in that conspicuous way people tend to whisper when they see someone to whom something terrible has happened. The newspapers wanted an interview. Maureen immediately forgot her sense of disappointment and sheltered her son. He was still her boy, her Firsborn. A gift from God. A man who could make things, anything it seemed, if you gave him the raw material. He was still the first fruit of her womanhood. Her love for him had no season. She knew he'd get another chance.

Firsborn never spoke to the papers. He never left Pompey Village. He stayed to himself most of the day sitting in the shade of the almond tree in the backyard. If he did go out, it was only to the clearing in the Big Bushes along a street with no name. The idle young men of the Village made that space so they could smoke weed, gamble, and talk hard without being seen by the police. Firsborn went there, smoked ganja, and tossed dice. But he said nothing. Everybody knew who he was but they asked nothing. Tree told his mother about Firsborn's trips to this place, but she never went there to fetch him. She couldn't shame him like that. She spoke to him one evening after she got home from work. She said only men with no hope went to such places and he was better than that. Said people who went to those places ended up shot in the streets or hanging from a noose. Firsborn just smiled that despairing, fearless smile that became his trademark and never answered.

Not long after his return, Firsborn and Kevin began to spar. It wasn't the same as in the old days when they fought each other, brother against brother, over foolish things. Now they fought over foolish things but they were serious. They didn't fight and make up the next day as they would when they were boys. They was both man now. And they blows was man blows.

It was as if each had sized up the other from the very first day of Firsborn's return, as if they both knew when they looked at each other silently that it would come to a blood-clash. Firsborn and Kevin were only a year apart. Firsborn was another John Bodie, only bigger and much stronger. Kevin was the spitting image of

Mercer Stone, only taller and more agile. The tension between them made Tree and Frankie scared. Maureen Bodie would lie in her bed and try to pray the evil away.

Kevin saw his brother as a failure and a fool. A good-for-nothing loafer and a parasite. After a few months he began saying things to stir up trouble. "How come he could sit on his ass for five months and don't do nuttin but slunk? Mamma, why you always gat to be makin' excuses for him? Ain' nobody fault but his own he ain' never finish school. Wouldn' listen to sense, das all. Now he sittin' 'round here spongin' offa oder people hard work!" Firsborn would only smile that smile. Everybody knew the time would come. There seemed to be no way of avoiding it. Blood-clash.

Then Kevin washed a cup, left it on the kitchen counter, and went to the bathroom. He planned to drink from that cup. Firsborn came in and filled the cup with switcha for himself to drink. Maureen was washing some clothes by hand in the backyard. Tree and Frankie were playing checkers on the living room floor. Tree was losing. Kevin went back into the kitchen.

"Nigger, das my cup."

"Your name on it?"

"I clean dat cup for me to use."

"I meet this cup sitting here."

"Das MY cup."

Then there was the sound of shuffling feet and of things crashing in the kitchen. Of bodies falling to the kitchen floor with great force. Of grunting and cursing. Tree got up ran into the kitchen and froze when he saw his brothers struggling over control of his mother's longest knife. The cup lay on the floor discarded, the switcha mixing with the blood.

Maureen Bodie ran into the kitchen screaming. Maureen separated her sons, and said out loud that the Devil done come in her house to cause trouble and vexation.

The sight of his brothers trying to kill each other was too much for Tree. In the middle of the cursing and screaming he slipped out into the backyard and ran to the steps of the Sinking Church with the dog, King. He stayed there for hours, until Maureen Bodie jumped in the car and drove through each street of Pompey Village in search of him. She found him sitting there, balled up, with the dog at his feet and his head on his knees, asleep.

After that fight Maureen decided it was time to do something for her son. The first thing she did was pay an architect to draw up a new plan for the Yellow and White House. It was time to expand. Two grown men cyaa live in one room for long wit'out comin' to blows. Once the plan was approved she set out to find a man to throw up the walls. After getting all the material, she discovered that she didn't have to find a man. Firsborn did the work himself. He worked day and night. The only thing she needed to do was bring men to help put on the roof. When the room was finished Firsborn moved in. Now he was out of his brother's way. But still he was restless. He would flare up suddenly if asked the simplest questions. He began to shout and curse at everyone, including Maureen.

She tried to get him a job. No good. He walked off every job or had disagreements with his bosses. Desperate, she went up to the Ministry of Education and tried to pull some strings. She got her son a job as a night watchman for one of the elementary schools not far from Pompey Village. That way Firsborn could walk to work. He worked the graveyard shift because Maureen thought it would be better for him—that way he wouldn't get himself into trouble. But the job was dull. After sitting in the security booth for two hours he would get restless and angry. He would leave before his shift was over and go to Fredricka's. He'd saved up his money for five months or so and bought old used cars. He would fix them up and destroy them soon after. In accidents. In frustration if they wouldn't run properly. Nothing gave him pleasure.

He started smoking even more ganja, started having it out with the roughnecks of the Southern District. Firsborn never backed down. The slightest challenge led to blood-clash. He would risk his very life to answer a smart-assed remark. He would rather die than lose face to some stupid sof' boy. No one could say anything to him that could be misconstrued as derogatory without paying a heavy price. Firsborn developed a reputation as a "bad head." The wise stayed clear.

Firsborn never stole anything from anyone. He didn't want anything anyone had. He never bullied. Never carried a gun. His one rule was that no one should fuck wit' 'im. No one. He made enemies of the police but admirers of his peers on the street and in the Bush. He never came home before dawn. He was never to be found at his security post at night, but he collected his cheque on time. And because of the teacher and woman Maureen was, Ministry officials were reluctant to punish him—many of their night watchmen were drunks anyway.

It looked like Firsborn's days were numbered. Bad heads all ended the same way in Santa Maria. He stopped cutting his hair and fingernails. His hair grew afro high, his nails an inch long. He walked around with the bugged-out expression of a man who had spent the night in a closet with a corpse. He could find no rest. One twilight, he was walking to work with a long knife in his back pocket for all to see and an orange in his hand. A policeman saw him and told him to give up the knife, it was against the law to carry such an object uncovered. It was Maureen Bodie longes' and sharpes' knife what she use for cuttin' she meat. Firsborn smiled that smile. "Come fuckin' take it if you is man." And he kept on walking. The policeman thought about it, then hurried off for reinforcements. He had heard of this dread nigger before. He came back in a car with three more Babylon armed with pistols. Firsborn spent his first night in jail.

That started Maureen's string of trips to the police station to post bail for her son. That started her going to court for him. Firsborn's reputation grew. Once, a house was burglarized on the Bodie's street. It belonged to an officer of the Criminal Investigation Department and his family. When the CID man was driving home from work late at night he noticed the light on in Firsborn's room. Everybody on that street knew it was Firsborn's room because Maureen had added it after his return and he could be heard shouting and blasting the radio from the inside. The CID man saw the light on in the room and when he saw what had happened to his home he decided Firsborn was his man. All he knew about Firsborn was that he had a bad head. That and the light in the middle of the night were enough to convince him.

The police came to the Yellow and White House and banged on the door about four in the morning. Maureen went to the door.

She let them inside. Four tall men in the dark. Firsborn wouldn't open the door to his room. They kicked it open. He fought them. They wrestled him to the ground, handcuffed him and took him to the station. Firsborn struggled and cursed and screamed as they dragged him out of the house. Tree stood in the corner of the living room crying. Kevin and Frankie stood by their mother powerless and afraid. Maureen say the Devil done come in her house to cause trouble and vexation.

When the police drove off Maureen jumped in her car to follow them to the station. The police had a habit of taking women's sons to the canals and telling them to run or be beaten to a pulp. Everybody knew that if you ran they would shoot you.

They took Firsborn to jail. They beat him up after Maureen Bodie left to go back home. He would not confess. They beat him some more. One officer spent ten minutes climbing up on a desk and leaping down, driving his elbow into Firsborn's shoulder like a pro wrestler. Another squeezed his testicles. He would not confess. He had been home all night. Strange for him, but he had. Stayed in his room the whole time. Three days later they caught a man burglarizing a convenience store and searched his room. They found the CID officer's video machine. The charges against Firsborn were dropped.

After that Firsborn slid even closer to the precipice. A fella from Jacob Road they called Einstein gave Firsborn a spliff. It was laced with cocaine. The next day Firsborn bought his first taste of freebase cocaine. Living for the rock. Hooked on the rock. Everything is the rock, the rock, the rock. Den people start sayin' he crazy.

That bugged-out look became calcified. No longer did he resemble a man locked in a closet with a corpse. Now he *was* that corpse, revivified by some accident of mad science. He started talking to himself. Loud. Not just talking to himself, but holding extended conversations. For most of the week he paid no attention to hygiene. And when he did take a shower, he used up the entire bar of soap in one go.

Firsborn started having passionate arguments with invisible people. He frantically searched the floor, the cracks and crevices of the walls, the windowsills, for minute things that he never seemed able to find. He began wearing his old winter clothes, the stuff he put on at the University in the North where it snowed. It was the middle of June. He quit his job. He spent all the money he was saving to build a house.

Then he got tired of the winter clothes. He stopped wearing clothes altogether. He walked about the front yard naked, holding his penis in his hands. Or, as in childhood, he went in the road barefoot, wearing the drooping, tattered gym trunks that were once part of his team uniform. The elastic in the trunks were slack. They hung below his waste, exposing his holey underwear.

He took to shouting at the Southern Road entrance to Pompey Village. He would gawk at women and curse loudly at no one in particular. His profanities became long and exquisite expressions that the children admired. He walked the streets shouting them as loud as he could, for no other reason than that they articulated something inside him that had to come out, that had to be heard. Parents heard their children repeating them and were incensed. When they saw Firsborn coming the little ones would try to shout it out like he did. He would smile that smile and show them how it needed to be done.

"OH-GOOD-GREAT-MOTHERFUCKIN'-GODDAM!!!!!"

If he watched a commercial on t.v. when he wasn't high, he would spend the entire day walking the streets of the Village reciting it over and over again.

Maureen Bodie felt no pain sharper in her entire life than that caused by her first born. She tried to talk to him. He nodded but didn't seem to be hearing her. She got up every morning at six and stood at his door. She would make the sign of the cross and say a silent prayer for her son. She called Mercer Stone at his house (she never ever called Mercer Stone) and told him that his son was in trouble and needed to hear some words of encouragement. After he got the call, Mercer Stone stopped coming to the Yellow and White House for close to four months. If he happened to be driving somewhere in his car and he saw Firsborn up ahead on the street he would turn at the first corner he could find and go another way. Mercer Stone would have nothing to do with the embarrassment that was his namesake.

Kevin's contempt for his brother grew stronger than ever. It seemed as if he vowed to kill Firsborn each and every day. Frankie hated Firsborn too, but he wasn't big enough to deliver. Even Tree hated Firsborn. He didn't hate him like he hated Mercer Stone. His hate for Mercer Stone was not informed by memory and experience. It was through his mother's hurt that Tree learned to hate the father he never knew. But with Firsborn there was the daily verbal abuse, the physical intimidation, the chaos he brought to the Yellow and White House, the embarrassment he caused the family. Where he hated Mercer Sr. because he felt he was expected to, he hated Mercer Jr. in spite of the love and patience his mother showed toward his brother every day. He hated Firsborn because he threatened to destroy the Yellow and White House and the safety it provided for all of them. He hated Firsborn because he seemed possessed by the Devil.

Firsborn brought havoc to his own home. He smashed things up without warning. He got into more blood-clashes with Kevin. He would shove Tree and Frankie violently if they got in his way. He drilled his fist through the thin sheet of wood that made the bathroom door when Tree didn't get out quick enough. He struck Frankie over the head with the telephone because he wanted to make a call and Frankie wouldn't come off. And worst of all, he would curse Maureen all the time and threaten to kill her. Tree hated Firsborn for this over all else. And without truly knowing how he would achieve it, he sometimes screamed, "I ga kill you! I ga kill you, buhy! I swear I ga kill you!" Firsborn would only look at him, look through him, and smile like the walking dead.

Tree hated Firsborn. He loved him also. He felt for him in a strange way he couldn't fully understand. Sometimes he would sit at Firsborn's door at night and listen to his brother mumble and curse to himself. He would cry for his brother. He would hate and cry for his brother. He loved him and swore he would kill him.

But being Firsborn's baby brother also protected Tree from all sorts of harm. No one in the Village would mess with him because he was "Miss Bodie crazy son brudda." Once Tree was on the basketball court across from Biggity Miss Francis's yard and a bully called Toker threatened to slap him in the face with a two-by-four.

Toker had been walking around the Village with the piece of wood all day long persecuting the smaller boys. Toker stood there with the two-by-four pushed up menacingly to Tree's face, daring him to say something. Firsborn came walking down the street. It took three fellas from the clearing in the Big Bushes to stop Firsborn from banging Toker's head into the lamppost onto which the basketball rim and backboard had been nailed.

Where once he had been famous because he was a great athlete, Firsborn was now famous because he was a crazy bad head nigga. Where once they considered him one of the best basketball players ever in Santa Maria, people now considered him one of the baddest men in the South. Badder than Raccoon and his brothers because he was plain crazy . . . Was only a matter a time 'fore he kill some woman chile.

Maureen, like many, employed a Haitian who did yard work for her because her sons didn't want to work in the sun. His name was Anton Bastien. Maureen "sponsored" Anton. In other words, she helped keep Anton in the country by paying the fee for his work permit. In exchange, Anton took care of her yard. Anton lived in a shack on the edge of the Pine Forest. He lived alone. His wife and children lived in Haiti. Anton sent all the money he earned to his family. When he began doing yard work for the Bodies he had already been away from his family for three years. Tree had been socialized to hate Haitians, to avoid Haitians because they were supposed to be nasty, disease carrying, uncivilized niggas. To be called a Haitian by your classmates in school was the greatest insult. To be considered a Haitian, to have someone say you dressed like a Haitian, was a disgrace. It meant you were the lowest of the low, a placeless person in a community that exploited you and despised you at the same time. Anton opened Tree's eyes. Despite their peculiar financial arrangement, Maureen treated Anton with uncommon decency and Tree learned from this. He was Anton, not "Daddy," which is what "Highshuns" were usually called. She gave him some of the food from her pot. Gave him a glass out of which to drink and did not toss it in the garbage afterward.

One day Anton was stopped in the street by Raccoon. He was on his way home after working in someone's yard. Raccoon ordered the stinkin' Highshun to give up the money he had on him or else. Anton refused and removed his machete from the brown paper bag which concealed it. Raccoon let him go.

That night Raccoon and some of his friends gave Anton his punishment. They set his shack on fire with him in it. They wouldn't let him come out. They carried guns and meant to shoot him if he tried to escape. He was burned alive.

The news of the murder spread fast but the police were slow to act. Raccoon came to the clearing in the Big Bushes and bragged about his feat. Firsborn, gym trunks drooping, barefoot, managing not to talk to himself and watching the men throw dice, heard it all. Two days after Anton Bastien's murder Firsborn took things into his own hands.

During the years that Anton had worked in the yard he and Firsborn had struck up a friendship. It was purely based on the casual talk they would indulge in whenever Anton took a break from work. Firsborn would give him the food and switcha Maureen prepared for him. A man with a good sense of humour and a fair command of English, Anton would joke with Firsborn. Firsborn used to call him Crocodile, because of an old alligator shirt he wore virtually every day he came to work. So when Firsborn concluded that the law was taking too long to act on Anton's behalf, he took the old pitchfork from underneath the almond tree in the backyard and marched to the Big Bushes where Raccoon was gambling. Raccoon had no gun on him that day. People had been saying Raccoon and Firsborn would come to blood-clash one day and they would see who was the true-true ragamuffin.

Firsborn walked barefoot and in the basketball trunks as usual. Gray clouds gathered for an impending thunderstorm. The pitchfork in his hand was like a spear. He hollered Raccoon's name all the way from the Yellow and White House to the clearing. Raccoon saw him coming and dropped the dice. At the same time Maureen Bodie turned off the Southern Road and into Pompey Village. Terrified, Raccoon began tossing rocks at Firsborn, but Firsborn stepped aside each one and kept advancing.

"What the fuck you want, man? Crazy motherfucker! What you want wit' me!?" Raccoon hollered.

"Youzza murderer." Firsborn's face was a blank but he answered in his booming voice.

"What the fuck you talkin' 'bout? Get out my face, man!"

"Youzza damn murderer."

The fellas said Firsborn took Raccoon in his hands and struck him to the ground. The sound of his fist against Raccoon's jaw caused a loud cracking sound. Raccoon grimaced and spat blood. Then Firsborn kicked him in his stomach several times as hard as he could. Raccoon coughed up something purple.

"Youzza damn murderer." Firsborn was saying it matter-of-factly.

With Raccoon writhing in the dirt Firsborn stood over him with the pitchfork up high, the four sharp points making a vertical line that pointed toward the criminal's chest. The fellas stood around in a circle, silent, their inaction serving as consent.

It was Maureen Bodie who jumped out of her car and ran screaming toward her son. It was Maureen Bodie who saved her first born from the gallows. The fellas said they didn't know the woman was so strong. That day under the eyes of the crowd Maureen dragged her son, so much taller and bigger than herself, and threw him in her car.

As the rain came down, falling like rocks as the thunder rolled through the sky, the fellas left Raccoon where he lay, writhing in the mud. Maureen drove straight to the Graylands Rehabilitation Centre, "Crazyhill," and admitted her son for substance abuse. Small Pint, who had seen the whole thing from the spot where he spied the gamblers, ran to the Yellow and White House in the downpour and told Tree what he'd seen.

That night the police went to the Stirrup Estate and carried Raccoon to jail. No one knows if Anton Bastien's family ever received news of his death. No one knows what became of his remains.

22

"We pull up in the squad car to see what was what and meet dem standin' dere buck naked as dey mudda born dem. Standin' at gun point wit' dey hand on dey head."

Stooley sucks his teeth and takes a drag. He keeps in the cigarette smoke for a second or two and then blows it out his nostrils. On the other side of the wall, Tree is sitting in the bed with his knees up against his chest, pensively listening to the story.

"Was like sumpm out a movie, man. One a dem movies where da white fellas 'bout ta lynch a nigga or sumpm. I couldn' believe it."

"You sure it was him?"

"I TELLIN' you man. Was him. Him an' dat fella . . . um-ah . . . what he name again? Lionel. Lionel . . ."

"McCartney. Lionel McCartney? His campaign manager?"

"Da two a dem, buck naked, dey clothes on da groun', and lookin' straight inta da shotgun barrel."

"Damn!"

"Das da same ting I say when I see it, only I didn' know it was dem at first."

Stooley clears his throat and takes another drag. The dew is falling.

"You and Monty pull up to see what's happening. You find these two naked men being held at gunpoint by another pair of police officers. Den what?"

"Like I say, earlier we notice Tall Boy get dis phone call an' den him and Jigger leave da station wit'out tellin' nobody where dey gone. Was a slow night so after a while, when dey ain' come back, we start to wonder what happen. We figure dey might be out Yearwood Beach, dis spot where we is go sometimes when tings slow, to chill out. Only ting, dey wuzzan at da spot at all. So we drive on and we see two cars instead a jus' one. Was totally a accident dat we come across dem at all, and we see Tall Boy and Jigger holdin' dese two fellas under arrest. Only, da fellas dem ain' gat no bloody clothes on.

"So first ting Monty say to me is, 'Dey mussie ketch some sissies.' So I say, 'Yeah, mussie.' But when we pull up 'long side, we see Tall Boy gat dem standin' dere at gunpoint. And das when I firs' get scared. 'Cause if all dese two fellas was doin' was boongiein', what you need a gun for? Jus' shine ya light on 'em, aks dem what da hell dey t'ink dey doin', and lock 'em up. Well, when Tall Boy see us, look like he get mad, like he wuzzan 'xpectin' nobody to come dat way. Yearwood Beach is be dark and it off da road, so only if you really desperate for a piece was you goin' to come 'round dere. You remember dat couple what get rob an' kill las' year?"

"Yeah."

"Well after dat errybody stop goin' to Yearwood."

"What you mean Tall Boy get mad?'

"I mean, if you t'ink 'bout it, catchin' two people in a car grindin' is a damn funny ting. And if is two man, den you ga want as many a ya friends to know 'bout da episode as possible. In fack, you ga wish dey was all dere to see it wit' you. But like I say, Tall Boy get mad. He tell us to go back ta da station, he gat erryting under control. And Jigger, who usually talkin' crap and all loosy goosy, he was jus' standin' dere sweatin' and gat dis nervous look on his face like sumpm was dead wrong."

"So wha' you do?"

Stooley discards the cigarette, crushing it with his boots to be sure it's extinguished. He leans on the wall beside Tree's window, putting one foot up against it. He puts his hands in his pockets. His voice is almost a whisper. No sign of nervousness. He has told the story at least one time before, Tree says to himself. Maybe to Small Pint or Yellow Man.

"I swear, I could get myse'f in some foolishness, ya hear Tree? Since I join da Force is been some seerus tings I see. Now you know, since I grow tall I don' tolerate no shit. Well, Tall Boy jus' as tall as me. An' bigger. He is a crooked nigga if I ever see one. One time he t'ief da video and t.v. out da station Rec Room and I see him. Fella t'reaten to *shoot* me if I talk. An' dealin' drugs? Shit. I even hear he is be robbin' some a dese stores in Safe Haven too. So you know, he's a rut'less sonofabitch. Da Police is a ting, I didn' know what it was like when I get in it. Some a dese fellas on da Force is worse hoods dan da set on da street! Seerus. So when I see Tall Boy gat dese two naked fellas at gunpoint I know some seerus shit was goin' down, an' half a me say 'Turn aroun' an' don' look back.'

"Anyhow, Monty ain' one ta stan' up ta nobody, so I aks some questions. I aks him what dey do he gat to point gun at dem? I aks him if dey resist arres' or if he suspeck dey have firearms. I aks him if dey search da vehicle or what. He ain' answer my questions yet. He jus' starin' at da two fellas who standin' dere buck naked in da draf', mosquita bitin' an' all. He say, 'Commissioner'—das what dey is call me 'cause I win da Baton a Honour when I was at Police College an' I is go by da book—say, 'Commissioner, go from 'round here now, I gat dis situation unda control. Me and Jigger ga bring dem in fa buggery, indecent sexual acks in a public place, resistin' arres', an' anyting else I choose to add ta da damn lis'.'

"An' das when Mr. Brown speak out. He say, 'We did no such ting. We was sitting in this car discussin' our campaign, nothing more nothing less. Mr. McCartney live just ten minutes from here. We been here since before sunset. Dis whole affair is a travesty and this bastard here is the one breakin' the law!' You know how dese lawyer what is go off ta England is talk, all proper."

"An' what Tall Boy say ta dat?"

"He slap Mr. Brown a cowboy slap. And by da looks a Brown and McCartney face, wuzzan da firs' one he get fa da night. But was too late, I done recognize who it was when he open his mout' to talk. Was Maxwell Brown, clear as day. Him and Lionel McCartney. And das when I start gettin' really scared, 'cause I was sayin' ta myself, 'If he could be beatin' up on famous people like dis, it mussie sumpm seerus up his sleeve.' So I walk up ta Tall Boy real slow, so he wouldn' do nuttin' hasty. And I say ta him, 'Tall Boy, you know who dat fella is who you jus' slap like you want all da teet' fall out his mout'?' An' he jus' keep he face screw-screw an' turn to me an' say, 'Hell yeah I know who it is. Is a faggit. A big fuckin' boongie bandit. An' he pick da wrong gaddam night ta catch a piece.'

"I say, 'Das Maxwell Brown, da FLP candidate for Hawkins Town. And das he campaign manager. Da man say he been here all night discussin' business. You sure you ketch dem breakin' da law?'"

"I cyaa believe I hearin' dis."

"Hmmph. Tree boy, I was up shit creek, an' dat snot Monty wuzzan no help ta me. He jus' talkin' 'bout 'Le's go, buhy, le's go.' But was too late for runnin'. I say ta Tall Boy, 'Look, dis man is a famous man. A man wit' money. He ain' gat to be out in da bush doin' foolishness. Dis man is a public figa. He da Shadow Minister a Education. Why you jus' don' put da gun down an' let dem go 'bout dey business? Some kinda misunderstandin' happenin' here.' And I turn to Jigger. 'Right Jigger? You meet dem boongiein' or what? Talk da trut'.'

"Tall Boy jump right in. Didn' even gee Jigger chance ta answer. Say, 'Ain' no gaddam misunderstandin'. Dem two big hairy man was in da back seat boongiein'!' And he put da gun to Maxwell Brown forehead. 'Go on, show dem what you was doin' Mr. Politician. Show dem. Do him right here and now!'

"But Maxwell Brown was calm. He ain' move. He look me dead in da eye. McCartney wuzzan sayin' nuttin. I could see he legs shakin'. Brown say to me, 'Constable, dis man drive up on us and wit'out aksin' any questions or stating the reason fa doin' so, pull us out the car. He force us to take our clothes off at gunpoint. You seen him hit me wit'out provocation. We was never questioned. Neider myself nor Mr. McCartney here have resisted arres'. An'

♦ 220 ♦

now you is a witness ta what he just order me to do. I insis' dat you not leave dis spot until you see us safely deliver to da Station. An' I hope you will report what you have witness here so that Mr. McCartney an' I could corrob'rate our story.'

"Dat time Monty dere, 'Le's go buhy, le's go.' An' Jigger ain' sayin' nuttin. He jus' standin' dere nervous, almos' like he ready to cry. Tall Boy scream at Maxwell Brown, sayin' he mus' shut his faggit ass up 'fore he shoot a road clean t'rough his head. Den Jigger shout out a nowhere, 'Dis ain' right, Tall Boy! Dis ain' right!' And Tall Boy say, 'Shut up, 'cause you jus' a big stinkin' sissy too! All a yall out here is a bunch a sissy!'

"And das when I pull out my rod."

"You pull out your gun? What for, dread? Dat nigga crazy. I hear 'bout him. He coulda shoot all a y'all."

"What I pull my gun for? What the hell else I was gone do? Wuzzan no tellin' what was gone happen nex'. An' Tall Boy didn' seem surprise at all ta hear who da two man was he had standin' dere in dey birt'day suit. Didn' seem to care too much about what I coulda go back ta da station to say neider. Was his word agains' mine, an' if da right people supportin' you on high certain shit will never see the light a day in Her Majesty Court. You know when it come to buggery errybody is see red. Maxwell Brown wouldna stand a chance. Some a dese old folks always sayin' he is sissy anyway.

"I put da gun ta Tall Boy head. An' I tell Monty pull his out an' take Jigger pistol."

"He do it?"

"Yeah he do it. Monty better or I was gone shoot him in the t'igh."

"You gat balls."

"Balls? My ass was *scared*. I pull one gun on Tall Boy an' Monty had Jigger cover—but I wuzzan too worried 'bout Jigger no how, jus' had to make sure. I say to Jigger, 'Jigger, talk da trut' an' maybe your ass won' be grass. When y'all pull up on Mr. Brown an' his associate here, was dey in da back seat commitin' a sexshul offense or was dey jus' talkin'. Shit. Kissin', huggin' even. Speak up!'

"First Jigger ain' say nuttin. He jus' lookin' over ta Tall Boy. Den I tell him he ga sleep in jail anyway, so he might as well let errybody know it wuzzan his idea ta do what dey was doin'. Might help him in court. He say, no dey wuzzan doin' nuttin but talkin' when dey pull up. He say dey come dere ta watch dem an' see if dey was gone do sumpm. Say dey pull up wit' da lights off an' sneak up close ta where dey could watch dem in da car. But Tall Boy get tired a waitin'. Say he get tired a sittin' dere 'cause all dey was doin' was jus talkin' talkin'. So he tell Jigger he ga go grab dem no matter what. Say Tall Boy say he didn' care wheder dey was boongiein' or not, dey is two damn faggits and dey gern ta jail."

A car passes. Stooley switches feet. Tree sits in the bed, rigid.

"So I tell Tall Boy drop da gun or I'll shoot him clean in da head. He drop it. Den I tell Jigger to come over an' cuff him while Monty keep me covered. Den Monty put Jigger in cuffs. An' I tell Maxwell Brown and Mr. McCartney ta put dey clothes on, get in dey car, and follow me ta da station."

"You gat balls."

"We lock Tall Boy and Jigger up for assault and battery, abduction . . . and . . . sumpm else, I cyaa remember. But I don' t'ink Jigger ga go to prison 'cause he squeal and he wuzzan aware a what dey gone out dere ta do. Maxwell Brown say he suin' da Police Force for wrongful arres' and he ga demand a investigation into Police brutality when the new Gov'men' get in power."

"Dat ain' ga happen. Sue the Police Force? Investigate the Police? Forget it, dat shit ga dead right dere. Watch. Dese people in power could stifle you in so many ways, an' ain' nuttin you ga do, man. Da PNF ga win ev'ry Election from now 'til Thy Kingdom Come. And as long as da PNF in power ain' nuttin ga change. Niggas in the force could do any shit dey please. These Santa Maria people? Dey don' *want* change. Scared a change." Tree sucks his teeth.

Stooley turns and peers through the window into the darkness of the bedroom. Frankie is working late at the casino so Tree is alone. "Don' be so sure, Tree. I for one votin' agains' dis Gov'men'. A change'll be good. I ain' no smart fella like you but is too much foolishness goin' on in dis place. People like Maxwell Brown . . ."

"The PNF will lose when Moses dies. Until the PM dies forget it. They love him too much. Shit don' never change aroun' here, man. Never. I don't care no more!"

Silence. Tree is sitting in the bed waiting, his chin on his knees, his hands clasped, his arms wrapped about his legs. He is hoping his words had a certain finality. Hoping they would communicate to his friend that he wishes the conversation to end. Hoping Stooley won't say another word. Hoping he'll turn and leave.

"Tree-o."

"Yeah."

"Sumpm else I gat ta tell you. 'Bout last night."

No sound.

"Word goin' round is you workin' on Thaddeus campaign staff so I t'ought you should know."

"What?"

"Well, I sure you know dat the PNF been publishing dese tings in da paper 'bout Maxwell Brown. Well, da people who supportin' im ain' takin' to it kindly. An' errybody know is Thaddeus who want the stuff spread over town. I don' know if you know who writin' it for him or what but . . ."

"No. I don't know . . . It's probably someone on staff at *The Clarion*."

"Yeah . . . Well . . . I jus' t'ought you should know dat if dis ting ever go to court, I mean if the PNF lose an' dis go to court, Thaddeus ga be in seerus trouble. You know why right?"

After a long pause the reply comes, reluctantly: "Yeah."

"I mean, it ain' da stuff in da paper what ga get him in trouble 'cause he ain' really call no names as such. Is what happen da oder night. You see, when Tall Boy get put in jail he say if *he* goin' to prison den da man who pay him ta lock up Maxwell Brown goin' ta prison too. Da person who call, who was followin' Brown and McCartney around and call Tall Boy on the phone when they pull up on Yearwood Beach. It was Thaddeus, Tree. Thaddeus McKinney."

Tree takes a deep breath and lets it out heavily. He takes his head in his hands and scratches his scalp as if to calm his nerves. He has given up.

"I know. From the minute you start tellin' da story I know. I know dat idiot gone too far. He better hope the PNF win. He better *hope.* 'Cause if dey lose his ass is grass. And I'll be right there to testify."

"It ain' right, you know."

"I know. They wuzzan doin' nuttin."

"No. I mean . . . The whole thing . . . I know what older folks is say 'bout him . . . An' is prob'ly true. He prob'ly a sissy. And he prob'ly was gone do sumpm if dat jackass did just wait. But so what, man?"

"I didn't know you cared."

"You ain' gat to get all sarcastic and shit. I seerus. I mean, if was a man and a woman out dere and dey was buck naked all over the backseat, you t'ink anybody was gone lock dem up? They was jus' gone shine dey light on em an' send up home. I mean . . . Maxwell Brown is a good man. He is talk sense, man. A radical, kinda. We *need* him in dis country. And plenty people 'round here, aldough dey'll say 'He is a sissy,' 'He like man,' when dey in trouble, who dey ga go run to for advice? For help? Him. It jus' don' seem right."

"Yeah. I know."

"I don' know if I tell you dis, but one time me and my frens was at Club Rendezvous and we see dis sissy couple outside holding hands under one palm tree. Was dark, an' we couldn' see dey face at firs'. We rush dem. We was drunk bad. One a my friends name Dexter, he break a beer bottle on one a da sissy head. Turn out the fella he hit was my cousin. My cousin, Harvey. You know? Da one I always jokin' 'bout?"

"Yeah."

"Me and Harvey cool. But from he was in primary school people was callin' him sissy. We use a play togeder when I go ta my aunty house. And we still cool. But when I in public and I see him I is don' be too friendly, ya know? I is have ta play it off 'cause I ain' want nobody call me a sissy too."

"Hmph."

A silence between them. Crickets. Potcakes barking.

"Tree-o."

"Hm?"

"Is you write dem tings 'bout Maxwell Brown for Thaddeus? Say, 'B. B. is at it again?' Say, if a certain candidate in Grand Santa Maria become Minister of Education all da muddas in da country gat to watch dey sons 'cause dey ain' ga get send ta da Principal Office no more, dey ga get send to da *Minister* Office?"

"He say he was gone mess wit' my ole lady. He say he was gone make sure I don' get no student visa . . ."

Tree's words are choked. Stooley puts his hand on the window-pane.

"Is O.K., man. Jus' tell him you ain' doin' dat kind a ting no more, das all. Jus' go t'rough da motions for da nex' four-five mont's an' it'll be over. Once he hear how dis ting backfire he ga lay off anyhow. And if not, let him bury hese'f. Don' let him pull you down too. He might a start off good long time ago but power is make people evil, man. Is like a gun. You always tempted ta see how much damage it could do."

"I fuckin' up erryting, man."

Stooley, looking into the darkness of the room: "Ga soon be over man, and you ga be off ta school. Right? Miles away from dis shit, you know. You wan' a cigarette?"

Tree doesn't answer.

"Tree, guess what man? I gat to work durin' Junkanoo, man. Boxing Day *and* New Years. Das a bitch, hey? I ga cyaa even spend a night wit' ma gal. And you *know* Junkanoo is my *one* excuse ta take her out her mudda house all night wit'out gettin' us bot' in seerus trouble." Stooley laughs, hoping to lighten things.

"Dis little life on dis speck a dust we call a planet. It ain' shit. It don' mean shit, man."

Stooley sucks his teeth.

"You know what your problem is, Tree? You is t'ink too much. And what you t'inkin' jus' ain' *right* . . . You want a smoke or what?"

The Fourth Part

♦

PASSAGE

We forced the doors.

The master's bedroom was wide open. The master's bedroom was brilliantly lit, and the master was there, very calm . . . and all of us stopped. . . . he was the master. . . . I entered. It's you, he said, very calmly. . . . It was me, it was me indeed, I told him, the good slave, the faithful slave, the slave slave, and suddenly my eyes were two cockroaches frightened on a rainy day. . . . I struck, the blood spurted: it is the only baptism that today I remember.

—Aimé Césaire, *And the Dogs Were Silent*

The darkies are fond of processions, and never miss an opportunity of getting one up. About Christmas time they seem to march about day and night with lanterns and bands of music, and they fire off crackers. This is a terrible nuisance, but the custom has the sanction of antiquity.

—L.D. Powles, *The Land of the Pink Pearl,*
or Recollections of Life in the Bahama Islands

First the goat
must be killed
and the skin
stretched.

—E. K. Brathwaite, *The Making of the Drum*

23

Junkanoo comes like an ambush. Drums, dance, street lights. And the masquerade is hot, bold. Bespeaking omens.

When they were slaves the backras did not pierce the drums. And to this day, they still dance, now at the year's end. Rushing to the sound of goatskin, cowbells, and whistles . . .

Is dem.

The "Holy Knights" and the "Mighty Men." The "Dragons" and the "Treasure Bandits."

Is dem.

I hear dem comin'.

Out of the West, dancing toward the sun. Coming to put the spirits at ease. Coming to venerate the ancestors. Coming to kill the sins of the old year before the dawn.

Is dem. Dancin'.

Dancing out of madness and into madness again. Dancing a dance of passage. Dancing the dance of Festival. Dancing to the confrontation of drums.

Dis dem nah!

On come the barefoot courageous.

Da bare-foot!

Dancing their way to the new year's dawn. On that stage without a stage. On that asphalt platform of the frantic horns. Dancing to the wailing laughing cursing lashing pounding drums. Dancing to the rhythm the child can beat with his little hands. The beat the old man can sway to in the mist and the dew of the birthing dawn. The beat the lovers sway to, backside to crotch, in the early morning rub of the rising sun. Are you dancing? Dancing to the liberation ring of the cowbells?

Dey comin'! Dey comin'! Dem damn big-assed barefoot picky-head black shiny ravers from Backadabush! Dey comin'! Dey comin'! Dey comin' to take ova da whole a downtown!

Who?

Dem.

Da dancers?

Da ravers?

The black people.

Dancing from present to past. From past to present. From present to future. And back again. And back again. And-back-again.

DIS is Junkanoo.

So on come the shadowprancers.

Da sha-dow-pran-cers!

Black sweaty faces seeping a year of fuckstration. A year of taking orders. A year of sinning and faking. (A year of being true too). And this is their reviving. This is their ghost-chasing. This is when they funk down Waterfront Road between fancy stores, telling white business owners, telling the tourists with their cameras, telling their friends and foes, telling the whole wide world, at three o' clock in the morning, to kiss their big black asses.

'Cause das how dey go.

And on come the magic makers.

Da ma-gic ma-kers!

Working that old obeah again with new incantations. Working that joy magic. That life magic. That I-sure-damn-glad-to-be-alive-magic.

And the street start shakin'. And the two-storey buildin's seem small.

For these are the magic makers. Bringing it forth for the owners, and the cameras, the friends and the foes, and the police with their billy clubs and riot-gear too. Bringing forth beauty from the shacks. Bringing forth fire and blood from the shacks. Bringing forth the music of magic from the shacks. From the hearts of the drummers and the cowbellers and the whistlers. Bringing forth life from the shacks for the living to live again!

And each time 'round the bend the groove is reborn. Each time the funk is funkier than the time before. And the heads must bob. And the white shining teeth in black wooly heads must shine under the drunk street lights. And the sweat must lather on the faces of the men carrying the big costumes. And the breasts must jiggle extra special and the asses must go zzzzzzoooom into the god-annointed dark. And the muscles must flex. And the crotches must be clutched. And the rum must run fast fast to the head like the kick from a horse's hoof. And the old and the young and the woman and the man must join in this special thing that is happening. This special happening that is happening which they can never get enough of, which they have crawled from their homes on Christmas night or New Year's morning to be a part of. Because they must come to groove in this people-gel. This people-gel that stays with the times. This people-gel that obliterates time. Like the last beat of a black hand on the heated goatskin obliterates the one that came before it. Like the last pa-pa-pa-pa-paaaaaaa of the whistle obliterates the pa-pa-pa-pa-paaaaaaa that came before it.

Das dem nah! Das dem nah gaddammit!

Yout' 1: Who? Who you for, buhy? Talk fas'!

Yout' 2: You gatta aks? I is a Holy Knight! We ga bus' y'all behind tonite!

Yout' 1: Don' talk too fas'! Don' talk too damn fas' an' ya have to eat ya words, nah. Take it easy. Any boongie gettin' bus' roun' here it gern be yinna own! TWO STRAIGHT FOR THE MIGHTY MEN!

Yout' 2: Who teach you how ta count nigga!? "Two straight fa da Mighty Men?" You mussie dotin' hey? Dis Festival belong ta da

Holy Knights! Looka dem colours buhy? You een blind yet? Listen ta dat music! I know you tryin' ta play it off, but I catch ya dancin' when we pass on Waterfront Road. Jesus could come down off his t'rone tonight and He wouldn' beat us! Dis OUR parade!

Yout' 1: Now I know you is take drugs. You is base, hey? How yinna 'xpec' ta win Junkanoo wit dat tired ass parade yall drag out here? Cheaper y'all burn dem costume now! Don' wait 'til tommorow morning. Burn um nah! "Fishes of the Sea?" How much damn times y'all gern come out Waterfront Road wit' "Fishes of the Sea"!? If I see any more shark, seahorse, coral reef, octapus, and grouper on Waterfront Road I ga dead! "Fishes a da gaddam Sea!" Yinna have nerve! Da judges ain' goin' fa dat out here tonight!

Yout' 2: Well muddow! Don' tell me you tryin' ta rear up nah! Le's face some facks. You talkin' 'bout our parade like is a damn disgrace. But from what I could see, if is anyone who's a poppy show out here is yinna. Sheeeeeet! Man I could see da damn spray paint drippin' off dem costume y'all CLAIM to paste with papier-maché from miles away! But you ain' foolin' a soul but ya se'f. Da judges done scope dat piece. And at least half a dem big pieces I see out dere even ain' look half way *real*. An' who you is to carry on 'bout "Fishes a da Sea" when y'all parade is "Is Better in We Country." How much Jesus-Christ-time yinna try pull milk outta tourism flabby breas'? Leave it 'lone, ma buhy. Leave it 'lone. All dem blackjack table and dice on Waterfront Road for the umpteent' time is enough to make a grown man cry!

Yout' 1: Man, I ain' wastin' no more a my time disagreein' witchoo. I ga let da judges say who is who. I gat odder problems to worry 'bout. Someone tell me they see my woman out here wit' Lincoln Jones!

Yout' 2: You seerus! Ogly Lincoln Jones who is work in Mr. Chang grocery store?

Yout' 1: That woman ain' no good, man. No good. I just-just buy her one gold chain wit' my last fifty dollars! I gattie find me a new woman for da New Year.

Yout' 2: Think is you! I where ya put ma.

And the street start shakin'. And the two-storey buildin's seem small.

Before Mudda Mae's roosters began to call the sun from its rest, Tree and Elsa caught Yellow's bus and got a free ride onto crowded Waterfront Road. Standing behind the barricades, Tree could see all his friends from Pompey Village, and he pointed them out to her.

Stooley was there on duty, dressed in riot gear and standing amongst the other young policemen, looking fierce and suspicious of everyone. Tree thought perhaps he had violated a code of male toughness when he called out to Stooley from the crowd and used his childhood nickname. He saw his friend wince, make eye contact, and then look the other way. "Cyaa talk now," he seemed to say in the instant their eyes met.

Later he saw Small Pint, obviously drunk, but handling the ropes for the Holy Knights, keeping the huge group separated from the one that preceded it in the parade; leading the way as the throng of Knights pushed forward with slow exuberance along the main street. No need to call out to him. He shouted over to where they stood behind the barricades and blew a kiss at Elsa, whom he had only seen once or twice before. The couple laughed at him when he tripped and got up cussing a man for getting in his way. The man had escaped the notice of the police and was trying to jump the barricade on the other side of the street. Small Pint, embarassed by the laughter of the crowd, cussed him so soundly that the man slunk away to a point further down the street and tried again to haul himself over.

And they saw Jahown too. Bedecked, solemn, majestic. Fulfilling his prophecy of long ago. He was wearing his bright, flaring costume of the African Warrior, the one he had been working on for so many seasons. His locks were unleashed for all to see. His cowbells ringing in his hands, he was dancing defiantly in a scrap group. He didn't seem to care what was going on around him. He was enraptured and transported in the thrill of his timeless moment. The vision of him moved Tree deeply. He felt he was seeing a prophesy fulfilled.

"What a beautiful man, hey?," Elsa said. Tree agreed.

But the big new Junkanoo group, Ashanti, was the talk of the town that morning. It was formed by defectors from both the Mighty

Men and the Holy Knights. This new group became a peculiar and powerful third force on Waterfront Road that had captured everyone's imagination. Everyone said they would sweep the New Year's Festival.

Elsa noticed that the Prime Minister was not rushing with the Holy Knights as he usually did. Instead he had found his way into the crowd of estatic cowbell shakers in this new group. She figured that the old man must have sensed the appeal this new group would have and decided to capitalize on it by attaching himself to the throng. Tree had yet to tell Elsa the truth about all the dirty work he had done for Thaddeus. Seeing the PM reminded him of his dishonesty. He tried to sound optimistic about the leader to see how she would react. He said he agreed that people were tired of watching Holy Knights and Mighty Men split the winnings year after year. Perhaps the PM still had some of that old magic up his sleeve? After all, New Year's Day marked the beginning of an Election Year. Maybe the PNF would make some meaningful changes? Maybe the PM was hoping this change of Junkanoo groups would symbolize his rebirth for the onlookers, his transformation from Moses to Joshua. Elsa only frowned.

"Don't fool yase'f, Tree. You better guess again," Elsa said wryly. "Is the same ole PM. He ain't change. Cat cyaa meow in the morning and bark like dog when the sun go down."

The multitide erupted after sunrise when it was announced that the Ashanti had won first prize in the masquerade. Tree and Elsa, who usually pulled for the Mighty Men, were as overjoyed as everyone else. It was the first time in years that a group other than the Mighty Men or the Holy Knights had won Festival. But no one thought that such an upset at New Year's Junkanoo might be a sign of greater things to come.

24

The Prime Minister was deformed. Tree noticed this when the leader stepped to the podium for his first campaign speech since his mysterious three month sabbatical. It came to Tree so suddenly that he began to laugh out loud and encountered suspicious glares which made him fix his face. He didn't laugh at the absurdity of it all but at the great amount of sense it made. Its cold, hard sense.

The Cabinet Ministers rose to congratulate the PM before he had even spoken a word. Sir Thaddeus was grinning from ear to ear. The women in straw hats at the edge of the platform waved their pom-poms in jubilation. The sound system boomed the campaign song. Tree sat there in the midnight dew, biting his lip and shaking his head at how foolish he had been.

It must have been so obvious all these years that it simply escaped his attention. He'd seen the Prime Minister so many times before: while sitting on the wreckage of the drug plane, every year at Junkanoo parades, in Victoria Square on the day of the demonstration, the night he introduced Sir Thaddeus, countless times on television and in the papers. Nothing had registered. Of course, everyone knew that something was *wrong* with the PM. It was all right there in front of their eyes. People joked about it all the time. It was a way of bringing the PM down to size. But Tree had never thought seriously about what it meant. He had never thought about what it *really* meant that something was wrong with the man. Not until now.

"The Prime Minister was deformed." He had to repeat it to himself, under his breath. Had to get used to the idea. And he understood anew why the man was so loved, why the man was worshipped and feared, why he was the embodiment of all they had been and still were as a people. He suddenly felt as if he had been let in on a terrific secret.

The Prime Minister's affliction was not his skin colour, although in complexion he was a very dark man. Light skin was usually a mark of beauty, but in Santa Marian politics the blacker you were the better. The malady was not the size or shape of his nose. The PM's nose was large and broad, the nostrils wide and flaring. But to the masses of Backadabush, a politician could have no more cherished facial characteristic. It signified class—underclass—for few who looked stereotypically "African" were well off. Neither was the Prime Minister's infirmity his stature, although he was a physically diminutive man. Who has not observed the Napoleonic aggressiveness of the short politician, his charisma, the commanding nature of his voice, the vitality and sweep of his gestures, his propensity for stepping to the forefront of crowds to see better and to be better seen? And it was not a failing that the Prime Minister spoke the creole of the masses at these political rallies. The high-sounding phrases of the Queen's English were good for the House of Assembly, but here in Backadabush, amongst the people, you had to speak like them or be rejected as a snob and a white man's stooge. No, the Prime Minister's deformity—and consequently, his mark of ascendancy— was a wound that could not have been mistaken by the people.

He had come out of his mother's womb uneven. A spinal defect at birth. It set one shoulder higher than the other and gave him the permanent posture of someone jerking backward as if avoiding a blow. Few knew the medical name for this birth-sign, but its cosmic significance grew clearer and clearer as the young man grew in fame and power.

First as a nettlesome student leader at the Government New School and then as a young barrister of great flair and charisma, the PM-to-be embodied the grievances of the people. His body was inscribed with the licks and wounds of the past. Skewed and stricken, his frame bore the scarifications of greed which could not physically pass through the womb but which were felt in the soul: the slaver's brand, the overseer's lash, the master's manacles. The sicknesses of soul and mind that four hundred years of servitude and filth had bequeathed to the people of Backadabush found in his twisted frame a quintessential metaphor. He was the sign and the signified thing. He was the living tool of their retribution, the walking evidence of their suffering. As bent as he was in body, so was he as straight as a burning spear in his words, his holy wrath, his deeds of symbol. His voice became the voice of the people, his physical deformity a harbinger of the white man's Judgment Day. From Parliament to platform to street corner to church hall, his words manifested the immovable rightness of the people's cause, the impatience of their demand for justice, the authority and consent of their ancestors, the force of a new history. Though he was a mere man—the least impressive of men in terms of his physicality—yet was he also the Elected, man above men, the instrument of God's Will. In the eyes of a people constrained by poverty and consoled by religion, the PM was the voice and hand of God. Why else, Tree asked himself, would these people have clung to him so, have continued believing in him, despite the defection of so many capable men from the ranks of the PNF, men who for twenty years now had been calling him a traitor, a liar, and a thief?

Fully aware of his place in history, the PM had manipulated everything at his disposal to ensure that the people of Backadabush never stopped believing in his command over the forces of the supernatural. There seemed no end to his clever ploys. But somehow everything seemed altered this go around. Having been in power for twenty-five years, the leadership of the PNF seemed to have gone about this final stretch toward General Elections all wrong, as far as Tree was concerned. Like Sir Thaddeus, the PM seemed to be making unsound personal and political decisions. In fact, other than rushing with the Ashanti four months ago on New Year's Day, it seemed as if everything the PM did or said annoyed and disturbed the people. Tree began having doubts. He reassured himself that despite it all the PNF would win. They always did. They had been through rough times before.

In fact, the decline in the Prime Minister's appeal had begun a full two years before the Election race began. It coincided with a US recession which caused the plunge in tourist arrivals the country was now experiencing. It also coincided with the establishment of Robert Curry's newspaper/tabloid *The Daily Report*, which, in addition to Tree's articles, featured a scandal about the PM or one of his right-hand men virtually every week. Curry's copiously corrosive rumour-spreading made it fashionable to say out loud what people only whispered. The private lives and suspect financial affairs of the PM and countless other politicians became front page news. True or false, once something appeared in *The Daily Report* it might just as well be fact, because people treated it as such.

Despite Maureen's passionate disapproval, Tree had gone to work for Curry because he promised him free rein. His Santa Maria College disappointments behind him, Tree envisioned himself as the courageous reporter covering the darker side of Safe Haven life, and Curry, an enigmatic half-a-Conchy Joe who spent most of his nights drinking Rum and Cokes at Tommie Tommie's, didn't seem to care. Word was that Curry had been living in England for the last fifteen years and had come back to settle an old score with the PM. No one knew where he got the money to start the paper. No one knew what the PM had done to Curry that would make the newspaperman attack him so ferociously. But they figured he must not have had much family left in Santa Maria if he could attack the Government with so little hesitation.

To combat the fall in tourism revenue and remind the people of just how important the industry was to their welfare, the Prime Minister thought it best to become Minister of Tourism himself. Santa Marians were becoming ruder and ruder to tourists every day and something had to be done. So the new Minister of Tourism dressed up as a bellboy at the Hotel Impérial. He was sixty years old. He carried people's bags to their rooms and took tips. There were pictures in all the papers of the smiling black Prime Minister of Santa Maria carrying bags for the white tourists, all of whom looked on quite pleased. "Oh, how sweet!" they seemed to be saying. "Yeah, what a marvelous idea!" "And such a charming guy, too!" The PM felt he had masterminded a public relations coup.

But for Backadabush people, their leader was supposed to be a warrior, not a stooge. For all these years he had served as the voice of condemnation against the white man, his money, his businesses, his crooked schemes. The whole hotel affair looked sweet, but was bitter-bitter to the stomach. "What the hell he doin' dat for?" they asked, gathering in circles to look at the pictures. "Look how da man makin' a ass a hissef for dem whities!" "Gat himself for a damn poppy show!" Things only got worse after that.

The Prime Minister's parents passed away. They had been with him during all his years in power and now they were gone. First his father, then his mother left the living. One year after the other. A people who should have been filled with sympathy for their leader became disturbingly callous. These funerals, and the visible grief they inflicted on the PM and his family, became a spectacle that the powerless soaked up like flies on waste. The nation ogled and whispered. *The Daily Report* led the way. Moses was becoming human. He cried like every other man. He was not invincible. For the first time, people noticed that their warrior-king was getting old. The man who was rumoured to swim for a mile every day at the crack of dawn, regardless of the weather, now seemed frail, exhausted, beatable for the first time.

Then he made what seemed to Tree to be three critical mistakes, mistakes which soured the entire Election campaign. The first mistake was deciding to celebrate the twenty-fifth year of black Majority Rule and of PNF power. The Government released commemorative stamps that immortalized certain scenes from the struggle. The Prime Minister and his first Cabinet figured prominently. Certain dead politicians were declared saints. The newspapers carried retrospectives. The PNF financed an ad campaign in which old men and women with white heads reminisced about the days of old, when blacks had nothing. These ads urged people not to forget where they came from, not to forget that it was thanks to the PNF that they had running water and electricity and schools to send their children to. A big celebration was planned in Safe Haven National Park. Free food and drink for everyone. One huge anniversary party. But Santa Maria people did not respond. Only stragglers and ragamuffins came to the party. They drank up the liquor, swallowed the food, caused a ruckus, and left. The Prime Minister was shocked. What had the PNF said or done to offend? Weren't the people grateful for all he had done?

The fanfare and commemoration created not gratitude and nostalgia but discontent. It was as if the people had been in a daze for twenty-five years and this anniversary business woke them up. Suddenly, a nation of somnambulists was roused and started asking questions. *Twenty-five years? Is been dat long? By damn. And I still strugglin'. I still ain' gat a job. But look how fat all dese PNF done get? And what dey celebratin' 'bout? Ain' no work. What dey do for me lately? Twenty-five years. Das way too long. Too damn long.* Tree didn't like what he was hearing in the streets and in the barbershops.

The second big mistake. Perhaps finally aware of his own mortality, the PM began thinking about his legacy, about what he would leave behind when his days were done. He felt that after twenty-five years as Leader he could now ask for something in return. He wanted his son to enter the House of Assembly. And rather than have his son run for an easy seat, he wanted him to be tried in fire. He wanted his son's victory to deal a blow to the FLP. He put him up against one of the most successful politicians in the Opposition, someone whom everyone in the country, regardless of their political affiliation, admired.

No one liked the idea. Even PNF supporters wondered what the hell was going on. Why do this, when other people had been waiting in line for so long, waiting patiently for their turn to get into Parliament? People wondered if he was using his son as a decoy; wondered whether the PM hoped that everyone would direct their contempt and frustration toward his son, that seeing his son lose would make it easier for them to bear a sixth straight PNF victory. Others saw it as down-right selfish and nepotistic. Who did the PM think he was, Papa Doc? Did he think people wanted to be living under his family forever? Again the Prime Minister could not understand it. Again he was appalled at the degree of ingratitude and disrespect these people were capable of, these people he had done so much for. The FLP had two father-son tandems, and no one seemed to be at all disturbed by it. Why was this one so outrageous? It wasn't as if he had named his son Deputy Prime Minister or anything like that.

Then the final blow. "How could he have done this?," Tree asked himself. "Why tamper with a machine that was working so perfectly?" It was this final act by the Prime Minister, when there were only seven months left in the campaign, which opened Tree's eyes and revealed the secret. Tree had never thought of the Prime Minister's scoliosis in symbolic terms because it was always there, it was so everyday. It had been in front of his eyes since boyhood. In front of everyone's eyes. It was such a part of the Prime Minister's image that Tree had been unable to dissect it, could not separate it from the man and think of it in terms of the magic it wielded. Not until the Prime Minister went away on a sabbatical to New York and had the spinal defect corrected. All the papers said was that the Prime Minister had gone away to have "a long-standing illness treated." It was totally out of character for the PM to leave the country so close to a General Election. People talked, but no one knew exactly what was happening. Now it was late May, and with the Elections only three months away people were getting edgy.

When he saw the Prime Minister walk toward the podium Tree knew immediately that something was different. He didn't have that usual jerking saunter. Somehow, he seemed slightly straighter. The immediate effect was devastating. Tree wondered if only he noticed the difference. Everyone seemed to be cheering as loudly as possible. Maybe they hadn't picked up on it. Maybe they felt they had to pretend not to notice. The PM is really trying to transform himself, Tree thought. To make himself into a new man.

The people will notice eventually. They won't appreciate it very much. They ga feel cheated somehow. Abandoned. Like he was no longer a part of them, no longer a fellow sufferer. Tree feared that this latest move would be greeted with even greater disapproval than all the rest.

But when he heard the giant speak, some of his anxiety slackened. The voice was the same. The gestures were the same. Still the righteous indignation. Still the talk of war, of confrontation, of struggle against the white man and his stooges, the FLP. The people must not be fooled, the PM was saying. The FLP had mostly black candidates, but they were still funded by the same secret hoard of Egyptians that had kept them in bondage for so long. The FLP served the ends of the white minority. Never mind you don' see them runnin' for office, backra controllin' tings in da background. Vote the FLP in and we will go right back to being hewers of wood and bearers of water. It was the same ole PM saying, "Let my people go." Tree relaxed. The Prime Minister and his party of Thaddeuses would prevail. Da more tings cheenge da more dey stay da seem damn way.

25

To come to a real understanding of the sense of joy and triumph Jahown felt in wearing his costume of the African Warrior
that New Year's Junkanoo—his thick, black locks dancing about
his shoulders and the muscles in his arms flexing as he struck the
cowbells together in syncopation with the drums that echoed and
re-echoed all around him, his heart pounding like the hooves of a
stallion at full gallop in the heat of confrontation—was to come to
a true knowledge of what the ancient masquerade meant to a people
robbed of the memory of their past, a people who had to make the
new soil on which they found themselves holy ground. Jahown
didn't care who won First Prize at the parade or about which of the
three big groups was awarded best costume, best music. This moment of Junkanoo was his moment, and he cherished it. It transported and transplanted him in an instant and forever. For it was
then and only then that he showed the world his true spirit, his true
self. Only then that he said loudly, yet without speaking, *"Dis me!
Dis me nah!"*

Passing through the burning portal of the music, he felt meta-
morphosed. Dancing in the majesty of his colours, with shield and

assegai strapped on, he was entranced, possessed by spirits the names of which he and his people had long forgotten. But the look of ecstasy and pain, of creation and terrible rage that ruled his expressions, that accentuated each movement of his awe-inspiring dance, was enough to prove to all the onlookers, if ever there was a doubt, that Junkanoo was, at its core, the highest expression of their free will, their dignity, their humanity. Junkanoo was more than license and clichéd acts of youthful defiance. It was life-giving. Junkanoo was the affirmation of the spirit that was in him and in all of them. And Waterfront Road, for those few hours of passage, became a luminous pathway upon which, his arms outstretched, lightning on his finger tips, Jahown was able to join his spirit with those of his countrymen, with those of the long gone.

That was the power of the masquerade. The power, in the moment, to weld the dancer and the dance, the mask and its wearer. It mattered not that to the outsider, to the tourist flashing his camera, scrambling to t'ief his soul, Jahown was simply performing a masque, was playing a role, that by eleven that New Year's morning the crowds of sweaty black people, exhausted and cleansed, would drag themselves home to sleep the best sleep of the year, that the streets would be swept and the groups would go back to their shacks and burn the costumes they had spent all year planning and building, that the night of make-believe would end and everything would be back to normal. For Jahown, there was no make-believe. He was as sure of the truth, the rightness of himself, as he was sure of his decision to leave medical school so many years before. That New Year's morning, that moment, that dance, melted together, became Jahown's declaration of self. That morning, moment, dance: the finest, surest, of his entire life.

And only by understanding that, by understanding how he had transcended the world in which he found himself, even as he walked on it and was a real part of it, can anyone hope to understand why Jahown did not wish the masquerade to be over, why he resisted the night dying into day, why he chose not to go home like everybody else and get some sleep.

It was because Jahown refused to have his sense of joy and triumph extinguished that he found himself, after the parade was over, walking in a different direction from everyone else. For while they were returning south to their homes in Backadabush, Jahown's face was turned west, along the shore. Away from downtown and toward the open beaches. Long after day clean, with the sun approaching its noontime peak, he walked the streets in full costume, not even removing his headpiece.

He was still in that trance, still possessed by the spirits of old forgotten things. The world all around him was silent. He walked in a cool stride for nearly twenty minutes. Buses taking tourists back to the hotels whisked by him, music blaring. Young people who had rented cars and hotel rooms for the night passed on the other side of the road, their night of license ended for another year. Time to go back home, reenter reality. When he got to Graham's Beach he took off his sandals and walked on the sand. He had never felt so contented. Bright-bright sun.

He show dem. Show dem what he really 'bout. He answer all they questions far as he concern. Show dem da time.

He paused and looked at the sea. A sloop could be seen on the horizon, its white sails taking advantage of the cool breeze that played with his dreadlocks. Jahown walked to the water's edge and let it come about his ankles. The sound of screaming broke into his consciousness, rupturing his peace.

She was standing all alone on the little dock that small boats sometimes pulled up on but which was mostly used as a diving board for boys in the summertime. She was a white woman. A tourist. Dressed as tourists dress, in khaki shorts, a straw hat, and one of those "Hey Mon" t-shirts they get from the souvenir shops. Jahown looked in her direction and then instinctively looked away once he saw who it was. But she screamed again. He turned. She was about one hundred yards away, jumping up and down on the dock's edge and looking in the water, at what he couldn't tell.

Jahown dropped his headpiece in the sand. His cowbells were looped about his waist and they clanked as he sprinted to the dock. The woman was blond and had a very bad case of sunburn. She'd been suckered into paying to get her hair braided. Now that he was on the dock he could hear what she was saying. There was no one else on the beach, but over her screams came the sound of something splashing in the water. He could not yet see it.

"Oh God! Oh God! He's going to drown! Do something! You have to do something! Oh dear God!"

"What happen woman? Who ga drown?," he shouted as he approached.

"My boyfriend, Todd. He's drowning! Oh God. You have to do something. Christ, you've got to help him!"

He was standing beside her now and he could see the man.

"He cyaa swim?"

"He's stoned. Said he just wanted to go for a dip. I can't swim . . . He's caught a cramp. Oh please mister, you've got to do something before it's too late!"

Jahown was standing beside her now. The man was about twenty feet away. He looked completely terrified and was getting tired. He flailed wildly, his arms reaching for something that wasn't there.

"Woman, I cyaa swim. I cyaa swim. Ain' nuttin I could do."

"Help . . . help . . . mister . . . Sarah . . . I . . ."

He was swallowing salt water and coughing. His face was red, and yellow mucus covered his nose and mouth. He spoke as if he hadn't much air left inside him.

"For Jesus sake! He's drowning!"

"Ain' nuttin I could do miss."

Jahown was on the very edge now and she was holding onto his arm, squeezing, urging him to jump in. Pushing him and he was resisting.

"Miss, I ain' never been in the sea in my life. I cyaa help him. Lemme go run to the gas station across the road and fetch somebody quick. Hol' on mister! Relax!"

"Listen you goddam nigger in a monkey suit, Get in the fuckin' water and save my fiance! Because if he drowns on this no good fuckin' shithole of an island, I swear I'll . . ."

She shoved him.

Jahown half fell, half jumped in the cold water.

Todd went down and came back up gasping for air, his eyes open wide in shock and hysteria, his arms reaching out now as if to God. Jahown moved toward him, swimming in a dog paddle. When he got to him the man held on with all the strength he had left in his body.

"Help . . . help me . . . mister . . . please . . ."

"Keep still man. Keep still. Stop actin' crazy."

"Oh God! Oh God! Bring him in! Bring him in!"

"I tryin', but tell him keep still!"

"Oh God! Oh Christ!"

"Help . . . Help me."

"Why you don' keep fuckin' still?"

Jahown was getting tired. The man was pulling him down. The blond named Sarah with the braids and the "Hey Mon" t-shirt kept screaming at the top of her lungs.

The man named Todd dug his nails into Jahown's flesh. The crepe-paper costume he had laboured over for so long was soaked through. Pieces of various colours broke off and floated atop the water.

Salt burns the eyes, the throat, the stomach.

Spit blood.

Jahown looked to the sky. Bright-bright sun.

26

Tree tried to excuse his behaviour since meeting Sir Thaddeus by telling himself that there really was no right or wrong way to live in Santa Maria, no right or wrong way to get what you wanted. He figured it didn't matter what he said or did, just as what he wrote in *The Daily Report* never seemed to matter. Because he had been Robert Curry's smart ass he was licensed. Whatever outrage or idiocy he might write about would be tuned out anyway. He believed, in spite of it all, that the PNF would do what it had always done: win. He could write about white businessmen burning down their own foodstores or social misfits sending out distress signals all he wanted. It would not change the world he lived in.

But Tree's grandmother Jewel once made an observation that he would only now appreciate. His mother was making one of her daily visits to Bell's house and had accused Jewel during their conversation of being too much of a softy. Accused her, in essence—while Tree looked on, sitting on the edge of the bed from which his grandmother had not moved in four years—of always letting people run over her. He wasn't quite sure who she'd been run over by because he hadn't been listening closely at first.

To this accusation Jewel calmly responded by reminding her daughter of the nature and ways of that scrawny but wise survivor, the potcake. This animal is constantly abused by its master. Its tail is always pulled by him in provocation, and the master enjoys this type of teasing immensely. The dog does nothing at first, appearing shocked that it is being victimized by the object of its devotion in so callous a fashion. Eventually it responds to these tail-pullings by feigning anger and acting as if it is going to bite the hand of its owner. This persists for a while, until the feigning of the dog is taken for granted. It is then that the potcake becomes sick of the master's abuse of privilege and the game is over. The dog buries its teeth in his outstretched hand. Tree was about to learn that Santa Marians were the potcakes of the world.

For a very long time, the cynics assumed that Santa Marians had done nothing about Government corruption because they were themselves a lawless people prone to disorder. That they were too fat, too docile to stand up, fight, and suffer the consequences. But the problem in Santa Maria was not lawlessness. Neither was the problem one of outright disorder, nor disorder grown unrecognizable by its permanence. The problem was not a lack of distinction between "right and wrong," nor the capacity to fight "wrong" when it revealed itself. Yes, drug dealers had been allowed to live the life of glamour virtually unmolested by police. Customs Officers continued to charge shoppers returning from the U.S. with boxes of goods large sums of money, while letting their families and friends go by free of charge. Politicians were awarding themselves free business licenses, free plane tickets, all-expense-paid trips, excessive pay increases, and extravagant pensions. People accepted bribes and gave bribe money to others. People bought licenses of every kind and government officials forged cheques, misappropriated funds, and awarded themselves interest-free loans at the Treasury's expense under embarrassingly false pretenses.

But there was never lawlessness as *they* understood it. Lawlessness to most Santa Marians meant gun-toting ruffians committing rape, robbery, and plunder. Lawlessness meant rioting and looting and burning. Lawlessness meant assassinations, coups d'état, civil wars, and mutilations. Lawlessness meant blowing up the hotels or raiding the cruise ships and holding all the white people hostage. Lawlessness meant riddling innocent men and women with bullets as they lined up to vote on Election Day. Behaviour of this kind required a sense of desperation that Santa Marians did not possess—yet. A faith in the redemptive power of violence that their history had never taught them. Lawlessness did not mean the breaking of laws that were inconvenient and counterproductive for poor folks to obey in the first place, laws in which they were never invested, that they had been given but had not themselves devised or accepted.

Severe conditions of physical brutality and despair, the kind of brutality and despair that might lead an entire people to believe in an apocalyptic violence, had not existed in Santa Maria. The absence of sugar and the failure of cotton in the islands had kept the plantations small and the incidences of men having gunpowder ignited in their anuses to a minimum. And because such bloodletting had never been an overwhelming part of black Santa Marians' history, it was never a feature of its recent political revolution. The ballot was enough.

The violence that most Santa Marians knew was the violence of the juvenile delinquent and the rogue, the violence of the streets of Safe Haven. Downtrodden people killing each other because they could not get at the real source of their troubles. Certainly, these incidents were sufficient to frighten many of the people of Maureen Bodie's generation, people who had no experience of the anonymous cruelty of cities. They had no frame of reference, no previous experiences which could help them to process this outpouring of exasperation: a criminal violence, a violence of smuggled weapons and Chinese grocery store robberies, of stabbings and cutlass slappings in public school hallways, of gang war. Tree witnessed shades of this at school and in Pompey Village. Firsborn had to an extent lived it during the years of torment. To some extent this violence was romanticization, a borrowing of gestures from the cities of America, gestures seen in rap videos and action movies, gestures of a gun culture glamourized in dance hall reggae tunes that had found themselves transplanted to Safe Haven's narrow alleyways. Some of it had that air of defiant fraudulence that characterized Small Pint's writing the words "No Law" on the school wall. Small Pint could never see that act during high school as somehow contradicting his sole ambition of being a Defence Force Officer because the words meant nothing, the act of vandalism was rebellion enough. But if they borrowed another people's gestures, it was only because it captured how they felt, because it was all they had at their disposal. The most hopeless of them made these borrowed gestures of rage their own. And meant them.

The truth was that the people had never been blind to anything. It was never the case that they hadn't noticed how these men of power neglected public education while sending their children to boarding schools in The States, Canada, and England. It was never the case that people hadn't noticed when, all of a sudden, in the last year or two of the PNF's fifth term, these same men had to make more frequent trips to Miami, Orlando, and Fort Lauderdale to buy diapers, soap, shampoo, cosmetics, school supplies, shoes, shirts, dresses, underwear, cars, even chicken, beef, and pork chops, because Santa Maria's wholesalers and retailers were raising prices too high. It was never the case that people hadn't seen the four Low-Price Food Stores go up in flames, only to be replaced with brand new ones without a single official entertaining the possibility that arson had been involved. It was not that people hadn't been aware of the Haitian immigrants who had been doing their gardening ever since black Majority Rule had made Santa Marians too important to pull up their weeds themselves. It was not that people hadn't noticed that the Prime Minister, and many politicians in both parties, had become millionaires and lived in mansions that could swallow a hundred of their clapboard houses. People noticed. Had always known. There was no such thing in Santa Maria as a secret.

What Tree and the politicians did not realize was that the people had remained obedient, even after Majority Rule, to an unwritten law they established for themselves long long ago. And it was this obedience, mistaken by some for lawlessness, which shocked the PNF and brought about their sound defeat on Election Day. It was this obedience which shocked and humbled the Prime Minister; shocked and humiliated politicians like Sir Thaddeus, who thought that Moses's mere presence at a rally in a poor area of an island would guarantee victory as it had in the past. This obedience is what surprised Tree when the Election results came in two weeks after the service his mother had organized for him in the Sinking Church.

When the service was held he'd already been notified that he would be receiving a Government scholarship. He felt terrible, and he fantasized about leaving Safe Haven and returning many years later, when he would be unrecognizable to everyone, even those closest to him. After betraying the cause they had fought for at Santa Maria College, after losing the respect of Jahown, of Stooley, and, he suspected, of Elsa, he could not trust himself to be true to any promise, could not trust himself to deserve anyone's admiration or faith. He expected only to bring his mother further disgrace, more than Firsborn had already given. He expected only to betray Elsa's trust even further. Not because he wanted to, but because he had no idea who he would become once he left home. He was afraid that he had no centre which might keep him strong, keep him whole in the years ahead.

* * *

Fruit Vendor 1: Bush crack and man gone, chile!

Fruit Vendor 2: Gal! You ever see?

Fruit Vendor 1: I hear his heart give out on him, too.

Fruit Vendor 2: No!

Fruit Vendor 1: Yes!

Fruit Vendor 2: Serve him right. Spreadin' dem lies 'bout Maxwell Brown. What go aroun' come aroun'.

Fruit Vendor 1: Jus' wuzzan right. Heeza good man. Decent. Never once open his mout' ta t'row lowness. How you t'ink his parents an' ting feel hearin' dat foolishness and seein' it all in the paper? An' it ain' true. Ain' true at all. He jus' ain' fin' da right gal yet. Das all. I hear dey even had da man and his campaign manager in custody, talkin' 'bout dey wan' lock dem up for buggery! If it wuzzan for Mr. Lightbourne boy from Pompey Village, da one who win da Baton a Honour, dey woulda had him in jail an' ting.

Fruit Vendor 2: What!? No!

Fruit Vendor 1: Yes! You ain' hear 'bout dat? I figure errybody in Safe Haven mussie hear dat piece a news by now. Had dem in cuffs and erryting, ready to t'row dem in jail.

Fruit Vendor 2: Jeeeeeesus!

Fruit Vendor 1: Come to find out dey was jus' sittin' in da car plannin' dey strategy. An' I hear Sir Tajus mix up in dat business too. Gal, he gone too far an' it all backfire in he face dis time. Dis new Gobmen' ga get tada bottom all dis foolishness! He mussie was gettin' desperate, try'na put da police up to arrest dat woman chile.

Fruit Vendor 2: Da people dem vote for Maxwell Brown jus' ta spite him!

Fruit Vendor 1: Ha haiiieee!

Fruit Vendor 2: Well chile, I glad to see Tajus lose. Was too damn cheap. All of a sudden he try'na give people t-shirt and beer. Where he was da las' five damn years! Too little too damn late, baby!

Fruit Vendor 1: I hear dat!

Fruit Vendor 2: Erry Christmas since da las' Election Maxwell Brown been in Hawkins Town buyin' people ham and turkey. Mudda's Day he is bring card and flower. You don' see Tajus Mckinney 'til Election two mont's away. An' dey ain' even pave Hawkins Town roads! What Election dey t'ink dey was gone win and dey ain' tar da roads?

Fruit Vendor 1: Well listen here, I hear say people was callin' up Tajus house all night once Election results was in. Callin' up ta he house and cussin' all kinda stink words. Tellin' him da PNFs was gone get wha's comin' tadem and he gern straight ta jail for what he do to Maxwell Brown. Tellin' him he better don' set foot out his house for least a week 'less he wan' get polt wit' rock!

Fruit Vendor 2: Lord in the mornin'. No!

Fruit Vendor 1: Yes! And I hear da police been ta he house firs' ting dis mornin' an' 'fore dey was half way finish sayin' what dey had to say ta him he fall out wit' heart attack or stroke or sumptin' and dey had to call ambulance forrim.

Fruit Vendor 2: Well what you t'ink do him so?

Fruit Vendor 1: Chile, I ain' know, but it couldn'a been good news what dey bring forrim dis mornin'. An' plus, dem people callin' his house all night and passin' by shoutin' had him on edge a'ready. I hear plenty a dem Gobmen' minister was gettin' harrassin' phone call an' ting all t'rough da night. Cyaa find none a dem 'round town today. Dey lock up in dey house wit' dey phone off da hook.

Fruit Vendor 2: Bush crack an' man gone, for true for true.

Fruit Vendor 1: And I hear dis new Gobmen' havin' Commission a Inquiry an' dey gone bring all dem PNF politician on da witness stand to accoun' for what dey t'ief out da people dem Treasury and for how bad dey manage we country.

Fruit Vendor 2: Well dey could have all da Commission dey wan'. I ain' interested. I jus' wan' wha's comin' ta me. Sissy or no sissy, Maxwell Brown bes' deliver on dat job tada Ministry a Works for my son or it'll be me and him!

Fruit Vendor 1: I hear dat!

* * *

What Tree had failed to understand, what he saw on election night with great clarity, was that in order to sustain themselves in this strange land, African slaves and the sons and daughters of African slaves had come to an unspoken understanding. The understanding was that in their newfound Egypt there were two laws: the law their masters laid down, and the law that they themselves, if they were to survive, should obey.

They could reject the Conchy Joe's sense of time, his sedate way of singing, his notion of the Spirit, his ignorance of the uses of roots and leaves, because these were laws that not even the power of force could make them obey. And, in a time when men of their own skin colour and texture of hair became the rulers, they could accept those who had nothing claiming for themselves that which had been denied them. They understood the overwhelming sense of past lack that came with the first opportunity at having. Had they not all been poor and hungry for four hundred years? Had they not all been forced to walk the roads wearing rags, eating pig's feet and sheep's tongues? Were they not all just now being called Sir and Ma'am and not plain old nigger and darky? How then could one complain about potholes, about streets without names and houses without numbers?

Their patience was monumental. But it was not infinite. That neurotic taking-in-a-hurry in which their leaders were engrossed was well noted. The people may have been taught to despise the colour of their skins, the shape of their noses, and the texture of their hair, but they were not fools. Jack dumb but he ain' stupid. They may have been obsessed with those trappings of the world outside that the revolution had brought with it, but they still understood betrayal. They had let these, their leaders, enjoy the stardom that power afforded. They had let them act as the chosen translators of the language and ways of the Outside World. But they had never let their politicians forget who it was that they served. Every Member of Parliament was accountable to the most lowly of any community, could be asked at any moment, in any place, for money, for a job, for compensation for the privilege of having. And any politician who valued his position was ready to oblige, ready to chew out any employer for firing a member of his constituency, no matter how incompetent or insubordinate that person had been.

In the people's eyes, the man who took was not necessarily a threat, as long as he did not stop others from taking when their time came. The man who took and took, and not only took but prevented, even hated to see others take, this man had gone too far. This man was not only breaking backra's laws—which only those who had never experienced having nothing obeyed anyway—but was breaking the law of the people. He was no longer Moses or one of Moses's men, he was Pharaoh, one of Pharaoh's men. He was a black backra.

In the days when Jewel Bodie and Maureen Bodie were much younger the Prime Minister had become the people's champion. He was a man who had nothing. Almost all of the men who followed him were the same way. The Prime Minister's having nothing had made him fearless. He and his men saw little consequence in being reckless. In the storybook past which Tree and his generation could only gain access to as schoolchildren in Social Studies classes, and by way of textbooks with black-and-white photos depicting the drama of a turmoil that faded with the victory of the people's bloodless revolution, the Prime Minister had carried out all the selfless acts required of a leader in a colony in crisis. He suffered imprisonment. He led marches. He disrupted the affairs of the House of Assembly. He tossed the ancient mace, symbol of the power of the Crown, the power of backra at home and abroad, out of the window of the House and into the waiting, shouting crowd of blacks in the street below: an act of intimidation and defiance; a show of deadly resolve. The white minority wilted. "This is the symbol of power. And power belongs to the people. But the people are there in the streets. Outside in the hot sun. The mace belongs there too." His words were memorized in Junior Schools everywhere. Blacks ruled.

The man with nothing became a hero. He became "The Prime Minister." He became the object of the affection and prayers of countless gray-haired women with their hands clasped. As the Prime Minister rode through the streets of Grand Santa Maria in his huge, navy blue, chauffeur driven limousine, he maintained the posture, through the tinted glass, of a man in deep meditation, contemplating the continued and justifiable scattering of his foes, the foes of the people: the Conchy Joe and his black puppets in the Opposition. That first election victory twenty-five years ago had come on January 10th, the tenth day of the first month; the descendants of slaves needed no other proof that the days of the Bible were again being lived, that as the Israelites had been delivered so too were black folk, that God had spoken, that He had picked his man.

But Tree's generation was born into black Majority Rule, born into Independence. They never knew what it meant to have nothing, to shit in the bush (except by choice) and sleep on grass beds, to be called nigger and darky (except by others who were also black). For them pig's feet and sheep's tongue had lost significance as the master's leftovers and had become delicacies. Their parents tried to give them everything they themselves had been denied. And the result was the migration from underdeveloped settlements on islands like Runaway, La Ventana, Little Santa Maria, St. Mark's, and Ferdinand, to Grand Santa Maria and its growing city, Safe Haven, to work as bus and taxi drivers, waiters, hotel maids, cooks, glass-bottom-boat skippers, straw vendors, police officers, civil servants, bank clerks, teachers, accountants, lawyers, doctors. The result had been cars, television, satellite dishes, VCRs, electricity, telephones, running water, and indoor toilets, where before there were only old story time, kerosene lamps, water from the well, and nannying in the outhouse.

The world of Bible-times began to recede. And although they could not totally dismiss it, this new generation became more and more cynical toward the notion of the Prime Minister's command over the supernatural. To Tree's generation, which read many books from many parts of the world and was going to Santa Maria College and University abroad in record numbers, was weaned on American television, and to whom growing yam and cassava in the backyard was not as important as buying hamburgers on Waterfront Road, their parents and grandparents' view of the world was something they could not relate to. It was fast becoming shadowy and illegitimate. The Maureens felt they were ungrateful, disrespectful of the struggles and achievements of their elders. But the truth was that in one generation people Tree's age were already far removed from the past that the Prime Minister and his aging disciples had shaped. They felt no covenant with them. They were impatient. They were hungry. They did not wish to be left out in the cold.

And it was Tree's generation which saw the Prime Minister—when the prosperity had dried up, when the drug planes stopped flying, when the hotels were empty, when the scandals that had always been taking place seemed more significant because no one had American dollars to burn any more—not as Moses but as Pharaoh. The young saw him not as the courageous, black barrister raising holy hell with backra, but as an old man. An old gray man who did not speak to them. Who lived in big Whitehall Mansion and didn't give a damn. An old gray man whose time was a time of storybook drama. An old man whose achievements took place before they were born. A man whose magic was withered and dead. A man leading a country whose finest moments, in only a quarter of a century, were already behind it. The young, and some of the older generation, now felt that the leaders of the country had gone back into the pot one too many times, that the game should end, and the dog should cease to feign on the next pull of its tail. The young and those of the older generation who felt they had been betrayed saw not Daniel but Nebuchadnezzar.

It did not matter by that time who the Opposition was. As long as its leader was a dark-enough black man they were satisfied. It helped that he was a protégé of the PM who had been expelled from the PNF years earlier for calling for Moses's resignation after the Commission of Inquiry. He was black and brass. Just how they liked it. To the PM's obeah snake the Opposition Leader responded with the power of his obeah hat. The PM was called Sweet Mout' for all the lies he made sound like truth. The Opposition Leader was called Mr. Biggity. In all the elections past the various light-skinned leaders of the Opposition had been unable to win the people's trust. This new man, this man reared by the PM, would do the trick.

A vote for the Opposition on that day, however, was really a vote against the PM and the PNF. The Opposition had promised jobs, pay cuts for the MPs, a proper programme to curb the influx of Haitians fleeing persecution and poverty, an end to victimization and corruption. But really, there was no difference between the parties. No one believed the Opposition to be populated by men any less corrupt than those who had been in power for the last twenty-five years. The issue was the unwritten law. The Opposition's greatest asset was that it had not been in power yet.

Santa Marians had needed and sought a Moses, had stayed with the PNF for twenty-five years because they, as a people, were faced with a common Enemy who plagued them; an Enemy that seemed aligned, synonymous with Evil itself; an Enemy that was responsible for them all having nothing. Back then they could be sure who the evil ones were on sight. Being black automatically numbered you among the saints, among the sufferers. Now, people weren't quite sure who could be trusted. Now you couldn't take anyone for granted.

● ● ● ● ●

FREE LIBERAL PARTY
WINS BY LANDSLIDE!!

—by Tree Bodie, Daily Report *Staff Writer*

Under light rain the citizens of Safe Haven City danced in the streets last night as the results of the Santa Marian General Elections were announced over Radio One. The ruling Progressive National Front, after twenty-five years in power, was soundly defeated 35 seats to 7. Ironically, the now former Prime Minister was correct in declaring during his campaign speeches that the people would be brought home to victory on "Flight 357." Unfortunately, it was his PNF that got the 7 seats and the Free Liberal Party that won the 35.

Only moments after the announcement the new Prime Minister gave a live interview at FLP Headquarters which was televised by Channel One News. The scene was one of jubilation as the new PM, in between being doused with champagne by supporters, declared that "freedom and democracy had at last prevailed in the Santa Marias." Urging his supporters to "celebrate peacefully," he asked for everyone's prayers as his party sought to right the wrongs committed by the former Government.

Later that evening, Radio One broadcasted the outgoing Prime Minister's concession speech via telephone linkup from Crab Bay to Safe Haven. The PM's usually resonant voice, which has been the trademark of the man many have considered the Caribbean's foremost head of state and most cunning politician, had more than a trace of sadness and exhaustion to it. He congratulated the new Prime Minister on his victory. After conceding defeat, he complimented the Santa Marian people for achieving a peaceful transition of power and successfully utilising the democratic process to express their will.

These are the final words of the new Opposition Leader's address: "Our people, the citizens of this wonderful little democracy we call Santa Maria, have spoken. We must heed their words, for they have spoken nobly. The voice of the people, as the elders say, is the voice of God. How then can I raise a fist in dissension? I give my utmost thanks to the people of Santa Maria who blessed me these past twenty-five years with an opportunity to serve them as best I could. For that opportunity I am eternally grateful. The new Prime Minister has defeated me fair and square and for that he deserves congratulations. Because of the economic hardships that we have suffered in recent years and his promises of employment and economic growth, he has achieved tremendous popularity throughout the nation. The problem with this popularity is that it has unleashed a wild beast. I only hope that he will be able to contain that beast. For if he cannot contain it, I think there will be very, very bleak days ahead."

So it was that on August 28th the PNF was voted out of power and the FLP became the Government of the people. Numerous PNF incumbents lost their seats this General Election. Especially surprising were pivotal seats in grassroots areas of Backadabush which were PNF strongholds. Among those former MPs who will not be retaining their seats in Parliament are Sir Thomas Smith, who lost Rolles Town; Sir Alfred Gibson, who lost Phillips Town; and Sir Thaddeus Rudolph McKinney, former Minister of Education, who was soundly defeated in Hawkins Town by a margin of 5 to 1.

Sir Thaddeus is said to have been committed to the Intensive Care Unit of Queen's Royal Hospital early this morning after being summoned to appear before Magistrate Helen Burrows in connection with a case of police brutality and unlawful arrest involving the new MP for Hawkins Town, The Hon. Maxwell Brown. Up to press time this afternoon no word has been given on Sir Thaddeus's condition, but he is believed to have suffered a mild stroke.

(Tree Bodie has worked for us for two years. He will be leaving to pursue a Bachelor's Degree in the United States. We wish him the best. R.C., Editor and Chief)

27
Mamma

Harrican come an' 'mos' bruck up all da land. Harrican come, dashin' and smashin' erry Chris' ting in sight. Never see nuttin like it in my born days. Mamma tell me 'bout storm like dis but I ain' never see none so. I 'member when lightnin' dance on da wall in da All Age School an scal' errybody back. Seerus business. But I ain' never see nuttin like dis here so in all my born days dis side a Creation. Tunda and lightnin' gone to bed. And rain so hard I t'ought ma windahs was gone broke.

Do Jesus, what a ting. Is a sign. I know is a sign. My people headin' for hard times. Hard times ahead, ah tell ya. Everybody know Santa Maria is a place don't have harrican. Sumtin 'bout da wind direction, da flat land, and the shallow water dey say, 'cause been only one or two seerus-seerus harrican since my mamma born. Hell fire.

Had to set dem lazy boy-chirren to work. Nailin' plywood over my windahs and cuttin' down dat ole pine tree what been standing dere since Noah build da Ark. When ya look dat ole tree fall on top my house? Do Jesus, no.

Never see win' and rain so. Air raw-raw from lightnin'. Rain drop like it ga cut you. What a time, what a time. I hear plenty dead. Mash up, shock up, and drown. You ever see? Ain' no one is dead from no harrican in Santa Maria. We too lucky, das why. Too damn lucky. God ga show us, dough. Show us straight. Errybody sittin here takin' storm warnin' for joke. Waitin' las' minute 'til the wind pick up to buy plywood, lantern, and radio battrie. Lord rest their souls who pass.

What a ting. An' my las' chile waitin' to go off to School. Is a sign. I want dis sky clear up quick-quick. I tell him he sittin' his narrow behind right here in Santa Maria 'til God business done do. When I see blue-blue sky I ga let him go. What he so hurry to leave his ma for I don' know. Hurry to go crash in plane, hey? Humph!

But what a storm, dough? And right dere so, two days after Election. Votin' even een finish good harrican come bus'in' up da place. I declare. God's will be done. These Santa Maria folk ga see jus' what comin' deir way, 'bout dey changin' Government. They ga remember when dey mout' turn white from hunger. Is a sign you see dis harrican business lick us just we done vote out the PM. God ain' please. Das what I say. New PM ain' scratch he head good yet he gat to go runnin' 'bout da place inspeckin' damage. Lord have mercy. Dese young people, man. Is dese young people vote the PNF out. Need a new breed. Too much gravalicious fellas hice up under the PM, t'iefin lef' right and centre. Is dem what cause him lose dis Election.

Never mind dat.

Thank you, Lord, for sparing my life. And ma boy-chirren. And ma Mamma, Jewel Macintosh Bodie. Send my las' chile off to School. Let him do right. He's a good boy. If he stick witchoo I know he'll be jus' fine.

What a storm dough. Tear down ma sour sop tree. Take so long for dat to catch and now it uproot. So be it. I ain' ga cry. Could plant a nex' one.

Had a seerus dream las' night, in da middle a dat storm. I swear. What a time.

See my Granma. First time since I was a little girl. See her clear as day. Standin' beside my bed, smilin' at me. See my mother's mother. Sure as day.

Wuzzan scared dough. What to scared for? I know what dey say. I know dey say when ya see um ya time near. But da Lord strong in me. And he ain' tell me say is my time yet. She just want to talk. I know say she just want to come tell me is all right. Erryting is alright.

Come to tell me a secret, see. Sumtin don' nobody know. Not even my Mamma. Is 'cause a man. 'Cause man gat bad ways. 'Cause the Half-a-Scotsman had bad ways. But he cyaa hol' her now. She in Guinea, where her people from. Cyaa hol' my Grammy no more. Half-a-Scotsman lock in he grave. Lock here, but my Grammy gone. Leave dat name they give her right there on the tombstone. Pick up her ole name again. Ha haieee!

Lord, I tell you. What a ting. Dis storm wuzzan no joke. Is seerus omens.

My Granma come back from Guinea to tell me sumtin. I goin' right now to see my mamma, Jewel Macintosh Bodie. Gone take dis benny for the benny cake, and gone tell her da news. Gone tell her what the Half-a Scotsman keep from the bot' a us all dese years. Tell me her name, man. Her real name.

Rachel? Humph! Better go from roun' here wit' dat. Fumi. Dat is da name of my mother's mother. We comin' full circle, we people, wrench from our place, born to make a new place home. Full circle. Fumi is my Granma name. Salt water, tunda and lightnin', blood an' da grave, bring us full circle. FUMI!

28

Firsborn began to heal. It was a gradual process. The hurried trip to Crazyhill was a beginning. Every day Maureen Bodie would visit her son in the hospital and take him food she had cooked just for him. She'd sit and talk with him, tell him everything would be alright and that she would pray. The doctors asked her permission to give him electrical shocks to the head. She refused. She said he needed healing, but not that kind. Deep down she knew that the anguish of her son was the anguish of the restless, of God's gifted who had failed and could not bear the sitting still; just as she, in her time, could not bear it. He was her son after all. She took him home.

She prayed at his door each morning and made the sign of the cross. She sang a hymn as she worked in the kitchen. She made him breakfast and gave him tea. He looked broken and lost. She would sit and talk to him in the early hours before she went to work. *You muss give up the poison.*

Firsborn stayed in his room. He refused to go out. He knew if he went out what would happen. He laid on the bed and fought the monsters in his head, in his body. Maureen brought him cigarettes each day and kept feeding him.

The voices were still in his head but he was fighting the body-thirst. He took to eating chocolate and other sweets, to drinking a six-pack of coca cola each day. Substitutes for the rock. Maureen got him another job. Working for a dry cleaner. He straightened himself up and started to work. The job kept his hands busy the whole day. That was good.

Still the voices in his head. How to stop the voices. A psychologist from Crazyhill suggested depressants. Maureen gave in because the doctor said it was harmless. He took them and they calmed him down. Got rid of the voices telling him to do this and do that. But he started gaining weight. The pills made him dizzy. He stopped taking them. Maureen did not argue.

Still she prayed and made the sign of the cross. Still she cooked him good food and made him tea. Still the hymn in the morning and the talks.

The boy need sumtin. Sumtin to live for.

That's when it hit her. Driving home from work she saw the land for sale and called the realtor the next morning. She made the down payment on the land and gave him the deed. *Dis for you. Dis yours. Dis sumtin you can do. Show people what you could do wit' your hands. Wit' what God give you. Make your self sumtin so people could see and say, "Dere is sumtin Firsborn do." Take dis deed and finish da payments. Buil' yasef a house. Each one a us muss have sumtin what ain' nobody own but ours. Yes?*

Firsborn threw himself into the land. He worked hard at the job and he saved his money. He made the payments. He drew a plan of his house and Maureen showed it to the architect. He bought a pickax and shovel. He dug his own foundation. Each day after work, each morning before work, each weekend, he laboured on the dream. He sweated the thirst out of his body. He worked the voices out of his head. The house filled him. He bought each brick, carried it to the lot, and put it in place. Maureen saw and said God is good. The house was inspected and approved. She brought in men to help put on the roof. Only the interior and the windows were still needed. Firsborn had been out of trouble for two straight years. He went to work on time. He came home. He bothered no one. No one bothered him. He got in no fights with his brothers. Then he saved two thousand dollars and bought himself a used car so he didn't have to ride the bus. One day they saw him driving in the new car with a woman in the passenger seat. Tree and his brothers were shocked at the transformation. They had all expected their brother to be dead by now. Killed or found in a gutter somewhere overdosed. Maureen saw and said God is good.

After the hurricane Tree went with Firsborn to see if the house had been damaged. Once they were satisfied that nothing had gone wrong they sat on the steps and talked. For years now Firsborn had not spoken to his youngest brother in a way that was not meant to intimidate or to threaten. He asked Tree where he was going to school and what he planned to do. They watched the birds in the twilight sky, their flight plans altered by the recent storm. The world around them seemed new somehow. Like it had been given a second chance. Like after the Flood.

Then suddenly Firsborn started laughing. Tree didn't understand.

"What happen Firsborn?"

"I was jus' t'inkin'."

"T'inkin' 'bout what?"

"You know B' Bouki and B' Rabby?"

"Yeah."

"'Member Mamma use to talk old story?"

"Yeah, was good."

"Yeah. I jus' remember one, das all."

"Which one."

"'Bout how Rabby make B' Bouki he cart horse."

"How it go?"

"You ain' never hear it?"

"No man, how it go."

"Lemma tell ya. Once upon a time dese two gals was livin' in a house on a hill. Nah, B' Bouki say ta hesef, I gern check one a dese set. So B' Bouki gone dere a-courtin'. Get all dress up in he Sunday best and chit chattin'. Nex' ting ya know, B' Rabby spy da same two woman, so he figure he ga cramp B' Bouki style. He gone up so

♦ 269 ♦

an' say, 'Why yinna even studyin' B' Bouki? He ain' no man. Heez my fada cart horse.' So de nex' evenin' B' Bouki gone back t'inkin' he in straight wit' one a da gals. De gal say to him, 'B' Bouki, I cyaa study you no more. I t'ought you was a man. B' Rabby tell me say youz his fada cart horse.' B' Bouki was well screw. 'Say what? I is his pa what? Cart horse? I gone fin' dat no good Rabby right nah. Talkin' 'bout I is his pa cart horse. Gern bring him right here so. Make him take dat foolishness back!' Dat time B' Rabby takin' stock. He see B' Bouki haulin' ass in his direction, looking well vex. So he lay down in de bed and play sick. He start groanin' like he half dead. Bouki buss in da house wit' he face all buil' up: 'B' Rabby, how you ackin to go tell dem woman I is ya ole man cart horse? You take me for poppy show?' B' Rabby roll over in da bed ackin like he on deat' door. Say, 'Wuzzan me, man. Wuzzan me. I been lay up here all week.' B' Bouki still screw dread. Say, 'I tell dem gals I was comin' here ta fetch you, so you gattie go if I hattie tote ya masef.' B' Rabby just smile to hissef. He tell B' Bouki, 'O.K. I could go if ya tote ma.' Bouki say, 'Good. Jump up on ma back. Le's go. I ain' gat all day!' Rabby hop on topparim. Den he do like he was gone fall off. Say, 'Bulla, I cyaa sit right here so.' Bouki runnin' hot. 'Well, what you want nigga?' 'I cyaa be fallin' an' breakin' ma neck. I need one stirrup to keep ma steady.' 'Go get it den.' B' Rabby gone get it an' come back. He still make like he fallin' off. Say, 'Bruh, I still cyaa manage.' Bouki gettin dead vex. 'Is what you want so, man?' 'Lemma jus' dash in da house an' grab dem ting what yuhz put on ya heel. What dey's call um again?' 'Spur.' 'Yeah, yeah, spur.' 'Sheeeet. Go on den. Time wastin' while you fartin' roun'.' B' Rabby come back wit' he spur an' ting and jump on B' Bouki back. 'Now I set. Giddiup!' Dey haul ass down da road. When dey reach da bend before the hill, B' Bouki get nervous. He say, 'Jump down now, man! We almos' reach.' 'Go on little furda, buhy! Ah comin' off soon tereckly!' Bouki eye get big big, cuz he see da gals dem walkin' down from da house to greet um. He sweatin' and breathin' dead hard. Say, 'No, dread. See da gals dem dere! Come off ma back, buhy.' When B' Rabby reach da gals he dig da spur dem in B' Bouki side an' he holler, 'Yeeeeeehah! En I tell yinna B' Bouki is my pa cart horse? Check him out! Yeeeeehah!

Giddiup boy!' Den he tie ole Bouki to a tree and he gone up ta da house wit' da gals to drink some switcha. Bouki rear up 'gainst de reins and break um. An' when he rear up he kick me so hard I fly right here to tell dis storee."

They laughed a long time after that, out of joy, out of fear. Pink and gold sky, the darkness encroaching.

29
Flight

The car is speeding. The suitcases are piled up on the backseat. Must not forget to buy chewing gum. The pressure in the plane makes his ears hurt.

"You have your Bible?"

"It in my bag."

"Shouldn't travel without it."

"I know."

"What time the plane leavin'?"

"Two thirty-five."

"Oh man, we have plenty time. Plenty time."

"You know dey is take forever to check you through."

"Have faith."

"You say good-bye to Granma Jewel for me?"

"Yes. But she was disappointed you couldn't come say so for yourself."

He says nothing.

"She give me some money for you."

"Tell her thanks. And sorry."

"Christmas will be here in no time and you can tell her yourself. She proud a you. Everybody is."

Silence again. He is looking out of the window of the car. He feels terrible now. He is sorry he has been so eager to leave. The glimmer of Lake Charlton makes the water look like undulating sheets of silver. It reminds him of the sun shining on the water of the canal on the day he went there all alone. He was such a fool back then, he thought. He was actually leaving now. To live amongst strangers and with no one to call family. He wants to cry already and he hasn't even reached the good-bye part. He thinks to himself that he cries too much. His mother never cries in front of people. She just so strong. Stronger than he'll ever be because he's had it easy all his life.

"Ya pa give ya anyting?"

"Fifty dollars."

"Humph."

Nuttin change, she seems to be thinking.

"You have your passport and visa?"

"Yes ma'am."

They have parked the car now. Taking the bags. He has never noticed it before, but his mother looks old. He remembers watching her breathe, thinking she might stop and leave him all alone. She is smiling at him and looking at him from head to toe. He feels self-conscious.

"You mus' call soon as you get in and let us know ya livin'."

"Yes ma'am."

"When ya classes start?"

"Nex' week."

"Good, good, I know you ga do well. You didn' never need me to tell you to work hard. Always self-motivated. Always did your best."

He says nothing. He looks down at his shoes. He watches her taking one of the bags. Though she looks old to me now, she still thinks she's twenty-five. Look at her totin' da bag like it light like fedda. Mamma, whuzz plumage?

"Where Elsa? She ain' come to see you off?"

"Hm? Elsa? Oh. She . . . She ah . . . she had to work."

You is lie. You is a damn liar. Tell da trut', tell her da truth for once. Tell da trut' for once. So could lie.

Elsa: I sure you ain' takin' this long ta tell me you was workin' for Sir Thaddeus. Dat you sell your soul an' vote PNF. I know all dat already. So it mus' be sumtin else.

Tree: Yeah.

Elsa: Well? What you have to say to me, boss man?

Tree: I ga tell you. Give me a secon'.

Elsa: A secon'? I been layin' here for half a hour waitin' on you to say what you gat to say. Anyting. Say sumtin.

Tree: Why you lookin' at me like dat? Smilin' like dat.

Elsa: Like what?

Tree: You know, like you expectin' . . . Like you know what I ga say.

Elsa: Talk boy, come. Say it, spit it out.

Tree: No.

Elsa: Look, I don't know what you're going to say. Seriously. I have no idea.

Tree: You just have that sarcastic look on your face.

Elsa: You're a man, aren't you?

Tree: Yes.

Elsa: Then I have every right to look at you sarcastically.

Tree: Shit.

Elsa: *(She places her hand on his face. On his lips. So she can remember.)* So, tell me. What you wan' say?

Tree: Elsa.

Elsa: Um hum. *(She is hurting. But still the smile. He can't look her in the eyes.)*

Tree: Elsa . . . I just . . . You know we're going to be apart for a long time and I just . . . Well, I was thinking we should . . .

Elsa: Say it. Go on. Say what I know you was gone say. I ain' surprised. I ain' no fool. I know just how y'all go. I should be happy, dough. You een as bad as da res'. They promise they'll be fait'ful. They write and call. But while dey over dere dey screw ev'rytin' what could walk. Then they come home and pretend they been fait'ful all along.

Tree: Don' talk like dat. You know I wouldn' do dat.

Elsa: No. Your method is more decent. You go out with a girl for four years and just when you're ready to go to school you dump her. You dump her so that when you get your hot little American girl you won't have a guilty conscience because Elsa, good ole Elsa, fait'ful Elsa, off somewhere waitin' to see her man come Christmas time. Been hones' ta her man da whole time. Ain't find it necessary to sleep wit' someone else just because she was lonely.

Tree: It ain' like dat. It ain' like dat, Elsa. Seerus. I just t'ink we should see oder people. I jus' wan' be sure.

Elsa: I *see* people ev'ry day. I *want* you. I gave myself to you. You are the first and only person I ever been wit'. And I sure a that. An' wha's more, I give myself to you jus' half an hour ago. That don' mean nuttin to you? You could jus' t'row all dat away? You jus' wanted a good-bye fuck?! *(She slaps him. Tears. She is out of the bed. Grabbing up her clothes.)* I guess Maureen will get what she want after all.

Tree: Wait! Wait, hey. Hol' on, man! We still ga be friends. We still could talk in the Christmas!

Elsa: Fuck you!

"That will be fifteen dollars Departure Tax, sir."

I tellin' you dese tings 'cause you too young to remember. I tellin' you dese tings so you'll learn the difference between real man and play-play man. You hear me? I tellin you now, while you still a green plant dat could bend.

"Are you carrying any fruits or uncooked food with you to University, sir? Sir?"

"Hmm? Oh. No. Nothing."

His mother is standing watching him. She can't cross the yellow line.

"Bye Tree. Go wit' God. Call me when you reach."

She don't seem phased. But what she feel inside? I ga miss her.

"Sir, could you pull your seat up, we're about to take off."

The plane is full of white tourists. Two or three students like himself. Doesn't know any of them. He wonders if it's their first time going off to school too. The tears are there in the back of his eyes again. Doesn't think he can stop them now. He remembers Small Pint. Didn't get to say good-bye. Erryting change.

He remembers Jahown. Never even cry for Jahown. He cryin' now. Like a baby. His shoulders shakin'. Wipin' his nose wit his hand. He don' care who see. He lookin' out the window like a child in a plane for the first time. He e'en cry for Elsa. How he get so col' hearted anyhow? E'en cry for Jahown. Elsa gone. Jahown gone. Pompey Village gone. 'Pose he don' never come back?

He could see Jahown in his costume, ringing his cowbells under the water. The white man stranglin' him. Hol'in' him down.

The islands look small. Green islan's. Sacred green bush. Home. Bright-bright sun.

Jahown ringing he cowbells. Kalik. Kalik.

Water smood-smood. Like glass. Sea a glass like onto crystal. Sea a glass surroundin' da t'rone a God.

Be bo ben,
My story en'.

Glossary

Benny: Sesame seeds.

Backra: The white man. From Igbo or Efik, "mbakara," which means "he who governs"

Biggity: To be arrogant, argumentative, abrasive.

Boongie: Backside, behind. From the Scottish, "bung hole." Also, sex between men.

Bouki: Character in Caribbean and Louisiana trickster tales. Usually the dupe of B' Rabbit, or Compair Lapin. The word is Wolof and means "hyena."

Buhy: Boy.

Chickcharnee: A legendary creature of the pine forest possessing magical powers, with the head of a man and the body of an owl.

Chimmey: The Banana Quit.

Conchy Joe: Refers to the white minority/white Creole class.

Cyaa: Can't.

Day Clean: Meaning dawn or daybreak. It is a literal translation of an expression existing among speakers of Yoruba, Mandingo, and Wolof.

Dread: A term derived from the Rastafari, used here as a form of address.

Duppy: In Jamaica the term refers to a roaming spirit. Here it means "to kill" or "to be killed." Perhaps from the Bube, "dupe" meaning ghost.

Fix: To work obeah on someone or something.

Fyak: Witchcraft.

Gravaliciousness: Greed or selfishness.

Hice: From "hoist." To be "hice up under someone" is to be jammed up under them. To "look hice up" is to wear clothes that are too tight.

Hougnan: A priest in Haitian vodun faith.

Johny Cake: A heavy homemade bread.

Jook: To stab with a knife or other sharp object. From Fulani, "jukka."

Junkanoo: Masquerade held at Christmas in the Caribbean and southeastern United States. Involves drums, horns, and masks. It is a New World synthesis of various African agricultural rites and processions.

Muddo: Exclamation expressing wonder.

Nanny: To deficate; faeces. From Twi, "nene," meaning to discharge the bowels; in Bantu it means "faeces."

Obeah: Traditional African religious belief system and bush medicine brought over from the Middle Passage. The word could be derived from Efik, Twi, or Akan.

Pawkin: A game usually played by boys that involves throwing a small ball into the air so that everyone has an opportunity of catching it when it descends and hitting the other boys with it as hard as possible.

Poppy Show: Puppet Show. To be made a fool of in public; loss of face.

Potcake: A small mongrel dog. The food caked at the very bottom of the pot.

Put Mout': To "put mouth" on someone is to pronounce a curse on them by predicting that something bad will happen to them.

Rabby: New World trickster figure among peoples of African descent. Called B' or Brer Rabbit in the Anglophone Caribbean and southeast United States and Compair Lapin in Louisiana and Francophone Caribbean communities.

Rush: To "rush" can mean to participate in a Junkanoo parade or to march and dance all night in a church during a concert or program in which spirituals are sung.

Slam Bam: A sandwich made of plain or "dry" bread and sausage.

Story: To "story" means to tell a lie. If you are lying you are "storyin'." To "talk old story" means to tell a tale, usually a folk tale, like the story of B' Bouki and B' Rabby.

Sucker: The shoot of a tree, especially sugarcane, plantain, banana.

Suckneck: Someone selfish, greedy, or inclined to betray his friends.

Switcha: Homemade lemonade.

Yinna: Means "you all." From a synthesis of African sources, such as Wolof "yena," Limba "yina," and Yoruba "nyin."

Note: In compiling this glossary I consulted Frederic Cassidy's *Jamaica Talk* and Schilling and Holm's *Dictionary of Bahamian Dialect.*

About the Author

Ian G. Strachan was born in Nassau, Bahamas, in May 1969. After graduating from the Government High School in 1985, he attended the College of the Bahamas, where he obtained an Associate of Arts degree in English and a Teacher's Certificate in Secondary Education. In 1990, he received his Bachelor of Arts degree in English from Morehouse College in Atlanta, Georgia. He taught at the C. I. Gibson High School in Nassau before going on to complete his doctoral studies at the University of Pennsylvania. He is currently Lecturer in English at the College of the Bahamas.

Strachan's first two plays—*Pa and the Preacher* and *Mister Maphusa*—were produced at the Dundas Centre for the Performing Arts in Nassau. In 1991, his political play *No Seeds in Babylon* was performed both in Nassau and in Edinburgh, Scotland, at the Edinburgh Festival Fringe. In 1992, his play *Fatal Passage* was televised nationally by the Broadcasting Corporation of the Bahamas. *God's Angry Babies* is his first novel.